DARCY COATES

THE VENGEFUL DEAD

DARCY COATES

Poisoned Pen
PRESS

Published by Poisoned Pen Press, an imprint of Sourcebooks
P.O. Box 4410, Naperville, Illinois 60567-4410
(630) 961-3900
sourcebooks.com

Cataloging-in-Publication Data is on file with the Library of Congress.

Printed and bound in Canada.
MBP 10 9 8 7 6 5 4 3 2 1

CHAPTER 1

A DROWNED MAN STOOD at Keira's window.

Water dripped from his hair and chin. His fingers, splayed, pressed against the glass, and small flecks of frost bristled outward from the touch.

He opened his mouth and a gush of water drained free. Then, slowly, he turned his head to stare toward the graveyard's entrance.

"Understood," Keira whispered. She stood in her dark cottage, holding a notebook. She'd been working when she felt the spirit's presence, but she put the book aside.

The ghost shimmered, then evaporated, like a wisp of mist caught in a chilled breeze. The only trace he left behind was the icy outline showing where his hand had touched the glass, and even that was beginning to fade.

His presence had been a warning.

Someone's coming.

Keira's cottage, hidden at the back of Blighty's cemetery, was hard to find if you didn't know where to look. And she was grateful for it. She'd made some enemies who would very much like to find her.

Six days had passed since she, with the help of her friends, had destroyed one of Artec's power plants and untethered a batch of ghosts they'd been keeping chained. It wasn't a fatal blow to Artec, but it would be a painful one, undoing years' worth of work and freeing hundreds of trapped spirits in the process.

But it came with a cost. Gavin Kelsey had died. And while he hadn't endeared himself to many people during life, he'd been a resident of Blighty. His death was all but guaranteed to lead Artec to her town, and probably soon.

She was taking whatever precautions she could. The groundskeeper's cottage was already well hidden, but Keira kept the lights dim and the windows covered. Only one curtain had its corner pinned back, exposing a pane of glass.

That was for the ghosts.

Her ghosts.

The denizens of Blighty's cemetery were never talkative and rarely interactive, but she'd managed to earn a small measure of their trust over her time in the groundskeeper's cottage. Without being asked, they watched the path leading into the graveyard and appeared at the window to warn Keira when someone approached.

She wasn't too worried this time. Mason and Zoe were coming to visit that morning to go over their plans. Keira checked the clock as she crossed the room. They were early, but—

Keira leaned close to the window and felt her breath catch. A single figure strode through the maze of grave markers. Morning fog clung to it, turning the edges hazy, but it was clear the silhouette didn't belong to either of her friends.

A visitor? The cemetery had plenty of those, but they usually stayed in the section closer to the town and the parsonage. All the recent graves were there. Back near the forest, where Keira's cottage was, were the old stone markers—cracked, faded, listing, and all but forgotten by everyone except Keira. It was rare to see a visitor make their way back here.

And the figure was moving with purpose. They weren't pausing to search the rows or read names on the stones. They faced forward, and their end destination was clear.

They were coming for her.

A faint, tense buzz built as Keira stepped back from the window. She was prepared for Artec to find her. She'd just been hoping for more time before they did.

The window in the bathroom opened wide enough for her to creep through. That was a modification Mason had made; before, the only way out was through the front door. The new casing was a tight fit, but she'd practiced and knew she could slide through in less than three seconds. That gave her a way to leave the grounds-keeper's cottage and get into the forest without being seen.

Next to the bathroom door was a backpack with spare clothes, toiletries, money, and a backup mobile phone. Zoe had planned the contents. Mason had bought them.

Keira hooked her fingers through the backpack's strap, her pulse fast, then hesitated. Some small glimmer of doubt drew her back to the window. She crouched, keeping herself hidden in the shadows as she peered through.

The figure was on its own. Keira had been prepared for Artec to send in a whole squad, armed to the teeth, when they finally found her. They'd never used half measures before.

It could be an ambush. There could be more of them in the forest.

Except…her ghosts would have warned her if there were more figures creeping through the trees. The graves spilled in between the trunks, burrowing deep into the forest, and the spirits' watchful gazes extended even further.

Keira glanced behind herself. Her small black cat, Daisy, napped on the lounge chair, twisted so that her chin was pointed toward the ceiling, two little white fangs visible as her lips twitched. She didn't stir.

Through the window, the figure began to resolve in increments as it emerged through the mist. It was a woman, Keira realized. She looked at least fifty. A tweed skirt perfectly matched her tweed jacket, and a crisp white blouse was buttoned high around her throat with a brooch. She clutched a small black handbag in both hands.

Misdirection? Keira's racing heart began to slow as confusion overtook any fear. *Are they trying to lull me into a false sense of security?*

The woman stopped at the low stone fence bordering the groundskeeper's cottage. She lifted her chin as she stared up at the building. Her nose twitched, and her lips, flawlessly covered in a muted red lipstick, pursed.

Keira let the backpack fall to the floor beside her. Whoever this woman was, she wasn't Artec.

The stranger set her shoulders, then stepped past the fence and up to the door. Everything was silent for a moment; then three quick, neat knocks echoed through the room.

Keira glanced back at Daisy. The cat had an uncanny ability to sense when danger was about, but except for the flick of one ear, she didn't move.

"Okay," Keira whispered to herself, then opened the door.

Up close, the woman made a striking impression. Everything about her was so *precise*. Her hair—short, dyed a golden brown, and permed—looked as though it had come out of a hairdressing tutorial. Her glasses were small and immaculately tidy. There wasn't a single loose thread or stray hair on the tweed suit, let alone a wrinkle.

She folded her hands, the small handbag hanging from the crook of one arm, and offered a restrained smile that didn't quite reach her eyes. "Good morning," she said, and her voice was every bit as controlled and exact as her appearance.

"Hey there," Keira said in return, trying not to feel self-conscious in her secondhand clothes and with hair that was definitely overdue for a wash.

"Miss Keira, I presume?" Eyebrows, tweezed into thin lines, rose expectantly.

Keira couldn't remember the last time someone had called her *Miss*. "Yep, that's me."

"Wonderful." The woman drew herself up another inch, though

she only came up to Keira's chin. "Please allow me to introduce myself. My name is Agatha Edith-Whittle, and I am the president of the Blighty Propriety Society."

"The…" It felt like the kind of tongue twister people forced on young children.

Then the implications of the name sank in. Keira felt hyper-aware of her surroundings as she sent a covert glance toward the weed-choked, crumbling graveyard, then a second, even more covert glance toward her cottage and the dust bunnies she knew had to be lurking under the mismatched furniture.

"The Blighty Propriety Society concerns itself with the respect-ability and overall wholesomeness of our lovely town," Agatha continued, her smile resolute and unflinching.

"Great," Keira managed. She wished she'd picked something other than the garish polka-dot cardigan to wear that morning. But then, her clothes were all secondhand, and her other options included things like an out-of-season and extremely ugly Christmas sweater and a T-shirt that read *Regional Halibut Preservation Society Team Camp 1989*. Somehow, neither of them seemed likely con-tenders to measure up to Agatha's flawless tailoring.

At least she can't see the ghosts. Silver linings, and all of that. The drowned man stood just a dozen paces behind Agatha, water trail-ing from his clothes as he watched her with sightless eyes.

"As president, I felt obligated to pay you a visit," Agatha said. "With, erm, the society's apologies for not formally welcoming you earlier."

Here it comes. Keira forced a tight smile into place as she waited for Agatha's verdict. *Does she want the grass cut? Are the gravestones an eyesore? Am I going to be labeled a menace to the town's reputation?*

Agatha cleared her throat and took a shuffling half step closer. She lowered her voice, glancing to either side, as though afraid someone might see her at Keira's cottage. "Actually, to be frank with you, this isn't a purely social call. I've come on a rather… delicate matter."

"Oh?" Keira waited.

Agatha fidgeted with her bag. She swallowed uneasily. "I have heard… I have been informed…that you are known to have had correspondences with the deceased."

Wait, what?

Keira's ability to see the dead was a closely guarded secret. To anyone outside of her immediate circle, the official story was that she was niece to the pastor, Adage, and had been hired as the cemetery's groundskeeper. She could count on the fingers of one hand the number of people who knew the truth, and none of them seemed the type to give it away so easily.

"Is that true?" Agatha was peering up at her, her blue eyes shrewd behind her glasses.

Keira felt too exposed standing in the open. She stepped back, opening the door wider. "Why don't you come in?"

CHAPTER 2

THE COTTAGE WAS KEPT dim to avoid attention; when she needed more than the half-open window provided, Keira would light a candle.

It didn't feel right to invite a guest into the gloom, though, so Keira reluctantly turned on the lights. She immediately regretted it as Agatha Edith-Whittle's eyes fixed on a cobweb in the corner.

"Should I remove my shoes?" the older woman asked, still in the doorway.

"Oh, no, probably best if you don't." Keira kept her home clean, but she had a strong suspicion that she and Agatha held very different standards for the word. "Um, can I get you something? Tea or…?"

Agatha entered with small precise steps. She moved toward the couches by the fire before seeing Daisy and the fur she'd shed during her nap, and she quickly turned to the wooden seats at the small round table. "Thank you, but I shan't take up much of your time."

She perched on the very edge of the seat, as though touching too much of its surface would contaminate her, and laid her handbag squarely in her lap before folding her hands over it.

Keira sat opposite, crossing her legs to strategically hide a stain on her jeans.

"It is true, then?" Agatha asked, her eyes strangely intense behind her narrow glasses. She leaned forward a fraction, her posture still rigidly upright. "That you have a gift to open dialogue with those not of our world?"

This is the most bizarre conversation I've had in a long while. And that's a high bar to hurdle over.

She had no idea what Agatha wanted. Was this the beginning of some campaign to drive Keira out of town? A modern-day witch hunt? Instead of answering, Keira hedged. "Where'd you hear that?"

Agatha's eyes narrowed shrewdly. "It came from…a somewhat reliable source."

Surely not Mason or Zoe. Would Adage tell one of his parishioners? No, he knows how important it is to keep this quiet.

Keira tried another tactic. "Are you curious about the dead? Or…did you want to speak to someone who's passed?"

Agatha looked scandalized. Her eyebrows shot up and one hand fluttered over the brooch. "Of course not. I would never!"

"Okay." Keira sighed. "Look, I've got a lot of work to get through today. Maybe we could—"

"You haven't answered my question." Agatha's jaw quivered faintly. "Are you able to help me or not?"

Keira had half risen from her seat, prepared to shepherd Agatha from her cottage. But that one word—*help*—hung in the air. "What kind of help do you need?"

"I…" Agatha glanced aside, color rising into her face. "I have recently begun to suspect…to have some concerns arise…that there may be some…some…*unworldly presence*…tangentially connected to my residence."

It took a few seconds for the words to make sense.

"Oh," Keira murmured, and dropped back into her seat. "You're worried that your house is haunted?"

The color on Agatha's cheeks was deepening into a flushed scarlet. "Please understand. As president of the Blighty Propriety Society, I absolutely cannot have any unwholesome connotations attached to my name. Something of this nature could call my entire character into question. This has been a source of great agitation to me. As it would be for anyone."

"Sure," Keira said, pretending she couldn't see the ghosts drifting around the graveyard through her window.

"You're the first person I've confided in," Agatha continued, her words hurried. "Because I was advised that you may be able to help. *Discreetly.*"

The Artec situation was already consuming all of Keira's time and energy. As far as stakes went, they were about as bad as they could get. Artec was absorbing a near-constant flow of dead bodies into their cemeteries, and the ghosts of those dead, once interred, were chained there for an eternity: human batteries, condemned to writhe and scream and beg, without anyone ever seeing or knowing.

Well…nearly. Artec knew. And Keira knew. And now they were locked in a deadly race. Keira, to destroy Artec and its cemeteries. And Artec, to get rid of Keira before she could do any more damage.

She knew she should turn down the request. She couldn't afford to spend her energy on anything else. She couldn't even afford a distraction when every minute might be the one that made the difference.

More than that, she wasn't supposed to leave her cottage unless absolutely necessary. There was always the risk that Artec's people were watching the town, waiting for her. She'd come too far to give her location away so easily.

But there was emotion welling in Agatha's eyes, even half-hidden behind the pristine glasses. To Keira, who was exposed to ghosts virtually every day, having a haunting in your house was extremely unremarkable.

But Keira wasn't Agatha. And, to Agatha, this was her whole life.

"Okay," Keira said, squashing down her reluctance. "I'll answer both questions. Yes, I can see ghosts. And yes, I'll come and take a look. I can't make any promises that I can help, though."

Agatha drew a deep, stuttering breath. Some of the flushed color was fading from her face. "I'm very grateful. All I need is a professional to confirm whether there are…any…any…"

"Ghosts," Keira prompted.

Agatha swallowed. "Yes. Any spiritual presences in the locality. I can pay, of course."

Keira waved the offer aside. "It's fine. I don't charge."

She hadn't given much thought to the ethics of billing people who needed help with the dead, but it felt dicey at best.

"Let's schedule an appointment," Agatha said, reaching into her handbag and bringing out a small crisp business card. "I would be grateful to make it as early as is convenient. Does your work require a specific time of day?"

"Uh…no, any time's fine." Keira took the card and squinted at the address. The street name seemed familiar, but she couldn't quite picture it. She'd ask Mason or Adage for directions. "I have to meet up with some friends this morning, though."

"The afternoon, then. That will work fine for me, as well. My neighbor leaves at two every day for his chess club. Let's set the appointment for three. It will be more discreet that way."

"Sure."

Agatha stood, bag clutched primly. She glanced toward the lounges arranged around the fire. "What is your cat's name, may I ask?"

"Daisy."

"Good morning, Miss Daisy. A pleasure to make your acquaintance," Agatha said. Then she turned back to Keira. "And thank you, Miss Keira. I'll see you at three."

Keira watched the older woman leave, walking carefully out into the cemetery. She was oblivious as she passed between the faint, shimmering specters dotting the overgrown grass. Keira looked down at the business card again. The printing was neat, modest, and very, very formal.

She hoped the job would be easy. If she was very lucky, she'd arrive at Agatha's house and find it completely empty. But, somehow, she suspected *nothing* about the woman would be simple.

"If Artec could see me now," Keira murmured, partially to herself and partially to Daisy.

She was still growing comfortable with her newfound memories and her newfound awareness of who—and what—she was.

She'd lost her memories while trying to destroy a power plant shortly before being chased into Blighty. The town had saved her. At first, physically—Adage, the pastor, had hidden her, and Mason, doctor-in-training, had treated her injuries. But it had also saved her in a far less tangible, and far more important, way. She'd found a home there. Friends. Purpose.

For a long time, she'd thought her memories might be permanently erased. But, as it turned out, the small black cat that had followed her to Blighty was also carrying secrets. A part of Keira had become locked away in the feline. They'd just needed a catalyst to reconnect.

Daisy was a paradox. Alive and yet not entirely. A cat but also harboring part of a human. Daisy and Keira were irrevocably linked, bonded together by the energy surge from Artec's collapsing power plant, and Keira was still trying to figure out the extent of their entanglement.

She crossed to Daisy, who was still napping, and gently scratched beneath her chin. Daisy shivered happily, her paws flexing and her whiskers twitching.

"I thought I'd have more of this figured out by now," Keira whispered, and even though Daisy didn't react, Keira knew she was listening. "I've got my memories back, and still nothing makes sense."

She didn't know what she'd expected in answer. The slow reveal of an eye, filled with knowing reassurance? Some sign that Daisy understood how she felt?

Instead, the cat hiccuped, then fell back asleep.

During the stretch of time Keira had spent without her memories, she'd believed that Old Keira had the answers, Old Keira would know how to deal with the ghosts, Old Keira would understand Artec. She'd been fully convinced that, if she could just unlock her memories, all her uncertainty and doubt would vanish.

But now she had Old Keira back, and it turned out Old Keira had been scrambling around in the dark just as much as New Keira was.

She had the runes, and she had a very small amount of knowledge about Artec, but that was it. There was no magic solution that could solve everything. No secret weakness in Artec she could use to break it apart.

And, if she was prepared to admit it to herself, that had been a slight motivation behind accepting Agatha's request, even though she technically couldn't afford to lose the time.

It was because Agatha's job would be easy.

Keira had been running into a metaphorical brick wall for days. There had to be a path forward—she *knew* there had to be one— but she just couldn't find it.

On the other hand, a potential haunting? That was easy. Cakewalk levels of easy, even. She just needed to visit Agatha's house and feel for the telltale prickles of electricity, maybe take a look through a few rooms, and she'd have answers.

To be fair, if it turned out there really was a ghost, removing it would be a whole other question. Sometimes it involved resolving unfinished business. Sometimes she had to physically untether them. The difficulty rating of *that* part of the process stretched from cakewalk to near impossible.

But at least the first half of the job would be simple. And she was craving some feeling of progress. Even something small.

Hairs on the back of Keira's neck rose. The soft thrum of electricity ran through the air, both feather soft and unmistakable. Another ghost was at her window.

She turned. This time, it was a woman. The right side of her face had been scraped away, revealing the white bone of her skull. The raw wounds held flecks of gravel, and Keira guessed her cause of death must have been a horrific car accident.

There were still so many spirits in the cemetery she hadn't yet talked to and whose stories she hadn't yet learned. So many still waiting for help.

One of the woman's eyes blinked languidly. The other no longer had an eyelid. The woman tilted her head toward the driveway, letting her hair drift about her shoulders, then faded from sight.

For the second time that morning, Keira checked her mantelpiece clock as she crossed the room. It was right on schedule for Zoe and Mason's visit. She leaned close to the window, her breath fogging on the glass, and smiled as she saw their two familiar silhouettes weaving toward her.

Mason carried a basket, and they seemed to be hurrying. They used their phones for any urgent messages, so she knew there wouldn't be any news that was *too* dire, but she was on the alert for any signs of danger, and *something* had made her friends quicken their pace.

She threw the door open before they even reached it. Zoe burst through first, her face bright and flushed and eager.

"That was a Beeps!" she yelled, so loud that Daisy startled and tumbled off the couch. "I saw her leaving. Did you seriously get a visit from a Beeps?"

"A…" Keira blinked rapidly, trying to catch up.

"Hello," Mason said, gentle and calm as he stepped in behind Zoe and closed the door. He set down his basket, then leaned close to Keira and pressed a quick kiss to her forehead.

Zoe spared just a second to shoot them a disgusted grimace at the overt affection, then her earlier excitement flooded back in. "The lady from the Blighty Propriety Society. Did she visit you?"

"Oh, right! Yeah. Agatha Edith-Whittle? I guess you know her."

"Know her!" Zoe threw her arms wide as she stalked through the cottage. "It's the Beeps! Everyone in town knows her!"

"Rewind a second: the Beeps?"

"The Blighty Propriety Society. BPS for short. Most people call them the Beeps because they sound like an especially annoying alarm clock when they talk: *beep, beep, beep, beep!*"

"Gotcha." Keira moved to put the kettle on while Mason bent

down to pet Daisy, who had trotted up to him to receive her obligatory dose of affection. "Yeah, she wanted to ask a favor. Are the BPS…" Keira scrunched up her face as she tried to figure out how to phrase her question. "Are they *okay*? I mean, should I be worried about helping them?"

Zoe began pulling mugs out of the cupboards. "Babe, you're infiltrating evil corporate lairs. Agatha should be easy mode for you."

"They're actually not as bad as they first seem," Mason said, still crouched to scratch around Daisy's ears. "They'll raise their eyebrows and clear their throats a lot if they see something they don't like, but they're not busybodies. They're more worried about how the town sees *them*. What was the favor?"

"She's worried her house has a haunting." Keira shrugged. "I'm going to check it out later."

"Her place is a short walk from mine," Mason said, and Keira realized that was why she'd recognized the street name. "I can drive you there when you're ready, but you can also get to it by following the trails through the forest."

"I love the idea of a lift, but honestly? I'm turning into a jittery mess being cooped up in here, so the walk's going to be my exercise for the week."

"Fair." Mason chuckled as he began unpacking the basket he'd brought. Keira was delighted to see scones, jam, and cream. "At least you'll know I'm close by if you need any help."

"Do you think she's actually going to have a ghost there?" Zoe asked.

Keira could only shrug. "I didn't get the chance to ask what was happening to make her worried. It might be a ghost. It might be rats. I'll figure it out when I get there."

Zoe tilted her head, her owlish eyes turning shrewd. "Hold up. How'd she know you could talk to ghosts?"

Keira grimaced as she began filling mugs. "Yeah. That was going to be my next question, actually. Have either of you mentioned the ghost business to anyone else? Even in passing?"

"Never," Mason promised, at the same time as Zoe said, "Over my dead body."

"Yeah." Keira felt faintly warmer at how quickly and intensely they'd objected. She knew, beyond a shadow of a doubt, that she could trust them. "I figured. But *someone's* said something to someone, and I'm desperately hoping it won't travel further than Agatha."

"Especially not right now." Mason rubbed the back of his neck, frowning.

"I've been keeping watch for any strangers passing through Blighty," Zoe added. "Especially strangers who ask a lot of questions. But Artec either hasn't scouted out the town yet, or they're doing it *very* discreetly."

None of them needed to finish the thought: even if Artec hadn't visited the town yet, it was only a matter of time before they did. Keira might have a couple more days. Or she might only have hours. But the longer she waited, the more precarious her situation—and *all* their situations—became.

"Why don't we get started?" Mason suggested, beckoning them to the table.

Keira felt her stomach twist. They'd been having daily meetings, and she dearly, dearly wished she had something to tell her friends that wasn't an echo of *I'm still working on it.*

Mason saw her expression. He reached out a hand, his smile warm and soft, and gently pulled her into a seat. "You're not in this alone," he said. "We're here to help, remember?"

"And that's exactly what we're doing." Zoe pulled a notebook out of her bag and slammed it on the table. "Get yourself a scone while you can still appreciate it, because once you hear my plan, nothing will ever be the same again."

Keira raised her eyebrows. "Huh?"

Zoe flipped open her notebook. "Get ready for Operation Obliterate Artec."

CHAPTER 3

"COME AGAIN?" KEIRA CRANED to read Zoe's scribbled notes upside down. They were erratic, overlapping in places, and Keira was fairly sure the red lines scored through them were supposed to represent red string.

"We've been approaching this from the wrong direction," Zoe said. "All three of us just took for granted that *you* had to be the one to fix everything. On the surface, it makes sense: you're the person who can see ghosts; you're the person who can control the energy. But just for a second, let's all revisit our ultimate goal: get rid of Artec."

She paused, waiting for her words to sink in, but Keira and Mason only exchanged a confused glance.

Zoe jabbed a finger into her notebook. "Get rid of Artec. Not *use our magical powers to get rid of Artec.* Think about it—companies fail all the time and for a thousand different reasons. If we can trigger something to push Artec into a downward spiral, we can halt their expansion plans and maybe even close the company, all without Keira having to lift a single magical finger."

"To be completely honest with you both, I don't think my fingers are especially magical," Keira said.

"But your magical fingers are the entire reason I'm dating you," Mason said, grinning. "Entendre only slightly intended."

Zoe hunched, massaging her temples. "I swear I am going to quit the team if you two can't figure out how to separate personal from business."

Keira chuckled, but her mind was whirling. Was Zoe right? Had she been coming at this from the wrong direction the entire time?

To the best of her knowledge, she and Artec's founder—a man named Schaeffer—were the only two people who could see the dead. They had both been exposed to enormous amounts of spectral energy: Schaeffer during his experiments and Keira before she was even born, as her mother worked on the project.

She'd believed that was her one advantage. She could see the dead. She could interact with them. She could free them.

But Zoe was right. Paring back all the distractions, she had only one purpose: to end the company. And a company could be killed in more than one way.

"First, we get rid of Artec corporate," Zoe said, raising a finger. "Then, make sure the connections to the cemeteries—the ones holding the ghosts there—are broken. Without guards and time crunches, that part should be easy."

"You're right that a thousand factors can go into a company's downward spiral," Mason said, "but ultimately, there's only ever one element behind a company's closure: lack of revenue. And that's a factor that will be *very* difficult to overcome."

"Not impossible," Zoe said.

"No. Not impossible. But Artec has dual streams of income. It earns money with every body it buries, since one of its branches is a legitimate cemetery service. Then it earns again from the energy those spirits generate. Artec has no direct competition for that structure. Its profit margins must be immense. At the very least, the company has enough money to begin expanding into international markets."

He was referring to Zoe's discovery that Artec had registered its name and purchased land overseas. Nothing had been built yet, but it wasn't far off.

"And we don't really have much time to play with," Mason added. He sent an apologetic glance toward Keira. "A company of Artec's size might be able to operate at a deficit for years by relying on loans and investors. And…even if we hopped towns and tried to hide, I don't think we could stay off their radar that long. Not with how aggressively they're hunting Keira."

"You're right about that," Zoe said. "We *can't* wait years. Which is why we're going with a much more immediate option: total reputation annihilation."

Keira plucked a scone from the towel-wrapped bundle, just so she'd have something to put her nervous energy into. It was still warm. Mason must have baked them right before coming over. "Talk to me," she said.

"Welcome to Operation Obliterate Artec." Zoe grinned, then grimaced. "I'm a little devastated that Artec's name doesn't start with an *O*. The alliterative element would have added so much to this presentation."

"Focus," Mason said.

"Right. So. The plan here is simple: tank their reputation so thoroughly and aggressively that they're drowned under a wave of public outrage. They'll be so busy scrambling to put out that fire—and hold on to their business relationships—that they won't even have time to hunt Keira. A normal dying business might need years. A public-shame campaign, when powerful enough, can functionally end them in a week."

Keira frowned as she leaned forward, picking at the edges of her scone. "Okay. I'm on board with that. But...what's our angle?"

"It's so simple and so, so beautiful." Zoe's wolfish smile widened. "We tell people about the ghosts."

For a second, Keira's cottage was perfectly silent.

"No one will believe us, though," Mason said. "We've grappled with this a few times. If people knew about the shades, *of course* Artec would be ruined. But no one else can see them. And we haven't been able to find a way to prove they exist."

"Ex-act-ly," Zoe said, stretching out each syllable. "You guys don't get it yet because you're part of the mainstream. But take it from me, if there's one experience that's universal among conspiracy theorists, it's having your beliefs mocked."

"Are you referring to the alien sighting you had two years ago?"

Mason turned grave as he leaned his chin on his folded hands, his elbows propped on the table. "Because I'm deeply sorry that no one took your experience seriously."

Zoe narrowed her eyes at him. "Leave it."

"I am also sorry your alien encounter happened on an extremely dark and foggy night."

"Mason, this is your last warning."

"I am even more sorry that a half-deflated metallic birthday balloon was later found in the tree where you for sure, definitely saw that alien."

Zoe swung toward Keira. "You need to dump him or else I'll dump him on your behalf."

"We can negotiate dumping my boyfriend later. Right now, I want the rest of your plan."

"Fine." Zoe groaned, then, with what appeared to be an enormous amount of effort, regained her composure. "Look, this just proves what I'm saying. *No one* takes the fringe stuff seriously. And what is more fringe than harvesting electricity from dead people? Think about Artec's tower. Think about what you found there."

"The archives," Keira said.

"There was enough paper in that basement level to keep a moderate-sized bonfire going all winter," Zoe confirmed. "All of it data and research on *ghosts*. If we got some of it and distributed it widely enough, Artec's reputation would be toast. People would think they were some new-age cult. Or that they're conning the public. At the very least, none of the respectable science-based power suppliers who are currently purchasing, quote, *renewable energy* from Artec would want anything to do with them."

"Huh." Mason frowned at his half-eaten scone. "There's enough evidence to back up our claims. We can link the cemeteries to Artec."

"And I can make sure the documents aren't ignored," Zoe said. "I have networks everywhere. Including a couple of friends in news broadcasting. If we can leak Artec's research, we have a way to make sure people pay attention."

"Getting the evidence is going to be the challenge," Mason said. "Breaking into Artec's tower the first time was difficult enough. Their security is going to be even tighter if we make a second attempt."

"I really wish I'd grabbed some of those papers while we were down there," Keira muttered.

She hadn't left empty-handed. She had slipped something very precious into her pocket: the only known photo of her parents. It was currently being kept hidden at Mason's house, where Keira knew it wouldn't be lost if her cottage was burned to the ground or if she was forced to flee without warning.

"I'm working on the impossible-tower situation," Zoe said. "But I need to know if you guys are on board before I take it too far."

"I actually am," Mason said. He sat back, arms folded. "I'm impressed. I mean, if we can manage it right, it might actually work."

Keira's mind had been ticking along as they talked. She tried to picture the future Zoe was painting: Artec, making every news headline in the country. The company that believed the dead walked among the living. The company that tried to extract power from graveyards.

It was the kind of headline people would love to share. The company would become a laughingstock overnight. Late-night talk show hosts would do bits.

Zoe was right. It would be enough to ruin the company. Artec could try to restructure and reemerge under a new name, but there would be no escaping the public scorn as long as Schaeffer, the owner, was still attached. And he wouldn't leave the company. It was his life's work. His obsession.

Keira's mouth turned dry. "We can't do it."

"What do you mean?" Zoe was flipping through her notebook but fell still.

"You're right about everything you said. It's a brilliant plan. But I made a mistake when I set our goal. I decided it needed to be *destroy Artec*, but it's not—not really. The more important goal— the goal that supersedes all else—is *stop ghosts from being harvested*."

Zoe tilted her head, her owlish eyes narrowed. "I'm not sure I follow."

"Artec has been pretty covert until now. For obvious reasons. They don't want anyone thinking too much about what they do or where they get the electricity they sell. If we make Artec's research public, they'll be shot into the public eye. People will laugh at them, yes, but some people are going to start asking a different kind of question. Artec is selling power, so where is it coming from if not ghosts?"

"Artec is lucrative," Mason said, catching Keira's drift. "And where there's a lucrative business, others will want to dip their hands in too."

"Even if we cherry-pick the documents we release, we'll still be dropping clues about how to replicate Artec's model. And some people will try it for themselves. Not many. Maybe no more than a handful. But…if Artec becomes internationally known, it'll be impossible to prevent copycats."

"Shoot," Zoe whispered, slumping back.

"Artec's secretiveness is the only thing that's stopped that from happening until now," Keira said. "But if journalists start prying and if employees start leaking details of their experiments…"

"There's no way to put the lid back on the box once it's open," Zoe finished.

"Yeah. For the remainder of humankind, ghosts will be subject to experiments. The average person might not be able to see a spirit, but the energy spirits can generate when harnessed correctly is real enough." Keira shrugged helplessly. "I might—*might*—be able to stop Artec, but I don't stand a chance against a dozen underground companies doing the exact same thing more stealthily."

Slowly, and with evident pain, Zoe closed her notebook.

"Sorry," Keira said weakly.

"Not your fault." Zoe sighed. "I didn't think that far ahead. But you're right. Getting rid of Artec isn't enough."

"We have to destroy their research too," Keira said. Her stomach twisted, and she put the half-nibbled scone down. "We have to make sure it's so thoroughly buried that no one can ever revisit it."

"Scorched-earth policy," Zoe said. "I'm on board with that."

Mason cleared his throat. "Keira, think about what that means.

You're not just talking about the paper trail in Artec's tower. You're talking about the scientists who worked on the research. What exactly does a scorched-earth policy mean for them?"

They were silent for a moment.

"Are we considering murder?" Mason prompted.

Prickles built in the back of Keira's throat. She wasn't sure if she could speak, but she tried anyway. "I don't know."

Mason shuffled in his chair, faintly agitated. "Please understand. I'm not…passing some kind of moral judgment. I understand the stakes, and I know the potential cost if we don't succeed. But… I don't think I'm capable of taking another human's life."

"No," Keira agreed. Mason was gentle. He was compassionate. He was not a killer.

And, she was pretty sure, neither was she.

How far would you go to save the damned?

Her gaze drifted to the corner of the window she'd left uncovered. When she opened her second sight, distant forms bled into view. Trapped but not suffering. Not like the spirits contained in Artec's graveyards. Or the countless others who would be trapped and experimented on if Artec's work ever leaked.

"Fine," Zoe said, raising her hands in resignation. "I'll take one for the team. But I'll need to source a rocket launcher first."

It was enough to draw a laugh from Keira, but she shushed Zoe regardless. "Look, I'll…I'll figure something out. Somehow. I just need more time."

"Sure." Zoe tucked her notebook away. "I'm going to see what else I can come up with. Maybe there's some way to enact

Operation Obliterate Artec but without using the ghost research. I'll think on it."

"Thanks."

"Well, my time's just about up anyhow," Zoe said, glancing at the clock above the cold fireplace. "I have a shift at the general store. As painfully mundane as that seems considering the circumstances, my boss is in crisis mode because the delivery of crunchy breakfast cereal is late, and I guess the whole town is going to turn feral if we don't get it back on shelves soon."

"Wait, did your boss put you back on the roster already?" Keira asked. Zoe had taken time off from the store after her mother's funeral, which had been just days before. Zoe was still deep in grief, even if she rigidly refused to talk about it.

"Relax." Zoe shook her head. "I put myself back on. I've already deep-cleaned my kitchen twice and fully revised eight hundred pages on the cryptid wiki I help manage; I'm physically going to explode if I have to sit at home for even one more day."

"Gotcha," Keira said. "But—"

"Put my needs first, I know, I know." Zoe made a face. "This is gonna be good for me. Now, come here."

Zoe reached out a hand. Keira took it, and then Mason took her other one.

"Remember where your escape bags are," Zoe said.

As well as the bag at the back of the room, Mason had left two others hidden near the town's exits just in case Keira needed to go on the run while she was away from her cottage. "Find the stop sign past the parsonage, take five steps away from the road, look under a large rock," Keira recited. "The second is at the Old Crispin Mill, hidden in the crates stacked at its back."

"Good," Zoe said. "Remember your messages."

Those were the agreed-on texts they could send to each other in the event of an emergency. Just one letter per message, when the situation was too dire to waste time on a fully typed memo. "*H* for *hide; suspicious figures spotted. R* for *run; they know where you are. M* for *meet up at the campfire in the forest.* And *E* for *emergency, I'm in danger; proceed with caution.*"

"Brilliant job." Zoe squeezed her hand. "You're a beast, girl— you're going to get through this just fine. Same time tomorrow?"

"Same time tomorrow," Keira confirmed.

"You coming, nerd?" Zoe asked Mason as she swung her jacket over her shoulders.

"I'll catch up to you later," he said, beginning to stack their dishes and half-eaten scones.

Zoe waved over her shoulder as she slipped out the door. Keira listened to the crunch of Zoe's sneakers fading into the distance. Something small caught in the back of her mind.

Zoe normally preferred boots over sneakers. She had a fashion style that was very uniquely Zoe—something that blended punk and theater kid and sparkles and thrift-store finds that somehow all worked together.

Keira had noticed less of it over the last few days. Zoe had been wearing sneakers and jeans. So was Mason, she realized, watching him stack the dishes at the sink. And they had both brought jackets, even though the day was relatively mild.

They were dressed for travel, she realized. They were both ready to go on the run with her at a moment's notice.

"What are you thinking about?" Mason asked.

"How grateful I am," Keira said truthfully. "And how much I wish things were different."

Mason crossed to her. His warm arms wrapped around her, and he rested his head on top of hers. Keira leaned into him, breathing deeply. She'd never gotten much practice with close physical contact. But with Mason, it felt *easy.*

"Sorry," she whispered into his chest. "Your life would have been a whole lot easier without all of this."

"Worth it," he whispered back.

Keira tilted her head back to see his face. His smile infused his whole expression: it was not just his mouth, but it was also there in the tilt of his brows and buried in his eyes.

She'd only just started to let herself get close to Mason. They should have been going to the café on dates. Cuddling up on his couch to watch cheesy movies together. Going on long drives just to enjoy each other's company.

Instead, with the constant threat of Artec hanging over them, they were snatching at precious moments spent together. A brief kiss here, the brush of a hand there. It was nowhere near enough for either of them.

But then, without Artec pursuing her, Keira likely never would have stumbled onto Blighty. And she never would have met Mason. Those stolen moments wouldn't have existed at all.

Maybe, like he'd said, it was worth it.

She rose up onto her toes to kiss him, and he bent down, meeting her halfway. He was warm and sweet and everything good, and Keira felt like she was being torn away from something precious when she finally broke off the kiss.

"Time to get back to work?" he guessed, breathless.

She could only nod miserably.

"I'll go back on watch," he said, stepping back and finally letting her go. Following their last clash with Artec, he'd rented a car and spent large parts of his day looping around the roads surrounding Blighty, watching for any vehicles with Artec's branding. "Text me after you visit Agatha Edith-Whittle so I'll know you're okay."

"I'll do that."

Mason sent her a final, fond glance, then gently closed the door in his wake. The cottage felt a fraction colder and a fraction smaller with him gone.

Keira stood for a moment and let the emotions run through her. The burst of joy that came from being close to Mason lingered, but the doubts and anxieties and frustration were starting to bleed back in, smothering it.

The small lithe black cat appeared from seemingly nowhere to weave around Keira's legs, and the darkness faded again. Keira chuckled, bending to scratch around Daisy's head. "You're ready to start, huh?"

The cat's only answer was to trot to the door and stare back at Keira plaintively.

"Right," Keira said. She set an alarm on her phone, then took up her notebook and satchel. "Let's get this done."

CHAPTER 4

EVEN DAMPENED BY WISPY clouds, the sun still felt good on Keira's skin. She wished she could bask in it for a while longer. But that would have meant being more visible than she could technically afford.

Instead of lingering in her front yard, Keira turned into the forest that pressed against the edge of the cemetery. Daisy frisked ahead, already distracted by the insects in the long grass.

The trees were ancient and twisted. The ground was a maze of exposed roots and hollows, all hidden beneath the leaf litter. Grave markers, so old that the names were near unreadable, were barely visible between the trunks.

It was a wild and unforgiving place to be, but Keira had taken that path a dozen times in the last week.

She wove between the trunks until she reached her clearing. It was far away enough from the cemetery that no one would hear her and secretive enough that she wouldn't be easy to find. The clearing was only about twelve paces across, and the trees at its edges showed signs of her experiments: small scorch marks and runes trailed across their surfaces.

Keira came to a halt in the circle's center. Daisy paused briefly at her side, then leaped for one of the fallen leaves, delighting in the way it crunched under her paws.

For a second, they were alone in the space. Then faint, wispy mist began to bleed out between the trees' roots. Keira pulled on the muscle behind her eyes that opened her second sight, and three ethereal figures swelled into view.

"Hey, gang," Keira said. "It's good to see you all again."

She'd found their gravestones and learned their names on the first day she met them. They were Jayne, Emma, and Henry Tillson. Three siblings, all young adults, all deceased from a wave of influenza that had traveled through Blighty in the eighteen hundreds.

As far as Keira could figure out, none of them had unfinished business. They didn't seem able to explain why they stayed. She thought it was possible they simply didn't want to be separated from one another.

Keira had a trick to untether ghosts who didn't have unfinished business. Each spirit had a delicate, tangled thread buried in their chest, close to their hearts. Keira couldn't see it, but she could feel it when she reached into them. Pulling on that thread would untangle it, releasing them from the earth and letting them pass over peacefully.

She'd offered to do that for the three siblings, but they indicated they weren't ready to leave yet.

Keira was grateful for that—because they'd also agreed to help her with her tests. And she really needed that help.

The journal in Keira's hands was small, but it felt like it weighed a ton. In the span of a week, she'd filled it two-thirds full with notes and sketches. In early morning and late at night, when she couldn't sleep, Keira would light a small candle and hunch over the pages, preparing her next attempts. Then, during the day, she'd come out to her clearing and test them.

Keira's gift let her see the dead, but it also gave her the power to create and use runes. They were images that, when drawn just right and infused with a whisper of energy, would give her a small amount of control over her environment.

She had a rune to unlock doors. A rune to quicken the speed she regained her strength when she was exhausted.

A rune to dissipate or redirect a spirit's energy. A rune that, when painted on her body, would help her see easier in low light. A rune that increased luck, by just a tiny fraction.

She'd also discovered a new rune while trailing Artec: a symbol they attached to the deceased to tether the ghost in place. That was how they ensured the spirits didn't dissipate naturally before they could be interred and turned into batteries. It had been an ominous discovery; it meant Artec had also been experimenting with the sigils. Keira dreaded what else they might have uncovered.

Artec's rune—the one that tethered ghosts—was the exact

opposite of Keira's mission, but she'd still dutifully copied it into the notebook.

That little leather-bound sheath of papers had become her lifeline. There was no other preexisting list of runes or any guide on how to use them. Zoe had scoured historical records, looking for anything that lined up with Keira's list and had come up empty. Every symbol Keira knew of, she'd discovered by accident.

Which meant it was possible she might find more.

Maybe even one strong enough to give her an advantage over Artec.

Keira flipped the notebook to the latest entries and knelt on the ground. Using her fingertip, she traced shapes in the dirt, waiting for any prickle of significance.

She could sense when a rune was working. Kind of. Just as she could sense electricity in the air that warned her when a spirit was nearby, she could catch a whisper of sensation when she hovered her hand over an active rune. It wasn't much—nothing she would ever notice if she wasn't focusing—but it felt almost like a soft breeze across her fingertips. And, for whatever reason, it was easiest to feel when drawn on organic matter, like the loamy earth in the forest.

This strategy—trial-and-error testing to find new runes—was the best one Keira had. While Mason watched the town for Artec operatives and while Zoe worked to dig up more information about the secretive corporation, Keira spent her hours crouched in the forest, scoring lines and circles and arrows through the dirt.

She was trying to work systematically. With each failed drawing,

Keira would cross it out in the notebook. The pages were becoming covered with thick *Xs*.

But not every test failed.

Three days before, Keira had discovered a rune made of looping circles. Finding an active rune was only half the puzzle, though. She also had to figure out what it *did*. She'd spent twenty minutes on trial and error before thinking to draw the image on her forehead.

The moment she did that, the three siblings spaced around the clearing's edges glowed as though a lamp had been brightened.

A rune to make ghosts more visible, she'd written in the journal. Keira wasn't sure what she was going to use that one for, but it would probably come in handy if she needed to communicate with a weak spirit.

In addition to the ghost-brightening rune, she'd found three additional active sigils. She just didn't know what to do with them yet. She could feel the whisper-soft energy bleeding off them, and she'd spent hours testing every angle she could think of. She'd burned them into the tree trunks, drawn them beneath and surrounding the spirits, and written them on herself.

In the end, she'd had to conclude that they likely required a specific scenario to work, like the rune to unlock doors. It might take an entire lifetime to uncover their purpose. Frustrated, Keira had noted those signs in the back of the book for more testing, then moved on.

Sometimes the spirits would drift nearer to Keira, as though they found her strangely curious. Sometimes they faded out of sight, as though wanting to have a rest. Most of the time, though, they simply stood and waited. Keira liked to talk to them when the work began to wear on her. They didn't talk back. The dead were not especially chatty.

Hours trailed by while Keira worked through the pages of options she'd lined up the previous night. Angle, angle, swoop, arrow. Angle, angle, circle, arrow. Angle, angle, circle, circle, arrow—

A whisper of sensation brushed Keira's fingertips as she hovered her hand over that latest rune. She froze, her breath held, as she made sure she wasn't hallucinating.

She wasn't. The rune was active. She'd found another one.

Keira quickly flipped to the back of her notebook. The final page kept notes of all her active runes. The ones with known abilities were at the top and the ones she didn't yet understand were below. Keira carefully transcribed the shape, then turned back to the earth.

"I think I have something," she called to the spirits. "Stand by."

They didn't react. But that was par for the course.

Keira let her hand hover over the marks again, half hoping their purpose would spring to mind. She didn't know if she was imagining it, but she thought the faint energy rising from the lines was different from the ones before. Stronger? More condensed?

Or maybe she was just making herself more sensitive to the sensations by focusing on them so much.

Over the course of that week, Keira had developed something like a routine set of tests for new runes. First, she tried standing on the mark. There were no new sensations. No increase or decrease in her tiredness or emotions. Keira stepped back, then began to draw repeat patterns of the rune in a circle.

"Who wants to help this time?" she called to the watching spirits.

There was a second's pause as the ghosts seemed to consider, then the eldest sister drifted forward.

She was the strongest and brightest of the trio that day. Keira moved back to give her room but still felt the faint wash of icy air coming off the specter as she took her place in the center of the circle.

"How are you feeling?" Keira kept her voice to a respectful whisper. "Anything?"

The ghost simply blinked once, lids closing gracefully over empty eyes, and Keira took that to mean *no*.

"Okay. Let's try…"

Keira began to draw the symbol in looping patterns. One thing she'd learned about runes was that repeating them often made them stronger. She didn't stop until she had nearly two dozen of the shapes, spiraling away from Jayne's smokelike form.

There was no response. The spirit simply waited, impassive and faintly unimpressed. Not for the first time, Keira got the sense that the siblings had expected the work to be a lot more exciting than it actually was. It wasn't a good feeling to be a disappointment to the dead.

"Right." Keira stretched her arms, trying to loosen sore muscles, as she crossed to the trees. She'd started wearing a small satchel filled with essential tools: pens, charcoal, and a tiny flashlight Zoe had given her. It saved her from having to hunt for writing tools whenever the need to create a sigil arose. She'd already used her own blood to draw the marks a few times; the satchel, in theory, meant she wouldn't have to bite through the sore skin on her thumb again.

She took out a piece of charcoal and used the ash to draw a repeat of the symbol on multiple trees, in case the rune's purpose needed something more solid than dirt to become apparent.

There were no exciting results. No smoldering, no sparks, not even a faint glow.

But Keira knew she was on the right path. She could still feel the soft, whisper-light touch of power when she pressed her hand into the drawings.

That was the last layer of her experiments: to draw the runes on herself. She rubbed some of the charcoal onto her fingertips, then awkwardly re-created the shape on her own forehead.

Nothing. No visions, and no change to the spirits' forms.

Come on, come on.

She drew the marks on her hands, then on her chest, just in case. Still nothing.

Keira was starting to feel desperate. When she'd discovered the rune that made the ghosts light up, it had felt like a euphoric victory. Everything since then had been a dead end.

And she was running out of time. She couldn't spend another week hunting for yet more runes that gave her no results.

The alarm on her phone went off, and the sound was so loud and sudden that Keira nearly choked. She scrambled to turn it off, then checked the time.

She'd set that alarm to remind her to visit Agatha Edith-Whittle. She'd figured tardiness would be deemed unacceptable by the head of the BPS. Almost as unacceptable as showing up to the woman's house grimy. She glanced down at her hands, which were coated with charcoal.

Oh, damn it.

"Great job today," she called to the ghosts as she snatched up her supplies. Daisy came loping back toward her, apparently ready to return to the cottage too. "A-plus, gold star. Did you guys get gold stars for your work when you were alive, or is this all nonsense to you? Doesn't matter. I'll see you tomorrow."

The three siblings gave no response except to tilt their heads a fraction as Keira sprinted out of the clearing.

There were no visitors in the cemetery, so Keira didn't need to keep herself hidden as she jogged straight into her cottage and into the bathroom, where she quickly scrubbed the marks from her forehead, chest, and hands. Even with soap, they didn't want to fully come off. She supposed Agatha Edith-Whittle would just have to deal with a somewhat grubby guest.

Then she threw on a jacket that she hoped would make her halfway presentable, scooped out some fresh food for the small black cat that was circling her bowls impatiently, and then looped back out of her cottage and into the woods again.

She was lucky that her intended address was on one of the roads that pressed into the trees; it meant she could avoid the main streets entirely. The forest was cool and quiet. It had begun to feel like a second home to Keira. She moved quickly and lithely, her paces long and near silent, until she saw the silhouette of houses through the trees.

She fished Agatha's card out of her pocket as she stepped between the trees and crossed to the street. House number 5. Though, as she lifted her head, Keira realized she could have found her destination even without the card.

Agatha's house was like a manifestation of its owner. The paint was so crisp and clean that it looked like it had been applied within the last week. The grass didn't hold a single weed and was trimmed so strictly that Keira felt she could go through the lawn with a measuring tape and not find any variation. The shrubs were perfect cubes, except for the ones that were perfect orbs. And the path leading up to the front door looked uncannily clean, like it had been scrubbed just that morning.

The nearby buildings were tidy but none to the obsessive extent of Agatha's. It stood, small and prim and perfect, between sprawling estates. The street, which also held Mason's house, looked to be one of the more expensive ones in Blighty.

"Well," Keira said to herself. "Let's do this."

She grimaced, knowing her shoes were probably going to leave flecks of dirt on the spotless path, as she crossed to the porch. She only had the chance to knock once before the door swung open.

"Thank goodness you made it," Agatha gasped, one hand pressed to her chest. "It's getting worse."

CHAPTER 5

KEIRA WAS ASSAULTED BY the scent of potpourri as she stepped inside Agatha's house.

She couldn't stop herself from glancing around surreptitiously. As far as she was aware, no one else could see or sense ghosts in the same way Keira could.

Though…that's not true, is it?

She'd met ravenous spirits in Dane Crispin's mansion. They'd latched on to their last descendant, draining him endlessly, and Dane had certainly felt the effects.

Keira shucked her coat, her guard high. "Tell me what's happened."

"Look at this." Agatha crossed the hallway, then extended a hand toward a small potted plant carefully positioned against the wall. A single leaf lay on the polished wooden floor beneath it. Agatha's voice shook. "My peace lily has been brutalized. I fear the spirits are growing angry."

"Oh." All the tension drained out of Keira. She'd yet to meet a ghost that had the ability—let alone desire—to prune plants. "Right. Um, let me take a look around."

Agatha took a hiccuping breath. "Of course. Anything you need."

The house's inside was just as precise and perfect as the exterior. The floors were glossy and dark; the walls were pristine white. There wasn't a single speck of dirt or any sign of dust. Every piece of furniture fitted into its space as though it had been custom-made. Agatha clearly was not the kind of person who tolerated irregularities.

Keira tilted her head back and opened her senses. She waited for the familiar prickle of spectral energy, the soft whisper of a presence nearby. The atmosphere was still. Keira stretched herself, fighting to pick up even the smallest trace of energy, but there was none.

That was her answer then. Case closed in a record one minute and twelve seconds: Agatha's house was confirmed to be perfectly, mundanely unhaunted.

It felt too soon to deliver that news to her host. She'd only just walked through the door, and she didn't want to look like she wasn't taking Agatha seriously. Instead, she hedged for time.

"Why don't you tell me what first made you suspect there was a ghost here?" Keira asked as she began to walk down the hallway, glancing into the rooms she passed.

"Well." Agatha stepped neatly behind her. "I've only had this house for a few years. My old home was on Magnolia Lane, across town you know, but then the council put up a lopsided signpost on the street corner and resisted my efforts to have it straightened, so I had no choice except to move."

"Sure," Keira managed.

"Before I purchased this home, I drew together a timeline of its most important facts—births, deaths, marriages, pets, where the kitchen tiles were sourced from. The builder's name and his extended family medical history. Things like that, you know, the basic background details."

"Yes," Keira said, doing her best to act like she hadn't just been subjected to some of the most bewildering concepts she'd ever heard.

"There was nothing that alarmed me excessively. The house was only built twenty years ago, you know, which makes it absolutely brand-new compared to most of our beautiful town. To the best of my knowledge, no one has actually passed away inside the building."

"Right." That tracked with what Keira was seeing. She passed by the bedroom and bathroom with her second sight held open, just in case, but she neither saw anything spectral nor felt any trace of energy.

"But I must have been mistaken." Agatha knit her hands together, growing anxious. "Lately, I've grown convinced there must be something…something *sinister* within my home. I hear it at night. It scratches at the walls. It moves through the roof. It rustles and thumps. And there's an awful smell, and no amount of lavender infusers can fix it."

"Huh," Keira said again as they stopped in the kitchen.

Ghosts generally didn't create sounds or smells. At least, not sounds or smells the average person could perceive. Keira struggled to find a way to broach her next thought. "Have you, uh…considered calling in a pest inspector? Maybe someone who can look for rats?"

Agatha gasped, her hands fluttering around her throat. Apparently, Keira had found something Agatha feared even more than ghosts.

"Mercy," she gasped, staggering and then slumping into a chair. "Not rats. My reputation will never recover."

"Well, uh…" Keira shrugged helplessly. "I'll keep looking, I guess?"

She'd nearly covered the whole house. Ghosts could hide when they didn't want to be seen, but their presence still left traces in the air. Keira could just about guarantee that Agatha's house was ghost-free, but she guessed it wouldn't hurt anyone to be extra thorough.

She looped around the kitchen before stopping at the door to the back garden. Through the glass, she could see a sitting area and neat rows of shrubs that had been trimmed into precise angles. And…

At last, there it was. Right at the edges of her senses, so distant that it could have been a memory of a memory, was the distant thrum of electricity. Keira reached out a hand, trying to sense where it was coming from.

"Hey, is it okay if I take a look outside?"

Agatha seemed faintly skeptical, probably because she'd

requested Keira visit her about a haunted *house*, not a haunted *garden*. But she still gave a curt little nod. Keira pushed on the door and stepped through.

The taste of electricity was a fraction stronger but still not close. Agatha's yard stretched ahead for about twenty paces before ending in a painted wood fence. As far as Keira could tell, the spirit she'd sensed didn't belong to Agatha's yard.

It wasn't a total surprise to pick up on a nearby spirit's presence. Many ghosts lingered at their grave sites, but others stayed at their places of death. Keira hadn't spent much time exploring what ghosts might be found within its boundaries, but Blighty was an old town, and she guessed there would probably be at least one or two ghosts on every street.

She pulled her second sight as wide open as it would go, trying to ignore the faint headache that flared whenever she overused the muscle, and glanced over the fences and into the neighbors' yards.

There was the flicker of a faint, transparent form in the garden to Keira's left. Unlike Agatha's tidy lawn, the house on that side was a sprawling tangle. Buried inside it was a building so large that she'd have to call it a mansion. It was three stories high, and the land around it seemed to stretch forever. If Agatha had a *yard*, then that house had an *estate*.

That's weird, isn't it? Keira craned to see some of the other nearby houses. They were large and probably expensive, but nothing as big as Agatha's neighbor's. *Guess every street needs a Jones to keep up with.*

The yard was badly overgrown, making it hard to see the dead resident. Keira slowly paced toward the fence as she tried to get another glimpse of it. Was it possible this ghost was causing Agatha's agitation? Probably not, since the symptoms were a better match for wildlife than un-life. But still…

A second form shimmered in the distance, and Keira pulled up short.

Okay. Two ghosts. It's a big house; it's probably had a lot of people live and die in there. And, honestly, the yard is large enough that it might even have a private family graveyard…

A third form drifted between the trees. And then a fourth. Keira's skin turned clammy.

One or even two ghosts would be fairly expected. But something was starting to feel bad, and Keira had learned a long time ago not to doubt her instincts.

She rested her hands on the fence and strained to see the specters between the long-neglected plants. The garden had been a formal space once. She could still make out a cracked and empty fountain and two stone seats, both overturned. Grass had overtaken a stone path until it was barely visible.

Keira tilted to look up at the house. It wasn't a mansion, she realized, but something more distinct. A hotel, maybe? Though something about that description didn't sit right either.

The building was elaborate, made of stone that had aged into a caustic shade of slate gray. A dozen balconies jutted out of its rear wall, facing the garden; each one was small, with wrought-iron rails running around its borders. Just enough space for a guest to sit at a small table and overlook the fountain.

Despite the balconies, the building didn't seem like a pleasant place to stay. It felt almost closer to a prison. The chills intensified, and Keira wanted nothing more than to back away and never set her eyes on the brutally rigid building again.

A ghost appeared. She emerged out of the air, directly in front of Keira, so suddenly that Keira's breath froze in her lungs.

Only the thin wooden fence separated them. Keira could feel the chill rolling off the specter, like a gust of icy air. It was a woman—probably no older than twenty-five—and long wispy hair drifted behind her as though caught in an invisible tide. Her empty eyes were wide. Her mouth was pinched into a hard line, and some dried liquid—phlegm?—crusted at its corners. A dirty nightdress swirled around her bone-thin limbs, weightless.

Keira still had her hand braced on the fence. The spirit reached out her own and rested it on top of Keira's. It was a strange, unpleasant sensation. Keira couldn't feel the ghost, but she could feel the *cold*, like plunging her hand into a bucket of ice.

The ghost's lips moved. The shapes they formed were blurred and indistinct, but the message was horrifyingly clear.

Save us.

"Oh," Keira whispered as something clicked in her mind. The other ghosts—the ones she'd glimpsed earlier—had emerged from the garden. They stood, distant but attentive, their unsmiling eyes fixed on Keira.

They were all women. All young.

All wearing the same nightdresses.

All horrifyingly thin.

This is bad, this is bad, this is bad—

"Miss Keira!" Agatha Edith-Whittle called, and Keira flinched. Her host stood by her house, hands clasped in front of her, a strained smile on her face.

The ghosts vanished, fading into nothing. The only trace they'd ever existed was the trail of melting frost on Keira's hand.

CHAPTER 6

"WHY DON'T YOU COME away from there?" Agatha called, beckoning to Keira. "We…we try not to bother our neighbors here."

"Right," Keira said. She gave the strange, elaborate house one final glance, then stepped away from the fence to join Agatha at her door. "I was just curious. What is that place?"

"Oh, I don't know." She was still smiling, but something about Agatha seemed strained. "The owner isn't a very pleasant man."

"What makes you say that?"

Agatha's eyes bulged slightly. She gestured toward his overgrown garden, as though that was the only answer Keira needed. To be fair, it was. The strange building was the opposite of Agatha's: everything she had kept meticulous and clean had been allowed to decay and run wild just across the fence.

"It's called The Home, and that's all I know," Agatha said. She sniffed. "Though there's not much homish about the place."

"Do you know the owner's name?" Keira pressed. "Or what his job is?"

"No. He's an unpleasant man, and it's an unpleasant place," Agatha said with the kind of finality that meant the conversation was over. "I avoid thinking about it. I suggest you do the same. I don't know why you're so interested in it, especially when *I'm* the one who hired you."

"Right. The ghosts. Yeah." Keira glanced back at The Home. She couldn't see the spirits, but she could feel their eyes on her. "I… I'll need to come back. Your situation is trickier than I thought it would be."

"There *are* otherworldly beings present, then?" Agatha asked, clasping her hands together.

It was a stretch of the truth, but Keira didn't see any way around it. She needed to revisit the neighboring ghosts, and having access to Agatha's home was likely the safest way to do that. "They're not dangerous," she promised. "They don't mean you harm."

"But the peace lily—!"

"An accident. Sometimes…sometimes ghosts are afraid of being forgotten, and so they'll try to remind us that they're here."

"Oh." Agatha's expression softened. "I didn't realize."

"There's nothing to fear about them," Keira said as they stepped back into Agatha's house and moved toward the front door. "But I'll help them move on, if I can. I have your number." She tapped the business card in her pocket.

"Very good," Agatha said. She seemed reassured, at least. "I'll wait for you to send me the schedule for our next appointment."

She waved Keira off, then carefully closed the door. Keira had barely taken two steps toward the road when she heard the faint but unmistakable sound of a broom swishing across the hallway where she'd been.

Keira forced her hands into her pockets. It wasn't possible to see much of The Home from the street; enormous trees had been grown to shield it from sight.

She needed to know what had happened in that place.

The spirits had all been wearing colorless nightdresses and had been barefoot, which made it nearly impossible to place their time of death. They could have perished a hundred years ago or the day before.

Mason's house was on the same street. She could see it, not far away. He might know more about The Home than Agatha. Keira moved toward Mason's place but slowed when she saw the driveway was empty and the lights were off. He would still be out, then, patrolling the roads around Blighty as he looked for any Artec-branded vehicles.

Zoe would probably give her answers too. If Blighty had any skeletons in its closet, she could rely on Zoe to know exactly how many bones they had.

But it was Zoe's first day back at the store, and Keira didn't feel safe venturing into the town's center.

There was a third option, though: Adage. As the town's pastor, he knew about every secret and every feud, though he took on the gossip with slightly less enthusiasm than Zoe did. But he was a reliable ally, and he was always happy to help Keira when she was working with the dead.

Keira reentered the forest and quickened her pace into a jog. Leaves rustled, and Daisy flicked out of the shadows to lope alongside her.

"We have *got* to figure out how this connection works," Keira whispered to the cat. Daisy's only reply was to flatten her ears and race ahead, a beast born of eagerness and joy at the sight of some imagined prey.

Keira emerged from the forest at the back of her cemetery. Graves spread out ahead of her in uneven rows. Mist had begun to gather as the sun fell behind the trees.

Specters were visible. Keira murmured greetings as she passed them. A few times, she stopped to ask the ghosts if they'd heard of a place called The Home, but they either blinked at her mutely or simply vanished from sight. Keira sighed and instead focused on the distant church and parsonage. If she was being honest with herself, she was a little bit jealous of the ghosts' ability to end an unwanted conversation by fading away.

The lights were on in the parsonage, but it turned out Keira didn't even need to knock. Adage was already in the garden, his cheerful maroon cardigan standing out against the green as he watered his plants. He raised a hand when he saw Keira.

"I was hoping I'd catch you," he called, setting down his watering can. "I stopped by your cottage, but you weren't home."

"Sorry, it's been an unexpectedly busy day." Keira leaned on the fence. "What's up?"

"Well, it's the strangest thing." Adage took his spectacles off and polished them with a small cloth from his pocket. His eyes were blue and a little watery but still perceptive as he peered at Keira. "I had a letter in my mail. It was addressed to you."

Keira's heart skipped a beat. "But…I didn't think anyone knew where I am."

"That's what I believed too." Adage lifted his shoulders in a shrug. "I know you said to call you if there was an emergency, but I wasn't sure if this counted. It's a letter, after all, not an invasion. I slipped it under your cottage door."

Keira rubbed the back of her neck as she tried to think. Zoe was the type of person who might send letters just for the fun of it. Mason, too—she could picture him writing her a note to show he cared. But if either of them were going to send her mail, she was pretty sure they'd warn her ahead of time so she could avoid exactly this kind of heart attack. They were all hyperaware of how cautious they needed to be.

But then…

"The library?" Keira guessed. "I signed up for a card there when I came to town, and I'm pretty sure I gave them your address."

"I can't say the library is in the habit of sending mail, but it's a possibility, I suppose," Adage said. "You haven't been holding on to overdue books, have you?"

Keira laughed. "I'm honestly looking forward to the day when I can borrow some novels just for fun. I think I've only ever used the library for research. Speaking of—I have a mystery. Have you heard of a place in town called The Home?"

"Oh, The Home!" Adage clapped his hands. "Yes, of course. It used to be one of the most recognizable landmarks of our town.

Though, The Home is only what the locals called it. It sounds a little warmer and friendlier than the official name and has the bonus of being less of a mouthful."

Keira's skin had begun to prickle again. "What's the official name?"

"Blighty Sanatorium and Rehabilitation Center." Adage tilted his head thoughtfully. "It's not exactly catchy."

The nightdresses. The pale faces.

"It was built as a sanatorium for those suffering from tuberculosis," Adage continued. "The country air was considered helpful. When antibiotics were developed as a more effective treatment, The Home was changed to a long-term convalescence hotel, especially for those with cancer and degenerative neurological disorders."

"How long ago did it close down?"

"That would have to be at least twenty years back now. You're stretching my memory, but I believe there was a scandal at the time. Something in the walls—mold or maybe asbestos—that was actually worsening the patients' health. They couldn't find a buyer, so it was eventually put in the hands of a custodian who continues to live there now. A Mr....Mr...."

Keira gripped the fence as she waited, eager. Adage frowned, staring blankly into the distance, before inhaling.

"Mr. Jensen! That's it. I rarely see him in town, and I don't think I've spoken to him since The Home closed down. Truthfully, I think he tries to avoid me if he sees me." Adage's bushy eyebrows pulled together; then he sighed. "I wish I could be a friend to everyone in our community, but I have to accept that not all my neighbors want the same."

Keira nodded, her mind swirling. Everything fit together. A rehabilitation center would see a lot of lives cut tragically short. It explained the clothes, too—if the women spent most of their stay in bed, they might only ever wear the long gowns.

"Have you found a new spirit to help?" Adage asked, picking up the watering can.

"Kind of. Maybe. I need to think it through."

"You know I'm always happy to help whenever I can. Ah—but I forgot to tell you. One of my parishioners and a very dear old friend is unwell. Her daughter has been staying with her but has a work trip she can't avoid. They asked if I would stay at their place to keep an eye on her. It's just for two days, and it's near the town center. If there's any trouble, call me. I can be home within ten minutes."

"No problem. I hope your friend is okay."

"I do as well," Adage said, and then gave a parting wave.

As Keira walked toward her cottage, her mind turned back to The Home. Adage's revelations should have been a reassurance. It explained the ghosts' appearances. But as she crossed between the gravestones, one image reared in the back of her mind again and again.

Save us.

She was sure that was what the ghost had said.

Is it possible she wasn't fully aware that she was dead?

Some spirits—the children especially—seemed to have a tenuous grasp of what had happened to them. Maybe the ghost refused to believe she'd died and was begging for the medical help that hadn't been able to save her during life.

But…

There hadn't been any fear or confusion in the ghost's expression. Her face had been hard. Determined. Angry, even.

As though she'd been wronged.

Save us…but from what? What does a ghost fear?

They feared Artec once they realized what was happening, but the ghosts at The Home weren't in any danger of being interred there; Artec only took fresh victims—bodies they could guarantee the spirits would stay attached to until Artec could… harvest them.

She'd seen ghosts afraid of the shade from the forest as it grew and consumed them. But shades were more powerful and far more noticeable than an average spirit, and Keira hadn't gotten any sense of one near The Home.

So then…what?

Daisy was waiting for her at the cottage door. Keira unlocked and opened it. Just inside, on the wood floor, she found the letter Adage had mentioned.

She picked it up and turned it over. The sender had handwritten her name—just *Keira*, no surname—and the address to the parsonage on the front. The scrawl was tight and angular, very different from Mason's neat print and Zoe's enthusiastic scribbles. It had been sent as priority mail, overnight delivery.

Keira's stomach twisted as she tore the letter open and pulled out a single sheet of paper. The message inside was brief.

"Oh," Keira said, a whistling sound rising in her ears as the words sank in. "Oh no."

CHAPTER 7

THE CAMPFIRE, STILL NEW, sent up a trail of smoke toward the forest canopy above. Mason had arranged three logs around it so they could sit, but Keira couldn't stop pacing in endless looping circles around the clearing.

"It might not be as bad as it looks," Mason murmured.

"Well, it's not *good*," Zoe said. She had the letter and was rereading it for what must have been the hundredth time.

They were at their secret meeting location. Night had fallen and the only light came from the flames.

Mason crouched near the fire, tending it. He'd brought food for dinner. Daisy lounged in the leaves at his side, soaking up the warmth.

"I can work on tracing the letter," Zoe said. She flicked the envelope around to point at the stamp and the barcode printed over it. "This little set of numbers will tell us which post office processed it. Though, if I'm being honest, we might not get far with that. If we were the police, we could scan the security footage to identify who mailed it, but, well, it turns out the average postal store isn't a big fan of giving their tapes to some random person who doesn't have a badge."

"You've tried?" Mason asked.

"Heaps of times." Zoe sighed. "So. We'd know where it was mailed from but not much more."

"And we don't really have time," Keira noted. She rubbed her hands on her jeans to stop them from growing damp again. "We'll need to make a choice in less than twelve hours."

They lapsed into silence again. Keira crossed to Zoe and held out a hand for the letter, even though she'd memorized its words already.

The note was written on a plain piece of paper with the same jagged hand as the letter's address.

I FOUND YOU, AND SO WILL THEY. WE NEED TO TALK.

Below that was an address and a time. Zoe had already looked up the location; it was a park about twenty minutes outside Cheltenham, the nearest major town to Blighty.

The meeting time was set for the next day. The unknown sender was lucky Adage was reliable about checking his mail.

"It's obviously a trap," Zoe said, not for the first time.

"But *why?*" Keira shook her head as she resumed pacing. "If Artec has pinpointed my location this closely, then why not just rush me while I'm in my cabin? Why try to lure me out to a new location?"

"You've evaded them quite a few times now," Mason noted. He'd started toasting bread over the flames, turning the slices carefully to avoid letting them burn. "Maybe they realize it's a mistake to try to catch you on your home turf, where you're prepared."

"But…I'm not going to be walking into this meeting blind. The letter isn't trying to disguise the fact that it's connected to Artec. If they wanted to lower my guard, they could have at least pretended to be a long-lost aunt or something."

"They probably want to guarantee you'll go," Zoe said. "I mean, *would* you have gone to meet a long-lost aunt you've never heard of before? Doubtful. But you don't really have a choice this way."

"Which means, if it's a trap, it's so foolproof that it doesn't matter how prepared I am." Keira stopped, then turned and started pacing in the opposite direction. "I just need to be in the vicinity and I'm as good as dead. But if they have a trap that effective, why does it have to be at Cheltenham? Why not set it up closer to Blighty? I just don't get it."

Mason had finished toasting the bread and began stacking layers of ham, cheese, and tomato onto it.

"You're awfully calm," Zoe said.

He smiled. "I've been thinking along some slightly different lines."

"Spill," she said dryly.

"I think you both skipped lunch today. Zoe, you were busy at the store, and Keira, you were busy with Agatha, and you both forgot to eat. I think some food is going to make this feel more manageable."

"Thanks, Mum," Zoe said, but she still grudgingly accepted the sandwich he passed her.

"I also think Keira has a habit of underestimating herself." Mason offered the second sandwich to Keira, and she gave him a tight smile as she took it and bit off a corner. The bread was still warm, helping to soften the cheese. He'd been right. She'd forgotten about lunch entirely.

"I've watched you climb a Ferris wheel and leap fences and do the impossible," Mason continued. "Artec is powerful, but so are you."

Keira forced herself to stop pacing and she sat on one of the logs by the fire. Mason thought she was underestimating herself, but she was more afraid that he was overestimating her. She'd only survived so long through a combination of luck and outside help. But she didn't know how to say that out loud, especially not when Mason was smiling at her so warmly.

"I also think it's possible that this is just what it looks like at face value," he added. "Someone who wants to help us."

"Not a chance," Zoe said.

"Artec is a powerful company. But it's also a *large* company. And when you have hundreds of employees, you're guaranteed to have at least one or two who fall out of love with the mission statement. Look at Keira's parents; they were high up in the organization but still left it, even knowing the risks."

Zoe spoke through a mouthful of cheesy bread. "They left

because they knew Schaeffer would want to experiment on their baby when he discovered she'd been exposed to the spectral energy."

"And no one else in the organization could possibly have an equally strong motive to break away from it?" Mason shrugged. "Remember, Artec's original prototypes didn't involve chaining ghosts to their graves. I'm sure there are people growing uncomfortable with the direction the research has taken."

For a second, they were all silent as they thought. Then Zoe said, "I still can't believe you're this calm, Mr. Play It Safe."

"*I* didn't skip lunch."

Zoe flicked a piece of crust at him.

"We have to go, don't we?" Keira asked as she took another bite of the sandwich. "At least one person knows where I am now. I can't hide any longer. But if we go to the meeting, we might be able to make it safer."

"That's a good question," Mason said. "It's impossible to eliminate all risk, but at least we can reduce the potential danger. We'll have the rental car, to begin with; it won't be familiar to them."

"We'll change the meeting location," Zoe said. "That's the best way to gain an advantage. I'll look through my supplies back home, too, and see if anything in there can help us."

"Okay." Keira nodded, tearing off a piece of ham and offering it to Daisy. "We can do this. Worst-case scenario, we're just bringing forward the inevitable. Best-case scenario…"

"This might be the advantage we've been looking for," Mason finished.

"Fingers crossed," Keira said.

Zoe kicked her legs out toward the fire, basking in its warmth. "While we're here, how did the meeting with the Beeps go?"

"Right, Agatha." The letter had almost knocked The Home out of Keira's mind. "I think she has rats."

"Yeah." Mason gave an apologetic smile. "That tracks. They come out of the forest sometimes. Poor Agatha; she won't like that news."

"She really didn't." Keira shuffled closer to the fire. The night was cooling rapidly, and small wisps of condensation floated from her lips as she spoke. "But while I was there, I found something else. Have either of you heard of The Home?"

Zoe and Mason exchanged a glance.

"That's next door to her, isn't it?" Mason asked. "It's so well hidden from the street that I keep forgetting it's there."

"Did you see something?" Zoe's eyes had lit up with curiosity as she leaned forward.

"Yeah. Ghosts. More than a few."

"It used to be a sanatorium," Mason offered.

"Right," Keira said. "I checked in with Adage when I got home, and he was able to tell me part of its history. But...there's something different about these ghosts. They're not lost. They're almost...angry?"

"I bet they know something we don't," Zoe said. "That place shut down to escape a scandal. The official story is that it was too old and too expensive to keep running without tuberculosis patients depending on it, but the nonofficial whispers say there was something more. Patients who were expected to recover died. Lawsuits were looming."

"I heard they found something toxic in the walls," Mason said. "Was it arsenic?"

"That's the thing." Zoe snapped toward him, her eyes huge and round. "I've heard about five different stories for what they found in the walls—lead, arsenic, asbestos. And even with the place being an alleged biohazard, the caretaker is still living there."

"Huh," Mason said.

"Though, I guess maybe he really is suffering some kind of chronic poisoning. He's the weirdest guy in town, and in a place like Blighty, that's saying something."

Mason grimaced. "I thought we learned a lesson about passing judgment on strangers after you accused Dane Crispin of being a vampire."

"Who says I was passing judgment on Dane Crispin?" Zoe folded her arms, looking annoyed. "A bit of vampirism would have instantly increased his coolness factor, something he desperately needed."

"Zoe—"

"No, seriously, I'm not trying to be mean to Old Man Jenkins or whatever his name is."

"Jensen," Mason said, looking pained. "You know his name is Jensen."

"You want to believe there's a good side to everyone, and I wish I could admire you for that, but there's something wrong with that guy." Zoe held up a finger to silence his protests. "You probably don't remember this, but when we were kids, Suzy Halstead slipped on the icy stones in the town center. She split her lip and knocked a tooth out."

"I do remember," Mason said sadly. "She was twelve. She was away from school for a week and needed surgery to reattach the tooth."

"Yeah. And I was there when it happened, sitting on the edge of the fountain. There was blood everywhere; people started yelling and running to help her. I was so shocked that I just kind of froze. Then I heard a strange sound. I turned, and I saw Jensen standing in the middle of the street, laughing. He saw all that blood and heard the screams and started to laugh."

Chills crept up Keira's back.

Mason knit his hands together, frowning. He took a slow breath. "I fully understand why that would be upsetting. But we all have different reactions to shocking events. Some people panic. Some people freeze. And, yes, some people even laugh. Not because they find it funny, but because their body doesn't know how to process what they're seeing, and it bubbles out in strange ways. It doesn't mean they're an awful person."

"I'm gonna let you believe that."

"I mean, it's a scientific fact—"

"Jensen wasn't in shock." Zoe shook her head. "Believe me, I was there. He was delighted."

They fell into silence. The fire crackled, sending up a small shower of sparks. Mason leaned forward to drop another piece of wood into it.

"Are you thinking Jensen has something to do with why the ghosts are upset?" Keira asked.

Zoe shrugged, relaxing a fraction. "He's a weird guy. The ghosts are mad. They might be related, or it might just be a coincidence. Correlation versus causation, and all of that."

"You want to help the ghosts." Mason said it as a statement, not a question.

Keira shuffled her feet. "Yeah. I know I shouldn't—I know it's a distraction we don't need right now—but…they asked. And it's hard to say no when there's no one else who can hear them."

He smiled. "I get that."

"So much for sticking to one crisis at a time," Zoe said, but a wolfish grin was growing. "I can't believe we get to investigate The Home."

"That might be a problem," Mason said. "Jensen keeps the place running largely the same as it did when it was an active convalescence home: the gates are always locked, and strangers are treated with suspicion. He's not the type of person who would invite a curious neighbor in to have a look around, so you'll need another form of access."

"Um." Keira cringed. "Okay, so, Agatha Edith-Whittle definitely has rats, but I might have told her I'd come back to deal with her ghost problem anyway."

"It's not lying if it's to a Beeps," Zoe said. "It's just…a tasteful omission for everyone's benefit."

"I can speak to the ghosts across the fence," Keira said. "So I won't need to do any trespassing. I just have to keep Agatha distracted long enough to find out what the spirits need."

"That'll be easy enough," Mason said, and the fire hissed again, shooting up more sparks. "Let's start planning for tomorrow. If we're going to meet your anonymous correspondent, we'll need to leave early, and that means we only have a few hours to figure out our strategy."

CHAPTER 8

LEAVES TICKLED THE BACK of Keira's neck. She lay on her stomach, staring down at the distant park where the letter writer had asked to meet.

The overlook was Zoe's find. Technically part of a hiking trail that looped across the foothills of a mountain, it let them surveil the area for unusual activity while still giving them plenty of concealment and multiple avenues to flee.

Mason lay to her right, binoculars held loosely in one hand. They'd been watching not just the park, but both roads that looped past it. As cars passed, Zoe would jot the license plates in her notepad. They were working on the theory that, if this truly was a planned ambush by Artec, they were probably going to see the same cars passing multiple times. The three friends had been there for well over an hour and hadn't yet recorded any duplicates.

"One hour to go," Zoe noted, checking her watch. "If I was

going to a clandestine meeting that I couldn't afford to miss, I reckon I'd plan to be about an hour early."

The park below them was empty, and it had been empty since they arrived. And it was only really a park in the most technical sense—it had a few picnic tables spaced around an empty patch of green and not much else. It was clearly intended as a place for long-distance drivers to stop and rest before returning to the road.

Not that the road was very busy. It was just before midday, and traffic was minimal. A car appeared in the distance, and Zoe clicked her pen as she prepared to write down its license plate number.

"Turn signal's on," Mason said, passing the binoculars to Keira. "Looks like they're stopping."

The car turned into the small dirt parking lot next to the park. It was a sedan, mid-tone gray, and while it probably wasn't the cheapest model, it didn't seem recent or expensive either.

"If this is our suspect, I'm surprised they brought a car instead of a van," Zoe said. "The windows aren't even tinted. It's a pretty bad choice if you're trying to abduct someone."

The car idled for a moment; then the engine turned off. A man stepped out. Keira held up the binoculars to see him more easily.

He looked like he was maybe thirty. His hair was blond and curly. A pair of perfectly round glasses magnified his eyes, and his jacket and pants were both a plain shade of gray.

"I don't think anyone else came with him," Keira said, scanning the car's insides through the windows. "Unless they're really dedicated about hiding and crawled into the footwells."

The man looked like he was trying to avoid attention. He glanced about, zipping his jacket up higher, then meandered toward one of the park benches. Before he sat, he pulled a scarf out of his pocket and looped it around his neck.

"It's him," they all said at once.

After listing the meeting location and time, the letter had included one final piece of instruction:

I will be wearing a blue scarf.

"An hour early, as predicted," Zoe said as Keira passed her the binoculars. "He looks so uncomfortable. He must have thought the park would be busy."

Keira had to agree. He was trying to sit nonchalantly, facing the road with his legs crossed and one elbow resting on the bench top behind him, but he kept fidgeting. Every angle of his body telegraphed awkwardness.

"The jacket's too thick to tell if he's carrying weapons," Zoe said. "How are you feeling about it, Keira? Any sixth-sense warnings?"

She narrowed her eyes as she watched their visitor. He shuffled, crossing his legs in the other direction as he stared down the length of the road, waiting for them.

"I'm good to go ahead," she said. "What about you, Mason?"

"If you're fine, I am as well."

"Right. One minute."

Keira closed her eyes and focused. For a second, all she could see was darkness; then blurry, desaturated images emerged.

This was the part of their strategy that was the most precarious: the segment Zoe had dubbed Operation Daze.

As far as Keira had worked out, she didn't have any kind of control over Daisy, but their link let her catch glimpses of the world through the small black cat's eyes.

More than that, Daisy seemed to share a part of Keira's mind. Or at least be aware of it. She'd saved Keira before when Keira had become lost. She'd appeared out of thin air when Keira was in Artec's tower. She'd given both warnings and help when it was most needed.

Keira couldn't give the cat instructions, but Daisy seemed to know what they needed to do, regardless. After a brief moment spent batting the piece of paper, she'd happily let them attach a note to her, using a loop of string around her neck.

Now, on cue, she trotted out of the trees where she'd been napping and approached the man with the blue scarf.

Keira opened her eyes and gave her companions a thumbs-up. They nodded in return; then the three of them shuffled back from the ledge. They didn't stand until they were on the trail, out of sight from the roads, then set out on a brisk walk to their new destination.

As they moved, Keira kept half of her mind on the cat. She watched as Daisy approached the man and saw a distorted view of his face, his faint eyebrows raised in surprise as he spotted her. Daisy wove around his legs and then held still as he took the piece of paper off the string. It held just two words: *Follow me.*

"He's on his way," Keira said, grinning despite herself as the man slowly, cautiously stood. Daisy trotted toward the trees, and after a second, the man reluctantly followed.

Zoe had been adamant that any meeting needed to happen at a place of their choosing. "Out in the open, we're exposed to snipers or to detonation devices hidden in the park," she'd explained. "If someone wants to meet us, it's got to be on our terms."

Our terms turned out to be an abandoned church Zoe had found in the foothills of the mountain. It was only a few minutes from their stakeout location, and Keira breathed deeply as they left the forest and crossed a weed-choked field to reach it.

The building wasn't large, but it had a crumbling spire stretching high above their heads. The doors hung open, allowing them to slip into the cool and slightly damp interior.

From what Zoe had learned, the church was once a meeting place for the farmers who lived in the region before larger agricultural companies bought them out. It hadn't been used in eighty years, and it showed; the pews were knocked askew and covered in debris, and the roof was collapsing in many places. They hadn't even needed to break in—the doors already hung loose on their hinges, leaving a gap wide enough to fit through.

Old faded graffiti and age-discolored bottles clustered in the corners suggested the church had been a clandestine hangout spot for young people before they, too, had forgotten about it. Now, Keira, Zoe, and Mason took their places inside: Keira, sitting in a pew facing the door, and Mason and Zoe leaning on the walls to either side as they waited.

"Still good?" Zoe asked.

"Still good." Keira let her vision go blurry as she watched the cat's progress.

Every few seconds Daisy glanced back to make sure the man was still following. He was, though he was looking increasingly uncomfortable. Keira guessed he was struggling with the mental gymnastics required to follow an unknown cat into the wilderness.

"There," Zoe said.

Daisy appeared through the overgrown, weedy field ahead. Her head was held high and her tail raised in greeting. She looked enormously pleased with herself as she trotted up the church's steps to reach Keira.

Keira bent forward to pick up the cat and let Daisy vanish back inside of her just as the stranger stopped in the church doorway.

He stood there for a second, blinking hard as he tried to see them through the gloom. Slender hands flexed nervously at his sides.

"Ah…hello?" he managed.

"Welcome." Zoe leaned forward, giving him a better view of her. "Please enter…The Murder Lair."

"We agreed not to call it that," Mason said patiently.

Keira braced her elbows on her knees as she watched the stranger. She normally had a pretty good sense of who she could trust and who she needed to be careful around, but the light was at the man's back, disguising his expression, and it was hard to get a read on him. "You wanted to meet me."

He made a faint, uncomfortable noise, his wide eyes darting about as he tried to see who else might be in the building.

"You *are* the person who sent the letter, correct?" Mason asked.

Zoe made a face. "We're going to feel real silly if you turn out to be just an unrelated commuter who likes blue scarves."

"No. No, it's me." He took a hesitant half step toward them. "I just… I thought the park would be a good neutral space. It's a public area."

"We prefer the theatrics that come with crumbling churches," Zoe said. "We meet here, or we don't meet at all."

He hesitated for one more second, then rubbed his arms. "Okay. Well, thank you for coming to talk with me. Even…even if it is in a crumbling church you call The Murder Lair."

"Did you want to sit down?" Keira gestured to the pew opposite her. With a final nervous glance toward Zoe, the man stepped forward and gingerly took his place.

"You won't know me," he said. "But my name is Mikhail. And I work with Artec."

"I kinda guessed," Keira said. "Your job, I mean. I didn't guess your name."

He chuckled nervously. "You're not at all what I expected."

Keira glanced down at herself. The previous night, Zoe had told her to dress to impress, and Keira had no idea what to do with that advice, so she'd worn the bug-eyed cat sweater. It was going to leave an impression, if nothing else.

"Schaeffer paints you as…as this ruthless monster," Mikhail said, and Keira suppressed the shudder that passed through her at Schaeffer's name. "He talks like you're a soulless machine bent on revenge. Like you're not even human."

"Ah, the cornerstone of propaganda." Zoe sat down next to Keira and crossed her arms. "Which begs the question: If you were taught we're bloodthirsty robots, why are you here?"

He knit his hands together, then unfolded them, then knit them a second time. "I'm going to be dead soon."

"Condolences," Zoe said with exactly zero emotion.

"If I can't get out of this, I mean." Mikhail was blinking very quickly. He took his glasses off to polish them on his coat, and Keira realized his hands were shaking. "Artec. The Reyes Protocol. All of it was a mistake."

Keira tapped her fingertip on the pew beside her.

The three friends had set up signals on the drive to the park that morning. Fingers crossed meant to be wary. Scratching the back of their necks meant *Get ready to run.* Tapping the pew meant Keira felt they were safe. Mason finally relaxed and crossed to sit next to Keira. He kept his hand in his pocket, though, around one of the small canisters of bear spray they all carried. They were a gift from Zoe. As she'd explained, they were both a better ranged weapon and less prone to user error than knives.

"Why don't you start from the beginning?" Keira said. She still knew barely anything about Artec, but she didn't want to show too much of her hand, if possible. "When did you join the company? What's your role? Why do you think you're going to die?"

"Sure." Mikhail swallowed thickly as he replaced his glasses. "Let's go way back to when I was first drafted."

CHAPTER 9

"I KNEW SCHAEFFER FROM my previous job," Mikhail began. "I was a recent graduate with a major in bioengineering, and Schaeffer was a consultant on the project my team was developing. He was already deep into his work at Artec, but he liked to regularly dip his hand into other companies by offering assistance. It was partially to learn what strategies other businesses were employing but primarily to find new talent for his project. Like me."

Mikhail's smile was shaky. "That's one of his greatest strengths: being able to identify and lure in effective team members. The core staff on Artec—and, yes, I am a part of the core staff—were poached from dozens of different companies in different sectors. And he can be shockingly persuasive when he wants to be."

Keira remembered when she'd encountered Schaeffer in his office. His voice had been compelling, even hypnotic. He radiated both authority and a strange friendliness, as though he was on the edge of inviting her into his inner fold.

"What he told me about his company was every forward-thinker's dream—an industry-disrupting breakthrough that would make energy nearly free for the entire world. Artec was poised to make history, he said, and I fully believed him. We would be this generation's Wright brothers. Edison and Tesla. Graham Bell. What we were creating would leapfrog humanity forward in a way that hadn't been seen in over a hundred years."

Even as Mikhail spoke, Keira's mind conjured up images of the shackled ghosts, howling, screaming.

Mikhail must have been able to read her thoughts. His smile was full of shame. "Yes. The reality turned into something very different from the dream. But it wasn't always like this."

"The ghosts weren't always sentient," Keira prompted.

"No. The early experiments—we call them marks—were a lot more rudimentary. We're currently up to Mark Five, the Reyes Protocol. We created…the memory of ghosts. They resembled the bodies they were conjured from, but they neither felt nor thought. I don't know if the word *humane* can be used here, but that was the intent."

Mikhail exhaled heavily. "Unfortunately, it turns out that the ability to *feel* and to *think* were vital to the energy production. No matter how many versions of the not-real ghosts we developed, none of them were able to produce power in an effective way."

Keira had seen those not-ghosts in the town and theme park surrounding Artec's headquarters. The company had shipped in thousands of cremated remains as it tried to develop a version that worked. The ghosts had been blank—staring but without seeing. Unresponsive. Empty.

"The strongest ghosts are the ones with the strongest personalities," Keira said.

Mikhail nodded eagerly. "Yes, precisely. It turns out their humanness—their emotions, their desires—were what created the most energy. And that was how we developed Mark Five. When a symbol is applied to a body shortly following death, the spirit remains attached, and the remains become viable."

"Viable," Zoe almost spat, and Mikhail blanched.

"Apologies. That was…*is*…how we talk in the company. I want to emphasize that many high-ranking employees were uncomfortable with the direction the project was taking. Schaeffer assured us that the spirits felt nothing, but…recently, some internal documentation leaked. It spoke about how units that are in distress are capable of creating up to two-point-six times the energy compared to placid units."

Keira felt faintly sick. None of the employees could see the state the ghosts were actually in. Only Schaeffer, overexposed to the energy during his tests, could sense them. And he didn't care.

Mikhail flexed his hands. "Of course, that caused some dissent. Schaeffer sent out a memo reminding us that neither our bodies nor our nominated relatives' bodies would be utilized in Artec's project after our deaths. It didn't pacify people quite as much as he'd imagined. It was virtually an admission—what we were doing was ethically wrong. Being excluded from the cemeteries was a perk of the job."

Mason swore under his breath.

"That's why you asked to meet?" Keira guessed. "Because of the leaked documents?"

He hesitated for just a fraction of a second. "Yes."

A lie. Her stomach twisted again, but she decided not to challenge him on it. Yet. "Okay. Keep going."

"Right." There was a rustling sound above them, and Mikhail glanced up toward the bats roosting in the rafters. "Are you sure you don't want to do this somewhere less…decrepit?"

"Sit in the dirt for a bit," Zoe said. "Your immune system will thank you."

He made a faint noise in the back of his throat but continued regardless. "I need to explain where Schaeffer's mental space is. He loves control. When he hired me, he talked about how Artec's technology would one day be used by every company in the world. But it soon became clear that wasn't truly part of his plan. He's gone to great lengths to keep our research proprietary. Secret."

"Because his peers would laugh him out of the industry if they learned he was using ghosts as batteries," Zoe offered.

"That's possibly a small part of it. But I believe his greater motivation is greed. Greed and a paranoia around having his discovery stolen. We all had to sign a small folder of paperwork before joining the company and then even more before being given clearance to see the research. Nondisclosure agreements, noncompete agreements, affidavits that we will protect the company's interests above all else…"

"Dang," Zoe said. "You're going to be sued into an early grave if Schaeffer learns about this meeting."

"He's not going to need to sue me to do that." Mikhail looked grim. "He is actively killing employees he believes are guilty of insubordination."

Keira's heart ached. "Like my parents."

"Yes." Mikhail sighed. "Your parents left the project before I joined, and I'm afraid I didn't learn of their fate until recently. They were key scientists on the project—two of Artec's four founding members—and when they fled, Schaeffer couldn't look past the risk they posed to the company's secrecy. From what I've been told, he hunted them down for years before finally finding them and having them dispatched."

It was such a clinical, cold way to speak about the murder of the only family Keira had. She balled her hands into fists but kept her face calm.

"Schaeffer's paranoia is escalating," Mikhail continued. "Mostly because of you, Keira. Your attacks terrify him. Your abilities even more so. Because you gained them from Artec's projects, but he does not control you. You're a wild card that could bring the whole house down."

"Don't worry, we've had plenty of experience in how much Schaeffer hates Keira," Zoe said.

Mikhail chuckled, but it was a dry, frightened sound. "You don't know the half of it. That paranoia is increasingly turning inward. My coworkers are going missing. We were always being monitored, but the intensity has escalated to unbelievable proportions. There are rumors that he's installed a doomsday device in the headquarters, whatever that means. It's supposedly something that would wipe out the whole company in a worst-case scenario."

Keira, Zoe, and Mason shared a silent glance. None of them dared say it out loud, but that doomsday device—if real—could be exactly what they needed. If they could just get to it.

"Schaeffer was always calculating to the point of being cold-blooded," Mikhail said. "But now he's begun acting more like a cornered animal. He reacts to any threat, real or imagined. He's growing frantic, and none of us are safe."

"*That's* why you're here," Zoe said, a perfect mirror of Keira's thoughts. "Not because the leaked documents or memo were weighing on your conscience, but because you're scared you're going to be next."

To his credit, Mikhail had the decency to look ashamed. "I made a mistake recently. It was just a bad calculation—I was tired and overworked and wrote a number down wrong. But there's new monitoring software on my computer. I've seen cars following me. And, yes, I'm not too proud to admit the truth. I'm here because I know I'm going to die if Schaeffer isn't stopped."

"You don't think there's any way to regain his trust?" Mason asked, speaking carefully.

"Not against this level of paranoia. Any mistake is perceived as potential sabotage. Any questions about the program's ethics are seen as insubordination." Mikhail's hands were shaking again as he squeezed them together. "He employs a company to take care of his dirty work. A black market, underground group that is not afraid of bloodshed. Supposedly, they're meant to be protecting us from you, Keira. But it's an open secret that they're sent after employees who threaten the company."

She knew exactly who he was talking about—the masked men who hunted her through the forest on her first day in Blighty. The same group that swarmed the motel where Keira had taken refuge.

Mikhail took a shuddering breath. "Three coworkers from my department have vanished in the last fortnight. I'm going to be next if I can't find a way out. And I realized there is only one person who has ever effectively stood up against Schaeffer: you."

Keira sucked on her teeth. "I really should have worn the Santa Claus sweater. I'd have looked a bit more legitimate that way."

They all laughed—shakily, and with a faint amount of panic in Mikhail's case. He'd really been hoping to meet with someone as ruthless and efficient as the picture Schaeffer had painted.

"You want to destroy the company," Mikhail said. "For what it did to your parents or for the units—uh, *ghosts*—it utilizes in its experiments. Or maybe just out of a simple grudge, I don't know. But you want to ruin it. And I want to help you."

Mason rested his chin on his palm as he leaned forward. "From my perspective, we might not have to do much at all. It sounds like Artec is already self-destructing."

Mikhail licked his lips. "That's true. It is. But please keep in mind that it won't go quietly. And it's the collateral damage caused in that self-destruction that frightens me. We're talking about not just my own life, but the lives of every other employee, not to mention the lives in the town you call home." His gaze fixed on each of them in turn. "Schaeffer is not afraid to kill. And I believe he is very close to killing on a far larger scale than we've seen before."

"I can easily imagine he's capable of knocking off employees one at a time," Zoe said. "But you're implying he might wipe out an entire town. There's no way he could cover that up."

"He can't, of course. But I don't believe he cares anymore." Mikhail looked miserable. "He'll cause mass destruction and accept life in prison or even a death sentence, just as long as he feels like he's *won*."

The words lingered over them. Bats shuffled through the rafters over their heads. Keira felt a horrible, horrible ache in her chest. She'd been able to pick up Mikhail's lie about his motivation earlier. But she didn't think he was lying about *this*.

She thought of Marlene, the moody barista. Dane, who had only just begun to live his life again. Polly Kennard and her son Harry. Everyone in the street who recognized Keira and gave her a cheerful greeting when they saw her.

She felt she had fairly good odds of evading Artec and keeping herself alive, at least for a while longer. She couldn't hide an entire town alongside her.

"You found me," Keira said. "How? And how far away is Artec from doing the same?"

"Not far," Mikhail admitted. "But I might have stalled it for a bit. The team searching for you—and, yes, there is an entire team working on it—have lots of lines of inquiry out, mostly focused on areas you're suspected to have a connection to. That includes Blighty. And, very recently, they got a hit. They intercepted a phone call, and someone mentioned *the new girl who lives in the cemetery.*"

Keira grimaced. Blighty's gossip network was both robust and dedicated. She just hadn't considered that Artec might be tapping phones.

"The team lead called Blighty's local police station. She has a few connections in the force, and she leaned on them to get confirmation that a visitor had arrived in town recently and was staying with the pastor, most likely in an old groundskeeper's cottage near the forest."

Constable Sanderson. Keira had mostly tried to avoid the head of the town's tiny police station, but she should have guessed he was keeping watch on any developments in Blighty…including her.

"I was with the team lead when she made that call," Mikhail continued. "And I convinced her to keep everything—the intercepted phone call and your exact location—a secret. At least, for as long as we can. It's a risky gamble, and we know it. But both she and I are next on the chopping block either way, so it's a gamble we decided to take."

So many lives were balancing on a knife's edge, and they were all relying on Keira having the answers. She clenched her hands. She couldn't bring herself to admit how powerless she felt or how far she was from being able to do anything material.

Mason, sensing her thoughts, rested a hand on her arm. "You mentioned you were going to help us," he said to Mikhail. "So I'm guessing you didn't ask to meet just to give us an update on how dire things are."

Mikhail chuckled. "You're right." He reached into the pocket of his jacket. Both Zoe and Mason tensed up, their hands moving to their bear spray, but they didn't need to use it. Mikhail removed a small slip of paper and offered it to Keira. "Here. I think this is what you're missing."

CHAPTER 10

THE SCENT OF MOSS and mildew was thick in the back of Keira's throat. Somewhere behind them, water dripped off the crumbling church's walls. The world seemed to be moving in slow motion as she reached out and took the slip of paper Mikhail offered her.

It held six numbers. Zoe leaned over to read them and inhaled. "Coordinates."

"Correct." Mikhail's smile was fleeting. "To Artec's base of operations."

Keira frowned slightly. "The tower in the abandoned amusement park?"

He just shook his head. "I knew you found that one. Schaeffer screamed at my team for hours after it. But that was the research department. This is the heart of the company."

"It makes sense." Zoe's eyes were huge as she stared at the coordinates. "The research station is remote. Far enough from any real kind of civilization that it can be easily hidden. But it's a nightmare of a commute. And it's expensive to ship food and living supplies to the people who live there permanently. So they just keep the stuff that needs to stay *really* hidden in it. Because it's only one limb on the monster, right?"

"Correct," Mikhail said. "The park tower is R and D. Their efforts are spent on developing new iterations of the protocol to make them more efficient. Then we have multiple locations called active sites. Those are the cemeteries—the places where units are installed to generate power. They connect to the power plants. And at the heart of it all is our central location, where most of the upper-level staff work is done. It controls the daily operations, the contracts with both our suppliers and our buyers, expansion plans—everything. If you're going to target anywhere, target that."

Keira tucked the coordinates into her pocket. "Can you tell me anything else? Does it have weaknesses? Or a way I can get close to Schaeffer?"

Mikhail's confidence faltered. "I…I mean…I kind of hoped you'd be able to take it from here. I thought—I thought you just needed to know where to focus—"

"We've got it covered," Zoe said with far more confidence than Keira felt. "Relax. Leave it to us."

"Okay." His smile fluttered up briefly before fading again. "I hope you do. A lot of lives depend on this. I'm sorry to put so much pressure on you, but…" He shuffled, uncomfortable. "Since you found Schaeffer at the R and D tower, he's kept a personal guard with him at all times. None of us can get close to him without them present. You're quite honestly our only hope."

Keira hoped he wouldn't see how terrified that made her. She gave a stiff nod.

"Okay," Mikhail said. He rose carefully, dusting his pants off. "I think my immune system has had as much strengthening as it can handle for one day. I can give you my number, in case you need to reach me. It's a burner phone."

"Give him your number too," Zoe suggested. "In case he finds anything else he can send us."

They exchanged details as the bats rustled overhead. Then, with a final grim smile and a wave, Mikhail stepped out of the church, his pale hair turning golden in the sun.

The three friends waited until he was out of sight, then they released a large collective sigh.

"It's good news and bad news," Mason said. "The good is that Artec is close to imploding and might only need a few taps to get there. The bad news…"

"The implosion is basically a bomb, and I risk destroying much more than just the company," Keira finished. She glanced at Zoe. "You sounded pretty confident back there when you said we had it under control."

Zoe grimaced. "Sorry. But the guy was panicking. And you know what panicking people do? They grasp for any life raft they can, even if it means selling out someone they currently consider an ally. I figure we're safest if our good buddy Mikhail believes we're going to save him."

"Good point," Keira said. He was helping cover up her location, but she couldn't rely on that discretion to last forever.

"At least we have one thing," Zoe said. "An address. Wish the guy could have just told us a street name instead of giving coordinates, but…" She glanced up at the church. "Guess I'm not the only one who lives for the theatrics."

"We can figure out where it is once we're on the road," Mason said. "Right now, I think it might be wise not to linger here."

"You're right." She didn't think the meeting had been an ambush, but they'd still be safer if they kept moving. Keira led the way to the open doors and, after a quick scan of the area around them, stepped out.

"You have Daisy with you?" Mason asked.

"Yep." She could still sense the cat. Daisy had heard the bats above them and was growing eager to be free. "Zo, lead the way."

While Mason drove, Keira took the passenger seat, and Zoe lounged in the back as she looked up the coordinates. Zoe had borrowed Mason's mobile for the job, since she staunchly refused to own a phone with internet capabilities, or as she liked to call them, identify theft dispensers. Keira listened to her friend's fingers tapping over the keys, then a faint noise of disbelief, then more tapping.

"What is it?" Keira asked.

"Eugh." Zoe squirmed, squinting at the screen. "I can't tell if we've just been pranked or whether the guy wrote down the wrong numbers. You won't believe where the coordinates are sending us."

Keira craned to see Zoe over her shoulder. "Where?"

"A shopping mall."

The words took a moment to sink in. Then Keira found herself snorting down chuckles. "Like, Artec just has a retail store…"

"You walk in and ask the sales assistant to show you the latest model of ghost-tethering technology," Zoe said. "Like you're browsing for a new laptop."

"Send them to the back room to check if they have any Mark Four Protocol left," Keira said, giddy and miserable and feeling utterly trapped. "But of course they're out."

"Heh. Exactly." Zoe tapped on the phone some more, then shook her head. "That's definitely it. Unless he wrote it down wrong, he wants us to go to a shopping mall."

"I don't know what I was expecting," Keira said. She stared at the sparse trees rushing past the windows. "Maybe an office in, like, an industrial zone. Or something remote and secret, like the tower was."

"Huh." Zoe tapped the corner of Mason's phone on her teeth. She took a slow breath. "*Huh.*"

"That sounds like a good kind of *huh*," Keira prompted.

"I'm just thinking. The research tower—it was important for Artec to keep that secret. So they built a whole entire amusement park and then abandoned it, all to act as cover for the real project: the hotel-slash-research department."

"Yeah?"

"What if they did the same here? What if they backed and funded an entire shopping mall, then hid their headquarters inside?"

For a second, the car was silent. Then Mason whistled. "Hundreds of shoppers would filter in and out of the parking lot every day. No one would notice if a few dozen of those cars belonged to Artec employees."

"Shopping malls get constant stock deliveries." Zoe ticked off points on her fingers. "They have security guards to keep the premises safe overnight. They're central enough for employees to commute each day. And there's even a food court for them to have lunch."

"Hiding in plain sight," Keira murmured.

"That's kind of genius, actually." Zoe frowned at the address on her phone. "Conspiracy folks *love* mysterious corporate buildings that don't advertise what they do. They'll stake them out trying to break the secret. But…no one's ever thought that a company might be hiding inside a regular, mundane, watch-a-movie-and-get-a-new-shirt shopping center."

"How far away is it?" Mason asked.

"Not far." Zoe kept tapping. "About two hours on the other side of Blighty. We could make it before sundown."

"Hmm." He frowned, looking dubious. "That means arriving after four, and that's if traffic is good."

"Which is still plenty of time to have a snoop around," Zoe said.

"Sure. But will it be busy? Or will we be walking down empty halls, in clear sight of any Artec employees who are leaving at the end of their shifts?"

Zoe scowled at him. "Okay, so *now* you decide you want to be Mr. Play It Safe."

He shrugged good-naturedly. "Sorry. But tomorrow is a Saturday. A shopping mall will be as busy as it ever gets, outside

of the holiday season. If we wait until then, we'll be better cam-
ouflaged *and* we'll have as much time as we want to case it out."

"Sure, fine," Zoe sighed. "That makes sense, I guess. But I want
to head out early, okay?"

"I'm on board for that," Mason said as Keira nodded.

"Even if we scratch the mall off the list for today, it's not like
we can't put the rest of the afternoon to good use." Zoe nodded
toward the shopping bags they'd packed into the car. "Are you still
game, Keira?"

"Yep." She felt a smile grow. "We should have just enough time
left to pay a visit to the head of the BPS."

CHAPTER 11

AGATHA, WEARING AN IMMACULATELY tailored suit and skirt, opened the door. She began to smile as she saw Keira, then her eyes darted to Mason and Zoe, and her hand fluttered to her throat. "Ah, is this truly necessary? I hope I impressed on you how important your discretion is—"

"Of course," Keira said. "These are my friends. They help me sometimes. And they won't tell anyone else about…well, any of this."

"*Discretion* is my middle name," Zoe said, winking at Agatha. "Along with *Danger*, *Spicy*, and *Lobster Disaster*. There's a fun story behind that last one, by the way."

Agatha's pursed lips made it clear that she did *not* want to hear it.

"Hello, Miss Edith-Whittle," Mason said smoothly. "It's good to see you again."

Agatha all but melted, an effect Mason seemed to have on half of the town's older population. "Mr. Mason. It's been too long."

"I'll get started, if you don't mind," Keira said. She held up some smudging sticks Zoe had gotten for her. The sticks didn't actually affect the ghosts Keira spoke to, but she wanted to look like she was doing something to help. "I just need to, uh, apply these…"

Agatha's eyes widened a fraction. "Those don't create smoke, do they? I absolutely do not allow any kind of smoke inside the house."

"Nope," Keira said, glossing over the fact that smudging sticks were most definitely supposed to smoke.

"Hmm." Agatha glanced from Keira's strained smile and over to Zoe's gleeful grin. "Hmmm."

"I just wanted to ask a question," Mason said, intercepting flawlessly. "What is the BPS's official stance on hedge sizes? Because I have a friend who says they should be no more than a foot wide…"

Agatha gasped. "My dear boy, a foot is far too narrow! Let me help—"

Keira seized on the distraction and stepped away. She waved the unlit smudging sticks through the air in what she hoped would look like an official way as she moved toward the back door. The charade almost wasn't necessary; Agatha was wholly focused on Mason and what she perceived as an urgent crisis.

Zoe gave her a discreet thumbs-up and turned to the kitchen to hide some humane rat baits. Keira slipped out the back door and into the picture-perfect garden.

Five spirits stood on the other side of the fence, facing Agatha's garden. They were staggered, with the woman Keira had spoken to standing closest.

She had the unsettling impression that the ghosts had been there since the previous day, unmoving, as they waited for her return.

"Hey," Keira whispered, pushing the smudging sticks into her pocket at she approached. "I don't know how much I can do to help, but I'm going to try. Okay?"

The nearest spirit—the one with dry crusts around her mouth—shifted closer to the fence. All of them had their empty eyes fixed on Keira. In tandem, the five women raised their hands.

They were holding small items.

This wasn't the first time she'd seen spirits carry objects with them into the ghost realm. An elderly ghost in the cemetery had a cane. Other spirits had trinkets or handkerchiefs. From what Keira could tell, the objects needed to be so closely tied with who the spirit had been during life that they almost acted as an extension of the person.

There was something uncanny about seeing all five ghosts holding objects, though.

One clasped a necklace. Another held an old fabric doll. Still another raised a journal. One had an ornate hair comb. And the nearest one, the one at the fence, held a pair of leather gloves.

The items all looked like they might have been important to the spirits at one time, and yet, they weren't the kinds of items Keira normally saw carried over.

There had to be some significance she was missing, though. The ghosts had been holding them as they waited for Keira, and now they clasped their items against their chests, as though emphasizing how significant they were.

THE VENGEFUL DEAD

Keira didn't know how much time she had. She wanted to figure out what the items meant. But, even before then, she needed to establish some basic context.

"Were you all patients at The Home?" Keira asked.

They nodded as one, the movement sluggish and blurred, their long hair drifting behind them.

"Okay." Keira swallowed and glanced behind herself. No sign of Agatha. Yet. "Were you staying here when it was housing tuberculosis patients?"

All five of them shook their heads.

"After that, then." Keira frowned. "While it was a general convalescence hospital?"

Every one of them nodded.

That gave Keira a specific time frame to work with, though she still had more questions than answers.

"Did you die from your illnesses?" she asked.

The nearest ghost—the strongest one—loomed closer until she nearly filled Keira's vision, and Keira realized she was answering for all of them as she shook her head. Icy air billowed out from her.

"You…" Keira ran her tongue over her dry lips. "You were supposed to live, weren't you?"

Yes. The woman's nod was rigidly sharp.

"There was a poison in the walls, wasn't there?"

This time, the ghost didn't respond.

Keira breathed quickly as the chilled air filled her lungs. "I heard there was something bad in the walls. Was it arsenic or mold or lead…?"

97

The woman's lips pulled back in a miserable grimace as she shook her head.

The Home killed them when they were supposed to live. But it wasn't poison leaking from the walls. Which means…

A door slammed. Keira's focus shot toward the hulking dark stone building the town called The Home.

A man stood there. Gray eyes, as dark as the stones behind him, bored into Keira.

Jensen.

Ice radiated from the ghosts, so suddenly and viciously that Keira's breath seized in her throat. Frost spread across the fence.

The spirits, in a single motion, raised their arms. They pointed toward The Home.

Toward Jensen.

No. No, no, no.

"What are you doing?" Jensen called. His voice was raspy and cracked, as though he hadn't used it in days. He started toward Keira, his steps loping. "Get away from my fence."

"I…" She didn't know what else to say. "I just wanted to admire your garden…"

The ghosts held out their arms stiffly, five fingers pointing in harsh accusation at the man drawing closer to them.

"You're not welcome here." His face twisted as Keira backed away from him. "Not you, and not that witch of a woman who lives there. *Get away.*"

The ghosts were no longer pointing at him. Each of them raised their hands in front of their faces. Their hands turned into grasping claws. Their mouths stretched wide open as they writhed. The chill burning out from them was so immense that Keira thought she was going to die from it.

What are they...

"Get away!" Jensen yelled, and in that second Keira realized what the ghosts were doing.

They were miming being smothered.

She bolted for the house.

Zoe was still in the kitchen when Keira burst through the door. She crouched by the fridge, the box of rat baits clutched to her chest, as she stared up at Keira. "You okay?" she whispered.

"Um." Keira carefully closed the door behind herself. Every nerve in her body felt like it was on fire. "Uh…"

"Hey." Zoe shoved the baits back into her bag and crossed to Keira. "Whatever's happening, it's okay. Just tell me what you need."

Keira pressed her hands to her face as she waited for her heart rate to slow. Then she took a shuddering breath. "I think we need to leave."

"Cool. Let's grab the distraction on the way out."

Zoe threaded her arm through Keira's for support as they followed the hall to the entryway where the distraction—Mason—was still speaking with Agatha.

"No, dear boy," Agatha said, one hand one her chest, the other reached out in supplication. "*No* lawn should have plastic flamingos."

"Really?" Mason scratched the back of his head, the picture of perfect uncertainty. "But my friend said I should have *at least* five."

Agatha's eyes fluttered closed. "Mercy."

Zoe cleared her throat to get Mason's attention. He glanced their way and gave a quick nod, then said, "You know what, Miss Edith-Whittle? I think you're right. No flamingos."

"Thank goodness," she managed.

"I'm done for today," Keira said, trying to force a cheerful note into her voice despite the way her hands shook.

"Really?" Agatha's eyebrows rose. "Is the spirit…gone?"

"I'm working on it." Keira began backing toward the door. "I might need to come back again. I'll let you know."

"Oh. Very well. Try to give me more notice next time." Agatha picked at the hem of her impeccable jacket. "I like to tidy before guests arrive, but you gave me almost no chance this visit."

Keira felt certain Agatha's house was still the cleanest she'd ever set foot in. "Sure."

"Until next time, then."

They spilled out of the house. Mason moved along Keira's other side, offering her his hand. She took it, grateful for the extra contact, and the three of them crossed to the car like that. Keira faced rigidly forward, trying not to react to the sensation of eyes on her back.

Not Agatha's eyes. But another darker, colder pair.

Jensen was watching her from inside The Home.

CHAPTER 12

"WHAT HAPPENED?" MASON ASKED as they spilled into the car and closed the doors.

Keira pressed herself back into her seat. She was struggling to find a way to put her thoughts into words. Her heart was still beating too fast. "I was told that Jensen became the custodian once The Home was closed," she said.

"That's right." Zoe sat forward, poking her head between the driver and passenger's seats to be part of the conversation.

"But he worked at The Home when it had guests, didn't he?"

Zoe and Mason exchanged a look.

"That was before our time," Mason said.

"It rings a bell, though," Zoe added. "What was he? An orderly? He had some connection to the place before it went under. I can double-check what it was."

Keira nodded slowly. "Do that. Because what caused The

Home to close…I don't think it was mold in the walls. That place saw more deaths than it should have. Patients who were recovering died unexpectedly. And I think that story—that there was something bad in the walls—was a desperate attempt to explain the high mortality rates. The walls were fine, and they knew it."

Mason stared at her. "You don't mean—"

"Jensen was killing the patients." She took a slow breath. "At least five of them. All young women."

Zoe slumped back, her hand over her mouth, and Keira knew she was remembering the image of Jensen, standing on the icy cobblestones and laughing at a girl who had fallen and split her lip.

"Okay," Mason said slowly. "Okay. Wow. Okay."

"Am I allowed to call him a weirdo now?" Zoe asked.

"Yeah." Mason swallowed. "Sorry, Zo. Yeah. I think you've earned it."

"So what do we do *now*?" Zoe turned to Keira. "I mean, we're not just going to sit on this knowledge, are we? From a technical viewpoint, Jensen's old as heck and he's probably not going to have access to any new victims now that The Home is closed, but…"

"I can all but guarantee the ghosts are trapped because they're waiting for Jensen to be caught," Keira said. "They won't move on until he's gone. So, no, I can't just ignore this."

"It's going to be tricky," Mason said. "We're looking at events that happened twenty years ago, at least. If the deaths weren't considered suspicious at the time, there probably weren't any autopsies, and any evidence that could have linked Jensen to the murders would likely be lost or destroyed by now." He hesitated. "Do you know how he killed them?"

"Suffocation." Keira closed her eyes and saw the women, all miming holding pillows over their faces.

"Dang," Zoe muttered. "Even if we could convince a coroner to disinter the victims for an autopsy, they'd all be bones by now. Suffocation can only be proven before the bodies decay."

"If Jensen really was employed at The Home at the time of the deaths, we can put him in proximity to them," Mason said. "But that's all we have, and it's not enough for any kind of investigation, let alone a conviction. Unless we can find something compelling, we might be stuck."

An image surfaced in the back of Keira's mind. The five spirits, all standing in five very precise locations, each holding a small item. Her pulse kicked up. "I think I have it."

"Yeah?"

"I think Jensen stole something from each of the women." The pieces were falling into place almost too perfectly. "And I think he buried them in the garden. Like little shrines to each victim. And it's probably a part of why he won't leave too. He doesn't want to risk those trinkets being discovered if a new owner digs up the garden during renovations."

Mason's eyebrows rose. "Okay. That's something compelling. If the items can be recovered, and if they can be linked to patients who died unexpectedly and without apparent cause, it might even be enough for him to be charged."

"Do you know where they're buried?" Zoe asked. "Do you think you could point to the exact place?"

Keira closed her eyes and visualized where each of the spirits had been standing. "Yeah. I think I can."

"That's all we need, then," Zoe said, growing excited. "I can put in an anonymous tip to the police station. Constable Sanderson's pretty reliable about following up on things like this and giving him very specific locations to dig will make it hard to ignore. As long as he finds those items where we say they are, that should be enough to kick off an investigation."

For the first time in a long while, Keira felt a swell of hope. They had a path forward. One that, she was fairly certain, would *work*.

"We don't even have to do anything illegal," Mason said, grinning as he started the car. "We can put it into official hands and let the process run its course."

"There wasn't even any trespassing," Zoe teased. "You must be loving this."

His grin widened slightly. "I think this is the least stressed any of our projects has made me."

As they coasted through Blighty's roads and toward Zoe's house, Zoe pulled a sheet of paper out of her notebook and passed it, along with a pen, to Keira.

"Draw a diagram," she said. "It doesn't have to be perfect, but the closer the better. Mark down any landmarks like plants or whatever."

"Got it." Keira clicked the pen and did her best to re-create her view of the yard. One spirit had been standing just beside a fern;

another was fewer than six paces from one of the broken stone seats. Keira drew it all with as much detail as she could remember, and she tagged each location with the item police should find there: *necklace, childhood toy, hair comb, journal, leather gloves.*

She passed the paper back to Zoe. "Need any help putting in the tip?"

"Nah, I've got it covered. The station still has a fax machine that's probably older than my grandmother, but I can scan all of this and zoom it over to them from an anonymous number. They should find it first thing tomorrow."

Mason slowed the car. They were passing through the town's center, and after a momentary hesitation, Mason pulled into the curb outside the florist's shop.

"What is it?" Keira asked.

His mood had shifted. Without speaking, he nodded to something across the road.

A figure walked along the pathway, carrying a bundle of papers under his arm. He was moving away from them, and it took Keira a second to recognize him.

Dr. Kelsey. The town's only physician, and the father of Gavin Kelsey, the boy Keira had very recently watched die.

Her stomach twisted into knots.

Dr. Kelsey stopped at a post, took one of the papers from under his arm, and stapled it to the wood. He barely broke stride before moving on.

A flutter of movement drew Keira's focus to the florist's wall, just outside their car. One of the papers had been taped there.

She wasn't supposed to be seen in town. Not when things were so precarious. But Keira couldn't stop her hands from opening the car door or from her feet carrying her toward the photo of Gavin Kelsey.

Gavin had followed Keira to one of Artec's power plants. She'd succeeded in overloading the structure and untethering a large number of spirits whose power had been funneled through its cables, but in the process, Gavin had been caught in the electrical discharge.

She still didn't know how to feel. Gavin had been a repulsive person. He'd graduated from killing animals as a child to killing humans as a young adult. That had been his entire purpose in following Keira. She'd wronged him, and he perceived her as an easy target.

Gavin had needed to be stopped. Keira just wished it could have happened another way. He deserved jail; she wasn't sure he deserved death.

The poster was simple. It held a photo of Gavin, apparently from his high school graduation. Below that was his name, the word *MISSING* in bold font, and a phone number to call with information.

"Dang," Zoe said softly. She and Mason had come to stand beside Keira. Together, they stared at the poster and considered every implication it held.

Because Gavin had followed Keira to the power plant hours away from town, and because the energy overflow had scorched him so severely that he was no longer recognizable, his body hadn't yet been identified. Dr. Kelsey didn't even know his son was dead.

The guilt-fueled knot twisted. Dr. Kelsey was not a pleasant person either. Keira was fairly certain he'd known about his son's crimes and had perhaps even helped to cover them up. But she still couldn't imagine what he was going through. His son had been home one morning, then, without a word, had vanished. It had been days. Dr. Kelsey would likely be fearing the worst, and those fears would soon become his reality.

A bell chimed. The florist's door opened. Keira turned, expecting to see Polly Kennard, the cheery owner, but instead found herself facing Polly's son, Harry.

He slouched. Everything he wore was a shade of black. His hair, flawlessly straight and dyed as dark as he could get it, hung across his face to obscure one eye. The only remaining visible eye was heavy-lidded and ringed in eyeliner.

"Horrible weather," he mumbled, squinting up at the clear sky. "Too bright."

"Hey, Harry," Keira said.

It was hard to imagine how such a dark, glum individual could come from one of the most colorful and bubbly women in town, but Harry had turned out to be a good friend. He'd let Keira have a skull he owned so she could try to eradicate a shade from Blighty's cemetery, and he'd been their getaway driver when they traveled to Artec's research base. Nothing seemed to faze him. Keira had gradually come to accept that his utter lack of emotions wasn't an affect but just a hard-baked part of his personality.

He joined the group, staring at the missing person poster taped to the window. Along with Zoe and Mason, he was the only other person who knew Gavin's fate.

"I saw him just a few days before he died," he said, his voice dull. "He came into the café while I was having lunch."

Keira swallowed around a lump in her throat. No matter her feelings about Gavin, he'd been a core part of the town. His absence wouldn't just be noticed, it would be *felt*. "It's hard, isn't it?"

"Not really." Harry sighed faintly. "He spat in my lunch."

Zoe and Mason made faint, commiserative noises. "He'd do that sometimes," Zoe said.

Keira grimaced. "Sorry."

Harry shuffled to face them. "The doctor has been coming into every business. Asking us about his son. Don't worry, I didn't say anything."

"Thank you." Another twist of guilt. She shouldn't need her friends to lie for her. But she was grateful for it, regardless.

The moment Gavin's remains were identified, Artec would know where to start searching for her. Another thing to worry about, on top of Mikhail.

Harry made a faint noise in the back of his throat. "It's nearly closing time. I get to throw the old flowers out. Best part of my day."

With that, he slunk back into the store. As the door rattled shut behind him, Keira turned to see the opposite sidewalk.

Dr. Kelsey was vanishing around the corner. His pose was rigid and his steps fast, but she could feel the agitation bleeding out of him as the stack of papers rustled under his arm.

"We should go," she said, and moved back to the car.

"Hey," Mason said as they opened their doors and climbed

inside. "I was thinking. Do either of you want to stay at my place tonight?"

Keira hadn't realized until that moment how badly she didn't want to be alone.

Zoe pulled a face. "What, and watch the pair of you make gross romantic eyes at each other across the room? Pass."

Mason held up both hands. "No PDA, I swear."

"That promise doesn't carry as much weight as you seem to think it does. You two have an atrocious track record."

Mason shrugged as he turned the car back onto the road. "It's up to you. But since we want to leave for the shopping mall early tomorrow, we could save some time by staying together tonight."

"Thanks for the offer, but I want to get back to my place." Zoe held up the map Keira had drawn. "I want to jump straight into this and get the tip submitted before the station closes for the night. Plus, the national Mothman phenomena committee is hosting a webinar tonight, and I don't care how important this Artec stuff is, I *cannot* miss that presentation. You two have fun on your date night."

"Sure thing." Mason turned onto Zoe's street, just outside the town's center, and cruised to a halt in front of her house. "Pick you up at eight tomorrow?"

"Looking forward to it." Zoe saluted as she climbed out of the car.

They both waved as Zoe jogged up to her home. As the door closed behind her, Mason started the car again. "How are you feeling? I can drop you off at the church, or…"

They'd spent precious little time together that hadn't been focused on Artec. Over the previous week, Keira's nightly routine had seen her crouched at the table as she created lists of potential runes to test, until her eyes turned too blurry and sore to stay open any longer. But now, they had something else to focus on. The shopping mall. For the first time, Keira felt she could rest, even if it was just for a few hours.

"Honestly?" She sent him a smile. "I'm kinda in the mood to make some gross romantic eyes."

"Hmm." He matched her grin as he turned the car toward his home. "I like the sound of that."

CHAPTER 13

MASON'S HOME WAS BEAUTIFUL and eclectic. His mother was a zoologist, and his parents both worked abroad for long stretches. Their home was full of gifts they brought back for him: taxidermy birds behind glass cases, paintings of creatures Keira couldn't even describe, and walls of photos of beautiful locations. Keira loved the way his home made her feel: both cozy and surrounded by good stories.

Daisy spilled out of Keira as soon as they arrived and vanished into the house, exploring. Keira and Mason settled into the kitchen. She chopped zucchinis into little cubes while Mason fried onions and watched a pot of boiling pasta. Music played from hidden speakers and they both sang along to it poorly.

"Here!" Keira called, sliding the chopping board of zucchini to Mason. He leaned down to press a quick kiss to her cheek as she passed, and Keira laughed. "Careful. We'll burn it if we don't focus."

"I'm not afraid of a few scorched vegetables," he said, scooping the zucchinis into the pan. "Hey, see if you can drain the pasta. I think it's ready."

A plume of steam spread above them as Keira emptied the pot over the sink. Both she and Mason whooped as it spread across the ceiling, then Mason snatched up a tea towel and began fanning it just below the smoke detector.

"This thing's so sensitive," he said, laughing as the steam dissipated. "Looks like we're in the clear, though. Oh, hey, this is a good song."

The music had changed, the upbeat dance tempo shifting to something gentle and sweet. Keira wasn't surprised he liked the tune; if Mason could be distilled into a song, she thought he would sound something very much like it.

He pulled the pan of cooking vegetables off the burner, then offered his hand to Keira. She took it and let him lead her into a dance.

His other hand went around the small of her back. She rested her head against the fruit-themed apron he wore. Even through the layers of fabric, she could hear his heartbeat, and it was a beautiful sound.

They stepped slowly, rocking together more than dancing, their dinner forgotten. Mason nuzzled against the top of her head, and she could feel his smile.

"I like this," she said, and she wasn't sure if she was talking about the song or the evening or just simply the feeling of being held. Maybe a little of all of them at once.

"I like this too," he said, and kissed her hair. "If we want to do the cheesy couple stuff, maybe we could make this our song."

Words nearly escaped her. *I don't want to ruin it for you.*

She kept her head down so he couldn't see the change in her expression. She wasn't sure she could explain what she was feeling. Or what she was thinking.

If I die, you'll never be able to listen to this song again without feeling pain. And that would be a tragedy. You like it. You should have things you like. You deserve good things.

"Keira?" His fingertips ran along her jaw, gently tilting her head back so he could read her eyes. "Talk to me. What's wrong?"

She looked up at him, the best thing in her life, and felt an unexpected surge of protectiveness. He didn't deserve this. He didn't deserve what Artec was doing to them. He didn't deserve to be pushed so far into danger, just to be with her.

"I'm never going to let anyone hurt you," she whispered, and pressed one hand to the side of his face. "I've decided. You and I will both live to be a hundred, and we'll be together, and we'll be *happy*, and I will utterly destroy anyone who tries to stop us."

His eyes widened in delight. "Oh," he said. "I have chills."

Keira found herself chuckling despite herself. Mason joined in, and they leaned against each other, laughing like giddy children.

A sudden, guttural scream cut through the silence, and they both jumped.

"What—" Keira started, but Mason was already jogging for the music player.

"Sorry," he said, mashing buttons until the shrieks cut out and another dance anthem started playing. "Sorry, that was one of Harry's songs. I promised him I'd add them to my playlist, you know, to support him. Probably should have curated it a bit better before you came over."

Keira leaned against the kitchen island, doubled over with laughter. "Oh, poor Harry. I should probably listen to some of his tracks too. I feel like I owe him at least that much."

"Well, he sent me a message yesterday. He's starting on a new concept album." Mason began to pull their ingredients together into a bowl. "It's apparently going to heavily feature 'monastic throat bellowing,' whatever that is."

"It sounds like a treat," Keira said. "An instant add to the playlist."

"Oh, for sure. Fifty percent chance the neighbors will call the police to report a murder in progress."

Mason circled the counter, carrying two bowls of creamy pasta, vegetables, and sausage bits. He passed one to Keira, then stabbed a fork into it for her.

"Do you think this counts as our second date?" Keira asked, scooping up some of her dinner as she leaned back against the kitchen island. "We decided that vandalizing that gravestone deserved to be the first."

"Oh, we're not counting that time we imploded the power plant?"

"I think we have to discount any activity that involves Artec. It feels too much like the company's third-wheeling."

"True." He lifted his bowl and cheers-ed it against hers. "To our second date, then. And to many, many more."

"I was serious when I said I expect you to make it to a hundred, so brace yourself for a whole lot of dating me."

He smiled, and she could feel the warmth radiating from him as he said, "I think I'd very much enjoy that."

Is this what it will be like? Keira wondered, leaning against Mason's shoulder as they ate. *When we manage to get free...if we manage to get free...will this be what it's like to live with Mason?*

I hope so. It's good.

Her eyes drifted toward the windows. Night had fallen, and the houses down the street had their lights on: little golden rectangles shining out like lamps from behind the trees.

Keira took a step toward the window. In the distance, she thought she could barely make out Agatha Edith-Whittle's home. Which meant...

Almost against her will, her feet carried her another step closer. The trees that were relatively well trimmed on the rest of the street had been allowed to grow thick and tall around The Home, but she thought she could still make out the silhouette of its roof.

"It's strange, knowing it's so close," Mason said as he joined her at the window. "It's been unchanged the entire time my family's lived here, and since it's so hidden, it's easy to just...forget it's there." He frowned. "At least, until now. I don't think I'll forget it again."

"I hope it won't disrupt your life too much—if it becomes a crime scene, if it needs to be demolished—"

"I'd be fine. Better to get the thorn out and let the wound heal than to leave it to fester." Mason reached past her and pulled on the curtains to cover the window. "No more work tonight, though. If the power plant thing didn't count, then I want to make this date a nice one. Hang on, I have something for you."

Mason put the bowl aside and vanished deeper into the house. When he returned, he carried a box under one arm and an assortment of items in the other.

"Do you like jigsaw puzzles?" He held up the box to show the design of a tropical jungle.

Keira blinked at it. She couldn't remember the last time she'd played any kind of game. "Yes!"

"Okay, good." He passed her a bundle of soft fabric. "I also have a change of clothes and a fresh toothbrush. If that's okay."

"Of course it's okay." She unfolded a set of pajamas that were, surprisingly, the right size for her. "Seems like date night has been in the plans for a while."

"Well." He shrugged, sheepish. "When we put together the escape bags, I made a spare one to keep in my home. It had clothes and supplies for both of us. Just in case…just in case you couldn't reach any of the other bags when you were leaving. I could bring it to you."

Clothes for both of us…

"You really committed to this whole ridiculous lifestyle, huh?" Keira said, feeling a swell of incredible fondness.

"If you needed to run, I wanted to be able to run with you."

She pulled him toward her and kissed him, sweetly and softly. They didn't pull apart again until Daisy began pacing impatiently and yowling for her own dinner.

"I think I like this date night," Keira said, finishing by trailing her fingers over Mason's jaw. "Let's feed Daze, then set up this jigsaw, yeah?"

CHAPTER 14

THE JIGSAW PUZZLE TURNED out to be far more challenging than expected. Although the rainforest scene had plenty of detail, the detail was all *plants*, all in very similar shades of green.

They sat on the rug in front of the fire, the half-finished puzzle spread out between them as they battled to line pieces up. It turned out they were both very similar levels of stubborn, and no matter how many frustrated groans the puzzle pulled out of them, they both refused to quit. It was all too easy to ignore the way the clock above them crept past midnight.

Occasionally, Daisy drifted in and out of the room, yowling mournfully. Something was bothering her that night, but they'd both tried to pacify her without much success. She ate her dinner and took as many treats as they gave her but always began her cries again immediately after. Mason had shown her the litter box and offered her toys. Keira had tried to cuddle the cat by the fire and lull her into sleep, but Daisy would only tolerate pets for a few minutes before squirming free and resuming her pacing.

"She probably doesn't like being in a strange house," Mason offered as the cat stalked into the room, screamed, and then immediately turned and left again. "Sorry, Daze."

Keira held up two promising pieces and sighed when the leaves didn't quite line up. "Maybe she's mad that she can't get to the taxidermy birds? She's usually so good about travel. As long as I'm calm about it, she's calm, too."

Mason found a matching piece and triumphantly slid it into place. "Does it work the other way? Can you sense her emotions?"

"Not really. I mean, I can feel a bit of what she can feel—like when she's cold or what sort of surface she's standing on—but it's all very vague and blurry, just like when I look through her eyes. I can't tell what she's thinking or anything. It's like she's connected to me, but she's still a completely independent cat. Just…a cat with a little bit extra hiding inside."

Daisy called from somewhere deeper in the house, then the soft patter of paws announced she was on the move again.

Mason watched as Keira slotted a piece in, nearly completing a trailing vine. "I'll give her another treat in a moment; maybe that and some extra pets will help her calm down. This is the first chance you've had to rest in a while, and I've been looking forward to making you breakfast tomorrow. Poached eggs and toast and salmon."

"I can't poach eggs to save myself," Keira admitted. "I've tried a few times. It just turns into boiled egg soup."

"My father loves poached eggs," Mason said. "He knows all the methods—stir the water, vinegar in the water, I swear he had a dozen different tricks he'd cycle through to get them just right—and he made me practice until I could match him. I guess that's the dad instinct kicking in, wanting to prepare his child for life in the world. Except, instead of teaching me how to change a car's tire or how to file my taxes, I learned how to poach eggs."

"Only the necessities," Keira said, laughing.

"Exactly. The tire changing came from my mother. She's a lot more practical." He rolled his shoulders in a bit of a shrug. "Most of her work happens in the wilderness, a long way from habitation, so if something vital breaks, she needs to know how to repair it herself."

"She sounds fun," Keira said. "I'd like to meet them both."

"They keep promising that this current job is nearly over," Mason said. "I want you to meet them too."

Tiredness was finally beginning to creep over Keira. She stretched, breathing in deeply, then fell still. "Hey, do you hear that?"

Mason tilted his head, listening. "I don't think so. What is it?"

"Silence." Keira frowned. "Daisy's not calling. I…I don't think she's here anymore."

"Do you know where she is?"

Keira closed her eyes and tried to focus. It took a moment to find the cat. "Huh. Back at the cemetery."

"She really can just…disappear and reappear wherever she likes, then?"

"Apparently." Keira could feel the cold dew beneath the cat's paws and see the slanting tombstones looming around her. "She doesn't do it often. But I guess she really did just want to go home."

"As long as she's okay." Mason smiled. He looked sleepy.

"I'm calling it," Keira said, sliding the box lid they'd been using as a reference away, and pulling in some of the pillows and quilts Mason had stacked nearby. "Good night, Mason."

"Good night. I love you." He caught himself. "Sorry. Was… was that too…?"

Surprise bubbled up in her, followed by a deep, rich joy.

"No. Not at all." She shuffled closer to him, kicking loose jigsaw puzzle pieces out of the way. His arm went around her as she spread a quilt over both of them. "I love you too."

"Poached eggs tomorrow," he promised her. "Look forward to it."

———

When Keira next opened her eyes, the fire had burned down to embers. Mason slept beside her, his arm draped over her, his breathing slow and steady.

Keira rolled onto her back. With the curtains closed and the fire nearly gone, she could barely see the ceiling. She felt warm and comfortable and sleepy, but also…unnerved.

Something woke me.

She held still, listening. The house was quiet. Mason's breathing created a soothing pattern. Outside, a cricket chirped, then fell silent again.

Then she heard it. A distant footstep, crackling on dried leaves. Keira's phone pinged.

She scrambled for it, finding it in her jacket pocket, and held it up to read the message. It was from Zoe and held two simple, horrifying words.

THEY'RE HERE.

Her pulse spiked. She thought of Mikhail, so hopeful and so frightened at once, and how he held the secret of her location.

She thought of Gavin Kelsey, dead at Artec's power plant, and how his identity would lead Artec right to the town.

She thought of every one of the hundred clues she'd left in her wake.

It didn't matter the cause. They'd come for her at last.

She put a hand to Mason's shoulder and shook him awake. Her other hand tapped at the phone as she replied to Zoe:

OK.

Mason stirred, blinking as he pulled himself free from sleep. "Mmn. Keira, wha—"

She pressed a hand over his mouth.

The house was as still and quiet as ever. But outside, something moved. The footsteps were slow and careful. Trying not to make too much noise.

Mason tensed, coming awake as suddenly as Keira had. She

switched her phone to silent, then held it out for him to read Zoe's message while she kept her eyes on the covered windows. The stranger was moving toward their home.

"We need to hide," she breathed.

They both grappled for armfuls of blankets. Keira kicked her jacket under the couch. Then they hauled the blankets into the hallway, where they weren't visible from the windows, and crouched with their backs to the wall.

The footsteps stopped next to Mason's house. Their owner was trying to move stealthily but was too heavy to stay fully silent. Trickles of light came under the curtains.

Mason found Keira's hand and squeezed.

The stranger moved again, pacing along the house's wall to reach the next window.

A message flashed up on Keira's phone. It was from Zoe again, and instead of words, contained a photo. It was taken from the second-floor bedroom in her house, aimed through the window to capture the garden outside.

A figure stalked the space below, craning to see through her windows, just like what was happening at Mason's house. The photo was dark and grainy but held just enough detail for Keira to make out the skull mask the stranger wore to hide his identity.

The photo caught a part of Zoe's neighbor's yard, and when Keira squinted, she saw the shoulders and head of a second figure.

They were the mercenaries Mikhail had spoken about. The same mercenaries who had chased Keira through the forest the night she'd lost her memories.

Stay safe, Keira texted back to Zoe. Keep hidden.

Lights flashed through the kitchen windows. The beam landed on the wall not far from Keira and she shrank back, doing her best to stay out of sight. Mason's breathing was quick and nearly silent; his hand was almost painfully tight over hers. She squeezed back, then closed her eyes and concentrated.

Daisy's vision was better in the dark. She was no longer in the grass but perched on top of one of the stone monuments to have a better view. Cold air ruffled through her fur.

In the distance, flashlights moved as two forms searched around the parsonage and church. Daisy turned to look to the right, and Keira could barely make out the dark shell of her cottage. It remained cold and undisturbed.

They've narrowed my location to the town, but they don't know exactly where to find me. Not yet.

She opened her eyes. The flashlight flickered across the walls, then vanished again, and she listened as the footsteps moved to the house's side.

They were no longer in danger of being seen, but Mason and Keira stayed where they were, pressed against one another, as the footsteps faded into the night.

CHAPTER 15

"DAISY KNEW THEY WERE coming," Keira said as they carried their bags to the car. "I don't know *how* she knew, but I'm pretty sure she was trying to warn us."

"Now I feel especially guilty for trying to pacify her with treats instead of paying better attention," Mason said.

"I mean, it didn't stop her from eating them."

They dropped their bags into the car's trunk and slid into their seats. Artec's mercenaries had hunted through the town for nearly two hours the previous night but left well before dawn. Keira doubted they would stay around town—not during daylight, not when they could be seen—but it was still hard to calm down. Every rustling leaf or snapped twig made her flinch, and she kept scanning up and down the street, searching for any hint of movement.

She was grateful they were going to be leaving town, at least for that day.

"Zoe thinks they had a list of items they were looking for," Keira said, reading the steady flow of texts that were appearing on her phone. Mason started the car, watching the road just as carefully as Keira had, as he pulled out of the driveway. "She thinks they were told to look for black cats and were given descriptions of clothing they've seen me wear, as well as a description of your car."

That car in question—badly damaged during their last escape from Artec—was presently hidden at the bottom of a lake.

"I'm grateful for the rental now," Mason said.

"They may also have been told to watch out for any collection of supplies that look suspicious: tools, plans spread out on tables, anything like that." Keira lowered the phone. "Daisy didn't see them near my cottage, which means my home's still a secret. At least for now. But Zoe thinks they'll be back again soon to search the town more thoroughly, and I have to agree with her."

"We'd better hope the shopping mall gives us a solution, then," Mason said. He gave her a tight smile. "Sorry about the poached eggs."

They'd both agreed to skip the cozy breakfast. They were safer on the road.

"I'll take a rain check." Keira craned forward, watching the streets and houses around them as Mason turned into the town's center.

Missing person posters, all bearing Gavin Kelsey's unsmiling face, were taped to stone walls, message boards, and wooden posts. It almost felt as though they were staring directly at her. Keira tried not to stare back as Mason navigated around the fountain.

Zoe had texted them to pick her up at the café instead of at home, and she was already waiting on the sidewalk, thick sunglasses over her eyes and a tray of three drinks balanced in one hand.

"Hey," she said, jumping into the back seat before Mason could even bring the car to a stop. The drinks tipped, but Zoe balanced them again before they could fall. "I got us caffeine. Because I'm going to go out on a limb and assume you both got just as little sleep as I did last night."

"Thanks," Keira said, taking the drinks Zoe passed to her and arranging them in the cup holders. "And thanks for the warning last night too."

"I have a motion-activated alarm system in my yard," Zoe said, sliding her sunglasses up to the top of her head and grinning. "I mean, I built it like five years ago when there were rumors that Blighty might be home to its very own Owl Man—I was *sure* I was going to be the first to photograph it—but turns out, it works just as well for shady corporate goons."

"The Blighty Owl Man thing turned out to be a teenager wearing an old Halloween costume, didn't it?" Mason asked.

"Evidence was inconclusive." Zoe waved a hand to shush him. "I didn't get the caffeine purely out of the goodness of my heart, by the way."

"Oh?" he asked.

"More gossip passes through the coffee shop than almost any other location." Zoe drank deeply, then sighed. She looked exhausted. "It's basically a drama superhighway. An hour spent quietly listening in there can give you enough insider information to fill a novel. Are you ready for it all?"

"Yes," Keira and Mason said in tandem.

"Right. Well, Mrs. Mulburry claims Mrs. Braye cheated at rummy last Tuesday and now she's refusing to tell her what book they're supposed to be reading for book club—"

"You know I could listen to this all day," Mason said, sounding pained, "but I was hoping the gossip might be a *little* more connected to our current situation."

"Are you sure? Because this story ends with someone getting a slice of cake smashed into their face, and you won't *believe* whose." Zoe waited, eyebrows high, then rushed ahead. "It was Marlene's. The barista. She was delivering their order and got caught in the crossfire. Anyway, yes, I did also get *plenty* of relevant gossip, don't worry."

Keira chuckled. The car coasted over the bridge leading out of Blighty, and simply being away from the town's boundary was making it easier to relax. "Lay it on me."

"You got it, babe. So, Gavin Kelsey was order of business number one. Apparently, for the first couple of days, the police wanted to treat his disappearance as a runaway situation. They figured he'd just turn up when he was ready, but this morning the investigation was expanded. Enough time has passed that *wait and see* isn't the most viable option anymore. The police are now actively searching for him, and that includes looking for matches with any recent unidentified bodies."

"I thought he might have already been identified," Keira admitted. "Artec's men never actually found the groundskeeper's cottage, and they didn't spend much time near the parsonage. Which means Mikhail didn't give them my location."

She'd kept watch through Daisy's eyes until the sun rose. The masked men had passed through the cemetery, oblivious to the shadowy cottage nestled in the corner, and then had concentrated on the town.

"They've narrowed me down to Blighty, but no further," Keira continued. "But *something* brought them there. I thought it might have been related to Gavin, but it sounds like he's still being treated as a missing person."

"Well, it's a bit more complicated than that." Zoe tilted her head to the side. "From what you said about Gavin's...*uh*...overwhelming crispiness, a visual identification isn't an option."

"Zoe," Mason said, grimacing.

"I was trying to be respectful!" She scowled. "What would you have used instead? Gavin's level of char? His altered state of matter? His universal barbecued-ness?"

"Just..." Mason flexed his hands around the wheel. "Let's move on, okay?"

"Sure. No problem. As I was saying, with a visual ID unworkable, the police are going to need some other link. That might be his personal belongings—can they identify his clothes? His phone? Anything else in his pockets? That might help them make the connection, but it's not enough on its own. They would also need to match Gavin's dental records or send for a DNA test to confirm his identity. Only then can they announce his death."

"And they haven't gotten that far yet," Keira said, thinking it through. "But there's a good chance they have a hunch."

"Exactly," Zoe said. "Right now, the body at the power plant is probably being considered *a potential match* for Gavin Kelsey. And if Artec has powerful connections with the police or any insider who can slip them information…"

"They could have learned Gavin's name before it's officially released," Mason finished.

Zoe shrugged. "That's my working theory. If I'm right, Artec might be casting a wide net. It's likely there are several missing persons who are considered potential matches for the body. Artec might have searched multiple towns last night."

"Either way, it won't take long for Artec to get confirmation," Keira said.

"Dental record matching can happen same day. DNA takes a while longer. But, yeah, most likely our timeline can be measured in hours, not weeks." Zoe took another long drink from her cup, then leaned back. "Right. Next order of business. We weren't the only ones who noticed Team Spooky scoping out the town last night. Except for Gavin and the rummy cheating thing, it was basically all anyone could talk about." She made a face. "We already know they came through town once before—right after you arrived, Keira—but this time was a lot less subtle, which isn't a good sign."

"Artec isn't caring so much about who sees them," Keira said.

"Exactly. It's like Mikhail said—they're getting desperate, and they're not afraid to break a few dishes to get what they want."

Keira picked up her drink to stop herself from fidgeting. "Did anyone get hurt?"

"Not that I've heard. A few people caught Artec's team snooping around their yards, though, and confronted them. And, get this, they all had the exact same story for why they were there. They said they were looking for a lost cat."

The hair on Keira's arms rose. "Did they say what color?"

"Yep. Black."

"Huh." Mason rubbed the back of his neck. "That's smart. It's both an excuse for why they're there and a fish for information, all at once. Do you know if anyone mentioned Keira's cat at all?"

Zoe shrugged. "I only know what I could catch in that hour at the café. I don't think too many people have seen Daisy yet, and no one mentioned Keira or Daisy within my earshot."

"At least my cottage is still a secret," Keira added. Daisy was napping in a patch of sun on the low stone fence. Keira could feel their connection, even as she moved farther and farther from Blighty. "I feel like, if someone had said something, they would have gone straight there."

"Give them time; they'll figure it out," Zoe said, grim.

Keira hated to admit it, but it was true. Her home was still a secret by sheer luck, and not much more.

"We'll get you somewhere to stay outside Blighty," Mason said. "I can book a hotel under my name. You'll be safer that way."

"No one else will, though," Keira said. If Artec was no longer trying to stay hidden, that meant they were only half a step away from outright violence. She could leave Blighty, but Blighty—and everyone in it—would pay the price.

And the people she loved the most were the most in danger. All it took was the wrong person to say the wrong thing and Artec would know who her friends were. And she might be able to keep those friends safe—she could bring Zoe and Mason and maybe even Harry with her when she left town—but then Artec would start going after her friends' loved ones instead. They had infinite ways to hurt her, even if they never touched her.

This is why I never let myself have friends. After her parents were killed, Keira had lived with her aunt, and after her aunt's passing, she'd kept herself as untethered as possible, drifting from town to town and never letting herself grow attached. *No friends meant no risk. And…no comfort. No joy. Not much of anything, really.*

Mason met her eyes. He reached across the seats and took her hand. "We'll figure this out," he said with far more certainty than Keira could muster. "We've done it before, we'll do it again."

"We have an entire shopping mall to raid," Zoe confirmed. "I looked it up last night, but I couldn't find *anything* exciting. It's unknown to any of the communities I dabble in, which means Artec has been pretty good at keeping its base a secret."

"Do we know what we should look for once we get there?" Keira asked.

Zoe shrugged. "I'm really hoping we'll know it when we see it. Artec's a large company, so it's probably going to have a large space for its operations. Malls usually have maps, so we can check one of those and see if there are any big empty chunks in it. Any area large enough to hold office space for a hundred or more people is my guess."

Keira nodded. That made sense; Mikhail said all the logistics, admin, and contracts happened through that base. That meant a lot of desk work.

"So, um." Zoe grimaced. "Aside from rummy-gate and Gavin and the whole deal with Artec's people, there was one more thing I overheard in the coffee shop. And it's the reason I got you both jumbo-sized drinks because you'll probably need them."

"That's not sounding good," Keira said, bracing herself.

"Yeah. Constable Sanderson came in. He looked awful, by the way. I feel like he got no more sleep than we did. Mostly because of the whole *weird people in Blighty* thing. He's worried it's someone casing for…I don't know, a mega theft spree? Like, he thinks they're burglars who are planning to rob the whole town in one go. Which is not the most awful theory, if we're being honest."

"It's more plausible than an underground organization searching for a fugitive," Mason agreed.

"Yeah, so that's what he's working with, and he's encouraging everyone to double-lock their doors for the foreseeable future. But while he was waiting for his coffee—double shot, extra cream, extra sugar, extra large—he started talking to Marlene about our anonymous tip. You know, the whole Jensen business."

"Oh, this was bad timing," Keira said. Between a decades-old cold case and a pending crime spree, she could guess which one would become his priority.

"It's worse than bad timing." Zoe pulled a face. "He's not going to investigate it at all."

"What?" Mason glanced at her through the rearview mirror. "Why not?"

"He said, and I quote, *those old rumors about The Home are circulating again.* He kind of rolled his eyes when he said it, then he asked Marlene to keep an ear out for who might be spreading the story, because he wanted to shut it down."

"Oh," Mason said softly.

"Yeah. Turns out, we're not the first people to raise red flags about Jensen. So I did some extra digging."

"How are you this productive?" Mason asked, sounding quietly stunned. "Keira and I tried to do a jigsaw puzzle last night and we didn't even finish that."

"Hey, it's not like I was getting any sleep anyway." Zoe shrugged. "Since I had some time to burn and the shopping mall didn't have any juicy leads to follow, I turned to The Home. And, yeah, Keira, you were right. Jensen *was* an orderly while the place was running. But you won't believe how he got the job."

"How?" Keira asked.

"His brother was a patient. Jensen visited it regularly over ten months while his brother stayed there and then applied for a job shortly after his brother's passing. The local newspaper did a story about it."

Rustling noises rose from the back seat as Zoe fished through her bag. She pulled out a sheet of printed paper and offered it to Keira.

It was a photocopy of a newspaper article. The headline read, *I Just Want to Give Back.*

Below that was a black-and-white photo of a man standing in front of a building that was unmistakably The Home. His lopsided smile sent ice through Keira's veins.

"My time spent with my brother in The Home opened my eyes to

what true kindness is," Zoe said, reciting quotes from the article. "*I want to give back to the community that showed me so much compassion.* They made it a feel-good story."

"He was a regular visitor over ten months," Keira said, putting the pieces together. "He would have seen the other patients on his visits. He would have noticed when they died and seen just how much attention was *given* to their deaths."

"It was a home for patients with serious illnesses, often terminal," Zoe continued. "There was a high turnover. So, yeah, I think he saw how readily the deceased patients were cremated or buried without any autopsy or suspicion, and he trained to be an orderly so he could take part in that process."

"He might not have even killed anyone at first," Keira said. "Maybe he just wanted to be *around* death. And after a while, that wasn't enough, and he wanted to take part in it too."

"And maybe he would have targeted people who were already close to passing," Zoe said. "You know, people who just had a week or two left. But it would take a while for patients to get to that state, and he would get impatient. So then he got bolder. And he stopped worrying about their prognosis."

"And he targeted victims who were recovering," Keira finished. She saw the ghosts in her mind's eye, insisting that they were supposed to live. "Nonterminal. And even then, no one raised too many red flags because even recovering patients might suddenly fall sick or pass away."

"But someone started noticing, eventually," Mason said. "The Home's death rates were too high. Patients who were nearly ready to be discharged died unexpectedly. And I'll bet the negative attention from those deaths harmed its already shaky ability to stay open."

"You got it in one," Zoe said, snapping her fingers. "The further I looked through records, the more news stories I saw about The Home. Rumors sprang up in town. People were going there to get better and were dying instead. Headlines like *House of Death* started appearing, accusing the place of negligent care. When the negative publicity got too great, the owners put out a statement about how something in the walls was making patients sick."

"That's the only rumor I ever heard," Mason mused. "That the building itself was poison."

"Because no one thought to point fingers at the staff." Zoe shook her head. "The owner tried to sell the place, but after claiming the walls were full of something toxic, no one would buy it. No one…except Jensen."

Keira felt her eyebrows shoot up. "Wait. I thought he was only the custodian of the property?"

"Oh, no, apparently not. The owners sold it to him for a pittance because simply owning an empty building that needed constant repairs was costing them too much, and no one else wanted the place. It's legally Jensen's home now."

"And he stays there because the town still believes there's something wrong with the walls and because he doesn't want anyone to dig up the garden," Keira said.

"Yep. You see, like Sanderson said, there were rumors about him," Zoe added. "I can't find out whether they sprang up *before* or *after* he bought The Home, but apparently, he's given people bad vibes for a while. Some rumors even included the detail of things being buried in the garden—which is why Sanderson didn't take our tip seriously."

"Because he's heard it before," Mason muttered.

"He's even *investigated* it before," Zoe added. More rustling, and she passed Keira another sheet of paper. It showed a photo of a dig team sifting through dirt under the headline *Search for Missing Possessions.*

"They already dug up the garden?" Keira asked, feeling shock sink into her bones.

"Not all of it. And not the section you flagged." Zoe took the papers back. "But, yeah, Sanderson and his team cordoned off a section and went through it, based on reports from the deceased's families that not everything had been returned to them."

"So as far as Sanderson knows, our tip is just a recycling of an old rumor he's already disproven," Mason said.

"Bingo." Zoe shoved the printouts back into her backpack. "He thinks it's just another of Blighty's urban legends, revived for a fresh generation."

"Huh." Keira let them sit in silence for a moment, then sighed. "Sorry, Mason, we might have to get illegal for this one after all."

"Oh," he said, sounding genuinely disappointed. "But we were being so civilly responsible."

"If it's any consolation, we'll need to save the criminal activity for another day," Zoe said, sliding her sunglasses back into place. "Because today? Today, we're going shopping."

CHAPTER 16

ZOE TOLD THEM THE bare-bones facts about the shopping mall on the two-hour drive from Blighty. It was two stories and advertised upward of a hundred and fifty retail stores. And…that was it.

"It honestly feels like no one's especially excited about this place," Zoe said as they turned into the town surrounding the mall. "Including the people who own it. They have social media pages but don't update them for months at a time. I'm not finding many tagged photos from inside the shops either. From what I can tell, everyone is just super, super apathetic about the place."

"Which makes sense if Artec owns it," Mason said. "The less attention it draws, the better it is for them."

"True. Maybe their mission statement is *Just Do the Bare Minimum*."

"I'm seeing some signs," Keira said, pointing toward an arrow hung over the road. Mason put on his turn signal.

They waited in silence as Mason navigated the last roads to the complex. Keira felt knots build in her stomach. This would be different from last time, when they'd infiltrated Artec's research tower, she promised herself. This time, they were entering a crowded public space. They'd be able to blend in and observe from afar. There would be no breaking locks or subterfuge required. No serious danger.

She hoped.

"We'll want to park somewhere in the rear two-thirds of the lot," Zoe said as enormous gray-blue walls appeared ahead. "Nowhere too close to the entrance of the store and its security cameras, but not right at the back either."

"Will do." Mason swung the wheel as they turned under a massive arch welcoming them to the mall. The knots redoubled as Keira got her first clear look at the building.

"What…?" Zoe craned forward, frowning. "It *is* Saturday, right?"

"It's supposed to be," Mason said bleakly.

"Then where is everyone?"

The parking lot spread on for what felt like miles, wrapping around the heavy concrete building. It was clearly designed for thousands of cars. Keira couldn't see more than eighty.

The cart bays were empty. The crosswalks were bare. There was no movement, no activity, no sounds even.

"Oh no," Zoe said. "Okay. I think I might have assumed *apathy* in place of what is actual, entire *disinterest*."

"What are you saying?" Mason asked. His eyes were narrowed with stress as their car coasted along the otherwise-empty path.

"This has got to be an abandoned shopping mall. Or very near it."

A tall narrow board ran up the side of the mall. It held twelve spaces for major stores to advertise their presence. Nine of those space were empty white holes. Of the remaining three, one was a grocery store, one was a clothing store, and one sold smoothies.

"I feel a bit stupid for not recognizing the warning signs earlier," Zoe said. "No one's talking about the place. Even corporate is doing the bare minimum on social media because they have nothing to show. I mean, it's not like this is the first or only abandoned shopping mall in the country."

"What do we do?" Mason asked.

Zoe was silent for a second as she chewed her lip. Then she nodded toward the parking spaces. "Scrap the plan of going to the back of the lot; that would look too weird. Pull in near some other cars. See if you can find a spot where we'll blend in."

"I don't know if that's possible if we're the only humans in the place," Mason said, but he still turned toward the area Zoe had indicated.

"It's not totally empty." She shook her head. "I've seen this kind of thing play out before. A mall doesn't just collapse overnight and shut its doors; it's a slow, painful decline. There won't be the crowds we were hoping for, but it's not like we'll be the only people there."

"It feels so…wrong," Keira said, staring out at the rows and rows of empty parking spaces.

"Yep. And get ready for a heck of a lot more wrongness once we get in there," Zoe said. "That's what causes the collapse. A few shops close. Maybe the center starts running low on funds for maintenance. Customers feel like the shopping mall isn't as friendly and exciting as it once was and stop coming as often. Which leads to more stores closing. Which means less money for repairs and maintenance. Which increases the feeling of uncanniness, and therefore results in fewer visitors, etcetera. It's a vicious death spiral and it's pretty hard to prevent once it starts."

"But no one wants to buy a dead mall and the building's owners have too much money invested to totally give it up," Mason mused. "Or I guess, in this case, Artec *can't* give it up."

"That's my guess, too."

The car pulled to a stop. Zoe opened her backpack. "I was hoping we wouldn't need to use these, but with how bare this place is, we don't really have a choice."

"What…?" Keira took a clump of curly blond hair Zoe passed to her. She turned it over. There was a mesh underneath.

"Disguises," Zoe said. "That's a wig. Put it on. Here, Mason, this is for you."

His trepidation turned to outright horror as he accepted an enormous bushy fake mustache. "No."

"Come on. They've seen our faces. This will be safer."

"This looks like something you'd buy at a joke store," he said, holding it up. "It's bigger than my entire hand."

"It'll hide your face better that way."

Keira tried pulling the wig over her head, but she got the angle wrong, and synthetic curls covered her face and made it hard to breathe. "Um."

Zoe sighed. "Do either of you have *any* experience in the art of disguises? Here, let me help."

A moment later, the three of them stepped out of the car. Keira's wig was *nearly* straight. Mason's mustache covered his mouth and most of his jaw, and the miserable tilt to his eyes suggested he was not especially pleased about it. Zoe had attached two thick caterpillar-like eyebrows over her real ones, and Keira had to admit, the effect was striking.

"Hell yeah," Zoe said, admiring the results. "I bet even your own families wouldn't recognize you."

"If I die looking like this, I think the shame alone would be enough to force me to come back as a ghost," Mason said.

"That's the kind of can-do attitude I'm looking for." Zoe gave them both a thumbs-up. "From here, the plan's pretty simple. We head on in there. We look for anything weird. And we hope for the best."

"And we hope certain facial hair extensions don't suffocate us," Mason muttered.

"Seriously, though." Zoe looped her arm through Keira's and began leading them across the empty pedestrian crossings and toward one of the archways into the building. "Try to act natural. Meander a bit. Look at stores but don't look *too* hard, if that makes sense. Even with the mall this barren, they probably still have a surveillance system, and we have no idea who's watching."

The automatic doors rattled as they approached. As the screens parted to let them in, Keira blinked up at a long hallway of white walls and dull signs.

It seemed like Zoe's assessment was right: the mall wasn't entirely barren, but it was coming very close to it. The hall held rows and rows of boarded-up stalls, interspersed with the occasional shop that was hanging on—either out of stubbornness, or a false hope that things would get better, or simply because their lease wasn't up yet.

The floor felt slightly tacky under their feet and many of the tiles were broken. Some storefronts were covered with plywood; others had just been left exposed, the shelves empty and the lights off.

"Guess that used to be the map," Zoe said, nodding to a free-standing sign in the center of the walking space. It held a glass case that might have once shown a color-coded display of the mall's layout, but management had evidently decided it was less depressing to leave it empty than to slowly keep blacking out the nonexistent shops.

In the distance, a few lone shoppers walked down the empty halls. If Keira had to guess, the store survival rate was less than one in fifteen. The ones still open were empty except for their one or two lingering staff. Some of them tried faking busyness by shuffling boxes behind the counter or wiping a dry cloth over glass display cases in languid, endless loops. Others simply stood and stared into the distance. No one looked happy.

Music was piped through overhead speakers, but it echoed strangely through the empty space. Fake plants and empty benches dotted the walkways, but they were all dusty and dull.

"This might just be my personal hell," Keira whispered.

"That's high praise from someone who lives in a graveyard," Zoe said. She was surprisingly chipper, a broad smile fixed in place as she gazed at the empty stores.

"Are you…having fun?" Mason asked.

"Oh, absolutely. There's a whole community online of people who explore abandoned locations, and failing malls are considered a gateway drug into it. This might be the most fun I've had all week."

Keira was glad at least someone was having a good time. They passed a dry water fountain and an escalator that was unmoving and cordoned off.

"Watch for any closed storefronts that look unusually well-worn," Zoe said. "Artec might be disguising its operations by blending it into the shuttered places, but the floor would probably look extra scuffed around it and any doorways might be chipped and frayed at the edges."

Keira nodded, but that felt a little like hunting for a needle in a collapsing mall of a haystack. Everything was dirty. Everything was worn. And the abandoned stores seemed to stretch on forever.

Her eyes fell to the floor and she drew a breath. "Look."

The floor's polished stone design was comprised of large repeating diamond shapes that stretched down the center of the hallways. Most of the diamonds were empty, but every fifth one held a decorative tile center. And the decorative element was unpleasantly familiar. Twisting leaf designs formed a circle.

"That's Artec's logo," Zoe said, and she sounded surprised. "Okay. Number one, at least we know we're in the right place. And number two, that's pretty bold for a company that wants to hide."

"That would have been added decades ago, when the mall was built," Mason said. "I get the feeling that Schaeffer was less obsessed with secrecy back then. He might have wanted to brag about what he'd created, even if it was in a discreet way that only people in the know would understand."

"I could see that." Zoe nodded as she gained enthusiasm for the theory. "And at this point, it would draw more attention to them if they tried to take them out, so they just do what they can to hide them instead."

She was right. The mall had positioned stands, seats, and even the occasional freestanding stores over the tiles with the logo. They occurred too often to hide them all, but they had still tried.

"I think I'm ready to start prying," Zoe said, scanning their surroundings.

"Wait, weren't we supposed to be trying to stay discreet?" Mason's mustache bristled with every word.

"Sure. But here's the thing—walking in endless loops isn't exactly helping us. We need to try something else. Most of the people working in these stores will have no idea who or what Artec is. But I'll bet they've seen stuff." Zoe raised her enormous eyebrows. "Minimum-wage staff who are bored out of their minds see and hear all sorts of wild things, and most of them aren't scared of gossip. We just need to pick the right target."

"What kind of target are you thinking of?" Keira asked.

"Oh, don't worry, I think I've found it," Zoe said, her grin turning wicked.

CHAPTER 17

ZOE'S GAZE FOCUSED ON one of the few open shops near them: a phone retailer that had banners offering repairs and accessories. The teenager slouched behind the counter looked as tired and sad as every other assistant in the complex, but he jolted to attention as Zoe sauntered up to him.

"Hey," Zoe said, slapping her flip phone onto the counter. "I can't get this to connect to the internet. Can you help?"

"Uh…" He blinked down at the brick of a machine. "Uhh… I seriously doubt it."

"Really?" Zoe pouted, which caused her caterpillar eyebrows to crush together. "But I was so excited to watch the latest hot vids and invite all the coolest tracking software into my life. I'm very into the idea of having no privacy whatsoever."

"How old is this thing?" The assistant—his peeling name tag said he was called Richie—picked up the mobile and flipped it open. He looked lost somewhere between morbid curiosity and horror. "Wait, I've never even heard of this brand before."

"Hmm." Zoe rubbed her chin, looking thoughtful. "How much could I get for a trade-in if I wanted to buy one of your latest government spy machines? I'll take the kind with the most human rights violations."

"A trade-in…" Richie seemed to be struggling to keep up with the words Zoe was slinging at him. He looked from her monstrous, furry eyebrows back to the phone. "For this thing? I'll be honest, it might actually be worth negative dollars. Unless you can find a historian who specializes in lost technology. How many of the world wars has it seen, again?"

"Cool, cool, cool." Zoe leaned an elbow on the counter and made a show of gazing about the mall, nodding slowly. "Nice place you have here. What's the deal with it?"

"Ugh." Richie rolled his eyes even as he leaned toward Zoe conspiratorially. Apparently, her assessment of the store workers' willingness to talk had been shockingly accurate. "I've been working here for three months and I'm already desperate to jump ship. This is the most depressing place I've ever seen."

"I hear you." Zoe kept nodding. One of her eyebrows had begun to peel free. Neither of them mentioned it. "What do you think the story is? Money laundering? I bet it's money laundering."

"My bet goes to secret FBI headquarters," Richie said. "Listen to this. There are the same fifty-odd cars that arrive at nine every day. Rain or shine, without fail. But they don't belong to the stores' staff and they're not shoppers. They're these intense-looking people wearing suits. They give me the creeps."

"Dang," Zoe said, fighting to keep her voice chill even as her eyes lit up. "That's weird, huh? Where do they go?"

"Somewhere upstairs, I think." Richie shrugged. "They get into the elevators. No idea what they're doing up there, though. I've taken a look around when I'm on break and the shops are all exactly as cool and hopping as mine." He gestured bleakly to the walls of phone cases and ads for data plans. "Look, I'm not meant to say this, but our stuff sucks. You'd be better off going to one of the places across town."

"Oh no, the privacy-invasion machines with built-in location trackers suck, tell me it isn't so," Zoe said with zero attempt to sound sincere. She picked up her flip phone. "Thanks for the tip, Richie. You deserve better than this place."

"And that's the truth," he said, giving them a halfhearted wave as they headed toward the elevators.

"Wow" was all Keira said as they moved out of earshot. "Just… wow."

"There's only one thing people love more than discovering a dirty secret," Zoe said. "*Sharing* it."

"Remind me to never try to hide anything from you," Mason said.

The elevator was in an alcove set back from the stores. Zoe mashed the button to go up and they waited, listening to its mechanisms churn. The doors rattled as they opened.

"They spared no expense," Zoe said dryly as they stepped inside.

The panel inside the door displayed *Level 1* in red. Below that were two buttons set into the bronze surface: one for their current floor and one for the level above. Below that was a decorative engraving in the metal. It held Artec's symbol.

Keira nodded to the panel. "Another one. I think you were right, Mason. I think, when they built this place, Schaeffer was almost bragging."

Zoe briefly fixed her floppy eyebrow, using the metal wall as a mirror, as the elevator rose. It was a short ride, with only two levels to choose from. The doors opened, releasing them into a space that was just as bleak as the lower level and somehow even emptier.

"Okay," Zoe said. She kept her eyes skipping from the floor to the walls to the boarded-up shops and even up to the mildewed, grimy glass panels in the ceiling that let in about half the natural light they should have. "We know they come up here. We *know* the entrance is on this floor somewhere. We just have to find it."

They trailed along the crackled floor, pausing as they pretended to look into the shops. Doubts began to grow inside Keira like small sprouting seeds.

The second floor was more open than the first. From what she could tell, the floor plan was entirely chopped up into retail spaces, none of them large enough to house part of a department, let alone a whole one.

"The walls are thin," Mason said, voicing some of Keira's growing concerns. "Even when the stores are boarded over, they're only using plywood that doesn't reach the ceiling. If there were people in here, we should be able to hear them."

Zoe huffed, lips pursed. "Good point. Something's not lining up."

"Hang on," Keira said. They'd covered nearly all of the second floor. Ahead was another elevator. She crossed to it and pressed the button to go down.

It rattled as it arrived. Keira pressed a hand over the doors to keep them open as she stepped inside. She took a breath, victory blooming. "Look at this."

"What is it?" Mason craned over her shoulder.

She pointed to the panel below the buttons. "There's no symbol."

They exchanged a glance, then turned as one and began marching back to the elevator across the building.

"I should have guessed," Zoe said. "There was an escalator just inside the doors. Sure, it was broken down when we saw it, but Artec has the money to fix it, no problem. So why would Artec's employees walk farther and wait longer just to use the elevator?"

"Because they weren't going to the second floor," Keira finished.

They arrived back where they'd started. The door pinged open the moment they pressed the button. "They're going *down*."

They stood inside the lift, staring at the panel beneath the buttons. Artec's symbol stood out on the bronze surface. It looked worn, as though it had been touched a thousand times.

"A basement level," Mason murmured. "Accessed only through a secret button. That makes sense."

"It gives them the space they need," Zoe added, bending down to look at the mark. "If they were co-opting one of the stores in the mall, they'd have to limit their footprint to not draw attention. But a basement can stretch as far as they need it to. And it allows for perfect soundproofing, assuming they put it far enough down."

She reached out, a finger poised over the button. Mason drew a sharp breath as she pressed it. "Don't—"

But nothing happened. There was no movement of the metal plate and no change to the elevator.

"Figured," Zoe said. "Of course, it wouldn't be a button. There would be too much risk of a casual shopper bumping it by accident."

"I can't believe you were willing to take that risk," Mason said, his mustache fluffing with each word. "You were fully prepared to plunge us down into Artec's headquarters—just to see if it worked."

"It's probably an electronic pass," Zoe continued as though she couldn't hear him. "Like a badge or a tag you press against the symbol to activate it." She ran her fingertips around the edge of the plate, using her nails to pry into its seams. "There might be a work-around, though. We could probably pop this off and fiddle with the wires below, if we really wanted to."

"That would just leave us in the same situation," Mason said. "The situation where we're plunging into Artec's headquarters with no plan."

For a moment, they stood in the closed elevator, staring at the panel.

"I wish we had a bear," Zoe said unexpectedly.

Keira squinted at her. "Sorry, like a real—"

"Yeah. A real bear. An angry one. We could stuff it into the elevator and send it down. Imagine how cool that would be. The elevator doors slide open and a whole entire bear spills out and wrecks everything in sight."

"We might have to temper our aspirations," Mason said, trying not to laugh. "Bears are in short supply in Blighty."

"Well, my unrealistic aspirations are still better than your plan, something that doesn't exist."

"Hey, don't pass judgment about the existence of my ideas *too* quickly." He folded his arms, staring at the button. "I have an alternate suggestion and it doesn't involve tampering with any potentially deadly electrical cables *or* bears."

"Yeah?" Keira asked.

"We assume Schaeffer arrives and leaves every day, like every other employee. We set up somewhere near the elevator. And we wait for him."

"Your plan," Zoe spoke carefully, "is to wait for the guy and maybe try to tackle him when you see him?"

Mason shrugged. "I think it would be better to have the confrontation up here, in the open, where we have room to retreat if something goes wrong. I'm working on the admittedly precarious assumption that he *does* have some sort of doomsday device, like the one Mikhail mentioned, and that he keeps it on his person, and that activating it would force the immediate closure of Artec's facilities. If that's all true, we might be able to wrestle it off him. Though, to be fair, those are just guesses."

"He won't be alone," Zoe said. "Mikhail told us he had a squad of those mercenaries with him at all times, and I can guarantee they'll be walking him to his car and following him home each day."

"True. But those mercenaries would be with him in the basement level, as well, along with potentially fifty other Artec employees blocking our path."

"And we don't actually know that he's here," Keira said. "We last saw him at the research tower. For all we know, he might even be working from a different, more secret location."

"That's possible," Mason conceded.

"No, he's going to be here, and I can all but guarantee it," Zoe said. "He views the tower as being compromised. Keira got in, and he's probably still not entirely sure how, so he's moved somewhere he perceives as being more secure. A place he thinks Keira doesn't know about yet." She held up a finger to make her point. "And you could make the argument that he might have other even more secure locations. But think about what Mikhail said. Schaeffer is paranoid. He's panicky. And *he calls his staff into his office to scream at them when they make mistakes.* Right now, he'll want to be here, where all the most important operations are happening, to hunt out potential insubordination."

"Huh. Yeah. It's a gamble," Mason said. "But I'm with Zoe on this one. I believe our odds of finding Schaeffer here are higher than anywhere else."

Keira chewed her lip as she stared at the symbol on the elevator. It was so temptingly, tantalizingly close. One press of a metaphorical button and she would be in the very heart of Artec.

"I can do it," Zoe said, unzipping her backpack to reveal a tool kit. "I came prepared. I can pry this sucker open and get us down there in two minutes, tops."

"We should play it cautious," Mason said, turning to Keira as well. "We have no idea what's down there. We lose nothing by waiting and watching who leaves."

"We lose time," Zoe shot back. "A resource that is shockingly finite right now. What if Schaeffer never leaves? We can't just go back to Blighty and wait out another night because I'm not sure Artec is going to give it to us."

"I want to fix this just as badly as you do," Mason started.

"Really?" Zoe threw her arms out. "Because it wasn't *your* mother who nearly got sucked into their hellhole of a cemetery—"

"No." His voice was growing louder. "It was my friend. And he's *still there.*"

Keira couldn't take it. She clapped her hands together loudly, startling them all and interrupting the rising voices. "Enough," she said, keeping her own voice gentle.

Zoe and Mason both slumped back against opposite sides of the elevator, breathing hard. Mason was flushed. Zoe's eyebrow was coming loose again.

"I'm sorry," Mason said after a second. "I shouldn't have raised my voice."

Zoe shook her head. "No, you should have. I keep forgetting you have just as much invested here as we do. I'm sorry."

"It's a stretch to even call him a friend," Mason said, looking uncomfortable. "I spent some time with him, but I didn't know him well."

He was talking about a classmate from his university who had been murdered. Mason had been walking close by when it happened, but he was hurrying to get to his next class and didn't realize what was happening. The guilt caused him to drop out of the university, and his search for that student's grave marker was what had first exposed Keira to Artec's cemeteries and the shades held within.

"You cared about him enough to change the trajectory of your life," Keira said. "I'd say he was plenty important." She took a slow breath. "We're all on the same team here. We're going to disagree on methods but only because we care so much about doing it right."

"It should be your choice anyway," Mason said, his smile strained.

"Yeah." Zoe nodded. "You're the one leading this. You make the call; we'll follow."

Keira stared down at the small symbol on the worn metal plate. It presented incredible potential but also incredible danger. Like a Pandora's box as yet unopened.

An idea was beginning to form. "What if there was a way to see inside the basement level *without* going down there ourselves?"

Zoe and Mason exchanged a glance.

"I'm listening," they said in tandem.

CHAPTER 18

THE ELEVATOR RATTLED AS they took it to the ground floor again. As the doors slid open, Keira explained her idea.

"We're pretty sure Artec's hidden itself in the basement level and there will be more than a few employees down there. Which means they'll need ventilation, and they can't let the ventilation system stand out or look obvious. It's probably going to be linked with the mall's own system."

"Makes sense to me," Zoe said. They stood outside the elevator, staring down the near-empty hallways at the few straggling shoppers. "But if you think we're going to be crawling along air ducts like they do in action movies, I have some bad news: those things are *always* smaller and *always* less well supported than the movies would let you think."

"That's fine; we're not going in them ourselves." Keira began walking, looking for vents as she moved. "We just need to find one with good access first."

Even with music piping out of the speakers, they could hear their footsteps echoing as they traced their way along the length of the mall. Most of the vents were up high and too exposed for Keira's liking, but as they neared the food court, the building's layout began to change.

The smoothie shop that advertised itself on the mall's entryway billboard was blasting techno music while the two workers stood there blankly, doing nothing. A couple of take-out places were still active, their lit-up signs offering burgers, fried food, and frozen yogurt. The far wall held the blocked-off entryway to what might have once been a movie theater. It was still before lunch, and only a few tables were occupied.

Decorative wood panels spanned the walls, taking up the places where vents would have otherwise been positioned. Keira scanned the area and found a vent close to the floor. A cluster of tables and large pots holding fake plants helped shield its view from the rest of the food court. She pushed a chair out of the way to crouch in front of the vent and held out her hand.

A gentle gust of air washed out of it, and every hair on Keira's body stood on end.

She could feel energy on that air. Not a massive amount, but…

"This one," she said, her voice a whisper. "It's going to connect to Artec. Zoe, do you still have that tool kit?"

"Heck yeah," Zoe whispered back, passing the pouch to Keira. Then she and Mason stood in front of Keira, shielding her from the rest of the food court.

Keira slipped a screwdriver out of the bag and pressed it into the screws holding the grate in place. They were stiff—they probably hadn't been touched since the mall was first built—but gave way with a bit of pressure. Keira carefully laid them on the grimy tiles at her side, then fit her fingers through the grate and pulled.

The vent cover popped free. More air drifted out, and Keira got another taste of the energy being carried on it. Artec's research was conducted at the tower, but she wouldn't have been surprised if Artec had kept a shade or two in the mall's lowest level.

"Now, for the moment of truth," she said, as Mason and Zoe watched her curiously. Keira placed a hand over her chest. She silently called for Daisy. As she pulled her hand forward, the small cat spilled forth.

Daisy landed on the tiles with a thud. The tip of her tail twitched as she gazed about, but she seemed neither surprised nor alarmed to be in the mall.

"Hey, Daze," Keira said, still on her hands and knees so she could talk directly to the cat. "I'm still not sure how this link thing works, but you've never let me down before. You know what we need to do, don't you?"

Daisy's liquid amber eyes met Keira's, and Keira was sure she saw a spark of acknowledgment in the cat's gaze.

Then Daisy languidly rolled onto her back, curled over, and began grooming her nether regions.

"Um." Keira glanced about, making sure none of the fast-food staff had seen the cat, then turned back to Daisy. "This, uh, this wasn't part of the plan."

The cat stopped her licking, her tongue still poking out from between her teeth, and stared blankly into the distance. Then she tumbled onto her side, reached out her front paws, and began scrabbling at Zoe's sneaker laces.

"Guess Daze really is just a normal cat at the end of the day," Zoe said, suppressing her laughter.

"Guess so." Keira scratched behind Daisy's ears. "It's okay, girl, we're not going to force you to do anything you don't want. How about you go back inside—"

The cat flopped around, exposing her stomach for scratches, then rolled back onto her feet. She was covered in a thin layer of dust she'd picked up from the rarely mopped corner of the floor. Before Keira had the chance to pick Daisy up, the cat turned and vanished into the open vent. Her happily flicking tail was visible for a second longer before it, too, disappeared.

"Oh," Keira said, her heart kicking up. "Okay, I guess?"

"Are you sure she knows the plan?" Zoe asked. "Is there any chance she's just being a perverse cat that can't resist the offer of a box, even when it's a long metal box with no end in sight?"

"No idea." Keira closed her eyes and tried to focus on what Daisy could see. The cat was moving, her little paws padding against the metal as she trotted down the vent. It ran downward at an angle, but the cat showed no hesitation as she followed the twisting route. "I…I think it might be working?"

"You keep an eye on her," Zoe said. "Mason, watch the food court. Signal me if any of the store staff look like they're paying attention to us."

"Where are you going?" Mason asked.

"The longer we stand here doing nothing, the more suspicious we're going to seem," Zoe said. "I'm going to get us some smoothies so we can at least have plausible deniability if a security guard comes by."

"Okay. Fair."

Keira stayed on the floor, her eyes closed as she struggled to track the cat. Daisy moved deeper, sometimes dropping down entire vertical plunges without skipping a beat. Keira would have been lost inside the vents, but Daisy apparently had no such qualms. She never hesitated, even when the pathways split.

Then, at last, sounds began to come through. They were distorted and wobbly, passed through whatever tenuous link existed between Daisy and Keira, but they were unmistakably human voices.

"Go slow," Keira whispered to the cat. "Go quiet."

Slats of light appeared in the duct ahead. Daisy slowed to a creep as she neared the vent. There was a room visible through it. Keira strained to make out the blurry, desaturated details. She saw desks and computers, their monitors lit up painfully bright. Men and women filled the space, either typing at the computers or trading sheets of paper.

Two taller, broader figures stood at the room's back wall. They didn't work but simply watched the figures at the computers. Their harsh dark outfits identified them as part of the mercenary team.

Mikhail wasn't exaggerating. Everyone in Artec is being watched.

Daisy didn't linger but kept moving. The ducts split, leading to more spaces in the basement level. Keira fought to keep a mental inventory of them all. Offices, workspaces, and then one massive, long room that was clearly a communal work area. At least fifteen people were there, their computers laid out on desks that had been squeezed in a haphazard arrangement. Daisy's eyes flicked to a gray shape at the far wall. The elevator. Two other mercenary guards flanked it, each holding rifles hung from their shoulders with straps.

Mason had been right to be cautious of plunging them into Artec's lair, as it turned out.

Daisy continued to move. Keira struggled to build her shaky mental map of the space. More offices passed beneath them: some designed for single employees, some for teams of four or eight. Many were empty, and Keira found it hard to guess whether Artec had preemptively built them to prepare for anticipated expansion or whether they had once housed staff who were no longer living.

Maybe a combination of the two.

Then, to Keira's surprise, they passed what seemed to be a bathroom and a bedroom. Both were empty and looked like they might have been belonged in a luxury hotel. The bed was a double, and the bathroom held a full shower and vanity.

A space for employees to rest if they're too tired? That doesn't feel right; it's too decadent. Every other room is concrete, but this is all carpet and real wood. It's not an employee space.

The bed looked rumpled, as though it had been slept in recently, and an open closet door revealed a flash of clothes inside. That was all Keira had a chance to see as Daisy continued along the tunnel.

She slowed as they approached a final vent. Keira fought to see through the slots as the cat neared it. When she did, her heart froze.

The vent looked down into an office space. It was large—large enough for a full team—but only held one desk and one computer. Elaborate wooden bookshelves ringed the walls. The furniture was significantly sleeker and more expensive than those in the standard offices. The reason for that was immediately obvious.

At the desk sat Schaeffer.

He was bent low over some paperwork, a pen scoring through printed lines and circling others. A horrible tension radiated from him.

She couldn't stop herself from glancing about the room—from the real plants in the corners, to the wall-to-wall books, to the plush leather surface on the desk.

Mikhail thinks he has a doomsday device with him. What would that look like? A remote? A box…?

Through Daisy's eyes, Keira strained to read the items on the desk: a paperweight, a pen, a quartz clock—

Daisy crept a millimeter closer to the vent. The metal creaked under her paws.

Schaeffer reacted instantly, snapping around to stare up at the vent.

Keira slapped her hand to her chest and immediately pulled it outward, spilling Daisy back into the food court.

She was breathing hard. The little cat's tail was bushy, and hairs stood up along her back. Keira ran shaky hands along the cat's body, trying to soothe her. "Good girl," she whispered. "Good girl—"

She wasn't sure if she'd gotten the cat back fast enough. She'd been prepared to recall Daisy at the first sign of danger, but Schaeffer had reacted frighteningly fast. The gaps in the vent were slim, but she thought he might have seen Daisy—or at least some kind of movement.

"Hey," she whispered to her friends. Mason still stood behind her, helping hide her from the rest of the food court, and Zoe had just arrived back, her arms full with three smoothies. "I think we need to go—"

A single, shockingly loud alarm blared out from the speakers above them, and Keira's mouth turned dry.

"Too late."

CHAPTER 19

KEIRA PULLED DAISY TOWARD herself, letting the cat vanish back into her body. Mason reached out to help her up. "We'll run."

"Nope." Zoe's eyes were huge beneath the bushy eyebrows. "No, they're going to have the exits covered. Running's the wrong move. We need to stay right here."

"What?" Keira asked, her heart thumping painfully.

"If we run, we make it clear we're trying to escape." Zoe slammed the smoothies down onto the nearest food court table. "It draws attention, and we won't be able to get to the car in time. We have to act like we're just any other customer. Keira, get that grate back on."

Keira swore under her breath as she shoved the metal plate back over the duct. She pushed the screws back into their holes but didn't waste time tightening them.

The alarm had cut out, but so had the music, leaving the mall eerily quiet. The handful of other customers in the food court all looked around, faintly bemused, then went back to their food.

"Sit," Zoe urged, still whispering as she shoved a smoothie toward each of them. "And act natural."

"How do you expect me to do that when *I'm wearing a fake mustache the size of a broom?*" Mason shot back.

Footsteps rang through the mall. Keira grabbed her smoothie and put her head down over the straw, pretending to drink as she let the wig hide most of her face.

Zoe had fallen into her role perfectly. She rested one elbow on the table, chin propped on her palm, looking bored out of her mind. Mason felt frighteningly stiff at Keira's side, but he kept his eyes down as he focused on his smoothie.

A guard appeared in the entrance to the food court.

Mason groaned under his breath. He found Keira's hand beneath the table and squeezed it. She squeezed back.

The guard moved forward. He wasn't dressed like the mercenaries downstairs, but Keira thought he must be one of them, regardless. He had one hand on a pouch on his vest, and she could only guess it held a gun.

He didn't seem in any hurry as he paced through the near-empty food court, glancing from table to table, looping increasingly close to them.

"And so I said to Makayla, I said, don't eat my lunch, Makayla," Zoe drawled, putting on an accent. "And you know what she said? She said, she told me right to my face, it was in the communal fridge, so that meant it was communal food; can you believe…?"

The guard kept walking.

Keira felt like her heart was going to explode. "It worked," she said, faintly stunned, as the guard left the food court.

"People who are looking for one very specific thing can easily overlook anything outside that description," Zoe said, using her thumb to make sure both her eyebrows were still attached. "Keep sitting and keep looking bored. We can't afford to move until the guards stop watching the exits."

"How long will that take?" Mason asked.

"We're going to find out." Zoe glanced at Keira. "How much did the people down there see of Daisy?"

"Not much. Schaeffer looked up at her in the vent, but I pulled her back right away."

"Okay, that means this alarm was probably for a precautionary search. We'll give it an hour; then we'll meander out of here." Zoe sucked in a deep breath…and let it out slowly and carefully. "Try the smoothies. It might help you stay calm to have something to focus on. I was kind of distracted when I ordered them, though, so I have no idea what they are."

Mason's hands shook as he lifted the drink. He made a face. "Maybe…kale and strawberries?"

"Yeah, that sounds about right." Zoe rested her arms on the table. "Keira, since we have some time to waste, did you want to tell us what's down there?"

"Guards by the elevator doors," Keira said, running through her mental inventory. "More guards in other major rooms. I'd wager there are at least a dozen mercenaries scattered through the basement."

"Schaeffer is *not* playing games," Zoe said. She tilted forward a fraction. "He's definitely down there, though?"

"Yeah. Definitely. He's at the back of the complex. We'd have to get through almost the entire space to reach his office."

"At least we know, for sure, where he is." Zoe worked her jaw. "So. Guards by the elevators. Guards through the offices. A long walk to reach Schaeffer. I hate admitting this, but Mason's plan is starting to sound like the better option."

"Waiting for him outside the elevator?" Mason glanced at Keira. "It's still risky, but…"

Keira felt her heart sink. "I don't think that's going to work."

"Talk me through it," Zoe said, leaning closer. Another guard had appeared in the food court entrance, but he stayed there just long enough to glance through the space before walking away again.

Keira waited until he was out of sight before continuing. "Schaeffer has a private bedroom and bathroom down there. And they looked used." She remembered the rumpled bedsheets and the shirts in the closet. "I think he's living down there full-time."

"Okay," Mason murmured. "I didn't think of that. But it's a smart decision on Schaeffer's part. I suspect he's a long way past taking risks. At least until he can catch you."

"This is ugly," Zoe said. "We *have* to go down there to get to him. But going down there means getting past a wall of armed guards." She paused, lips pursed. "Really wish we had an angry bear right now."

Keira tried her smoothie. She thought she caught the taste of oats and carrots. Zoe really had just pointed to random words when placing her orders.

"What about looking for other ways in?" Mason asked. "Like a stairwell? We've only seen the elevator so far. But legally, buildings are required to have emergency exits."

"Not sure Artec is inviting fire marshals and zoning supervisors down to its secret lair to check for compliance," Zoe said. She paused, then frowned, the hairy eyebrows doing a strange dance. "It's something I could look into, though. I found barely anything about this place when I was researching it last night, but surely there must be a building contractor with old plans, or…" She sighed. "Time. That's our only real enemy right now. If I had even one more day, I think I could dig some stuff up, but we can't gamble that much time."

Keira chewed on her lip. "How tired are you both?"

"Yes," Mason said bleakly.

"I feel like I am literally on the verge of dying," Zoe added. "What's your plan?"

"I think I can buy us some extra time—not just for us but for Blighty." Keira took a deep drink of her smoothie and pulled a face. "But it means another very late night."

"Hit us with your worst," was all Zoe said.

———

Leaving the shopping mall was less eventful than Keira had feared. They waited in the food court until Zoe decided enough time had passed, then carried the half-drunk smoothies with them as they aimed for the exit.

A security guard stood near the door. He was texting on his phone. Zoe set the pace, walking ahead with slow, lazy strides while taking another drink and keeping her focus straight ahead. The guard glanced up as they neared him, but Keira didn't think he even registered them. His gaze went straight back to the phone as the three friends spilled outside.

"You don't want to know how badly I'm sweating under this mustache," Mason said as they crossed to the car. "I'll need to wring it out before I give it back to you, Zo."

"Relax." Zoe dunked her drink into a bin as they passed it. "They're looking for fugitives, not shoppers. You've just got to act confident to sell the lie."

"Great advice, except you're forgetting my one weakness: lying."

Zoe snorted as they got back into the car. "That is *hardly* your only weakness."

Keira covertly watched the mall as Mason guided the car out of the parking lot. It seemed quiet. No alarms. No sudden flurries of activity. Zoe had been right: playing the part had gotten them out.

As they reached the main roads again, Mason tore the mustache off and passed it back to Zoe. It left his upper lip looking red and sore. "Right. Let's go make a scene."

Keira's plan was simple enough, as long as they could pull it off. She'd memorized the location of all Artec's power stations—before she'd learned just how dangerous and risky it was to target them directly.

One of those stations was nearly six hours' drive from Blighty. And Keira planned to pay it a visit.

She wouldn't try to break it—that was playing a little too close to fire—but she'd make it clear that she'd been there. If the scene was convincing enough, Schaeffer might believe she'd moved to a new area. It wasn't out of character for her. She'd hopped from town to town fairly frequently before arriving at Blighty.

And if it worked, a convincing sighting should pull Artec's attention away from her current home and toward the regions surrounding that new plant. At least for a few days.

While Mason drove, Keira and Zoe tried to get some sleep. Keira was tired enough to fall under easily, stirring only when Mason stopped for fuel. Her dreams were plagued with images of the endless hallways and looping rooms in Artec's underground bunker, punctuated by the flash of Schaeffer's eyes as he whipped toward her.

"Hey," Mason said, one hand gently pressing Keira's shoulder. "We're almost there."

She startled awake and shuffled to sit up in her seat. It was already dark out. Streetlights cast a pearly glow over the road.

They'd left the freeway and the suburbs behind. The road they were cruising along was rural, with thick, sticklike trees pressing in close to the asphalt.

"I wasn't sure if you wanted to stop for food first," Mason added. "But we passed a place just a little while ago, and there's still time to turn around."

Keira pressed the heels of her hands into her eyes to rub the lingering tiredness from them. "I'd probably feel better if we did the hard work first. I'm not sure I can keep much down right now."

"Ditto." Zoe, in the back seat, stretched her arms as far as the car would let her. "Let's knock on some doors first."

It was a good time to make the attack: just after dark, on an overcast night. Keira hoped it would give the appearance of a plan, rather than a spur-of-the-moment decision.

Artec liked to choose relatively remote areas for their power plants, where there were fewer prying eyes to care about what happened there. The company avoided cities and towns, and instead bought land at the edges of rural communities, in places where its structures would be largely hidden from public sight.

Keira had learned as much about the locations as possible before her very first disastrous effort at destroying one. That attempt had cost her her memories and in return had given her Daisy.

The power plant they were now weaving toward was the second one Artec had built. That meant it was older and slightly smaller than the newer versions. The company hadn't left it neglected, though. While it had originally been designed with a chain-link fence around its perimeter to keep trespassers out, Artec had upgraded that to a solid concrete wall. Guard towers were positioned around the edges, watching over the strips of bare ground encircling the walls. As far as Keira knew, there was no easy way inside.

Mason switched the car's headlights off and slowed to a creep as they neared the power station. When the high towers and imposing concrete walls began to appear over the trees, he stopped the car entirely.

"Decoy bag time," Zoe said. She tipped the contents out of her backpack, then began judiciously placing items back in. The tool kit, a set of thick markers, and a map of the local area—collected from a service station by Mason during their last fuel stop—went inside. So did a small rolled bundle of money they could justify losing and a canister of bear spray from their meeting with Mikhail.

Finally, Keira pulled the two smudging sticks out of her jacket pocket, where she'd tucked them at Agatha Edith-Whittle's house. She'd forgotten they were there until she felt them poking into her side while she was napping. They were functionally useless for the kind of ghost hunting she did, but Artec didn't know that. If nothing else, it would give them a lot of questions.

"Two minutes," Mason said, fixing Keira with a hard glare. "No more, okay? We just want to draw attention, not paint a target on ourselves."

"I could say the same to you," Keira said. She took his hand and squeezed as tightly as she dared. "Two minutes. No more."

"I'll see you then." He leaned in, stealing a quick, desperate kiss. "Be safe."

CHAPTER 20

KEIRA TOOK THE DECOY backpack from Zoe, then slipped out of the car. She glanced back just once before stepping into the trees. Zoe and Mason were lit only by the car's interior overhead as they collected their can of gasoline and a lighter.

Fast. Keira's heart was in her throat as she moved into the trees, her footsteps quick and nearly silent. *Be fast. Sting them like a bee, then vanish again. That's the only way you're getting through this intact.*

She'd managed to bring down one power plant by going unnoticed. She doubted Artec would leave any of its remaining ones so carelessly guarded again.

The trees ended. Keira lowered her body and moved smoothly and quickly as she covered the stretch of bare ground to reach the wall. Her clothes were dark. In the heavy gloom, she would look no different than a shadow.

Keira reached the wall and dropped into a crouch. It was a massive block of concrete stretching in every direction, guarding the power plant nestled inside. Faint scraps of moonlight bled through the clouds and cast a sickly blue shade over it.

If she were truly trying to cause damage, she would have needed to find a way under or over. But that wasn't necessary tonight. Keira dropped the bag at her side, then unzipped it and took out a thick marker.

The bag wouldn't be coming back with her. It would act as proof she'd been there—something tangible for Artec and Schaeffer to scrutinize—and the map would sell the story that she'd taken up at least temporary accommodation in the area.

She uncapped the marker and began to draw. The concrete was cold and rough under her hand. She fought to keep her patterns clear as she created them with large looping swipes.

Some were runes she'd used at the previous station. Some were repeating elaborate shapes with no real purpose—yet more red herrings for Artec to waste time chasing. She drew them hastily, covering as much of the wall as she could within her limited time.

Keira spared just a second to glance back. A distant red light was visible through the trees.

Zoe and Mason had lit their fire. Fueled by the gas, it grew fast.

They'd lit a fire at the previous station too.

If they were sticking to the plan, her friends were already back in the car and navigating toward their pickup location.

They'd agreed on two minutes—just long enough to leave a signature that unmistakably pointed toward Keira—and then they would bail. They were already past those two minutes. She'd covered a medium-sized section of the wall with runes. And yet, Keira hesitated.

If one of the guards spotted her, that would really sell the encounter.

Just the runes and the backpack alone were compelling, but not convincing. Artec already knew she was working with friends. Schaeffer, paranoid as he was, might think Keira had sent someone else in as a decoy.

But if there was a sighting…

A guard tower was perched along the wall, high above, but not far from Keira. She kept one eye on it as she continued scrawling.

Come on, come on… I know you've seen the fire…

She'd promised two minutes. She was pushing four. But there were no alarms. No sirens nor voices nor lights.

What are you waiting for? You must know I'm here—you must—

As though to answer her question, a blast of glaring, bright light hit Keira.

They had a spotlight. Its beam, brilliantly harsh, created a perfect circle around her, nearly blinding her.

That was the cue she'd been waiting for. She responded instantly, leaping away from the wall and dashing back toward the darkness and the trees. She was just a second too slow.

A distant popping noise exploded through the cold night air, and then a streak of white-hot pain cut into her side. Spots of vivid red blood splashed across the ground and were then smeared under her boots.

They shot me.

Breathing hurt. She hoped it was from the shock, not the bullet. The spotlight followed her, a harsh and angry circle of brilliant white illuminating her and stretching her shadow out far ahead.

She ran in an all-out sprint, ducking and swerving in sharp, darting movements. More popping noises came from behind her. A puff of dirt exploded in the earth nearby. The pain in her side was excruciating. She took it and forced it into a little ball in her stomach, using it to fuel her.

The gunshots faded as she leaped between the trees. Jagged slashes of the spotlight tried to reach between the branches to keep up with her, but she only needed a few sharp swerves to escape it completely.

They would be following her on foot, though, and she was probably leaving a trail of blood for easy tracking.

Keira clamped her hands over her side, trying to stem the flow. Her shirt was already saturated on that side.

That was fine. She didn't need to get far.

The pickup location was close. Mason had kept the car lights off, but she could hear the engine idling. She burst out of the trees and hit the side of the car, her breathing shallow and pained, and pulled the door open.

"That was a bit more than two minutes—" Zoe started, then cut off. "Oh, damn."

"Drive," Keira said, lurching into the passenger seat and slamming the door.

Mason had blanched a pained, terrified white. He reached for her side, which was covered in red. "Keira—"

"It's just a graze," she said, hoping that was true, and moved her arm to cover the wound so that he couldn't stare at it any further. "But they're following me. We have to go. *Now.*"

Mason set his jaw. He slammed a foot onto the accelerator and the car leaped forward, engine growling.

"Zoe, there's a cloth in the back," Mason said without taking his eyes off the narrow path they were following through the trees. He'd had always been a cautious driver, but he was gambling as much as Keira had ever seen him, rocking the car through the dark bushes and low-hanging branches to reach a main road. "Pass it forward. Keira, I need you to press it into your injury. It's going to hurt, but I need you to apply as much pressure as you can. We have to stop that bleeding."

"Here," Zoe said, reaching between the seats with a blue hand towel. "What else can I do? Do you want water or…?"

"I'm fine." Keira took the towel and forced it against her side, just a few inches below her ribs. She bit back on a groan as the pressure made the pain bloom across her skin like a nest of angry fire ants.

Zoe clung to the back of Keira's seat to balance against the way the car rocked over uneven terrain. "What happened out there?"

"Eh." Keira tried for a shrug and immediately regretted it. "I pushed my luck. I got a little bit shot. Standard weekend activities."

The car burst from the forest and Mason corrected his steering as they scraped back onto a near-empty highway. Keira blinked hard as Mason finally switched the headlights back on.

"Keep the pressure up. As much as you can take." Mason faced forward, but his eyes kept darting toward her, scanning the blood leaking between her fingers and her face in turns.

"Sorry about the car," Keira managed. "You're probably going to get charged a cleaning fee."

"It's a rental. I'm sure it's already had plenty of bodily fluids scrubbed out of it." One hand left the wheel, reaching toward her. "Hold on a moment. I'm going to find a place to pull over. I have my kit in the back."

"Not yet. We're still too close." Keira crushed the cloth into her side, hoping it would slow the bleeding, and swallowed a groan. "This can wait."

"But—"

"Mason, I love you more than anything, but right now I need you to worry less and drive more."

"Okay. Okay." He grimaced. "I'm trying *very* hard to trust your judgment. But I need you to tell me if you feel dizzy or like you might pass out, okay?"

"Yes, I promise I'll give you advance warning if I think I'm dying." Keira tried to smile, but it probably came out more like a grimace. "We're good."

For a second, the car was quiet except for Mason's tight, anxious breathing. Then Zoe said, "So you guys are up to *I love you*s already? Moving a bit fast, don't you think?"

"We have been facing imminent death since we started dating," Mason retorted. "Forgive me if I'm not exactly meandering."

Keira leaned back and closed her eyes. For all his worrying, Mason was doing a good job of moving them away from the power plant in an efficient but unpredictable route.

The ache in her side refused to abate and refused to stop

bleeding. But she didn't think the bullet had gone deep enough to hit anything vital. She was still alive and still conscious and, most importantly, she'd gotten away from Artec. All things considered, they were lucky.

Luckier than I deserve. She squinted her eyes open and watched the streetlamps wash over them in undulating waves. They were aiming toward the town again. *I shouldn't have taken that risk. It was stupid.*

But, she hoped, it might also work in their favor. Artec not only had the decoy bag and a sighting, but they had a splatter of blood too. They would think she was too hurt to go far. If anything was going to move the search away from Blighty, that would do it.

"This is far enough," Mason said, turning into the parking lot for a fast-food outlet. The drive-through was lit up and a slow procession of cars crept along its channel as the dinner rush moved through. Mason navigated toward the back of the parking lot, away from too many prying eyes. "Zo, take my card and get some food. It might help Keira with the shock."

"On it." She snatched a card out of Mason's wallet and turned toward the garish building.

"I'm not in shock," Keira grumbled. Mason only made soft agreeing noises as he fetched his kit and came around the car's passenger side.

He eased the cloth out of Keira's hands and peeled up her shirt.

"Oh," Mason whispered as he saw the injury. "Oh, Keira."

Keira dared herself to look down. Her side—from her shirt to her jeans—was saturated with blood. And the reason was clear.

The bullet had cut along her side, just below her ribs, taking out a four-inch slice of flesh.

"Hey, that's good, right?" she managed. "No bullets to fish out. No punctured internal organs. Pretty clean, everything considered."

"You know I'm going to say the same thing I always do," he said, crouching outside the open car door as he examined the gash. "You really need a hospital."

"And you already know I'm going to shoot that down," Keira replied. "Put a bandage on it or whatever you want. We need to get back on the road before it's too late."

"Do you want to go back to Blighty?" Mason asked. He seemed more intent on pulling bottles of antiseptic out of his kit than on hearing the answer. She guessed he was making small talk as a distraction technique, to keep her mind off the injury. He gave an apologetic glance as he unscrewed a cap. "This will hurt. Sorry."

Keira grit her teeth as he poured antiseptic over the gash. The pain redoubled, and clammy sweat drenched her. She waited until the pain subsided, then lifted her shirt out of the way so Mason could work over her side. "I guess…I just assumed we would be going back." She hesitated. "Zoe and I slept on the drive here, but you haven't yet."

He drew a needle out of the kit and unpeeled the sterile casing. "I was a med student, remember. I've had plenty of practice with all-nighters. I can get us back to Blighty. As long as that's where you want to go."

"Yeah," Keira said, then flinched as the needle pricked her skin.

"I think all of this—the sighting, the bag—will keep Artec away. But in case it doesn't…"

"You think it's better to be closer?" he asked.

"If Artec is planning to burn the town, I want to be there to stop them."

"Some days I wish you were a little more self-serving." Mason kept his head low as he worked on the row of stitches. "But I'm also glad you're not."

Keira chuckled, then suppressed the sound when the movement hurt. "Does this count as our next date?"

"I thought we agreed we weren't allowing any Artec third-wheeling."

"True. True."

Mason finished the row of stitches and cut the thread. He reached into his bag for clean bandages. "Though, to be honest, I don't think dating can get more romantic than this. Medical surgery performed in a fast-food parking lot in a town whose name I can't remember. Maybe we can forgive a little third-wheeling this time."

Zoe appeared from seemingly nowhere, her arms ladened with bags. "*Speaking* of third-wheeling, I hope you wanted me to buy literally twenty burgers when you gave me your card, because I bought literally twenty burgers."

Mason looked pained. "Why?"

"One of the cars in drive-through honked at me when I passed them, so I figured they could suffer through an extra-long wait for their order." Zoe shrugged, dropping two of the bags onto the ground next to the car. "Don't worry. I also got a bottle of water to wash the bloody handprint off the car door, so we don't look quite as unnerving when we're cruising down the highway."

"Sorry about that," Keira said.

"What's the prognosis?" Zoe leaned over Mason's shoulder, her owlish eyes scanning Keira's blood-soaked shirt. "Are we gonna have to dig a shallow grave?"

"It's bad, but it could be worse. Lean forward, please, Keira." Mason wrapped a final bandage around her middle to hold the cloths in place. "I'll need to keep a close watch on it. But the bleeding's slowing, which is a hopeful sign. You'll need as much rest as you can get. And you'll also need to move as little as possible to give it a chance to heal."

"Well…that's not really an option right now, is it?"

He glanced up at her, his eyes filled with pain, before returning to tying off the dressings.

The ramifications of her mistake were starting to set in. The sighting at the power plant might only buy them a few days. And Artec would be searching for her even more feverishly now that they knew she was injured.

Staying at home and resting wasn't really something she could do.

Artec was close on her heels. She needed to be at her peak. Instead, at that moment, even shallow breathing hurt almost too much to stand. She wasn't able to run. She wasn't able to fight. And Mason didn't seem to expect her recovery would be anywhere near as fast as she needed it to be.

"Oh," Keira muttered. "This… I…"

"Hey." Zoe leaned over Mason's shoulder to see inside the car. She tenderly placed a wrapped burger in Keira's lap and patted its top for emphasis. "Here. I'm told this might help the shock."

"Um." Keira felt moisture prickle in her eyes as she faced forward again. A sickly kind of panic had begun to set in. "How… how are we going to…?"

"And water." Zoe unscrewed the cap on a bottle and delicately pried Keira's fingers apart so she could slide the drink into her hand. Then she leaned close, filling Keira's view so thoroughly that it was impossible to look anywhere else. "Don't think about it. Not right now, and not even a little bit. Okay? Right now, all we care about is sleeping through tonight. Tomorrow, when we're rested, and when our brains have some juice, we're going to figure it out. And we *will* figure it out. But tonight, we're not going to think about it. Okay?"

Keira swallowed thickly. Zoe's tone had been gentle but held so much conviction that it was impossible not to listen. She looked at the burger and drink in her lap and then back up to Zoe's raised eyebrows and expectant gaze.

"Okay?" Zoe prompted.

"Okay," Keira said. She knew she was only delaying the inevitable, but Zoe was right. She had no energy left to worry right then. They had to focus on getting through the night; everything else would come after.

Zoe gave her a smile, then slid back out of Keira's way and fetched a second water bottle to pour over the door.

"We were talking about making the drive back to Blighty, as long as you're okay with that," Mason said to Zoe. "There's plenty of room in my house, and Keira shouldn't be left alone tonight. It might be good for us all to stay together."

"That works for me." Zoe used her sleeve to rub at the wet door. Her lopsided grin was back in place. "But I reserve the right to dump a bucket of cold water on the first person who tries to get cute with their significant other."

"Sure." Keira managed a weak chuckle as she tugged her shirt back over the stack of bandages. "That's fair."

"We've got a long trip to get back." Zoe stepped away from the door to admire her handiwork, nodded, then hefted the multiple bags she'd gotten from the take-out place. "Hope you're both hungry."

CHAPTER 21

OF THE TWENTY BURGERS Zoe had bought, they managed to make it through three and a half on the drive home. Even though their fuel that day had consisted of coffee and smoothies, none of them seemed able to stomach much.

The pain in Keira's side turned into a steady, gnawing thing. She clutched the water bottle in her lap, taking small drinks occasionally because she knew it made Mason happy. Dark circles had formed around his eyes. He watched her closely, stealing little glances in between trying to focus on the road.

The highway gradually emptied as the early evening hours bled away. Mason made two stops along the drive to check on Keira and to get more drinks, and she was silently impressed by his ability to keep moving, even with how little rest he'd gotten over the previous two days. The dashboard clock was creeping toward ten in the evening when a phone chimed from the back seat.

"Oh," Zoe said, speaking very softly.

Keira couldn't turn far enough to see over her shoulder, but she asked, "What is it?"

Zoe, chuckling, leaned forward and extended her phone to show Keira the screen. "All my digging actually paid off."

Keira squinted but still couldn't read the tiny text in the dim light. "Digging? Oh, you mean with the mall!"

"Bingo." Zoe pulled the phone back and began typing. "Guess who has the actual number for someone from the construction crew? Someone who, in a shocking and exciting twist, is willing to speak to me?"

"Zo, that's fantastic." Mason looked dead exhausted but still smiled at the news.

"Yeah, usually people stop talking the moment they realize you have nefarious motivations, but this guy doesn't care." Zoe's fingers flew across the keys. "Ready for the bad news?"

Keira and Mason exchanged a glance.

"He was a subcontractor for the concrete," Zoe finished. "No, let me clarify. He was hired to do pickup work by the subcontractor for the concreting."

Mason looked just as uncertain as Keira felt. "What does that mean?"

"He has access to nothing. No plans, no contact details for any of the other crews, nothing that came after the foundations were laid." Zoe made a face. "Apparently, he was only on the job for, like, two weeks to help them catch up when one of their regulars got sick. Which is part of why he doesn't mind talking; they stiffed him on part of his wages."

"Can he tell us anything specific?" Keira asked. "Anything we might be able to use?"

"Maybe." Zoe's face was screwed up in concentration. "He made some comment about the project being a disaster waiting to happen, so I'm prying around that. I'll report back when I have something more."

"Thanks, Zo." Keira clenched her hands around the water bottle, focusing on the tactile sensations to keep her mind off the ache in her side.

It was after midnight by the time they arrived back in Blighty.

They finally rolled into Mason's driveway. Keira was halfway out of the car before Mason made it around to her and gave her his arm to lean on.

"I'll get some blankets," he said, half supporting and half carrying Keira into the living room, where they'd slept the night before. She could still see a few stray jigsaw puzzle pieces scattered about the floor.

A small cat came meandering out of the kitchen, stretching languidly as though she'd just emerged from a long nap. Keira choked on a laugh despite herself. She hadn't even noticed when Daisy split away from her, but apparently the cat had known where they would end up.

"Hey, beastie," Zoe cooed, rubbing around Daisy's head. The cat yawned, then flopped down in front of the unlit fireplace, sending them all intent glances to convey her message.

Daisy got what she wanted. By the time Mason had retrieved three sets of blankets and pillows, Zoe had started the fire.

Keira sat on the edge of the couch, trying not to get stains on the fabric. She pointed toward the bathroom. "Okay if I clean up?"

"Absolutely. I'll help." Mason had been crouched as he shook out the bedding material but stood to offer her his arm.

Keira shook her head. "You're dead tired and I'm going to be slow. Get to sleeping. I'll see you tomorrow."

His expression tightened with worry. "Keira—"

"No, seriously." She smiled as she stood and shuffled toward the hallway. "I'm doing okay, and I'll be careful not to get the bandages wet."

"Okay," he said, relenting, and offered her a bundle of pajamas, which he'd brought out with the bedding material. "There are plenty of towels in the cupboard under the sink, and don't worry about making a mess of them. But you have to call me if you start feeling dizzy, okay?"

"Mm." She gently squeezed his arm as she passed, and he bent down to press a featherlight kiss to her cheek.

From across the room, Zoe shot daggers at them. *Cold bucket of water*, she mouthed, and Keira gave her a thumbs-up before shambling into the bathroom.

She moved gingerly as she changed out of her clothes and used warm water to wipe up the streaks of blood that had stained her side.

It was the first time she'd seen herself in a mirror since leaving Blighty. She looked as tired as she felt—grayed out and somehow less solid, as though her skin had turned papery. But she was standing. And that felt like a victory, even if it was just a tiny one.

Spots of crimson were visible through the bandages, but the worst of the bleeding seemed to have stopped. The stitches ached every time Keira moved her side or breathed too deeply.

She'd promised Zoe that she wouldn't think about what her injury would mean for their plans or for Artec. It was enough that they'd gotten home alive and had at least a few hours where they could rest. Zoe had been right. They could face everything else in the morning.

When she emerged from the bathroom, significantly less grimy and significantly more tired, she found Mason sitting on the floor, his back propped up against the corner of the couch, his arms folded. He'd tried to wait up for her but had fallen asleep, his chin resting on his chest.

"Shh," Keira said as she gently nudged him to lie down. He made a faint noise, his eyelids fluttering, but didn't properly wake. He must have been dead on his feet.

Zoe was already under, lying out flat on the bed, limbs thrown out.

Keira settled down beside them, careful not to disturb either of her friends, and closed her eyes. The gash in her side still hurt, and she slipped into an uneasy, fugue-like rest. Voices whispered to her through her dreams. They were the voices of the dead, pleading with her. Begging not to be forgotten.

Keira snapped awake as something cool and damp grazed her side.

The dead, trailing their fingers across my skin.

She stared, wide-eyed, at the ceiling. Then she blinked. There was no hum of electricity in the air warning her that there were spirits about. No chill in the room either. Keira craned to look down at her side.

It was still night. The fire had reduced to coals, and its dim light bled across the room. Daisy crouched at Keira's side. The pajama shirt had ridden up, and Daisy licked at her exposed skin.

Keira sighed and reached down to stroke around the cat's face. "I thought I washed all the blood off. At least we know that, if I really died, you'd wait no more than three hours to chow down on my corpse."

Daisy purred as she leaned into Keira's pets, her tongue still poking out from between her teeth.

That was when Keira felt it. A soft, almost painful prickle in her skin, like a needle being threaded into her.

Keira pulled her hand back. As soon as the pets stopped, Daisy bent down and began licking again.

But…it wasn't mindless lapping. Her cool tongue was tracing a pattern.

Careful not to move her torso or disturb the cat, Keira reached over Zoe's sleeping form to find her bag of tools. Even just stretching that far made the pain flare through her side, but Keira was too full of bursting hope to care.

She slid a piece of charcoal out of the pouch. Then she used it to trace a replica of the pattern Daisy was creating, copying it onto her side, near the bandages.

Prickles of electricity ran through her skin. Dizziness rose, and she sucked in a sharp breath as she squeezed her eyes closed. The sensations faded.

"Oh," Keira whispered, looking down.

Daisy, no longer interested in Keira, sauntered away. She stopped near Mason's head, considered him for a moment, then flopped over his face, extracting a muffled noise from the sleeping man.

Keira couldn't stop staring at the mark she'd replicated. She knew it well. It was one of the runes she'd written in her book: a rune with no known purpose. One of the first ones she'd discovered.

And Daisy—the cat that seemed to know what she needed, even when Keira herself didn't—had re-created it. With, admittedly, cat saliva. But Keira supposed it wasn't like Daisy had many alternatives.

Moving carefully, Keira unwrapped the bandages from around her torso. Mason had been strict about not exposing the cut, but when Keira peeled back the cotton pad, she saw that the injury beneath no longer looked as gory and raw as it had before.

The stitches were still present. They were neat and careful, the way all of Mason's work was. But the gouge they were holding together had deepened in color and begun to scab at the edges.

Keira, still not fully believing it, prodded at the wound. The two sides of the gash should have slid apart easily, but they didn't. And they hurt a lot less too.

It was a hard angle to work at, but Keira re-created the rune four more times, surrounding the injury. Each time she completed the design, the aching, burning sensation wound through the cut some more. And each time, some of the color bled out of the injury, fading it from angry red to pink.

She couldn't stifle a shocked grin. They'd discovered a healing rune.

That's something. It might not be bring-down-Artec *powerful, but it's powerful, nonetheless.*

"Hey," a groggy voice murmured. Zoe, head still pressed into her pillow, squinted up at her. "You good?"

"Very good." Keira didn't bother trying to replace the bandages before tugging her shirt back into place. She didn't think they were needed any longer. The clock above the fireplace said it was nearly two in the morning. "Zo, I've got something I have to do. I need to speak to a ghost. I'm probably going to be gone for a few hours."

"Huh?" Zoe squinted, using her palm to rub at her eye. "Really? Now?"

I'm no longer hurting. We've bought Blighty some time but probably not nearly as much time as it needs. Yes, I think, if I'm going to do anything, it has to be now. "I'm just heading back to the cottage. If Mason wakes up, try not to let him worry too much, okay? I'll keep my phone with me."

"Okay, I guess." Zoe looked confused, but she also seemed like she was already halfway back asleep. "Didja want me to come…?"

"Get some rest," Keira said, standing. Daisy flopped off Mason's face and trotted up to her side. She seemed to know they had a job, and her tail twitched eagerly. "I'll be back by dawn."

CHAPTER 22

THE STREET WAS DARK. In the distance, The Home stood, barely visible behind its screen of trees.

For a second, Keira was tempted to go there. She needed to see a ghost, and those were the closest spirits she knew of. But they hadn't offered to help, and it felt unfair to ask for favors when they were waiting on her to free them.

Instead, she turned to the forest. Daisy loped ahead, her curved tail bobbing like a lure in the dark, leading Keira to her destination.

She wore a change of clothes from the emergency bag Mason kept at his house. Her satchel of tools was tied around her waist.

The air felt thick. Almost oppressively heavy, like a storm about to break.

They were on the cusp of something, Keira sensed, as she broke into a jog. Something big. She felt like she was chasing the missing piece of the puzzle, her arms stretched out to grasp it before it flitted out of reach forever.

She was breathless when she burst into the clearing. That, by itself, felt amazing. She could run, and the injury she'd sustained less than twelve hours before barely ached.

She stood for a moment, letting her eyes adjust. The air prickled faintly. The three Tillson siblings emerged from the darkness, their fog-like forms seeming to glow in the moonlight.

Keira lifted the hem off her top to show them the injury that was gradually fading into a scar, and the ring of marks she'd drawn around it.

"We found one." She kept her voice quiet, as though raising it too high would ruin some kind of magic that presided over the night. "A rune."

Daisy wove between the three motionless spirits. She was nearly invisible—one shadow blending into a multitude of others. But her steps were quick and her whiskers twitched. She was eager.

Keira dropped her shirt and reached into her pouch for charcoal sticks. "I need another one. And I need to figure it out tonight."

She knew which one she wanted to focus on. It was the last symbol she'd identified—the one she'd found on the morning Agatha Edith-Whittle had visited. It had felt strong, she thought, based on what she could sense of it.

She circled the glade, scratching the mark into every tree she passed.

"We're going to figure this out," she said, speaking to herself more than the ghosts. "Even if it kills us."

She kept one eye on Daisy as she worked. The cat scurried around the clearing, following small bugs. She didn't seem especially interested in helping.

That's fine. Trial and error, it is.

She drew the mark on her chest, and then on each of her palms, using herself as a living canvas.

"Okay," Keira said. "I need a volunteer."

One of the spirits—the younger sister, Emma—stepped forward. Keira reached toward her.

Cold prickles spread through her hand, concentrating on the mark on her palm. It did *something*. She just wasn't sure what.

Does it…make it easier to feel the energy? She flexed her fingers as she pressed them into the ghost. It was like dipping her hand into a freezing pond. The prickles intensified, concentrating around the rune.

"Can you feel anything?" Keira asked.

Emma tilted her head, her loose hair flowing around her shoulders, but gave no response. That wasn't a surprise. *Chattiness* was a rare trait to find among the dead.

It confirmed that there was no immediate, obvious reaction from the contact, though. And so Keira tried pulling on the energy.

It was like touching an electric fence. White-hot electricity coursed up Keira's arm.

They staggered apart. The spirit clutched her hands against her chest, where Keira had touched her, as shock flitted across her pale features. And she *was* pale. The ghosts were always transparent, but now the youngest sister was barely a whisper of herself—a breath of mist that faded from sight entirely if Keira didn't fight to keep her eyes focused.

"Sorry!" Keira said, breathing hard. She could feel the extra energy moving through her, like electricity trapped in a closed loop—racing along her limbs and through her lungs as it looked for a way out. It sizzled in the runes she'd drawn on her side, the skin heating as the cut knit together some more. "Sorry, sorry, I didn't mean to—"

The other two siblings came up alongside their sister, brushing shoulders with her. The three of them stared at Keira. She braced for fear or hatred, but it wasn't there. Their expressions only held the same mild curiosity they always had.

I've taken energy from spirits before. She'd learned that trick a while back. She could push or pull on the energy the ghosts held, borrowing it and giving it back. But it had always been slow before, and she was limited in how much she could take.

This experience…it reminded her more of touching the raw wires running through Artec's graveyards and being flooded by energy she couldn't control.

She breathed deeply, feet braced as she felt the excess power. It wasn't as bad as it had been after Artec's cemetery, but it was still too much to sit with comfortably. If she gave it enough time, it would dissipate out of her—fading away in tiny pieces with every exhaled breath—until she was back to her usual levels. Or she could release it on purpose.

Keira held her hand out toward Emma Tillson. "Here. Let me touch you again, and I'll give you the energy back."

There wasn't exactly mistrust on the ghost's features, but she didn't move closer either. Slowly, and in unison, the three siblings turned their heads until they were facing away from her.

Keira felt a twinge of guilt. They didn't *have* to take the energy back. Emma would slowly regain it on her own. At least, as long as the rune didn't have any unforeseen consequences. She assumed it was somehow amplifying her ability to draw energy, but she'd need more tests to be sure.

She hadn't meant to upset the siblings so badly, though. They wouldn't even meet her eyes. They…

Keira's mouth turned dry. She'd misunderstood. They weren't rejecting her, as she'd first assumed. They were staring toward something else. Something between the trees, something Keira couldn't see. And they were fixated on it.

The phone tucked into Keira's pocket buzzed. She fumbled for it. *Did Mason wake? Or did Zoe…?*

She raised the screen. The number displayed was unfamiliar. And no one except her closest friends had this phone's details. No one except—

The message flashed up.

I'm sorry. I gave you as much time as I could. But they were coming for me. I had no choice.

Her heart froze. She raised her head to see that all three siblings, still staring into the distance, had lifted their hands. All pointing.

Someone was coming.

No. No. Not now.

A hundred thoughts raced through Keira in the span of a second. She had to warn Mason and Zoe. She had to run. She had to get one of the escape bags. Not the one in her cottage, though. That was where Mikhail would have sent them. But—

A branch snapped behind her.

Keira ran. She reached out a hand to Daisy as she passed, and the cat vanished inside of her, merging into the excess energy until Keira felt half-wild from it. Her path carried her straight through the three siblings, and she felt blistering ice rush across her skin before she broke free and burst into the trees on the other side.

It was impossible to be silent in the forest, but Keira moved lithely, keeping the sounds to a minimum as she ducked and wove. She was good at that. Breathing through clenched teeth, she kept her body small as she fled.

She'd have to give up the emergency bags. It would be too risky to circle back for them. She'd stick to the forest instead, using its cover to conceal herself until she was far enough away that Artec had no chance to close its net around her.

Keira had survived in the wilderness before. She could do it again. She'd text Mason and Zoe to let them know she was safe, but then…

Her footsteps faltered.

How much did Mikhail tell Schaeffer about my friends?

Her mouth turned dry. The fear she'd felt just a moment before—the fear of being hunted—had been sharp and alarming. But this was a different kind of fear. Thick, slick, coiling dread.

She'd survived on her own in the past. But that had been before she'd had friends. Before her mere existence could put the people she loved most in danger. She shouldn't have left them alone that night.

Keira bit her lip hard enough to hurt as she pulled her phone from her pocket. They'd agreed on a set number of brief, one-letter messages in case of situations exactly like this.

H for *hide; suspicious figures spotted. R* for *run; they know where you are.* The phone lit up Keira's face as she hastily created a message. Adage was safe; he was staying with a friend. But both Zoe and Mason were vulnerable as long as they were in Mason's house. She could only hope that the chime of the arriving message would be enough to wake them. She couldn't lose the time it would take to make a call.

She typed *R*, then moved to hit *send*. Her finger hesitated over the button as a wash of horrible premonition crashed over her. She recognized the sensation. It was something she was already highly attuned to, magnified by the extra energy she'd taken on.

She was being watched. She was certain of it.

Every hair on Keira's body stood on end. Silently, she pressed her hand over her phone's screen, blocking its light.

She couldn't tell which direction they were coming from. Or how far away they might be.

She just knew they were close.

Almost no moonlight made it through the forest canopy. Keira's wide eyes took in the strange, shadowed silhouettes of trees around her, searching for any aberrations. Every nerve was wound tight enough to snap.

A twig cracked to her right.

Keira shot forward, away from it.

She was too late.

A gloved hand snagged around her jacket, hauling her back.

Her legs slipped from under her. Keira twisted, trying to fight her way out of the jacket. There was no time. The attacker was already on her, grabbing at her hair.

Keira gasped and thrashed, ducking low as she tried to pull free. The grip only tightened, sending pain sparking across her skull as he pulled her back.

She kicked out, aiming her boots toward the stranger's legs. She connected solidly with a shin, but it didn't feel like the usual thin layer of skin across bone. The sole of her shoe hit something thick and solid instead, and the figure holding her didn't even flinch.

Armor. They're wearing armor.

Keira tilted back just far enough to squint up at the stranger. He was huge, towering at least a full head and a half above her. Where his eyes should have been were two glowing disks of green, reflecting the forest like sheets of glass.

Night vision.

Artec had taken no risks. They'd sent their men in with every advantage possible. She shouldn't have expected anything less.

The stranger's other hand—the one that had grabbed her jacket—snaked toward Keira's throat. She had no way to escape it. The grip crushed around her windpipe, bruising her, and she could only writhe as the attacker shoved her into the forest floor.

He pinned her there, one hand on her neck, one knee pressed

into her sternum so hard that she couldn't have breathed even if her throat were open. Then he reached back, and through the pain and rapidly vanishing oxygen, she realized he was reaching for his walkie-talkie.

No.

However bad her odds at fighting a single figure were, she had even less hope if more of them closed in around her.

Keira slammed her hand into the stranger's chest. Her fingertips pressed into a hard, armored plate, and she hoped her abilities would be enough to affect him, even through the layers of shielding.

She concentrated the excess energy she'd gained into her hand, bundling it until it was overwhelming, and then forced it out as a shock wave.

It hit the stranger's chest hard. He lurched back as his grip on her throat loosened. The communication device tumbled from his other hand.

Keira had a second where the pressure let up. Just enough to gasp in a thin breath. Then the hand tightened again, forcing a whine from her as the mercenary regained control.

It hadn't been enough. She'd put every ounce of excess energy into the attack, and it had barely made the figure falter.

And she had nothing left for a second attack.

CHAPTER 23

SPARKS DANCED AT THE corners of her eyes. Panic rose. She tried to claw at his hands, but his gloves were too thick to get through. Desperate, she reached for his face. One swipe nearly dislodged the night vision goggles. The figure twitched but didn't release his hold.

She swiped again, and this time her fingertips caught in his mask. She pulled, yanking it down, and exposed a sliver of skin.

A rune to move energy. Not in a trickle, but in a deluge.

It was still painted on her hands. She hoped it would be enough. The sparks were creeping in across her vision as her oxygen faded. Keira pressed her palm against the inch of exposed skin. The attacker tilted his head away but refused to budge farther.

She could feel the energy flowing beneath his skin. Keira reached for it and pulled. Not just a little. Not like when she'd been experimenting with the ghost and wanted to be cautious. This time she pulled as hard as she could.

Lava and ice poured through her veins, terrifying and intense and overwhelming. The hands around Keira's throat released her in a pained twitch. She didn't give the stranger any room to pull away but lurched up after him, her hand clenched into his face to hold the connection.

She could feel the electricity searing through her. It made her heart ache. Burned the edges of her mind. Flooded her lungs and nerves.

Keira broke the connection right as she reached the point where she couldn't take any more.

They collapsed apart. Keira dropped to the ground, gasping as she desperately tried to get air back into her body. Her throat ached where it had been crushed. As the dizziness began to fade, she forced her eyes open to see the stranger.

He lay shockingly still, crumpled on the forest floor. One arm was draped over his chest, the other thrown out behind him. Keira, still gasping, waited for him to move.

He didn't.

Wind rustled the trees above them, and a few small leaves trailed over them, landing on the man's body.

Oh no. Please, no.

Keira scrambled toward the figure. She pulled on the mask, wrenching both it and the night vision goggles off.

Stubble covered the lower half of his face, but his skin looked frighteningly gray. His jaw hung slack.

And then his eyelids twitched as he tried to look at her.

He's not dead. Not yet.

The relief hit her like a crashing wave. Keira tossed the helmet aside, still drawing in thick gasps of air.

She'd been too frantic in the moment to think about how much energy she was taking. She hadn't realized she would *need* to.

It was impossible to destroy a ghost by reducing its energy. When a ghost became drained, they simply vanished and returned once they were stronger. She didn't think the same was true for a human. She was pretty sure that, if she'd drawn much more, the stranger on the ground would have been dead.

His lips twitched as he tried to speak. His eyelids fluttered.

"Okay," Keira muttered to herself. She ran her hands through her hair as she struggled to think. The energy hummed through her, too dense and too sharp, and it felt like she was trying to strategize in the middle of a storm. "Okay, okay, okay. What do I need to do?"

Get away from here.

That was obvious. She'd taken down one mercenary, but more would be coming.

Keira's mobile lay half buried in the leaves. She snatched it up and turned to the forest, then hesitated.

The mercenary lay on his back. She could hear him breathing, but the sounds were thin and gasping and sickly.

She suspected he'd recover with enough time. But…

Guilt twisted in her stomach. He couldn't move. Couldn't speak. She had no idea how long it would take others to find him… or even if they ever would.

She circled the man until she found the dark gray walkie-talkie.

He'd dropped it when she hit him with the first shock wave. Keira crouched down in front of him and pressed it into his limp hand.

His fingers twitched, but that was all he could manage.

Keira swallowed, torn between doing what was best for herself and doing what she knew was *right*, and then pressed her fingertip into the center of the man's forehead.

She let a little of the energy trickle back into him. Not a lot. Not enough for him to get back onto his feet. But enough to keep him going. Enough to let him call for help.

She waited until she heard him draw in a proper, deep breath and saw his gloved fingers curl around the walkie-talkie, then she took her own hand back.

"I'm sorry," she said simply. "Call someone who'll help."

Then she turned and slipped between the trees.

Overcharged as she was, her senses seemed heightened. The forest felt more alive than it ever had before. She touched a tree as she passed it and swore she could feel it growing.

Keira ran until her lungs burned and her heart felt like it was ready to burst, then stumbled to a halt. She didn't think she was being followed any longer. Every time she inhaled, she tasted the world around her: the insects burrowed under the fallen leaves and the night owls perched high in the trees, still and silent as they watched her pass. She even caught the faint sense of a deer a long way away, its ears pricked high as it listened.

No other humans. At least, none closer than the man she'd left on the ground.

Keira bowed over, bracing her hands on her knees. Cold sweat covered her—partially from what she'd just survived and partially from the power channeling through her.

She placed one hand on the center of her chest and pulled it outward. Daisy flowed out of her, landing neatly on the ground and twisting in a circle. The cat had gotten a taste of the power too. She was frisky and bristling, her pupils dilated and her ears pricked high.

"Hey, Daze," Keira managed, her heart still galloping. She swallowed and closed her eyes, trying to collect herself. "What am I going to do?"

Asking the cat for advice was almost a habit. For a long time, Daisy had harbored Keira's old consciousness and had seemed to know things Keira didn't. Often, asking her for advice had yielded results.

Now, though, Keira herself had all the missing pieces. Daisy couldn't give her any kind of answer that Keira couldn't find herself.

She flexed her hands. The runes painted there were growing smudged but still worked.

"This is what we've been searching for, isn't it?" she asked Daisy.

The small black creature skittered forward an inch, paws grasping for a cricket hiding under the leaves. Her tail thrashed.

"It is," Keira answered herself, straightening. She breathed deeply and tasted the night's chill. "We needed a way to fight Artec. We needed something powerful. And this…"

Her throat tightened, and the bruised muscles ached. She saw the mercenary in her mind's eye, gasping and helpless, barely able to twitch his fingers.

This was more power than she'd wanted. A dangerous amount. A frightening amount. The kind that could destroy lives.

Repulsed shudders ran through Keira. She didn't want to hurt anyone. She didn't want to have to kill.

But Artec's increasing pressure was draining her options. Blighty was marked now. The town wouldn't be safe. Not if she didn't strike Artec first.

That very morning.

The realization came as a relief. It was cathartic, even. Whether she lived or died—whether Artec won or lost—would be decided that day.

She'd discovered the tools she needed. She had the missing pieces.

All she had to do now was hold her breath and take the plunge.

Keira pulled her mobile out. She'd never gotten to send the single warning letter. Instead, she deleted it and sent a full message to both Zoe and Mason.

Artec has found me. They might know where you are too. But I have a plan. Meet me at code word Sparkles in an hour. Stay safe.

Code word Sparkles was Zoe's invention. One of many. They were secret names for locations, both inside and outside town, that—in theory—the three friends would recognize, but Artec would find impossible to parse if they somehow managed to steal or hack into their phones.

In reality, there were so many code word locations that Keira kept getting them mixed up. She remembered code word Sparkles, though. It meant the lamppost partway between Mason's house and the town center. It was a quiet location without many residences around, and the post stood alone, long defunct. According to Zoe, she'd seen the moment it had died, and it had gone out in a shower of sparkles. Hence the name.

It wasn't a perfect hiding spot. Far from it. But Keira could reach it on foot, and it would at least get her friends away from the house and put them somewhere off Artec's radar for the next hour.

She got a series of replies, almost simultaneously. A thumbs-up emoji from Mason, followed by: Be safe, I love you.

Something bittersweet—deep affection mixed with deep grief—swelled inside Keira. Mason would have been asleep when his phone pinged. She could picture him fumbling for it in the dark, hazy and foggy and not properly awake, and still making sure to include the *I love you*. Just in case. Just in case that was the last thing he ever said to her.

Then a deluge of messages began to spring up from Zoe. Reminders of where to find the escape bags. Impromptu instructions for how to most effectively break a person's nose if Keira got involved in a fight…ironically, arriving just a few minutes later than would have been helpful. And then a series of reminders about how and where to hide, how to disguise herself with limited supplies, how to travel long distances without money…

Keira sent a smiling emoji so they both knew she was still safe, then beckoned Daisy back inside her and tucked the phone away.

She didn't need Zoe's instructions. Not that saying that would prevent Zoe from sending them.

She had an hour until she needed to meet her friends. That had been deliberate. There was a promise she needed to make good on.

For the first time in what felt like an eternity, Keira's path looked clear.

It was a horrifying path. The kind that she didn't know she would ever return from.

But at least she could see it.

And it started with The Home.

CHAPTER 24

DAWN WOULDN'T ARRIVE FOR hours. The streets were empty, the buildings dark. Keira stood in the center of the road, staring up at the old iron gate and the thick barricade of trees blocking The Home from view.

It was a nightmare hidden away in the midst of suburbia, its worst secrets jealously guarded by the man responsible. And not even one of its neighbors knew.

A distant streetlight lit up Keira's back as she approached the gates. They were tall, the iron spikes topping them nearly twice as high as her head. She could scale them, she was fairly sure; there were enough handholds and she was good at climbing. But the metal was covered in deep brittle rust, and Keira didn't like the idea of climbing it in full view of the street, no matter how sure she was that the denizens were asleep.

Instead, she followed the sidewalk until The Home's high metal fence gave way to Agatha Edith-Whittle's low brick affair, edged by a soft shrub. There was no scrambling or climbing required. Keira simply leaped over the fence and let the shadows of Agatha's yard cover her as she slunk alongside the house.

The Home's fence was high and imposing at the front but gave way to a lower wooden design at the rear yard. Keira had easily seen over it on her previous visit, which meant she could easily scale it too.

She moved carefully, hyperaware that Agatha's constant vigilance would probably make it easy to spot any changes to the garden. Even a single damaged shrub branch would alert her that someone had been there.

Keira kept low to the ground as she skirted under windows and reached the backyard. She could feel the ghosts' chill even before she saw them, turning the night air uncannily cold and causing gooseflesh to rise over her arms.

She approached the fence and stood to see over it.

The five ghosts were waiting for her, standing where she'd last seen them, the spectral memories of their stolen items clutched in their hands. Their heads turned to follow her, each set of dead, empty eyes fixed on Keira's every movement.

"Hey," she whispered, leaning forward to rest her hands on the wooden fence. "I'm going to be honest with you. I'm doing everything I can to help, but I'm running low on options. And now I'm also running low on time."

No guarantee I'm coming back from Artec. No guarantee I get to see any dawn past tomorrow's.

"This is…" She cast around for the right word. "A last, *desperate* option, I guess. It might not work. It very likely *won't* work. But…"

But I'm out of choices. The police won't dig up the yard without more evidence. And evidence is going to be hard to find.

"As slim as the odds are, I'm willing to try, as long as you're all on board."

As one, the five spirits took a step closer. Their billowing nightgowns and long loose hair undulated behind them, caught in a current that Keira couldn't feel. That was as close to an agreement as she could hope for.

"Okay." She cast one final look back at Agatha's house—still dark, still silent—then hopped to hook a leg over the fence and tip herself into The Home's back lawn.

The grass was dry and crackled under her boots as she landed. Attempts at maintaining the landscaping had been halfhearted. Even in the pale, weak moonlight, Keira could feel how claustrophobic the space was. It would have once been the size of a small park, but plants had been allowed to spread until very little clear ground remained.

Keira stepped between the spirits. As she did, she got a closer look at the spaces they occupied. Even as the wilderness had been allowed to take over the rest of the garden, those five spots had been preserved as bare patches of grass.

She could try to dig up the trinkets herself, but that would only open up a whole new slate of complications. There was no way to bring the salvaged items to the police without admitting to trespassing. And, even then, it would be difficult to prove the items were genuine and had come from The Home's yard. If the rumors had been so pervasive that Constable Sanderson found it easy to ignore them, then he might assume any excavated items were props bought at a vintage store to use as a prank.

If she was going to get proof, it needed to be something more concrete.

And that, she was sure, would only be found inside the building.

Jensen wasn't just guarding the garden. The iron gate and biting hostility were also protecting something inside The Home.

At least, that was her hunch. And she had to hope her suspicions would lead her to something concrete; otherwise, the five murdered women would likely never see justice.

Keira approached the rear door. Her plan involved being very quiet and very quick and, she hoped, going undetected...but she couldn't guarantee any of that. Which meant she couldn't afford to leave fingerprints behind. She pulled her cardigan down and used the fabric to cover her hand as she tried the door's handle.

Locked. No surprises there.

Keira slipped the charcoal out of her kit and used it to draw a rune above the handle. This was one she'd known most of her life, and while it wasn't as flashy as the rune that drained energy, it was no less useful. As she finished the markings, a quiet click echoed and the latch unlocked.

This time, the handle turned easily, and the door opened at a gentle nudge.

Keira took a cautious step inside. Her shoes crunched on years' worth of dirt that had built up inside the door, tracked there every time Jensen left his home to pace the garden. The house was almost pitch-black. Heavy drapes covered the windows, blocking out every scrap of moonlight.

Keira felt blindly inside her kit and found the small penlight Zoe had gotten for her. Its beam wasn't strong, but that suited her just fine. She didn't want to draw Jensen's notice if she could help it.

She clicked the light on.

Shapes loomed out of the shadows. Hulking, distorted, twisted figures surrounded her.

Keira flinched back, her heart thundering, as her light sought out details.

They weren't people. She was looking at furniture that had been covered in heavy white drapes. Every object in the room had been blanketed as the items were put into what was effectively long-term storage.

Carefully, Keira crossed to the nearest shape and picked up the edge of the sheet. Beneath it was a wingback chair, its cushion's padding limp and its fabric faded. She dropped the cloth and moved to the next item—a coffee table. Small scratches and stains marked the wooden surface. A bookshelf was pressed into the back wall, also covered.

Strange. Keira had heard about covering furniture to preserve it, but The Home's possessions all seemed so well-worn that there wasn't much to save. And the books... Who covered a bookcase when it was still heavy-laden with dog-eared novels?

A quiet shiver of superstition passed through Keira. Jensen wasn't trying to preserve the items, she thought. He only wanted to hide them. As though the mere sight of them brought up some kind of discomfort.

The space had to be a sitting room—a communal area for patients to rest and socialize. The doors at its rear gave easy access to the garden.

When he looks into this room, does Jensen see his victims in it? Does he picture them the way they once were, alive, lounging in the chairs as they read or played board games?

Something icy passed across Keira's shoulders. She knew the sensation too well to flinch. One of the spirits had come to stand beside her.

"Are you coming with me?" Keira asked, and each word turned into a tiny sliver of mist that faded into the darkest recesses of the room. The ghost was dropping the temperature. And not by a small amount.

The woman didn't answer, but she didn't leave either. Something about her expression was uncannily keen as she watched Keira.

She turned. The other four specters had also followed her inside. They stood like statues, their arms limp at their sides, the long hems of their dresses undulating about their ankles.

She was grateful. The dead might be poor company when searching a derelict mansion, but at least she didn't have to be alone.

Keira lifted her cardigan sleeve to cover her hand again before pushing on the sitting room's door. Its hinges were old and in desperate need of oiling. They groaned as they turned, and it sounded like the house itself was crying.

A hallway speared out ahead, too long for Keira's light to reach the opposite end. As she stared into the inky black abyss, she became convinced that something stood there, staring back at her.

A lump formed in Keira's throat. Her palm turned sweaty where she held on to the light. Almost against her better judgment, she took a step forward, and then another step. A floorboard groaned under her feet. The pale light fought against the darkness, but instead of vanishing, the distant figure seemed to be growing clearer. She could almost, almost see the edges of its form—

A crack rang out through the house. Keira jolted, turning in a sharp motion and pressing her back to the wall. A mirror was hung opposite her. The surface was old and foggy, and it reflected Keira's face back to her as a vague, ghastly phantom.

A crack ran across the glass, splitting it from one side to the other. Frost lingered at the metal frame's edges.

The ghosts had actually dropped the temperature far enough to break the mirror.

They were furious.

Slowly, dread creeping up in her stomach like a rising tide, Keira turned her light back down the hallway. Where she thought she'd seen the figure was only a patch of wallpaper, discolored from the slow seep of some broken pipe. It was almost as tall as a man, but blurred around the edges, making it hard to fix on the shape.

Keira swallowed thickly. Her mouth was paper-dry.

She pressed on, following the hallway. The wallpaper was peeling off in clumps. The plaster behind was hideously discolored. Keira thought of the rumors about poison leeching out of the walls, and she had to suppress the impulse to hold her breath. The five spirits trailing in her wake told the true story. They just needed a little help opening the door so the rest of the world could see.

Keira passed a dining hall and the kitchens. The passageway twisted multiple times. There were more rooms—some that looked like they might have been staff offices, but the furniture was all shrouded in white sheets and the rooms seemed unused—and then the hall ended in a set of double doors.

Through those, she found the foyer, with a wide stairwell in its center. The carpet runner was so worn down in the middle that the pattern was no longer even visible. Around the foyer's edges were what looked like stacks of covered furniture: chairs, lamps, coffee tables. At one point, visiting family might have sat there as they waited for their loved ones to meet them. Now, the furniture was piled up and barely recognizable through the coverings and the gloom.

The Home would have been luxurious at one point. Now, it was a crumbling, withering shell.

Keira exhaled and watched as a cloud of condensation rose toward the high ceiling.

She didn't need to ask the spirits for advice on where to turn. Even as she stood, staring up at the wide staircase, the ghosts began to ascend it. Single file, they created a line of glimmering, transparent forms, their bare feet tracing over the runner that must have been all too familiar to them in their final months.

They knew where to go, even when Keira hesitated.

She tightened her hold on the light and began climbing the

stairs, joining the procession. Moving to the higher level—where, presumably, Jensen would have his room—was risky, but she didn't think she had any choice. The downstairs felt too disused. Too forgotten. If Jensen had secrets hidden in the house, they would be kept somewhere more personal and more intimate.

At the top of the stairs, the first ghost turned right. Her delicate fingers trailed over the banister and left a line of glimmering frost that rapidly melted. She held herself with incredible poise, but the furious energy rolled off her so intensely that the house seemed to shrivel from it. She was reaching for the catharsis that she'd been denied for decades.

Keira watched as the spirit turned to face a door halfway along the hall. She stepped into it, and her transparent form vanished through the wood.

The other four women moved back, making room for Keira to follow. They stared at her, blank-faced and hard-lipped, waiting.

Keira swallowed, adjusted her cardigan over her hand, and reached for the door's ornate handle.

CHAPTER 25

THE DOOR CREAKED AS it moved. Dust reached Keira's nose first, followed by the scent of mildew.

She stood, frozen, in the entryway. The room was deathly dark and deathly quiet. Her light caught on the edge of a bare mattress and a stark, wooden bed frame.

"Oh," Keira whispered.

The ghost had brought her to a bedroom. The bed had been stripped—the sheets used to cover furniture about the house, Keira guessed—but otherwise it almost existed as a time capsule of when The Home had been active. A bedside table held a lamp, now draped in cobwebs. The window overlooked a balcony and, beyond that, the gardens. A faded chair and rug formed a sitting area.

The walls were bare white. The only relief was a single painting hung above the bed, depicting a tree.

The ghost who had led Keira into the room stood at the foot of the bed, staring up at the painting. Her expression had been fixed with resolution before, but softened fractionally into something tinted by grief.

"Was this your room?" Keira guessed. "Was this—"

Was this where he killed you?

There were no pillows on the bed. Keira wondered if the sight of them had filled Jensen with guilt…or whether he was long past such emotions.

Slowly, the spirit raised a hand to point at the painting. Her fingertip quivered. Keira stepped closer to it, raising her light and squinting, as she tried to find what it was that the ghost wanted her to see.

It wasn't a true painting, she saw, but a print. The tree inside was just slightly too abstract to feel comforting, but not abstract enough to feel fun. It was a dull, slightly depressing piece, and as Keira hunted through its smaller details, she couldn't even begin to guess what it meant to the ghost.

Wait…

There was a smudge of something on the frame. Dust, she thought, but not the same kind that blanketed the rest of the room.

And the frame was hanging crooked. Just slightly.

Keira glanced back at the ghost. The woman remained stationary, her long arm stretched out to point accusingly at the image.

"Okay," Keira said. She tugged the sleeves of her cardigan down to cover both hands, then gripped the frame and pulled it from the wall.

It had been hung on a single nail and came away in a small shower of dust. Keira placed the painting on the bare mattress and then stepped back, frowning at the secret it had kept hidden.

Someone had attacked the wall. Gorges and gashes dug through it, chipping off the pristine white paint to reveal wood behind.

The attack was chaotic, but also, somehow, seemed deliberate. As though…

No. Not just a wild assault on the wall. An etching. A carving.

There was dust on the picture frame, but Keira felt certain that the damage wasn't as old as the rest of the building. It had been created within the past decade, after The Home's closure.

She blinked, and the image resolved. The lines were too jagged and too erratic to be more than a blurred impression, but it was clear what the carver had intended. Jensen had drawn a face. A woman's face.

Cold air billowed through the room from the bitter spirit, and it wasn't hard to guess whose likeness he'd tried to capture.

Because he wanted to remember them. As he grew older and his memory began to fade, he carved their faces in their rooms so he would never completely forget who he'd taken, and where. A permanent memento.

Keira instinctively knew The Home would have four other carvings scattered through it, hidden behind identical motel-art prints. Forgotten by everyone but Jensen. And the ghosts.

Is this enough? Is this my proof? She could take a photo of the drawings with her phone. Surely the police would have to investigate then, wouldn't they?

Wouldn't they?

A sound came from somewhere deeper in The Home. The sigh of a support beam shifting; the pop of a floorboard releasing pressure. Keira froze, her heart thundering, as she listened. The space was silent again.

It's an old building. It will make small noises sometimes. Don't panic.

Through the open doorway she saw the other ghosts. They each held their hands out toward her, palms up. Urging her to them. Begging her to follow.

"Okay," Keira whispered.

The ghosts flowed together, their forms overlapping, as they wove along the hall. Keira walked behind them, and every inhale tasted like breathing in pure ice.

The wallpaper used to plaster the upstairs hallway was horrific. It was supposed to be something sumptuous and floral, but in the low light, it looked like an endless loop of screaming faces.

She couldn't shake the sensation of eyes on her. She looked over her shoulder, only to see the fifth ghost—the one who'd shown her the room—walking behind her. Keira tried not to feel trapped.

The spirits turned into a stairwell leading upward. It was narrower than the first set of stairs. She was fairly certain that meant they were leaving the patient portion of the hospital and entering the staff areas.

Running at capacity, The Home would have been buzzing with doctors and nurses, cooks and cleaners, specialists and admin… Now, it was empty. A cavernous building inhabited by one bitter, lonely man and the collection of secrets he jealously hoarded.

At the top of the stairs, the spirits turned right. The doors along that hall were plainer and more reserved, confirming Keira's suspicions that they were in an employee section.

The ghosts didn't stop until they'd reached the door at the hallway's end; then they flanked it, two positioned on either side of the hallway, creating a path between them for Keira.

She looked back and saw the final spirit was still behind her, standing statue-still in the hallway's center. The ghost wasn't trying to block her retreat, Keira knew. But she still felt squeezed in on all sides.

There was only one clear path. Forward. Toward the door and a bronze handle that seemed far more tarnished than in any of the other rooms.

Because it's one of the only spaces still being used, after all this time.

Keira's mouth tasted like acid as she reached a covered hand toward the handle. She turned it, and the grating metal seemed louder than it should have been. Then the door slid inwards, gliding silently, and revealed the space beyond.

It was a bedroom.

But wholly unlike the impersonal, unlived-in room she'd visited before.

Piles of unwashed clothes had been kicked into the corners. Empty jars were stacked haphazardly against a wall. The floors were worn down and covered in a mix of dust and dirt.

A mattress lay on the floor, covered by an old and worn blanket. A closet was opposite it. Beside the bed were a table lamp and a stack of old journals.

A desk sat under the only window. It was old and looked like it might have once been a consultation desk, but it was now bare except for dust.

The window was uncovered, and moonlight poured in. It was the first natural light Keira had found since entering The Home. She clicked the penlight off and tucked it into her pocket.

She had no doubt she'd found Jensen's room. While the rest of the building seemed nearly forgotten, this one was stained with decades of use. There was something sad and unpleasant about that thought. Jensen had an entire mansion…and yet he sequestered himself into such a small space.

It was very likely the room he'd worked in when he was on staff, Keira realized. The only place he truly felt comfortable.

Then Keira glanced back at the empty, unmade bed, and realized what it meant. This was the caretaker's room. And it was empty.

She remembered the silhouette she'd seen at the end of the hallway. The soft creak of floorboards echoing from deeper in the building.

Jensen was roaming The Home.

Her mouth turned dry and her heart kicked up a notch. She'd been trusting in the idea that he'd be asleep, but either insomnia or some perverse sixth sense that Keira was coming had kept him up that night. Which meant she couldn't afford to stay inside the house any longer.

Her eyes drifted toward the stack of journals, even as her feet itched to back toward the door.

Journals could contain anything.

Including a confession.

Something like that would be more than enough evidence to get the garden dug up.

The spirits lined the hallway, blank eyes watching her. Keira held her breath, listening intently, but the house remained deathly silent. She gritted her teeth, then crept forward, around the end of the mattress, trying not to bump any of the stacked cans. The room wasn't big.

As she stepped over the loose blanket, she heard an odd sound. It was a click, like a light switch being turned, except the house stayed just as dark as it had before. She froze, waiting, but it didn't repeat.

An insect?

The sound had been soft. It could have been a moth beating itself against the window. She looked toward the ghosts, watching for their reaction, but they only stared.

The journals were close. She reached out a hand, her breath held, and plucked up the top book.

The click repeated.

Hairs rose on the back of Keira's neck. She turned, but the room appeared unchanged. Dirty floor. Dirty walls. Empty desk. Lone closet.

The extra energy was making her twitchy and jittery and almost too bold for her own good. She opened the journal. There were no words on the pages, though. Only scribbles.

She flipped...and didn't stop flipping until she reached the back cover. Every sheet had been filled. Sometimes she thought she could see images inside the jagged lines; sometimes they just looked like Jensen had taken a pen and stabbed it into the papers and scratched away at it until the fibers tore. Multiple pages had holes in them.

Click.

Keira bit her lip so hard it ached. She couldn't tell where the sound was coming from. The Home was eerily silent, and even the smallest noise carried.

The ghosts gave no reaction. Not to the journals and not to the sounds.

She needed to get out of there. She needed to find her way back to Zoe and Mason.

But not unless she was certain she had something to link Jensen to the murders.

She dropped the first journal and picked up another. It was filled with more scribbles. She tried the third, but with the same result. The harder she looked, the more she began to see images emerging out of the feral scrawls. Screaming, howling faces. Mouths stretched wide, teeth gleaming. Hands twitching and grasping out of the darkness.

She thought some of the faces might be women's faces. Perhaps the same ones he'd carved into the walls.

Click.

Keira didn't even turn around. She picked up the fourth journal, then the fifth. She checked as quickly as she could, but didn't leave a single page unsearched. All she needed were a few words. It didn't matter if they were buried inside walls of scratchy ink; even just a victim's name might be enough.

But, although each of the journals had lines to guide a writer, Jensen hadn't used any of them to write.

Click.

Keira placed the last book back into its pile, her heart racing and her mind buzzing.

Jensen could return to his room at any moment. She couldn't linger. But, if she left then, she was leaving empty-handed and with no guarantee that the five women waiting in the hallway would see any kind of justice.

Click.

They'd led her to this room, though. Why? Had they, like Keira, hoped the journals might yield something? Or had they simply wanted her to see where Jensen lived?

Click.

Or…

She looked at them. They stared back, their eyes an empty, inky black but stretched wide. The chill billowing off them was enormous. They didn't move. Didn't blink. They were waiting.

For what?

Was there something else in this room she needed to find?

Click.

Keira drew a whisper-thin breath. She finally placed where the mysterious noise was coming from.

The closet.

Carefully, Keira raised a hand to point toward it, her eyebrows held up in question.

The ghosts didn't respond. But the room grew a degree colder.

Click.

There was no mistaking it now. The sound came from just behind the closet's double doors. Keira edged toward them, torn between a need to get outside and a need to get answers.

She reached for the handles. They were cold enough to make her hand ache.

Click.

The sound was sharper. Louder. Mist had begun to spill across the floor, poured forth from ghosts too agitated to be kept contained.

Click.

Keira tightened clammy hands on the handles. In one sharp motion, she pulled.

The doors swung wide open. And she found herself inches from the bulging, bloodshot eyes of Jensen.

CHAPTER 26

HE OPENED HIS JAW and snapped it shut again. His teeth echoed with an awful clicking sound.

Keira lurched back, twisting away, but not even her reflexes could make up for Jensen's advantage.

He held a sledgehammer. And, as the doors opened, he swung it.

It hit her back, just below the shoulder, and sent Keira sprawling on the floor. Incredible pain bloomed through her chest. She tried to draw breath, but the impact had made it impossible.

"Wicked girl," Jensen muttered, and his voice was so disused that it sounded like rusty gates. "Come into my house. Touch my things. Wicked, wicked."

He stepped out of the closet. His feet crunched on the filthy floor. His undershirt and jeans were dirty, his hair unkempt. Thin arms bulged with sinewy muscles as he raised the sledgehammer.

Keira tried to scramble back, but every time she moved, it sent splinters of agony through her ribs. Her shoes slid on the greasy, dusty floor.

"Wicked girls deserve what's coming to them." There was something deeply pleased in the way he smiled as he said that, and Keira didn't have time to question if he'd repeated the same phrase to his victims just before pressing the pillows into their faces.

The sledgehammer arced toward her. Keira rolled. The weapon's blunt metal end slammed into the floorboards hard enough to spread cracks through them.

She felt the reverberations run through her bones. And something else as well. Pure, freezing ice drenching her limbs.

The ghosts were there. They clustered around her, crouching, their hands over her. Panic twisted their faces.

They hadn't realized what they were doing by leading her into Jensen's room. All they'd wanted was justice. For someone to understand. They hadn't meant for Keira to be hurt.

Ghosts couldn't interact with the physical world beyond influencing temperature and sometimes weather. When they touched Keira, she felt the incredible cold of their hands, but instead of applying pressure, their fingers simply plunged through her.

And yet, they still grasped at her, trying with all their might to pull her, to drag her to safety.

To save her from the fate they all shared.

Jensen raised the sledgehammer above his head. One of the ghosts turned to face him, hands outstretched, body between Keira and Jensen.

The spirit couldn't stop him. His sledgehammer would pass

through her just as easily as it would pass through mist. He couldn't even see her.

But Keira could.

"Who was she?" Keira yelled, her voice cracking from the pain of speaking. "The woman with the beautiful comb?"

Jensen froze, the sledgehammer held high. Something passed over his face. Something like shock.

"What about the one with the leather gloves? You stole them from her when you killed her, didn't you?" Keira's arms shook as she braced herself on the floor. The ghosts clustered around, attempting to shield her. Their icy touch was actually helping to numb the pain in her back. "Or the woman with the necklace. Or the one with the stuffed doll she'd owned since she was a child. I know all of them. I *see* all of them. And I see what you did to them, all those years ago."

The skin on Jensen's forehead was growing shiny with fresh sweat. The sledgehammer, still poised high over Keira, wavered a fraction.

"They haunt you," Keira said. "You can't see them, but they're a shadow on every step you take. They whisper your secrets to me. They tell me what you did."

"Little girls shouldn't lie," Jensen hissed, but he seemed frozen where he stood, doubt and fear warring over his face. Fog, created by the ghosts, billowed around his legs, and his gaze kept flicking down toward it, the doubt growing stronger with every look.

"You smothered them," Keira said. Her pain was still there, but sizzling electric zaps crisscrossed it as the healing runes she'd drawn on her side began to work. It was growing easier to breathe. She began inching her feet under herself, gathering her strength. "You went into their rooms while they slept and pressed a pillow over their faces. You thought no one would know. But *they* know. They're still here. And they've come for your reckoning."

"Liar!"

All the tension holding Jensen in place seemed to snap. He swung the sledgehammer down. But Keira was ready this time. She skittered back, out of reach, and gained her feet.

Pain radiated down her right side. Her leg threatened to collapse. The whole house seemed to shake with the impact of the sledgehammer on the floor, but Jensen's attack had been frenzied and panicked, and it had thrown him off-balance.

Keira ran for the open door.

The ghosts moved with her. Keira's vision was filled with clouds of transparent hair and swirling nightdresses as they flanked her. Freezing hands pressed into her back, urging her forward. Toward the stairs. Toward escape.

But Jensen was following. His paces were slower than Keira's, but each stride was longer. The sledgehammer whistled through the air as he swung it. And Keira was stumbling as her body tried to cope with the pain trailing down her back.

They were almost at the stairs. Keira could see the edges of the railing.

Jensen was too close, though. There was no way she could navigate the steps in the dark. Not without feeling the bite of the sledgehammer partway down.

Keira feinted toward the stairs, then ducked away at the last second. The sledgehammer whistled as it missed her head by inches. The maneuver achieved her goal: it threw Jensen off-balance, his sinewy muscles fighting to keep hold of the heavy weapon.

But it wasn't quite enough. He caught himself just in front of the stairwell.

Keira's back hit the wall across from him. They froze there for a second, Jensen blocking the stairs and Keira with few options left, and stared at one another.

It was too dark to see much except the gleam of Jensen's eyes and the shimmer of his teeth. The sledgehammer swung as he braced his legs, sizing Keira up.

The ghosts pressed close. Their faces were contorted with urgency and anger and desperation.

Keira had spare energy. She'd used up some of it on the healing runes, but there was still plenty left. More than enough to do a lot of damage.

She blinked and saw the guard's face. The fear in his expression. The twitch of his fingers.

She wasn't a killer. She couldn't take a person's life.

But she had no options left.

"Here," Keira said, spreading her hands out to the ghosts. "Take whatever you need."

The runes that accelerated energy transfer were smudged, but enough remained to still work. As Jensen paced forward, his eyes glinting in the cold light as he aimed his next strike, Keira released all her extra energy, and let it flow into the ghosts.

The effect was immediate. The unearthly currents that caused the spirits' hair and clothes to drift turned into a typhoon. Their features became sharper. Brighter. Harder. They seemed to move a fraction closer to being physical beings.

Frost poured across the wall, across the carpet, across the ceiling. It burned on Keira's lips and in her lungs.

Jensen felt it. He had been bunching up, preparing to strike, but took a step backward as the ice spread over his shoes. His glinting eyes widened, darting from side to side, as he tried to understand what was happening.

That step backward took him a step closer to the stairs.

The ghosts left Keira's side. They lunged forward, their hair whipping as though in a storm. Their faces turned cold and furious as their hands pressed into Jensen.

And, in that second, he saw something. Or *felt* something. Or *understood* something. Keira heard a wailing scream build inside his chest as he stumbled backward. The sledgehammer was no longer raised in threat, but in self-defense.

The back of his foot grazed over the edge of the top step.

And the ghosts refused to give him even an inch.

Their hands pushed into him. Their empty eyes bore into his. The glass on every photo and every mirror along the hall cracked.

And then Jensen lost the battle against gravity. He tipped backward, and the ghosts followed him down as they plunged into the darkness below.

CHAPTER 27

KEIRA SLOWLY SLID DOWN the wall. She was breathing faster than she needed to, but she couldn't slow it down. Now that the extra energy was gone, she felt shaky and clammy, and the entire right side of her back ached.

The Home was very, very quiet. The darkness pressed in around her like a blanket, both comforting and frightening in how immense it was. One minute passed. Then two. Still, the building remained silent.

She had put her light in her pocket when she found Jensen's room, and she took it out now. Even its weak beam was better than the darkness. She used it to see the shape of the hall and then aimed it at the stairs opposite.

The top step came into view. Its edge seemed too sharp. Beyond was nothing but endless night.

Slowly, Keira got to her feet. She didn't want to follow Jensen down the stairs. But she also knew she had to.

Each step groaned as she pressed her weight into it. She took the descent carefully, staying off the worn part of the runner as though it would be disrespectful to trace where so many pairs of feet had been before.

The climb down to the lower floor seemed longer than it had when she was going up. But, at last, she reached the worn stone foyer—and the things that waited for her there.

Jensen lay sprawled on his back. One arm hung at his side; the other stretched above his head, as though he was still reaching for the sledgehammer that lay several feet away.

His eyes were open. His jaw was slack. A pool of shockingly red blood spread around him.

The five spirits stood in a semicircle behind Jensen. They had faded. Not just faded compared to the infusion of energy Keira had given them, but from even before. She could still see their faces, but they were beginning to blur, the details vanishing into the dark.

Keira's gifts let her see ghosts in ways no other person could, but when it came to identifying a living person from the dead, she had to rely on the same skills as anyone else. She moved with agonizing care to avoid stepping in any of the blood, then crouched and reached out a hand to touch Jensen's neck.

He was warm. His skin was pliant under her fingers. Her first impulse was to snap her hand away in horror, but Keira pushed through it and focused, feeling for a pulse.

There wasn't one. She searched again, then once more, to be absolutely certain. The pool of blood continued to inch out in increments, but that was the only sign of movement she found.

Keira took her hand back and used the sleeve of her cardigan to gently brush at his skin, wiping away any trace of herself. She then focused her second sight to pull any unseen spirits into view.

The five women flared brighter, but they were Keira's only companions in the cold house.

Jensen was dead, and he had left no ghost.

That was about as much of a mercy as Keira could hope for that night. She stepped away from the body, and then pulled her phone out of her pocket. She had told Mason and Zoe that she'd need an hour. That time allotment was nearly up, so she sent a brief message.

Need a few more minutes. Everything's okay.

That last line was a lie. Nothing about what had happened felt *okay*. A man was dead.

That wasn't the first time she'd witnessed the loss of life. Gavin Kelsey had died in front of her, and he'd died horrifically.

Except, in Gavin's case, Keira had tried to save him. She'd begged him to move away from the dangerous electrical currents. She'd done everything she could.

With Jensen…

Her throat burned. Her stomach turned over, and she had to look away from the body to stop the nausea from rising.

She hadn't pushed him. But she hadn't tried to save him either.

If she hadn't come into his home that night—if she hadn't been so hell-bent on finding justice for the ghosts, if she hadn't given the spirits her power—Jensen would have still been alive.

Did he deserve to live, though?

It was an ugly thought. He'd killed before. And he'd shown a willingness to murder again, given an opportunity and a motive.

Maybe he hadn't deserved to live. But…that wasn't Keira's call to make. She was a messenger for the dead, not a judge, and especially not an executioner.

The ghosts stood still, watching her, their faces once more impassive.

"We need to finish our work," Keira said. There was no one else in the house she needed to hide from, but Keira kept her voice to a whisper. It didn't feel like the kind of situation where a person should talk freely.

The spirits followed behind her, silent as whispers, as she climbed back up the stairs.

Everything felt harder and slower now that she'd given up her energy. The hallway seemed longer. The room at its end was darker and sadder. The air still felt cold from the spirits' exhausted anger, but even that was beginning to fade.

Keira used her cardigan sleeve to wipe the closet door handles. She'd touched them with her bare hands and, especially now, couldn't afford to have her fingerprints found anywhere inside Jensen's house.

Then she took up five of the journals from the stack beside the unmade bed. She held them close to her chest as she retraced her path back along the hall and down the stairs.

The pool of blood had seeped onto the edge of the sledgehammer, which meant Keira couldn't move it without leaving evidence that someone had tampered with the scene. She didn't know what the police would make of it, but that was out of her control at that point. She skirted around Jensen and then wove back through the house to reach the door to the rear gardens.

From among the cluster of pots and gardening supplies near the rear entrance, Keira scavenged five stakes and a ball of twine. Then she faced the lawn and whispered, "Show me where."

The five spirits flickered a fraction, then, as a group, moved forward. They spread out across the lawn and took up their positions like eternal sentries.

Keira crossed to the nearest ghost. It was the woman who held the necklace. She clasped it ahead of her chest, and, as Keira neared, let go. The ghostly object fell, disappearing into the earth.

Keira stabbed the first stake into the ground where the necklace had vanished. She wiped one of the journals clean of any fingerprints, then used the twine to lash it to the wooden post.

That first ghost gave her a thin, sad smile. She reached out. Icy fingers trailed over Keira's cheek: a bittersweet sign of thanks. Then the ghost shimmered and faded away.

Gone. Forever.

As the spirit faded, the staked journal seemed to age. Its pages curled and darkened as though water damaged. Traces of moss and rot spread over the stake. It looked as though it had always been there.

Slowly, Keira moved through the garden. At each site, the ghost released their lost item, and Keira marked its location with a stake. As they left, decay bloomed over their markers.

It should be enough, she thought. Coupled with Jensen's death, the journals positioned across the lawn would be hard to ignore.

They looked like a final confession from a man who'd been hollowed out by guilt for decades.

Zoe's tip had been anonymous. The included map was precise. It might even be believable that Jensen himself had sent it in.

Keira tied off the final marker. The ghost standing over it—the one who had owned the gloves—smiled, bowed her head, and then faded like a rush of condensation on a cold morning.

Keira was, at last, alone.

Dawn was close by. She could see the earliest hints of light ghosting across the horizon, erasing the stars one at a time. People in Blighty liked to wake early. She'd need to hurry if she wanted to be away from The Home before the joggers and early-morning shoppers emerged.

Keira crossed to the fence and clambered over it, wincing as her back ached, and tumbled into Agatha's yard.

From there it was a short silent walk to the street. As she dropped over Agatha's hedged fence and onto the sidewalk, Keira froze.

She could see Mason's house in the near distance. There were lights inside. Not his regular house lights, though, but the jagged dart of flashlights. At least three that Keira could count. Even as she watched, a silhouette passed across one of the windows.

Instinctively, she shrank back into the shadows. She tried to talk herself down from panic. Zoe and Mason were safe. They'd gotten out in time. She just needed to reach the car before Artec gave up searching the home and widened its net.

Keira kept her movements slow and subtle until she was out of sight of Mason's home, then broke into a jog. The meeting location wasn't far; within minutes, the defunct streetlight came into view. Keira felt the last of her fear fading as she spotted Mason's rental car parked beneath it.

He must have been watching for her. The door opened while she was still twenty paces away, and Mason ran to meet her, arms outstretched.

"You're safe," he whispered, pulling her into a hug. "Thank goodness. You're safe."

Keira clutched at him, burying her face into his knit sweater. He was warm. Solid. Slightly disheveled but completely Mason, and she hadn't realized how badly she'd missed him until that moment.

Something snapped inside her, a wall she hadn't even realized she'd been propping up. A rush of aching, horrific emotions poured free, and heaving sobs gripped her.

"It's okay, it's okay," he murmured, tightening his hold as he kissed the top of her head. "You're safe now."

She was so tired. Not just physically, but in every single fiber of her soul. Tired of running. Tired of being afraid. Tired of feeling like she was an inch away from losing everything.

Tired of feeling like the fight against Artec was changing her. And that it was changing her into something that frightened her worse than the company itself.

"I've got you," Mason said, and he ran his hands up and down her back, soothing, and Keira wasn't sure she deserved it.

"I killed someone," she said, tilting her head up to see his expression.

There was a flicker of surprise, but it immediately turned resolute. "Are you hurt?"

"No." She winced at the aching bruise on her back. "Not much."

"Right now, right in this moment, that's all I care about." His hand pressed against her cheek. She shivered as the calluses on his thumb brushed at the dampness. "We're going to worry about everything else later. I love you, and I'm here now, and nothing that happened tonight can change that."

She let her eyes close as she leaned into his touch. "Artec found your home. I'm sorry."

"Let them have it. Possessions can be replaced."

"Not your mother's taxidermy duck," Keira said.

He considered. "You're right. We probably can't replace that. But the sentiment stands. I'm still going to prioritize my friends."

Friends...

She leaned back. "Is Zoe here?"

"Present and unimpressed," Zoe said. She was propped against the car, arms folded, the previous day's eyeliner smudged around her eyes. "Let's count the ways this morning sucks. It's an unearthly hour to be awake. There's a good chance Artec is in my home, too, which means they're probably pawing through my Bigfoot research folders and, heaven help me, messing up my meticulous Dewey decimal system. And now I'm forced to watch the two of you get goopy. All in all, not the best start to the day."

"Sorry," Keira managed. Mason was still holding her, and she wasn't ready to let him go either.

"Eh. Whatever." Zoe shrugged. "Sounds like you've been through hell. You can have a little PDA. As a treat."

"Zoe inadvertently brought up a good point," Mason said. "If my home is compromised, it's likely hers is, as well. And your cottage…"

"Mikhail sold me out," Keira said. "Yeah. The cottage is lost. Adage is away from the parsonage, at least. But we can't go back there."

"We knew this would be a possibility," Mason said. He kept his arm around her, and Keira couldn't express how grateful she was for that contact. "We have funds for a hotel."

"Though…" Zoe pulled a face. "We'd probably have to reach one on foot. There are only two roads out of Blighty, and I'd be shocked if Artec wasn't watching them both."

Keira shook her head. "We don't need to move to a hotel. I have a plan. One that's going to happen today. But…we do have to get off the roads. As soon as Artec finishes searching your homes, they're going to start canvassing the rest of the town. Which means we want to find somewhere secluded and private. Somewhere Artec won't think to look. Just for a few hours, while I prepare."

Zoe's eyes lit up. "Oh, I know something that fits the bill. It's quiet. Very secluded. And the owner just happens to owe you a favor."

Keira narrowed her eyes. Mason started, "You don't mean—"

"Yeah. I think it's time we pay a visit to Ol' Crispy."

CHAPTER 28

"HEY," KEIRA SAID. "I'M so sorry. I know it's early."

Dane Crispin stood in the enormous arched doorway, blinking hard against the slowly rising sunlight. It had taken him several minutes to answer their knocking, though Keira thought that was probably due to the size of his mansion and how far he had to walk to get anywhere. He'd tied a faded maroon robe tightly around himself, and a pair of unexpectedly fuzzy slippers shuffled against the floor.

"Mm. Keira." He still seemed half asleep as he squinted at them. "And companions. Good morning."

"Depends on your perspective," Zoe said. "We're currently fugitives and there's a decent chance certain individuals are reading my Mothman manifesto and they're probably making fun of it. So. *Good* is debatable."

Dane Crispin stared at Zoe, his expression blank as he tried to make sense of her words; then he turned back to Keira. "Are you in trouble? Do you need help?"

"Yeah." She grimaced. "Yes to both questions. I'm so sorry, I—"

"Come in," he said immediately, stepping back and beckoning them into the mansion.

They crossed the threshold, Mason carrying his medical kit.

"I know it's a lot to ask," Keira continued. "I wouldn't disturb you except—"

"Anything you need." Dane closed the door behind them. "After what you did for me, I'll help in any way I'm able."

Keira hadn't been inside the Crispin estate since she'd cleared the ghosts from it. They had been parasitic beings: the spirits of the legendary Crispin empire, descendants of the town's original family that had learned to latch on to and leech off the living. Dane, as the final Crispin heir, had spent his life being consumed by his ancestors. Until Keira had gotten rid of them, at least.

Symptoms of that past were visible even now in both the building and its owner. The estate—ancient, crumbling, dim—was still a heavy presence. Dane was still gaunt, his clothes worn and faded. But Keira noticed small changes were beginning to stack up too.

A potted plant stood on the foyer's center table, a breath of life in the otherwise oppressive building. And it was flourishing. The floor had been swept. Keira thought the windows might have been washed—there was more light.

And Dane's hollow cheeks were beginning to fill out. His movements were smoother and easier. His clothes were old, but he'd cut his hair and was clean-shaven.

Keira had always known recovery would be gradual. It was impossible to spend a lifetime under his ancestors' control without those effects lingering. But she was relieved to see how much progress he'd made in such a short amount of time.

"The paintings are gone," Mason said, pointing to a large bare wall. Outlines showed where the family's portraits had once hung. There had been hundreds of them.

"They're all in storage," Dane said, leading them toward a door in the back of the foyer. "While I decide what to do with them. I'm leaning toward a bonfire."

"I wouldn't blame you," Keira said.

"That one is the exception, of course." He nodded toward a single painting that had been moved to the foyer's back wall. Keira recognized the woman in it. Josephine Crispin, a resident of her own little graveyard. She was the only Crispin ancestor who had not stayed in their collapsing estate.

Dane reached for the door, then hesitated. "Ah, I should probably warn you, you're not my only guests this morning."

"Oh?" Keira's footsteps faltered. She had a sudden mental image of Artec mercenaries waiting in the room beyond—there to question Dane, or possibly because they'd guessed Keira might go there to hide. But then the door swung open, and she let the tension drain away.

Beyond was a small but cozy kitchen. Dane's efforts to improve his house had apparently been concentrated in the spaces where he spent the most time. The foyer still felt austere and intimidating, but the kitchen was lovely: Cast-iron pots hung over the stove.

The benches and round wood table were all clean. A vase held fresh flowers, next to a cutting board with bread and a small plate of butter.

And at the table, clasping a ceramic mug full of coffee, was their town's sallow barista, Marlene. Her eyeliner looked freshly applied, and she wore an identical robe to Dane.

"Oh, hey, Marlene," Zoe said as though by rote memory, then she blinked, catching herself. "Oh? Hey? Marlene?"

"Ugh," Marlene said. "You manage to track me down even on my days off. Hello, Zoe."

Zoe's eyes darted from Marlene to Dane, then back again. Her lips pressed tightly together, and Keira knew she was fighting to contain an absolute avalanche of questions.

Dane cleared his throat. "Can I get you all some coffee?"

"I know how they all like it," Marlene said, rising. She rested a hand briefly on Dane's forearm as she passed him. "Though you'll have to do without your triple shot of caramel syrup this time, Zoe."

"I can survive that." Zoe's voice sounded faintly strangled as she took a seat at the kitchen table. She glanced at Keira and Mason and mouthed, with very little attempt at being subtle, *I called it.*

"Tell me what's happened," Dane said, pulling out his own chair. He glanced toward the medical kit Mason still carried. "You said something about...fugitives?"

"Uh. Yeah." Keira had been ready to tell Dane everything. He'd already seen evidence of the supernatural, and that went a long way to help when she started talking about the dead being held captive.

But…

Marlene stood by the sink, preparing drinks. Keira had seen her plenty of times at the town's central café. She, Zoe, and Mason had spent hours there, strategizing about how to handle Artec. In some ways, Marlene felt like an honorary member of those meetings.

But she was still Marlene. Keira rarely had a conversation with her that extended any further than her drink order and sometimes their respective opinions on the weather. As far as Marlene knew, Keira was simply working as the cemetery's groundskeeper, nothing more.

"So…" She tapped her fingertip on the table, choosing her words carefully. "You know I'm interested in…dead things?"

She'd hoped Dane would get her meaning and suggest they move the conversation somewhere more private, but he only waited, eyebrows heavy over gray eyes, as he nodded for her to continue.

"Um." Keira glanced at her friends, but Mason could only offer a small uncertain shrug. "Well…did I tell you about this other group that is also…interested in dead things? And how…they're getting…uh, annoyed with me?"

"Is this about the ghosts?" Marlene interrupted, placing a mug of tea—exactly how she liked it—in front of Keira.

Keira opened her mouth, closed it again, then cleared her throat.

"Oh," Dane said, suddenly realizing what was happening. He blinked. "I told Marlene about the spirits. She knows my full story."

Marlene handed off the rest of the drinks and dropped back into her chair. Keira watched her, waiting for some kind of emotion:

doubt, or scorn, or hidden laughter. All she could find was Marlene's usual dispassion. And a tiny bit of annoyance. Which was probably because Keira had interrupted an otherwise cozy morning.

"You…believe in ghosts?" Keira tried.

"Sure," Marlene said. She glanced at Dane, and a whisper of a smile crossed her face. Keira was amazed by how much softer she seemed in that moment. "I believe him, at least."

"I've been trying to tell you about the supernatural for *years*," Zoe muttered. "And *he's* the one who convinces you?"

Marlene scoffed lightly. "I've always believed in the supernatural. This is nothing new."

Zoe's expression was pained. "But—"

"If you don't want people to mess with you, you shouldn't make it so fun." Marlene turned back to Keira. "My mother made charms to protect our house when we were growing up. My sister reads tea leaves and carries herbs in her pockets to ward off bad things. If you want a private conversation, I'll happily shuffle off. But if you don't mind the extra company, I'm not always as frosty as I look."

Keira felt like a weight had been lifted off her shoulders. Marlene gave her a very thin smile, and Keira smiled back, and she realized she might have just made a new friend. She placed her hand on her chest, then pulled it away, and let Daisy tumble free and land neatly on the floor.

Dane twitched but recovered quickly. Marlene simply stared at the cat for a long beat, then said, "All right."

Keira pulled her mug of tea closer with unsteady hands. "There's a company called Artec. And they've figured out how to trap spirits after death. When they do it in a specific way, they can harvest energy from the dead, but at the cost of the person never being able to fully move over to the next life."

"Huh," was all Marlene said.

Keira took a deep breath, then told both Marlene and Dane about the company, her encounters with them, and what was at stake. They were a good audience. Dane asked a few questions—mostly about Artec's capabilities and size—but otherwise, they listened intently.

The mug of tea was empty by the time Keira finished. Sunlight—proper, strong sunlight—came through the kitchen window.

"So…" Keira spread her hands. "Artec is on the verge of expanding internationally, and once they move overseas, there's nothing I can do for the spirits they trap. I've run for as long as I can, and I've hidden for as long as I can. The more it draws out, the more people die. I'm finishing this today."

Marlene and Dane exchanged a glance. Then Dane said, "You have a plan, I assume?"

"Yes." Keira nodded toward Zoe. "We're going to do exactly what you suggested when we first visited the mall. We're going to put a bear in that elevator and send it down to tear the place apart."

"Oh, *hell* yeah," Zoe said, her face lighting up. "Heck. Yes. Wait—is the bear a metaphor? I feel like the bear has to be a metaphor."

Mason watched her curiously, eyebrows raised, clearly trying to figure out how worried he should be.

"Yeah," Keira said, answering them both. "We're sending a bear down. It's me. I'm the bear. And Artec is going to regret ever crossing paths with me."

"Are you bringing allies with you?" Dane asked.

"Yes." That was the most crucial part of her plan. And it was also the riskiest. "I'll need to use their energy."

"Then I will help, and gladly." Dane rose from the table, and the gray in his hair caught the morning light. "As long as you can give me a chance to change first."

"Hah." Keira had almost forgotten her host was still wearing his robe. "Yeah, I think we can spare the time for that."

Marlene's face was as impassive as ever, but there was an unnerving light in her eyes. "Count me in as well."

Keira was caught off guard. "Ah—are you sure? What we're doing is dangerous. You don't owe me anything."

"I know it looks like we were having a relaxing breakfast when you interrupted, but the reality wasn't quite so fun," Marlene said. She pulled her mobile out of her pocket and held it up. "I've been getting messages. Masked intruders have been breaking into houses. Dane and I were trying to figure out who they were and what they were doing. It sounds like we got the answer to both questions."

"Oh," Keira said, her stomach dropping.

"Blighty is my home." Marlene tucked her phone away. "It's the only place I've ever belonged. And right now, it's afraid. If I can do something to stop that, I will. So, yes, count me in."

"Okay." Keira swallowed thickly. When she'd arrived at Dane's house, she'd only been planning to bring Zoe and Mason with her to Artec's base. But…two additional helpers would increase their odds. By a lot. "Thank you. So much."

Marlene stood, stretching. "If we've got some time, I'm going to take a shower. And I'm borrowing some of your clothes, D."

"By all means." Dane glanced back at the three friends and gestured to the kitchen. "Please, help yourself to food. There's meats and cheese in the fridge. You're welcome to anything here."

He followed Marlene out of the kitchen, leaving Keira alone with Zoe and Mason.

For a moment, Keira just breathed, enjoying the brief seconds of silence as she tried to unravel her thoughts and feelings. She felt as though she'd lived an entire year in a single night. And she still couldn't rest. Not yet.

"So." Zoe folded her arms on the table and leaned forward. "It's really happening, huh? We're going to torch the place."

"Yeah," Keira said, and she'd never felt so certain of anything before. "We're going to burn it to the ground."

CHAPTER 29

"I'LL GET FOOD," MASON volunteered. He picked up their empty cups as he went, and then set the kettle to boil again. Daisy trotted about his feet, tail high as she requested pets.

"So." Zoe leaned over the tabletop, fingertips laced as she propped her chin on them. "You buried the lead earlier. But you maybe probably potentially killed someone? Someone from Artec?"

Keira grimaced. She could still picture the guard in her mind's eye, but at least he was alive and breathing in that memory. "No." The words tasted like poison. "Jensen's dead."

Mason leaned back against the kitchen counter, slices of bread held limply in one hand. Keira couldn't read his expression.

"*Jensen?*" Zoe pressed, her eyebrows pulled so high they seemed to carry the rest of her face up with them. "It was Jensen? Wait—is he for sure dead or only maybe possibly dead?"

Keira grimaced. She couldn't look at either of them. "For sure."

"Okay, fantastic. Please tell me why you're guilt ridden about it, because good riddance."

"Zoe," Mason said gently.

"No, I'm serious. Do you feel like you need permission or something? Because I'll give you all the permission you could want to fully annihilate that creepy, leering—"

"Zoe, I'm not sure this is helping." Mason exhaled and put the bread down. His voice was almost painfully gentle as he turned to Keira. "Do you feel like you can tell us what happened? Or is it too much right now?"

Keira didn't want to talk about it. She was afraid of how the words would sound. More than that, she was afraid of seeing Mason's expression change into something colder, steelier.

But keeping it inside would have been so much worse. So she told them everything. About breaking into the house. Searching Jensen's room. The race along the hallway. And then offering the ghosts her energy, only to watch them crowd Jensen over the edge of the stairs.

As she talked, Mason prepared sandwiches, which he carefully set in front of them. He didn't try to interrupt. Keira finished her story weakly, explaining how she had cleaned up any evidence that she'd been there—it felt so *dirty* phrasing it like that—and how she'd left the mementos in the yard.

Their silence lasted for barely a second once she was done.

"You have the worst moral code," Zoe said bluntly. She picked up the sandwich Mason had given her and bit off a corner. "The *annoying* kind of moral code. You didn't kill anyone. The ghosts did it. Conscience cleared."

"But I gave them the energy to push him." There was a lump in Keira's throat that wouldn't go away. "If I hadn't been there, he'd still be alive."

"And if he hadn't been a serial killer, the ghosts would have never existed either." Zoe looped a finger through the air. "That's what the professionals call circular logic."

Mason frowned. "That's…not what circular logic is." He shook his head, dispelling the tangent. "That aside, Keira, I think you're facing something that has weighed on nearly every powerful individual throughout history. Your choices carry ramifications that the average person never has to think about."

"Yes." The lump still wouldn't go away. Keira gave her friends a watery smile. "How do I make it stop?"

"Develop a sociopathic streak," Zoe suggested nonchalantly.

Mason gave her a brief baleful glance, then settled in opposite Keira. His green eyes were too deep and intense; Keira almost didn't want to meet them, but once she did, she couldn't look away.

"Kings and queens influenced the lifespans of the lower classes with nearly every edict they issued. Leaders who pushed for war are responsible for the lives those battles have cost. Even today, governments can add or subtract actual years from a country's expected lifespan based on how much they spend on healthcare and education."

"But those are *leaders*," Keira said, desperate to make him understand. "I don't want that! I don't want to be weighing up lives with every choice I make!"

Mason reached across the table. Keira met him halfway, and he rubbed her numb fingers, pushing life back into them. "That's the tricky thing," he murmured. "The responsibility grows smaller the less power you have, but it never really goes away. In med school, we sometimes talked about medical liability. Even the most experienced, well-meaning surgeon will make mistakes—sometimes mistakes that cost lives."

"Med school was the first mistake," Zoe muttered. "Pharmaceutical lemmings, all of them."

Mason ignored her. "Every day, we get to choose how we influence the world. Sometimes that influence is negligible and leaves no lasting impact. But sometimes it snowballs into something bigger. A kind word to the right person at the right moment could change the trajectory of their life." He squeezed her hands. "What I'm trying to say is…I understand why you want to escape this kind of responsibility. I think most people would if they could. Having power over another person's life is a terrifying prospect. But it's something we all have, in smaller ways or larger, and it's something we all have to figure out how to carry."

"But—"

Mason leaned forward a fraction. "You were in a dangerous situation. One with very few options. And you made the best decision you could in that brief window of time. You gave your energy to those women. They had the choice of whether to show mercy. And they chose not to."

"I can't do this again," Keira said. The thought of Artec hung over her, and she was too afraid to mention them by name. "I can't watch people die because of something I did. I don't want to be a killer."

Even if it's Schaeffer.

"Yeah." Mason's smile was full of all the warmth and comfort she'd always associated with him, but there was a tinge of grief there, as well. "I wish I could write a path forward for you. But I can't, because everything ahead looks just as murky to me as it does to you. But if nothing else, you won't be alone this time. I promise you that."

Keira nodded. The lump made it impossible to speak, but she pressed Mason's hands instead, silently thanking him.

She hated it. But he was right. The harder she searched, the more she began to fear there was physically no way to keep her hands clean when it came to Artec, no matter how much she tried.

Artec was killing its employees. It had been for years.

Keira might—*might*—have a chance to stop them. To prevent further deaths. To save the ghosts trapped in endless torment. And she was one of the only people who might be capable of achieving that.

There was no other way. She needed to strike hard. Do as little damage as possible, but give no ground. Stop it from getting worse.

And just pray that the cost wouldn't be too high.

"You know what's easier than trying to navigate a whole new moral code?" Zoe asked, breaking through the moment. "Cultivating that sociopathic streak I mentioned earlier. All your choices will get *so* much simpler."

"Good advice," Keira managed. "I'll keep it in mind."

"You want me to call Adage?" Zoe offered. "It's after dawn now, and he usually wakes up early."

"Ah!" Keira snapped up, then flinched as the bruise on her back twinged. "Yes. Please. He needs to know it's not safe to go back to the parsonage. If he needs somewhere to stay for today, I'm sure Dane would let him come here."

"Got it." Zoe finished her sandwich in one large bite and hopped out of her chair. "There's no one else we need to give a heads-up to, is there?"

Keira considered. "Maybe…Harry? I don't think Artec knows about him yet, but he *was* there with us at the tower. He should probably know he needs to be on guard, just in case."

"Yeah, that's a good call. I'll take care of them." Zoe was already dialing on her flip phone as she stepped out of the room.

Aching warmth pooled in Keira's stomach. It was an almost painful sense of gratitude and admiration for her friends. Neither of them had been searching for danger when she had stumbled into their lives. But they had risen up to face it with more competence and focus than she ever could have asked.

"We have some time," Mason said. "Let me take a look at your injury. I still can't quite believe everything you've done over the last night; it must be agony."

"Actually…"

Keira pulled up the hem of her top, just far enough to reveal the bullet wound on her side. The ink sigils were growing smudged around it, but the wound had knitted together. The skin was beginning to discolor as a scar formed.

Mason drew a sharp breath. He crouched, then gently, cautiously pressed his fingers against it. The injury still ached but nowhere near like it had before.

"Keira…" He seemed to be struggling to find words. "This looks like it's at least a fortnight old. Maybe more. How…?"

"Yeah. I figured out a new rune. Or, well, Daisy did. It speeds up healing."

"That's amazing." He looked at her, and his eyes were shining. "I've been so worried. This is fantastic. *You* are fantastic."

He moved up to kiss her, and his hand pressed against her back, right over the fresh bruise. She couldn't repress a shaky flinch.

"Let me see," Mason said instantly.

Keira tugged her shirt higher. Mason hissed as the bruise on her upper back was revealed. His careful fingertips fluttered around its edge. "What—"

"Jensen managed to land a blow," Keira admitted. It was the only part of the story she'd held back before, knowing it would derail Mason. "It's not too bad."

"I have more painkillers," Mason said, reaching for his medical bag and rattling it open. "And a cream that might bring down the swelling. Are you having any trouble breathing? Any sharp stabbing pains?"

"No, and no."

"Then we're not likely dealing with broken bones…which is a miracle," he muttered as he pressed two tablets into her hand. "Take these. And give me a moment here."

"Hey, can you try something?" Keira still wore her small satchel of tools, and took the pen out. She uncapped it and offered it to Mason. "See those marks around the earlier cut? Can you try replicating them near the bruise?"

He took the pen. "Will it still work if I'm the one who draws them?"

"I actually don't know." The bruise was too far back for Keira to reach, at least without a lot of pain. "But it's worth trying."

She was low on energy again after feeding so much to the specters at The Home, but as the cold ink dried on her back, she felt the runes crackle with a tiny bit of energy. Keira smiled. "Okay. They're active. That'll help."

Mason continued to draw. His spare hand pressed gently against her back, a few inches below the bruise. She could feel the warmth of electricity running between them, she realized. He was offering her some of his energy, to speed up healing.

"Not too much," she whispered. "We'll need as much as we can spare later."

"I know." Mason finished the last mark, then handed the pen back to Keira. As she recapped it, he pressed a kiss into the top of her head. He still hadn't moved his hand.

She wished they could stay there for a thousand years. She wished she could close her eyes and never have to think about what they were about to do.

Then the kitchen door slammed open, and they both jolted from the noise, letting Keira's shirt drop back into place. Zoe, either failing to notice or choosing to ignore how badly she'd scared them, held the phone up in victory.

"Harry and Adage are on board," she said, triumphant.

Keira blinked rapidly. "On…board? To hide until it's safe, right?" Zoe's smile just widened. Keira, growing increasingly nervous, pressed. "They're on board to *hide*, right, Zoe?"

"You said you needed human batteries." Zoe tucked her phone into her pocket, remorseless. "All I did was mention your plan. I can't help it if they both volunteered. Now, I hope you're done with that sandwich because we have a carpool to figure out."

CHAPTER 30

BLIGHTY FELT *WRONG.*

Marlene had offered to drive, since her van—used to collect supplies for the coffee shop—was both unfamiliar to Artec and large enough to fit them all with space to spare. Dane rode in the front with Marlene; the rest of them were in the back, sitting on whatever was available: a bag of laundry for Keira, an empty crate for Zoe, and the floor for Mason.

High tinted windows gave Keira glimpses of the town. It was still early morning, but Blighty's residents woke early. They weren't following their usual routines, though. She saw clusters of neighbors gathered on the sidewalks, some still wearing slippers, as they talked and gesticulated.

"A lot of people saw Artec's men last night," Mason said. He was scrolling through his phone, his eyebrows pulled down low as he read a series of messages. "They weren't trying to be discreet.

It sounds like they actually broke into houses. And not just Zoe's and mine."

Keira's mouth turned dry. "Is anyone hurt?"

"I…" He kept scrolling, not even blinking. "I don't know. I'm not seeing any reports. But the police have been nearly powerless. It's just Sanderson and two other officers at the station—Blighty's crime rate is so low that we've never needed more than that—and even though they tried to respond, they couldn't get to even a fraction of the reports. And never fast enough to catch Artec's people while they were still there."

The van pulled to a halt outside Zoe's house. Keira craned to look through the tinted windows.

Zoe's front door hung open. Through it, she could see a hall table tipped on its side. Books were scattered over the floor beyond that.

"Damn it," Zoe spat. Then she tilted her head to either side, cracking her neck. "Okay. Let's do this."

If they were serious about getting into Artec's base, they needed supplies. Supplies that Zoe just happened to hoard. They'd already agreed that Keira would need to stay hidden, which meant remaining in the van. Dane stayed with her. Zoe, Mason, and Marlene leaped out the sliding door and vanished into Zoe's house.

The five minutes they spent inside were some of the most stressful Keira had ever experienced. She couldn't stop her eyes from darting over the garden—trampled by heavy boots—and the toppled furniture in the hallway. That had been Zoe's mother's house. Zoe's mother's plants.

The minutes stretched on.

Keira could barely keep still. What if this had been a mistake?

What if Artec's men had decided to wait inside Zoe's house, knowing she might come back to it eventually?

Then Zoe appeared in the doorway, her arms full of equipment, closely followed by Mason and Marlene, and Keira let herself breathe again.

They piled back into the van. Zoe didn't say a word about the state of her mother's house, but there were scorching embers in her eyes and a furious tilt to her lips as she sorted her equipment into a duffel bag.

The van coasted into the town's center. Keira saw a familiar shop sign through the high windows and glimpsed an overflowing display of flowers. Then the sliding door scraped open, and a black-clad youth stepped in.

"Hey, Harry," Keira said, half rising from her seat. "Are you sure you want to do this? You don't have to."

He shut the door behind himself and slumped, sinking down to the cargo area's floor. It was then that Keira realized his black fringe—designed to cover one eye entirely—wasn't as sleek as usual. His eyeliner was faintly uneven. And she didn't think the dark circles under his eyes were created with makeup, for once.

"What happened?" she asked, dreading the answer.

"People came into the shop last night." Harry's shoulders slipped up into a halfhearted shrug and slumped again. "Knocked over the displays. Mum called the police, but no one answered. She didn't let either of us sleep for the rest of the night."

"I'm so, so sorry," Keira said. She sat back down as the van pulled back onto the road. "Is she all right now?"

"Visiting her sister," Harry said simply. His voice remained a perfect monotone, and it was hard to gauge how badly the night had affected him. "She thinks I'm staying with friends." Slowly, his heavy-lidded eye gazed around the van, unblinking. "Which I guess is the truth, for once."

"Hello, Harry," Dane called from the front passenger seat, followed by a grunt from Marlene.

Keira's stomach twisted into knots. Even if no one had been hurt overnight, home invasion was an ordeal. It could leave mental scars that were hard to recover from. The town had welcomed her more warmly than she could have hoped for, and so far, her presence was only bringing it pain.

Mason found her hand and squeezed it tightly. He didn't try to speak. He didn't need to.

The van slowed again. This time, the door opened more gently. Adage blinked at them, adjusting his glasses, then smiled.

"Good morning, all." He stepped in, and Zoe hopped off the crate to give him a seat. He sighed as he reclined against the van's wall, his familiar cardigan adding a spot of cheer and brightness to the van's insides. "I hear we have a journey ahead of us."

"Two hours," Dane said from the van's front. Keira had given him the address. "Are we ready to go?"

"Just a minute," Keira said. The knots in her stomach wouldn't relent. She took her hand back from Mason as her palms turned clammy, and she clenched her fingers together in her lap and gazed at the van's occupants.

When she asked Zoe and Mason for their help, she'd known they would agree. They'd committed to the fight against Artec as thoroughly as Keira had. They'd seen the stakes; they'd gone through fire and were still willing to do more. They knew the situation as well as anyone could.

The others, though? Harry had come with Keira to Artec's tower, and Adage had helped her at points when she needed transport or shelter. But none of them truly understood what she was asking them to risk.

"This is dangerous," Keira began. "If you think I'm exaggerating, please know that, if anything, I'm failing to convey just how bad it is."

Adage watched her calmly. Harry slumped, staring at the van's ceiling. In the front seat, both Dane and Marlene were silent as they listened. Keira swallowed.

"We'll be facing numbers far greater than ours," Keira said. "And people far more ruthless than any of us know how to be. They've killed before, many times, and they are both prepared and eager to kill again."

"I've heard this spiel before," Harry said, sounding bored. "I've already told you, I don't need the sales pitch."

"Potential death isn't meant to be a sales pitch," Keira said weakly.

Harry just sighed.

Keira shuffled her shoes against the floor, willing herself to keep speaking. "I want to be clear. I'll try to keep you as safe as I can, but there might not be much I can do when the time comes. I'm immeasurably grateful that you've all offered to help. But it's okay to take a step back. We'll drop you off somewhere safe, and no one will think less of you because of it. If you have any doubt at all, now's the time to speak."

Adage raised a hand, and Keira smiled at him.

"Of course, it's okay! Do you feel safe staying with a friend for today—"

"Oh, no," Adage said. "I don't want to get out. I just wanted to know: Is this connected to the people who tore through our town last night?"

Keira nodded.

"I heard them coming and locked the doors," Adage said. He took his glasses off to polish them. "But they circled the house and shone their lights through the windows. My friend was unwell, and it terrified her. She didn't deserve that."

"No," Keira said softly. "No one in town did."

"What you have planned today—will that prevent those people from coming back to Blighty?"

"If it works, yes." They were mercenaries. They did Artec's bidding but only as long as the bills were being paid. Cut down Artec, and, in theory, the hired hunters would vanish.

"Very good." Adage folded one leg over the other and settled back. "That's all I needed to know."

Keira gave him a thin, tight smile, and the smile he gave back was warmer and more generous than she thought she deserved.

"Harry—?" she tried.

"You have to promise not to leave me with the car this time," he grumbled.

Keira turned toward the front seats. "Dane, Marlene—"

Their reply came in the form of the van rumbling to life and turning onto the road.

"Two hours," Dane said. "I'll give you a warning when we're getting close."

"Okay." Keira nodded, and her heart both ached with gratitude and felt like it was almost bursting from fear and hope and the incredible, immeasurable relief of knowing the war was close to being over, one way or another. "Okay. Two hours. If you're going to join me in this, you all deserve to know what's happening and why."

She talked for most of the drive. She told them everything she'd learned about Artec. The cemeteries of trapped spirits. The aggressive expansion model that relied on agreements with hospitals and cheap burial contracts. Artec's plans of international expansion. The research tower they'd visited. Then she talked about the core base, hidden in the basement level beneath the shopping center.

As she recounted the story, she set to work on her companions in the back of the van. Her black pen danced over their skin as she covered them in runes. Runes of protection, runes of healing. They formed trailing lines that looped, again and again, over their arms and legs and faces and backs. She gave them everything she could, layering up the effects until she knew there was nothing more she could add.

They asked questions as she worked. She answered them as fully and truthfully as she could. If they were going to do this for her, they deserved to know everything she did.

Halfway through the trip, they stopped by the side of the road so Marlene and Dane could move into the van's back for their own marks. Mason, already covered, took the driver's seat.

Rain started falling as they neared the shopping mall. Keira finished writing on her friends and turned to herself. She used the same healing and protective runes but added an additional set: the new sigil she'd discovered, the one that allowed her to drain and expend energy. Those went over her hands—repeating circles of them—and then onto her feet, her elbows, and across her arms.

At last, she finished her story and clipped the cap onto her pen. As she admired her companions, it was hard not to smile. The markings actually looked like they fit on Harry. His Gothic aesthetic and black ensemble made them seem like a fashion accessory.

They felt the least appropriate on Adage, in his comfortable suede shoes and drooping cardigan. The pastor adjusted his glasses again and again, and every time his cheeks bunched up with a smile, the marks on his face distorted as the skin moved.

"Healing," he repeated, pointing to the images threading around his forearm. "Safety. Luck."

"That's it."

"And they're *definitely* not occult," he pressed, his bushy eyebrows tilting up at the corners.

Keira could only shrug. "Zoe hasn't been able to find them in any kind of historical document or religious text. So I don't think so?"

"Despite popular belief, pastors don't encounter things that are *truly* occult very often," Adage said.

"Shame," Harry whispered.

"But, from what I understand, you generally need to show allegiance to something evil to gain its power, and you haven't done anything like that."

"No," Keira confirmed. "This was all trial and error to find symbols that work."

"Well, that's fine for me, then." Adage folded his hands, careful not to smudge the drawings.

"We're here," Mason said from the driver's seat. The van slowed, and the engine turned off.

Keira craned to look through the window. Trailing rain streaked over the glass. It was turning into a storm, and heavy clouds transformed the world outside. Ahead stood the shopping mall. Its facade was grim, with trails of water dripping from the concrete.

"Everyone's comfortable with the plan," Keira checked, one last time. It was a loose plan. A very rough, very flexible beast that she knew would need to be disassembled and regrouped depending on what they encountered down there. A chorus of assent came back from her team. "Final chance. Anyone who wants to stay in the van can."

She gave them a searching look, watching for any flicker of regret or uncertainty. She saw none. In each of their expressions was tension—the same bone-jittering, heart-pulsing anxiety she felt leaping through her veins. But there was also conviction.

"Okay." Keira took out her phone. She had a message already cued up and pressed *send*. She watched the screen until it was delivered, then tucked the phone away.

Zoe was passing out black hoodies. They were from her *covert surveillance* collection, as she liked to call them: oversized ensembles that covered their hands and with large hoods to shadow their faces. Keira slid hers on. They would help hide the sigils and, more importantly, their identities. For at least a few minutes.

Then they picked up their equipment. Mason brought his medical kit, something Keira hoped would prove unnecessary, but that she feared might not be. Zoe had a duffel bag of supplies.

She'd wanted to equip the others with weapons. Not to fight—she was going to be the only one doing that—but to defend themselves, if it came to it. A baseball bat or a crowbar could do a lot to block blows and keep attackers at a distance.

But she'd been forced to give up on that idea. They wouldn't make it far through the mall if they were carrying large visible weapons. And a crowbar would make for a weak defense when the enemy was using guns.

Gummy fear stuck in the back of Keira's throat. Not fear for herself, but for her friends. Friends she'd protected as well as she could…but still not well enough.

Her phone buzzed as her message received a reply. It came as a single word: OK.

"We're ready," Keira said.

She pulled the hood up to cover her face, then stood.

Dane wrenched open the van's doors. And, for the final time, Keira stared up at the enormous hateful shopping mall that housed Artec.

Then she stepped out, into the rain, and toward the end.

CHAPTER 31

MASON HAD PARKED CLOSE to the entrance. There had been plenty of room; the lot was as barren as it had been when they'd first visited.

A dozen or so discreetly colored cars were scattered farther back in the rows—likely Artec's employees. More cars clustered near the entrance. Ninety-nine out of every hundred parking spots remained empty.

A tired-looking man wandered through the sliding glass doors. He put his head down and pressed into the rain. Otherwise, the world felt empty. Silent. Almost apocalyptic as heavy drops beat against the back of Keira's hoodie.

Her companions gathered close behind her. The van's door snapped shut, signaling they were ready. She moved forward, leading them in a spearhead formation toward the mall's entrance.

The glass doors rattled as they parted to let them in. Worn

carpet felt rough under Keira's feet but was quickly replaced with dull tile.

A security guard stood just inside the door. They'd anticipated that. Keira kept herself facing forward, her head slightly down, relying on the hoodie to hide both her face and the markings.

The guard turned slowly to watch them pass as suspicion tightened his features. One hand moved to the walkie-talkie attached to his hip, but he didn't unclip it.

Keira had known they would draw attention. The mall saw too few customers. A group of seven, all wearing matching hoodies, all hiding their faces, wasn't going to go unnoticed.

The only thing that might buy them time—even just a few minutes—was the size of their group. Artec would have given its guards instructions to watch for either a sole individual or three young adults.

Schaeffer knew her as a lone wolf. But that had been Past Keira. The Keira who ran and hid and stayed horribly, miserably isolated from even the smallest amount of human contact.

Now, though…

Even without turning to look, Keira could feel her companions behind her. She could hear their breathing, their footsteps. She could feel their resilience and focus and loyalty and goodness.

The guard continued to watch them as Keira led her group deeper into the mall. She kept their pace steady. Not rushing, but not slow either. Past the stand that should have held a map of the mall's layout. Past the broken escalator to the second floor. Past the dingy phone retailer and its tired, bored-looking teenage employee, Richie.

Zoe snapped her fingers at him as they passed. He lifted his head, and she pulled her hood back just far enough to show him her face.

"Run," she whispered, the runes stark against her skin. Then she turned and merged back into the group, leaving Richie speechless in their wake.

Another security guard appeared from behind a scuffed pillar. He was listening to something on his walkie-talkie. The staff were being alerted to an unusual gathering.

But the guard only watched them. He was suspicious but not yet fully alarmed. Which meant they still had time.

Keira didn't break stride as they crossed into the food court. It was still well before lunchtime and the area was nearly empty. Rain trailed over the glass-domed ceiling high above, and it did something queasy to the lighting, dulling the colors and thickening the shadows.

The smoothie shop was open. Staff at the frozen yogurt store wiped down the counters. Two mothers sat off to the side, strollers next to them, as they chatted over a coffee. And…

Straight ahead, sitting next to a cluster of fake plants, was Mikhail. He clutched his mobile, and Keira suspected he'd been reading and rereading the message she'd sent him. Meet me at the food court if you want to live.

He looked terrified. Mikhail saw her and jumped to his feet. His eyes darted to the group of hooded figures that followed Keira, and his mouth gaped open, then snapped closed again as the little color remaining in his face faded. He looked like he was one sudden movement away from bolting.

"Hey," Keira said mildly, and slipped into a seat on the table's opposite side.

"I'm sorry," he said instantly, and the words tumbled out in a deluge as he sank back into his chair. "I'm sorry I gave them your location. I...I panicked... They were going to... I didn't think I had much time left—I'm sorry." He swallowed. "You're angry, aren't you?"

"Yep," Keira said, keeping her voice light. "The whole town was searched. My friends had their houses ransacked."

Zoe and Mason took their seats on either side of Keira. Zoe glared at Mikhail as though hatred alone could set a person on fire.

"I'm very sorry," was all Mikhail could manage. He kept glancing across at each of them but was unable to meet any of their eyes. "I...I bought you a yogurt..." He cringed at his own words. "I know that doesn't even begin to make up for...but I...I..."

Keira glanced at the three cups of frozen yogurt sitting on the table, then back at Mikhail's face, which was covered in beads of perspiration.

She'd lived the largest part of her life in fear. Fear of Artec. Fear of being found. Fear of losing what little she had. She knew the emotion very well, and she could see Mikhail was crumbling under it.

That was going to end today. For both of them.

"I didn't make the drive just for yogurt," she said, nudging the cups toward the group standing behind her. Marlene, Harry, and Adage murmured among themselves as they each took one. "But if you want to make amends, there *is* something you can do. Three things, specifically. And with a little luck, they might be enough to break you free from Artec."

Mikhail watched her carefully. "You…okay. Yes. What three things?"

"You have an access pass to Artec's elevators," she said, and held out her hand.

Mikhail stared at her palm blankly for a second, then jolted with realization. "Oh! Right!" He fished in his pocket and brought out a small laminated card. It had a photo of him, as well as his name, employee number, and codes detailing his security clearances. He passed it to Keira, and she tucked it away.

"Second: I want you to be completely honest with me." Keira leaned forward, closing the gap between them. "Schaeffer has no remorse over what he's done, does he? He's never going to give up on using ghosts as batteries."

"That's correct," Mikhail said. "It's like it's become his life's mission. He believes this is the thing he'll be remembered for. The thing that will put him in history books. And he *wants* to be remembered, even more than he wants the money or the power he expects to gain. No, I don't believe he'll ever give up, no matter how many setbacks he encounters."

Keira nodded. She'd been afraid of that, but she also knew it was the truth. She just needed someone else to confirm that there was no chance of redemption for Schaeffer.

"What about the other employees?" she asked. "How many of them are loyal to Schaeffer? How many would leave Artec if they had the freedom to? Is anyone in the office below us innocent, or are they all complicit in what's happening?"

Mikhail hesitated, his jaw working as he measured his words.

"Honesty," Keira reminded him. "Your life hinges on giving me the truth."

He nodded, his hands shaking as he picked at skin around his fingernails. "Well. It's complicated. Artec expects unwavering loyalty. Staff who voiced dissenting opinions too loudly started to vanish. It created a culture of performative enthusiasm, where we act as though we live and breathe for Artec's cause. Myself included. Staff are afraid to show how they really feel, even to people they trust, because Schaeffer is desperate to weed out traitors, and it's very likely there are recording devices scattered through the offices."

Keira nodded, encouraging him to keep speaking.

"*But*." He swallowed, frowning. "Last year, when the memo about the spirits being sentient was leaked, we came very close to something like a rebellion. Everyone I spoke to either wanted to jump ship or pressure Schaeffer to scrap that current processing model and revert to an earlier mark. That was when the mercenaries were brought into the office. And that was when he stopped hiding the fact that he was disposing of people he no longer trusted. Everyone went quiet after that."

"You didn't answer the question," Zoe said. She continued to glare at him, totally unsoftened.

"Right. Because I don't have any answer." He gave a fleeting smile as he looked between them, but it quickly vanished. "Uh, let's see—you wanted to know if anyone was truly innocent or if we were all complicit. The staff that don't have any clearance—cleaning, maintenance, low-level admin, those sorts—to the best of my knowledge, they don't know anything. But anyone with even one or two clearance levels understands, even just vaguely, what's happening in the graveyards. The more clearance levels, the more hands-on they are with the process. Level Seven includes Schaeffer and just five other employees. They are actively developing the systems used to process the units and increase output."

Keira nodded, the knot in her stomach turning cold and heavy.

"But…" Mikhail fidgeted. "You also asked if anyone would leave if they had the freedom to. And, yes, emphatically yes. We can't discuss our sentiments freely for fear of being found out, but I've spent years with the people inside Artec's center, and I genuinely believe that almost all of them—perhaps the entire staff, even—are desperate to get free.

"Schaeffer's idealistic promises have turned to poison. He used to talk about striving for free, safe, limitless energy for the world, but the company has become increasingly focused on profits alone. And the deaths… We've all known someone who vanished and had their desk cleared out overnight. So, yes. We are all complicit. But, no, we don't want to be."

"Okay," Keira said. The knot in her stomach loosened a fraction. "Okay, that's good. That's what I needed to know. What about the mercenaries?"

Mikhail's mouth twisted at the mention of them. "There are at least a dozen at any time inside the base. Perhaps as many as twenty. They flank Schaeffer whenever he leaves his office. I don't know how you'll get past them."

"Do they know what's happening with the graveyards?"

"Probably not. Maybe the leader does. That's Bridge, the one with a scar on his temple. He and Schaeffer are close."

"And what about their willingness? Their job involves killing employees for minor infractions. Do any of them seem uncomfortable with that? Would any of them walk away from the job, given the chance?"

His lips pursed. "I doubt it. Bridge hires them not just for their *willingness* to do the dirty work but their *eagerness*. I've never seen even a scrap of empathy in any of them. Bridge runs the crew rigidly to keep them in line, but he's not forcing them to do their jobs, not like Schaeffer. The opposite. They want to do *more*, and some days it's like Bridge is a handler holding back hungry dogs."

Keira thought of the men hunting her through the forest. The way they'd torn through Blighty, looking for her. The pop of gunshots. Mikhail's opinion—that they enjoyed what they did—resonated.

"That's all I needed to know before I go down there," Keira said, and rose. Mason and Zoe stood alongside her. "Which leaves just the third and final favor you owe me."

"Yes?" Mikhail stood as well, though he seemed a little wobbly.

"You need to empty this place out."

Mikhail glanced from the two mothers who were talking over coffee, to the security guard eyeing them warily from the food court's entrance. "You mean—"

"The shopping mall, as well as the staff in Artec's basement level," Keira said. "You have some way to pass a message to them, right?"

"Uh, I suppose—we have work phones, but our calls might be monitored—"

"That's fine. Once I leave here, count to one hundred. Then send them a mass message. It's going to get dangerous down there, so you need to tell them to get out of the building. I won't stop any of the staff from leaving."

Relief flooded Mikhail's face. His fear hadn't been for just his own life, apparently. "Thank you."

"And after you send that message, I need you to clear out the shopping mall, as well," Keira said. She could still see the mothers out of the corner of her eye. A lone teenager, likely skipping school, examining the smoothie menu board. All innocent, all in more danger than they could ever guess. "I don't know what's going to happen. So you have to get them all out. Whatever way you can. Pull a fire alarm, maybe."

"Or," Harry said, slowly poking his spoon into his frozen yogurt, "you could skip the alarm and instead start several large fires." He blinked, unrepentant, as the group's eyes turned on him. "It's cathartic."

"Stick with the fire alarm," Keira said. "Or call in a bomb scare, or say you're from the gas company and there's a massive leak. Anything to force an evacuation. Do you understand?"

"Yes." Mikhail took a half step toward Keira, reaching out, then hesitated. "Look. I know you think it's just a platitude, but I really am sorry. I shouldn't have tried to trade your life for mine. That's going to haunt me for a long time."

"Okay," Keira said, while Zoe stared pure murder at him.

"I know I don't deserve forgiveness—for that, or for any of the work I've done under Artec—but…" He fidgeted, fighting with his words. "I want a chance to make amends. I…I want the chance to be a better person."

"Bless you, son," Adage said softly.

"No mercy," Harry said, and licked the last of the frozen yogurt off his spoon.

Keira gave them both a small smile, then turned back to Mikhail. "You're getting your chance. Clear out the building. I'm counting on you."

He half raised a hand in goodbye as the group turned away. Keira kept her head high as she passed the wary guard in the food court's entryway. It didn't matter how suspicious they were now. There was no longer anything Artec could do to stop what was coming.

She pulled Mikhail's access card from her pocket as they neared the steel doors of the elevators.

CHAPTER 32

"LAST CHANCE," KEIRA SAID as the elevator doors slid open.

There was a beat of silence. She turned. Her friends stood gathered close by. She glanced from Adage's pale face to Dane's clenched jaw to the way Marlene pressed her lips into a hard line. She could feel their tension almost as much as she could feel her own.

"I have no idea what will happen once we go down there." The elevator doors began to close. Keira reached out a hand to block them, and they rattled back open. "I can't promise that I can keep you safe. Anyone who wants to can take the van's keys and wait in the parking lot."

"I'm here to the end," Dane said. "However it turns out."

"Me, too," Marlene said, and Adage nodded in agreement.

Harry lobbed his empty yogurt cup toward the nearest bin. It sank in effortlessly, and he gave the tiniest whisper of a smile before his face fell back to neutrality. He didn't bother answering Keira's question.

Finally, she looked to Zoe and Mason. They met her eyes, and each of them gave a brief, firm nod.

"Okay," Keira said as the elevator doors bumped against her hand again. "Let's drop an angry bear into their bunker."

Thunder rumbled. It was loud, even through the building's thick walls. The air seemed to crackle with the storm's energy. Keira breathed it in as she stepped into the elevator, drawing the atmospheric charge into her bones.

Bodies packed in next to her. Adage, Harry, and Dane in the back row; Marlene, Zoe, and Mason clustered closest around Keira. They began fumbling for their hoodies, unzipping them and then dropping the damp fabric onto the floor. The disguises would be more of a hindrance than anything once they got to the lowest level.

The elevator doors rattled closed. This time, Keira didn't try to stop them. She took one more deep, stabilizing breath as the metal walls tapped together, sealing them in. Then she pressed Mikhail's access pass against the small worn panel beneath the number pad, where Artec's logo had been discreetly inscribed.

As her fingers brushed across it, a small flicker of something stirred inside Keira. Something like…confusion?

No. More like…inattention.

She clenched her teeth against startled laughter. She couldn't believe she hadn't seen it before. But then, she'd only started paying serious attention to the runes when it became a matter of life or death to find a new one. She hadn't picked up on it before, but Artec's logo wasn't just a logo. It was an active rune.

And it was designed to distract.

It wasn't strong enough to impact Keira, not when she was already laser-focused on Artec and everything they did. But she was fairly certain the mark could dampen a lot of casual curiosity.

Competitors in the energy generation market would probably pay less attention to Artec. Maybe safety inspectors could be lulled toward vague disinterest as they did their rounds.

And the employees…

Having Artec's sigil on their vans and their uniforms would help make them less noticeable in public. People would remember them less easily and ask fewer questions. It was actually a genius move to turn a rune into their logo, and it fit perfectly with Schaeffer's preference for secrecy and privacy.

They have one rune in their arsenal. Does that mean they have more?

The elevator beeped as it accepted the access card. Keira tucked it back into her pocket as the box rattled and began to drop downward.

"Artec knows how to use the runes," Keira warned her companions. "Perhaps not as much as I can, but…be on the watch for symbols."

She received a brief murmur of acknowledgment. None of them seemed quite up to speaking in that moment. She knew their stomachs had to be twisted in knots. Their mouths would be dry, their hearts racing, their breathing shallow. Just like her.

They were seconds away from the basement level. There was no time left to prepare. But Keira still snatched for what she could. She closed her eyes and tried to breathe.

She couldn't afford to be scared once she got down there. The others were relying on her—to lead them, to instruct them, to keep them safe. She needed to be focused. She needed to be able to pivot without breaking stride. And, more than anything, she needed to be able to charge forward without faltering because the element of surprise was their key advantage, and hesitation would be the first thing to kill them.

She needed to be an angry bear. Just like she'd promised Zoe.

Keira snapped memories of her parents into the forefront of her mind. They'd been kind. They'd loved her so deeply that they'd hidden her, at the cost of their own lives. She remembered her mother's laugh—snorting, cackling, not at all ladylike but fantastic because of it. She saw her father dancing to a cartoon's theme song with her. They had been complex and beautiful people.

Fresher memories flowed in. Adage, offering Keira a place to stay because she didn't have anywhere else to go. Zoe, stubbornly befriending her when she'd arrived in town as a frightened stranger. Mason, always so calm and patient and kind, talking her through her doubts. Smiling at her. Brushing his hand against hers.

She thought of them—any of them—ending up in one of Artec's cemeteries after death. Chained there, forever, voicelessly screaming for mercy.

The fire she needed roared to life inside her. It burned through the knots in her stomach, devouring the chill in a blaze of focus and anger and a deep, undeniable need to make things right.

Artec had cost her everything in the past. She wouldn't let them take any more.

"Marlene." Keira reached behind herself.

Zoe and Mason had offered to give the first energy donation, but they both had jobs to do in the basement level: Mason to give emergency medical care and Zoe to work on the technology side. They needed to keep their energy as long as they could.

Marlene had volunteered to go first instead. She slapped her hand into Keira's.

The elevator was slowing, nearing the final stop. The rune on Keira's palm burned with electrical charge as Marlene's skin made contact. Keira pulled, channeling through the markings, and Marlene gasped as the energy rushed out of her.

It was a flood of power. The fire in Keira's stomach became an uncontrollable inferno. Her nerve endings sizzled. Her lungs were scorched.

"Okay?" she asked, as the elevator touched down with a soft *ding*.

"Okay," Marlene said, though she sounded shaken. Keira had tried not to take too much. But she also couldn't afford half measures. Not with this much at stake.

She focused, shifting her weight and leaning forward, like a runner at their mark. The steel doors ahead shivered, then rattled open. Light flooded through the widening gap.

Angry bear, Keira thought, and launched herself through the opening.

CHAPTER 33

HESITATION MEANT DEATH.

And so she didn't hesitate.

Flashes of her surroundings came through. She assessed and processed the information faster than should have been possible.

A reception desk stood ahead, with a young man behind a modern monitor. He looked toward her, his attention drawn by the elevator's ding, but that first glance was vague and indifferent. He was expecting an employee. Which meant Mikhail hadn't given her away. Her presence would still be a surprise.

Behind the reception desk was an open office and a cluster of workstations. Out of the eleven employees there, she could see six ID badges pinned to their lapels. All low-level ranks. No risk from any of them.

There were doors behind those workstations, and another next to the reception desk. Only the one by the desk held an access pad, which meant it led to higher-security rooms.

Two of Artec's mercenaries stood by the elevator, one on either side. A third was positioned near the back of the open office. They were easy to spot; unlike the employees wearing plain business shirts, they were dressed in shades of black. And all three mercenaries wore military-style machine guns, carried at their side by a strap slung over their shoulders.

It was no wonder Mikhail had shuddered when he talked about them.

The mercenary at the room's back was looking away. But the two stationed by the elevator—guards, tasked with monitoring anyone leaving or entering the office—were already facing the doors as they opened.

They weren't ready for her, though. Despite the hours Artec must have spent drilling them on the danger Keira posed, they'd never actually expected to see her come through the elevator doors.

Keira saw them process what was happening. A flash of confusion—they'd been expecting Mikhail, most likely, who had probably made an excuse about getting a snack—followed by alarm as they saw the size of the group. Then outright shock as their focus locked on Keira and recognition flooded in.

Shock was as far as they got. And it all happened in less than a second as Keira came through the door.

She aimed for the guard to the left. He had the faster reaction and was already reaching for his gun. She concentrated her excess energy into her palms and slammed them into him.

He buckled, mouth gaping open, as electricity shot through him. Keira hadn't given him the full measure of her charge; it wouldn't be enough to keep him down permanently. But it would stun him. At least for a minute.

As he crumpled to the polished tile floor, Keira swung to the other sentry. He'd been slower to react; he was trying to take a step back, his gun rising, fingers reaching for the trigger, but Keira was faster. She darted her hand beneath the gun's barrel and gripped the mercenary's wrist. And then she used the rune to pull.

She'd been careful with how much she'd taken from Marlene, but she didn't use any of that restraint on the guard. She didn't want to kill him. But she also didn't want him to be able to move for a good long while.

Her nerves sizzled at the sudden onslaught of power. Color drained from the guard's face as his eyes rolled upward. She let go of the connection as he toppled, and he hit the floor hard.

A loud crack echoed through the space, and Keira snapped her head up.

The room blurred with movement. Employees yelled as they scrambled to find cover, pressing themselves under desks or behind filing cabinets or running for the doors in the back of the room. The third guard, the one farthest away, had his gun up. He aimed, and Keira launched herself forward as another vicious crack temporarily deafened her.

She saw a puff of plaster explode out of the wall to her side. There was no way to get to the guard without giving him opportunity to fire again, but she'd prepared for that. The energy from both Marlene and the second guard was overflowing her. She concentrated it forward, focusing it into the smallest, tightest space she possibly could, and then released it outward in a sudden rush.

It burst from her like a shock wave. Desks skidded. Papers flew upward and then began cascading back down like snow. The water cooler in the back burst, sending a gush of water across the floor.

The shock wave had been focused on the guard. He squeezed the trigger just as it hit him, and the shot went wide, chipping a chunk out of the ceiling. His feet left the floor as the impact threw him backward, and he slammed into the tiles with a grunt, his gun pinned under his back.

He'd been too far away to be properly stunned by it. Even as he landed, he began to roll, reaching for his weapon with one hand and the communications device with the other.

Keira couldn't let him use either of them. The disturbed desks blocked her path, so she pressed a hand to the center of her chest and then pulled it outward, spilling Daisy into the office space. The little cat darted ahead, weaving through narrow gaps, while Keira leaped on top of the desks and bounded across their surfaces, skidding from one to another and scattering papers.

Daisy reached the guard first. Keira caught glimpses through the cat's eyes: the guard was trying to pull his weapon free from under him. Daisy landed on his chest, claws extended and fur puffed as she hissed in his face. He snapped back, startled, and Daisy frisked out of reach before he had a chance to react.

It bought Keira just enough time to leap from the final desk and land next to the mercenary.

His eyes were watering and full of both hatred and fear as he squinted up at her. She felt him preparing to move—to throw a fist at her, maybe—and she darted in before he had a chance. She slapped a palm to his cheek, then pulled. He spasmed, once, then collapsed back onto the floor.

Panting, Keira slowly turned to check the room.

Pale, wide-eyed faces watched her from every dark corner. The staff had taken shelter wherever they could get it. The earlier shouts had faded into an eerie silence. None of them dared to move.

She hated the way they looked at her. As though she was the most frightening thing they'd ever seen. As though she was death personified, materializing in their office to swipe her scythe through their midst.

Daisy roamed the space, slinking through the narrowest gaps, tail frisking as she acted as Keira's second set of eyes.

Keira turned back to the collapsed guard at her feet. He was still breathing but wasn't moving much. She pulled the gun free, dragging it out from underneath him, and unclipped his walkie-talkie. Then she tossed both into a back corner of the room, away from anyone's easy reach.

Two of the guards were out of commission. But the first guard—the one who'd been fastest to react—had only been stunned.

Through Daisy's eyes, she saw her friends all clustered near the elevators. Adage was holding the doors open—just in case—while the others stood in a tight group.

Mason knelt near the guard she'd drained. He was checking for a pulse and didn't notice that the guard behind him, the stunned one, was trying to rise.

Keira drew a sharp breath. She leaped onto the desks and, moving faster than was probably safe, ran.

Daisy hissed as a sliver of shiny steel glinted at the guard's side. He was unsheathing a wickedly jagged hunting knife. Mason looked up, but he wasn't moving fast enough.

Keira vaulted past Mason and used her momentum to slam into the guard.

He was easily double her size, but he was still under the lingering effects of the shock. They hit the floor and rolled. Keira heard the knife scrape against the tiles, heard the furious rumble deep in the guard's chest. She grappled to get a hand on his exposed skin. A fist hit the side of her ribs, but it wasn't a strong blow. She wrapped her palm around his wrist and activated the runes.

It was over quickly. As he dropped, boneless, Keira kicked the knife out of his reach. The blade held a smear of blood. She looked down and saw red dripping off her elbow.

He'd managed to catch her, though she wasn't sure exactly when. The overcharge of power was sharpening some senses but numbing others.

She was hyperaware of every small movement in the room. She could hear the panicked breathing of the staff. She could feel her companions right behind her, could even sense their tension. But the pain barely registered, even after seeing the cut.

Mason had noticed it, though. He was at her side in an instant, wrenching open his medical kit. "Here—"

"Later." She placed a hand on his arm. Her senses were so

enhanced in that moment that she could feel not only the goose-flesh on his skin, but the pulse of blood through his veins.

The healing runes Keira had crisscrossed over her body were kicking in, stemming the bleeding. The longer she waited, the more time Schaeffer would have to assess the situation and react. They had to get to him before he realized just how much danger he was in and found a way to make himself unreachable.

A dozen soft dings and chimes echoed through the space, coming from a dozen different directions.

Text notifications. Several employees furtively reached for their pockets. Mikhail had sent his message, as he'd promised.

"Marlene," Keira said. She needed the energy she'd taken from the guards—it was too precious to just release into the atmosphere—but she also couldn't think properly with how much she was carrying. Marlene, tired from the measure Keira had taken from her in the elevator, stretched out a hand. "This is going to feel weird," Keira warned her, before pressing their palms together and sending some of the extra charge back.

Marlene gasped but managed to stand steady. The pressure flowed out of Keira, leaving her head a fraction clearer. She didn't give Marlene all her excess—not even most of it—but enough to let her function again.

Faces peered around the edges of the desks and filing cabinets, watching her closely. She saw a couple of them fidgeting with their phones.

"You're safe to go," she said, and her voice filled the open office. "Use the elevator, get to your cars, and leave. I won't stop you."

Then she beckoned to her group and strode toward the door next to the reception desk, the one with the access pad beside it. Even as they crossed the room, she heard the scramble of staff rushing for the elevator and the quiet ping as the doors opened.

Keira pulled out Mikhail's access pass but hesitated before pressing it into the device by the door. Daisy continued to roam the space, looking into places Keira couldn't reach. And the small black cat had spotted something behind the welcome desk.

The receptionist had ducked beneath it to hide when the gunfire started but had begun to creep out. Instead of aiming for the elevators, though, he was reaching for something else. A round red button was concealed next to his computer. It was unlabeled, but Keira had no doubts about its purpose: a panic button that, when pressed, would signal that the office had been breached.

She crossed to the desk and leaned over its counter. The receptionist froze, his hand outstretched, his eyes wide and terrified. Keira felt her heart break. He was young, and the name badge held only the lowest security clearance. He didn't deserve this.

"I know you're only doing your job," she said, keeping her voice soft. "But please don't tell anyone I'm here. I'm trying to help."

He hesitated, and his throat bobbed as he swallowed. Then, still without blinking, he slowly withdrew his hand, slid out of the chair, and backed toward the elevator.

Keira gave him a very small smile, then pressed Mikhail's pass against the reader beside the door. It beeped, and the light on the handle turned green.

She shoved through and into the main offices of Artec's operations.

CHAPTER 34

A LARGE RECTANGULAR ROOM spread out ahead of them. Office cubicles had been packed in, and they created hallways between them that crisscrossed the area.

More doors were scattered across the walls, leading to private offices. Keira was fairly sure she'd seen inside some of them when Daisy had gone through the ducts on their first visit. A printer whirred in the back corner.

Staff were spaced about the cubicles, either at desks or leaning over partitions in small clusters. Many held their mobiles. A buzz of quiet whispers fell silent as Keira stepped through the door.

They'd gotten their warning, but they still seemed shocked to actually see her.

Keira took in the environment in a fraction of a second. Then her focus narrowed in on the guards. Five of them. Three to her left, two to her right. None close enough to reach. That presented a challenge.

"Go!" Keira called, gesturing toward the cubicle straight ahead.

As her group ran forward, Keira whipped left and sent a shock wave down the hall.

It rippled along the edges of the partitions, cracking the material and knocking decorative trinkets free, and hit the guards just as they started to move toward her.

Her group had reached the cubicle and had taken shelter behind the furniture. Keira plunged in after them, her hands shaking. She'd put more than she'd intended into the shock wave. "Marlene," she mumbled, reaching out blindly. "Harry."

Two hands closed around hers. Keira drew from them, and sudden vertigo crashed over her.

The flood of power was immense, but at the same time, it felt worse than it had before. The fire in her nerves wasn't just burning but felt like rows of needles stabbing into her flesh.

She'd taken and given power before, but never so much, so quickly, or so repeatedly. And she suspected it was doing damage.

There wasn't time to think through potential consequences. As her friends clustered in the narrow gaps around the desk and filing cabinet, Keira threw herself back into the hallway.

The two standing guards had closed the gap. They were just five feet away: too close to avoid but not close enough to touch.

Keira didn't have any alternative. She concentrated her energy forward and sent it outward as a desperate, hastily aimed shock wave.

Darkness fluxed into the edges of her vision and then faded again.

Nearby lights burst. Guns fired, the bullets peppering the partitions and ceiling as the wall of energy slammed into the guards, throwing them backward. Staff yelled from inside the cubicles, but none of them sounded pained, so she could only hope no one had been hit.

Her ability to focus the blast had been compromised; the flux of power had stripped small scraps of paint from the walls but hadn't hit the guards as hard as she'd wanted. They collapsed but didn't stay down.

A headache began to throb in the back of her skull as Keira leaped forward. She pressed a hand against the closest guard's face. It only took a second to drain out his energy, but that was enough time for the other guard to regain his feet.

Keira lurched toward him just as his gun came up to point at her. She ducked under the muzzle. Gunfire went off next to her, and even though the guns must have had noise-dampening equipment, it was still loud enough to hurt.

She barreled into him, reaching for bare skin. The butt of the gun hit her stomach, winding her. They tumbled to the floor together. One of his hands fastened across Keira's throat. It was a sharp, nightmarish reminder of her encounter in the forest. Panic spiked as she clamped a hand over his, and her already bruised throat closed over.

Keira didn't think. She just reacted on impulse, sending a shock wave directly into the guard's chest.

She felt it as his bones snapped. The hand vanished from her throat. The guard lurched two feet into the air, like a crash test dummy, before slamming back into the floor. The impact was marked with a sharp, barking scream before he went completely silent.

Keira keeled back, panting, her heart throbbing. She hadn't meant to make things so extreme. The guard lay crumpled, and for a second, she thought he was never going to move again, but then he groaned as he rolled over, taking pressure off his injured side.

The office space was deathly silent except, inexplicably, for the printer in the back corner that was still chugging through its job.

Keira clambered to her feet. There was still the first group of guards to worry about—the ones she'd hit earlier on entering the room. But, when she turned toward the space where she'd last seen them, it was empty.

She staggered toward the cubicle that hid her friends. As she did, she craned, searching for the three missing guards, but couldn't see anything except the occasional bob of an employee's head, peeking over their walls to watch her.

As Keira entered their temporary hiding spot, Daisy snaked out past her, vanishing along the hallway to explore.

"Are you okay?" Mason whispered, reaching out to support her.

"Fine, I think. Just…dizzy."

Dizzy wasn't even the right word. She felt like her body had been put in a jar and shaken hard. Draining power from the guards was effective, but she didn't know how many more rounds she was capable of.

"Sit a moment, child," Adage said, pushing the desk chair toward her. "You look pale."

She'd feel better if she rested, she knew, but there wouldn't be an opportunity to do that—not until Schaeffer was dealt with. Whatever that entailed. She still didn't have any idea of what she might be forced to do once she encountered him.

It was only then, in a moment of quiet, that Keira became aware of a faint sound bleeding through the office's thick walls. It was dulled until it was nearly unrecognizable, but she thought it sounded like an alarm.

"Mikhail's clearing the mall," Zoe said, faint wonder lighting up her face as she heard the noise too. "He must have pulled the fire alarm."

"Or maybe he took my advice and started several large fires," Harry said. He paused, then whispered under his breath, "I *hope* he started several large fires."

Keira tried to focus on slowing her breathing as she took stock. They were all unharmed…except for the cut on her arm and a few new bruises. She could deal with that. Harry and Marlene had already given Keira their energy, but she still had Dane, Adage, Zoe, and Mason. Upstairs, Mikhail was keeping his side of the bargain.

With a little luck, they might still get through this.

Daisy darted through the office, weaving between desks and past hiding staff, and only paused for a second to bat at a scrunched-up ball of paper before refocusing on her job. She'd covered most of the space without seeing any trace of the three missing guards.

That was more than a mystery. It was a pressing anxiety. If Keira didn't know where they were, she couldn't protect against them.

"I've lost the first set of guards. Did anyone see where they went?"

She'd aimed the question at the group clustered around her, but after a beat, a shaky voice answered from two cubicles over. "They left."

Keira craned to look over the wall and saw a woman in a blue blazer, clutching her mobile against her chest. "Into one of the meeting rooms, I think. They lock from the inside, so…"

"Oh."

They'd felt the shock wave. They'd seen what had happened to the two other mercenaries.

And unlike the guards at the elevator doors, they'd had the option to retreat. Self-preservation was a powerful force, and that was apparently true even for Artec's hired hands.

The woman in the blazer looked down at her phone, then back at Keira. "He says you don't want to hurt us."

"No. I don't."

"We can…leave?"

"Yeah." Keira pointed toward the door that led to the reception room and elevator. "Just…step over the guards and let yourself out."

For a second, the space was perfectly silent. Then there was a soft rattle of chairs being pushed aside and the tap of hushed, quick footsteps as various staff exited their workspaces and began speed-walking toward the exit.

Keira frowned as she turned in a slow circle, staring at the myriad cubicle walls and closed doors. Daisy was working her way through the areas she could access, her second set of eyes feeding Keira glimpses of each office and passageway. The underground fortress felt larger than she'd thought it would be.

She glanced behind herself. Employees rushed past her, heads down, most of them just trying to avoid being noticed as they made their way to escape. "Hey, quick question before you all go… Which way is Schaeffer's office?"

Several of the staff paused just long enough to point in unison. Down the work area, toward one of the farthest doors.

"You'll need to go through the research division," the woman in the blue blazer said, right on the exit's threshold. "He's in the back of the complex. Take the doors that need higher security clearances."

"Thanks," Keira said, but the blazer had already vanished.

She glanced back at her companions. Her body still ached, and the headache was still threatening to worsen, but time was of the essence. She couldn't stop. Not until the job was done. "Let's go."

CHAPTER 35

KEIRA LED THE GROUP toward the doors at the back of the office area. She kept the pace quick but not so fast that anyone had trouble keeping up. It was vitally important that they stayed close together. It was the only way Keira could keep them all safe.

They passed by the two guards Keira had taken down. The first—the one she'd drained—seemed unconscious but was breathing. The second squirmed sluggishly. One hand reached toward his dropped gun.

"Nuh-uh," Zoe said, and kicked the gun out of reach as she passed. "Not for you."

She swallowed thickly as she passed him. Draining the guards immobilized them without causing permanent damage. But she'd messed up with the last one. She'd felt ribs break. She hadn't meant to hurt him like that. She could only hope his coworkers would get him help.

As they neared the back doors, Keira glanced down. The worn carpet was tiled and had an odd pattern in the center of each square. She'd spent so much time working on finding runes that she wasn't sure if she was starting to imagine them in places where they didn't exist, but she didn't think so. Not this time. Keira crouched and pressed a hand over one of the designs.

Compliance. Obedience.

Like the rune Artec had incorporated into its logo, this one wasn't something that would drastically change anyone's behavior. But with hundreds of them layering the floor and with the employees unaware of their purpose, they would have an insidiously subtle effect.

It reinforced two suspicions: Firstly, that Schaeffer, on some level, understood how runes worked. And, secondly, that his focus was likely on passive runes. Keira's arsenal was mostly active: runes to drain energy, runes to unlock doors, runes to stun.

She suspected Schaeffer hadn't been able to fully explore those, since he'd never had the same exposure to spectral energy that Keira had. Just like the way he saw a shimmer of movement where Keira saw a full ghost, his senses were similar to hers but blunted.

Or, perhaps, he'd never seen a purpose for the more active runes. He wouldn't have much use for a mark that unlocked doors when he already held a key card for them all.

Either way, his runes seemed to be implemented into environments. Passive and weak, but persistent. Just enough to give his business a little edge. Just enough to dampen some rebelliousness in his staff.

"Anything dangerous?" Zoe asked. She must have guessed what Keira was doing, even though, to anyone else, it would have looked like Keira had spontaneously stopped to pat the carpet.

"It's a rune to encourage compliance." Keira stood. "Nothing we need to worry about. But I'll keep watch for anything worse."

Ahead, four doors blocked their path. It wasn't hard to guess which one they wanted, though: only one was made of solid steel and had an access panel above the handle.

She held up her card. The door beeped and opened into a long metal hallway. A second door with its own access panel waited at the end. The passage worked like an air lock, designed to prevent any unwanted personnel from slipping through unnoticed by trailing behind a higher-ranking staff member.

That meant they were past the routine, low-clearance areas. They were entering the parts of the complex Schaeffer truly wanted kept hidden.

Daisy trotted behind them as they pressed along the passage. The fire alarm from the shopping center above created a dull pulsing noise that barely penetrated the walls of concrete separating them. Keira unlocked the air lock's second door as she reached it and, like before, stepped through without hesitation, hands raised as she prepared for a confrontation.

It wasn't needed this time. She was in a long concrete hallway, and it was empty. Unlike the earlier areas, which had been carpeted and held the types of desks and swivel chairs that Keira could have found in any large office, this section felt utilitarian.

The lights were harsh. The walls were bare. Each step echoed uncomfortably. The hall split in three: one path led straight ahead, and others to the left and to the right.

She hesitated. It hadn't been hard to tell where to go in the previous rooms, but this hall offered no clues. There were no signs on the walls. No arrows. Each passage ended in a turn, with no indication of what might be beyond.

"Um." Keira stared to the left, then to the right, while the others grouped in so close behind her that she could feel their clothes brushing against her back. "Anyone getting a good feeling about any direction in particular?"

There was a beat of silence as they all craned to look down the barren concrete halls. Then Adage spoke. "The floor is more scuffed to the left. Perhaps it gets more traffic?"

He was right. The plain floor held small marks, showing where it had been worn down by hundreds of sets of feet.

"That's good enough for me." Keira turned left.

Everything sounded too loud in the halls. Their footsteps overlapped, creating an awful drumming sound. Daisy trotted ahead to peer around the corner, and Keira got a second-long glimpse of another hall filled with metal doors before Daisy looped back to weave between their legs and smell the floors.

Distant sounds began to bleed into Keira's awareness. She thought she caught distant voices, but the hall distorted them, and it was impossible to tell whether they were coming from ahead or from behind. She reached the corner and leaned around, bracing herself.

The hall was identical to the first one, except it held rows of metal doors. And they were opening.

A man wearing a lab coat stepped out of the nearest one, clutching a binder of papers to his chest. He saw Keira, pulled up short, and immediately turned and walked back into his office, feigning nonchalance despite the sudden grayness that flooded his skin.

Two more employees in long white coats had just entered the hallway. They stumbled to a halt as they saw Keira, and she was struck by how uncertain they looked. They were watching her with the same wariness that they'd watch a large dog: on high alert for signs of aggression, ready to run if it came to that, but trying to avoid any sudden movements that might break the temporary calm.

Beyond them, at the end of the hallway, Keira saw another keypad next to a door. Their way forward.

She took a risk and began walking. Her group, as they'd promised, stayed close at her back. She stared straight ahead, as though she couldn't see the two staff in their path and kept to the right-hand side of the hall.

After a second, the staff began walking too. They mimicked Keira's body language, facing forward and clinging to the wall. The two groups passed one another, and Keira resisted the impulse to glance back as the staff members broke into a trot as soon as they were away from her.

It was like opening the floodgates. More employees began appearing in the doorways. Some waited, eyes averted, until Keira had passed them. Others walked past her, staying silent and keeping their heads down as they moved aside to give her room.

They were all trying to reach the exit. A flood of Artec's

high-ranking workers, fleeing a sinking ship, spurred on by messages instructing them to get out, and get out fast.

Keira's group was nearly at the next level of access restriction. The card reader next to the door glowed faintly, beckoning her toward it.

"Hey," Zoe said, pulling to an abrupt halt. They were passing a set of double doors. Employees rushed through, shoving them open and giving glimpses of the room beyond. It was large, and full of so many flickering lights that it almost looked like Christmas. "I think that's the data center."

"That's—" Keira blinked at it. She'd been hoping to find some kind of sign pointing them toward it, but Artec didn't seem to believe in those. Stumbling on the room was a relief. "Great, let's go."

The doors held a card reader, but Keira didn't even need to activate it. The staff members who were trying to leave backed away as Keira pressed between them, her companions flowing through in her wake.

The room was large enough to be command center for a shuttle launch, and had enough technology packed into the rows of desks too. Computers were scattered throughout. Walls of imposing, blinking machines Keira couldn't even name stood like sentries.

"Do you need anything?" Keira asked, trying not to notice the room emptying around them.

Zoe unzipped her backpack. She pulled out a series of small devices and cables, a wicked grin lighting her face. "Nope. Give me fifteen minutes. We're going to give my favorite pet a new home."

Zoe had explained what she needed to do on the drive to the mall. It wasn't enough to bring down Artec, the company; they also had to prevent anything like its cemeteries or its tethered ghosts from happening ever again. And that meant they should concentrate on three main areas of risk.

The first was Schaeffer, the mastermind behind it all. The second was the staff themselves and the knowledge they'd accrued. And, finally, there was the data: all the documentation from the different rounds of research, all stored on Artec's servers.

"I can take care of that," Zoe had promised. "You've just got to get me to the data center. I've got a lovely little worm in this backpack, and it's hungry for a treat."

That statement had been met by a lot of blank looks. Zoe had begrudgingly explained. She had a computer virus contained on a disconnected hard drive. It had been a gift from a friend she'd met on some of the less savory parts of the internet, with the promise that it was one of the worst creations he'd ever encountered. Once installed, it would worm its way through every computer in the network, corrupting files and erasing years of history. And, once in, it was virtually impossible to fully eradicate.

Keira watched the last staff rush from the room, leaving them alone with the banks of computers. The double doors had bar handles on the inside. They looked about the right size to jam with the legs of a metal chair, and Keira shifted one to lean next to the door for Zoe.

This was her least favorite part of the plan. It involved splitting up.

"We're going to keep moving," she said. "Seal the doors behind us. I'll ask Daisy to stay in the hallway and keep watch in case any guards start closing in on you. If that happens, I'll see it through her eyes, and I'll get back to you as fast as I can. But…I don't know how long that will take. You might need to shelter for a bit. Okay?"

"You got it." Zoe was pale, but her eyes were brighter than Keira had ever seen them. She saluted with one hand and began plugging cables into a nearby computer with the other.

Keira shoved open the door and leaned into the hallway. The door they needed to go through was protected with an access pad, and they only had one card for it.

A few straggling staff were moving past as they tried to get out. Keira pointed at the nearest one, an older man with shaggy gray hair. He froze, staring at her finger as though she was about to cast a magic spell at him.

"What level of access do you have?" Keira asked.

"Uh…" He blinked. "Five."

That was the same level as Mikhail's. "I need your access card. Please."

The man looked from her finger to her face, then fumbled in his pocket to take out his pass. He leaned forward, arms stretched out, to hand it to Keira without physically getting any closer to her than he already had.

Keira took the card, leaned back inside the room, and tossed it across the desk to Zoe. "Here. Just in case."

Zoe caught the card without even looking up from the computer. The screen's glow reflected off her owlish eyes as she feverishly clicked away at something. "Roger. Fifteen minutes."

"Barricade the doors. Text if you need me. Stay safe."

"Ditto to you."

Keira led the group back into the hall. The older man with the shaggy hair was speed-walking away and had nearly disappeared around the corner. Keira glanced down at Daisy, who was weaving around her legs. "You know what to do, right?"

If the cat understood that she was supposed to be Zoe's guard, she showed no signs of it. She found a discarded paper clip and began batting it along the hall.

But the small black cat hadn't let Keira down before. And this whole exercise was based around trust. Trust that her friends would stay close to her, even when it got dangerous. Trust that Zoe would be able to wipe Artec's data. Trust that Mikhail wouldn't betray her a second time.

So Keira left Daisy to the paper clip, marched toward the next door, and pressed her access pass into it.

She felt a subtle shift in the atmosphere even as the door beeped and opened. A slight crackling sensation. The tang of energy in the air.

This section held ghosts.

CHAPTER 36

KEIRA INHALED THE HUM of energy into her lungs. The environment had changed yet again. The metal walls seemed dimmer, colder. Meaner, somehow.

She was so attuned to the sense of spectral energy that she barely saw her surroundings. She turned right, following the energy, barely noticing the staff who moved out of her way. There was a double set of doors ahead. As at the IT center, it held an access pad. The energy bled out from underneath the doors like a gas.

Keira pressed Mikhail's card into the reader. It beeped, but instead of turning green, the light became red. Keira tried again, then a third time, for good measure.

Mikhail had a high level of access. But even *he* hadn't been allowed in this room.

Keira pulled her pen out of her back pocket. She'd just started to draw the rune for unlocking doors when someone burst outward, slamming into her.

"Ah—" A shocked staff member wearing a lab coat stared down at Keira while Keira pressed a hand against her aching face. "Ah—"

"It's fine," she managed, already feeling small sparks dancing through the fresh bruise as the healing runes worked. "Not the worst I've had today."

The staff member shuffled around her, hands raised apologetically. The doors were beginning to close. Keira grabbed one, stopping it from locking again, and nodded for her companions to follow her inside.

There was no other staff inside the space. The message network had been effective at clearing them out. It left the room's main feature entirely unobstructed, and the view was horrendous.

A platform was raised in the room's center. On it, five spirits writhed. Their forms were ribbons of inky dark smoke. The strands melded together and then rippled outward again, flowing in strange currents as they made the approximate shape of a human.

The shades' mouths yawned open, stretched into silent, agonizing screams.

Console tables were spaced around the raised platform. They held strings of data. Machines whirred, measuring energy output.

This is the department my mother worked in. A lump formed in Keira's throat as the raw, brittle electricity snapped through the air around her. *This is where she unknowingly exposed me to dangerous levels of spectral energy before I was even born.*

This is the entire reason why I can see ghosts.

Artec wasn't finished with its experiments. Mark Five, brutal as it was, still wasn't enough to satisfy Schaeffer. He wanted more.

The ghosts screamed and screamed and screamed.

Keira's face felt wet—tears or perspiration, she wasn't sure. It would be smudging the runes, but she didn't care about that either. She crossed to the platform. There had to be a way to shut it off. To free the ghosts.

Beneath each shade was a small metal box. They each held a plaque with a seven-digit number on it. The boxes would contain the spirits' cremated ashes, Keira realized. Five people, stripped of their names, each reduced to a number.

"Where…?" She blinked from the consoles to the platform to the writhing, twisting shades. The energy flowing through the air was so strong, she couldn't tell where the cables were hidden. Except…

She reached for the platform. It was metal, like every other surface. But as she touched it, Keira felt the rush of power moving through.

"I need energy," Keira said. "And I need a lot. There are ghosts here. I…I know I'm not supposed to be wasting energy, but…I can't just leave them here… They…"

Adage stepped forward. He placed his hand in Keira's. Dane appeared on her other side and pressed his palm to her shoulder.

"Be careful," Mason whispered. He lingered close. "I know this is important, and I know you need to do this, but don't let it hurt you."

She'd been trying to hide it, but he knew her well enough to see she was struggling.

Keira nodded, to let him know she'd heard, and leaned forward. She pressed her hand into the cold metal surface and felt her skin buzz.

There were cables underneath. They both measured the spirits' energies and delivered a charge to keep them trapped. If she could do this just right—if she could deliver a large enough shock to the central part of the system—she might be able to break the link holding the shades in place.

She closed her eyes and concentrated. Both Adage and Dane maintained contact, offering her everything they had. She took it.

Vertigo crashed through her head like a breaking wave. Every nerve burned, all acid and knives. Patches of dark bled in at the farthest corners of her vision, and it took a second for them to recede.

Channels of energy mapped themselves beneath her fingers, creating a maze of lights in her mind's eye. She couldn't afford to get this wrong. It was already a waste of their precious resources; she wouldn't get another shot at it.

"Hey," Harry said, but his voice sounded very distant. He wasn't staying close to the group as he'd promised.

She couldn't respond, not even to tell him to get closer. She couldn't afford to break her concentration. The map of cables was growing clearer. There was a nexus beneath her hand, one that controlled all five shades. Keira continued to draw from Adage and Dane, not in a rush like the rune allowed, but slowly, carefully, as she built a charge.

"Hey," Harry repeated, slightly louder. "I think someone's coming."

Not yet—please, please, not yet—

She was so close. The charge felt like an inferno in her chest, burning hot and bright. Voices behind her were speaking, but they overlapped until the words became lost.

She couldn't turn away from the shades, though, and she couldn't hold on to the energy she'd taken. This would be the only chance she'd ever get. And she was almost there—

The power peaked, growing so painful that Keira thought her head was going to split open. She shoved it out of her, slamming it into the bundle of cables tethering the ghosts in place. They were already carrying a dangerously high current. She just hoped she was giving them enough to force their overload.

Keira saw them light up in her mind, burning and melting and sizzling. She forced her eyes open. The spirits above her twisted violently, their smoky forms billowing and undulating and then, all at once, collapsing in on themselves like a supernova. She felt, more than saw, their spirits snap free from the restraints. The howling mouths vanished. The smoke condensed into a tight clump, then burst outward, spreading thin and, within seconds, fading into the ether.

"They're free." Her voice cracked. If she hadn't already been kneeling, she thought she might have tumbled over. The room seemed blurrier and dimmer than it had before.

But the shades were gone.

Adage and Dane were still on either side, but they seemed unsteady. She'd pulled a lot from them.

Mason dropped into a crouch next to her. He touched her arm, gentle but insistent. His eyes tightened with worry as he took in her face. Worry and…a flicker of panic?

"We need to run," he said, his voice a whisper. "Keira, hold on to me. I'll get you up. But we need to—"

"Hey," Harry called. Keira made herself lift her head. He stood by the doors, his hair a little mussed from its usual style, but his features as flat and unemotive as ever. He raised a hand to point to the locked metal doors. "There's someone out there."

"Harry—"

The room rocked. Keira's first instinct was to think it was her vertigo again, but Mason gasped and Dane barked out a sharp exclamation. A booming noise came from the doors, and Keira flinched as they were blasted from their hinges.

Then the lights went out entirely, plunging them into horrible, eerie darkness.

Tremors ran through Keira's limbs as she fought to get to her feet. Everything was noise and chaos. Her friends yelled to one another, trying to locate each other in the dark. Dust filled her lungs when she inhaled.

And then, a new noise joined the cacophony. Heavy boots beating against the cold metal floor.

One of the bulbs set into the ceiling flickered. It gave them a second of light, thin and paltry, and Keira took in the scene around her.

Adage and Mason were crouched on the floor beside her, Adage shielding his head. Dane and Marlene were close by, pressing back against the wall. Desks and consoles had been knocked over by the explosion that had taken out the doors. Parts of the ceiling had collapsed, forming mounds of rubble.

The doors—Harry—

The light flickered again. Her eyes lit on a pale hand with black nail polish, half covered by shattered concrete. A streak of vivid red dripped from one finger.

And ahead…

Artec's guards had arrived.

They marched through the door, weapons raised. Dark armor covered their bodies. Visors were set across their eyes. Night vision, she was sure.

Even with the identical uniforms, Keira recognized the nearest form. He was taller than the others, and something about his stance felt more aggressive. The leader. Bridge, Mikhail had called him. She'd only encountered him twice before. She would have preferred to avoid this third meeting.

He raised his gun and aimed it toward the flickering light. There was a bang, and Adage gasped as a shower of sparks trailed down. The light went out completely.

This had been their plan. Rob the group of sight. Leave them trapped and blind, unable to even see their way out, and then pick them off one by one.

They thought they had Keira cornered. They thought they had tilted the odds overwhelmingly in their favor.

But they'd underestimated just how furious she was.

Keira reached for Mason. She found his hand, and he wrapped his unsteady fingers tightly around hers.

She inhaled deeply as she took his energy.

And then she lunged forward.

CHAPTER 37

THEY'D EXPECTED HER TO be helpless. They thought robbing her of the overhead lights would leave her fumbling and lost.

They didn't know she could see their energy.

It wasn't much. The energy they held was weaker than what had run through the cables in the platform. But Keira could close her eyes, open her second sight, and glimpse the very faint shimmer of each advancing form.

There were five of them. The leader stood back while his four mercenaries marched inward. They were intending to take their time. To pick off the group methodically.

Keira balled up all her anger and fear and desperation and used it to fuel her.

She slammed into the first guard before he realized she was coming. She shot Mason's borrowed energy into him, stunning him. His armor grated against her hands, scraping skin off, but she barely noticed as she clawed around the mask. She found his skin. There wasn't much access, but that was fine. She just needed a finger's touch.

The next nearest guard was turning his gun on her, a bark of alarm echoing from under his helmet. Keira swung her other hand toward him. And, as she pulled energy out of the first guard, she funneled it out to the second, forcing him back.

He stumbled on an overturned console. The gun skittered from his hands. It bought her a second, not much more.

She hurled herself toward the remaining guards.

Gunfire flared. *Snap, snap, snap*, echoing around her. Small sparks of light danced as bullets glanced off metal. It made it harder to see the energy, but not impossible, as she toppled another guard, straddling him, and wormed her hand under his protective gear.

Her limbs were shaking. Her head burned. Her heart skipped every second beat. She tasted metal and instinctively knew her gums had started bleeding.

But she didn't stop moving. She was a bear. A tornado. Unrelenting.

Two guards were down, and she moved toward the third. He was backing toward the door, one hand raised. It only took a second to pull his energy, then she spun and sent a shock wave toward the fourth guard, who had been coming up behind her. He hit a wall. Fell. Didn't get up again.

Cold metal touched the back of her neck. She'd lost track of Bridge during the commotion, and he'd taken advantage of that opening.

A thousand thoughts flashed through Keira in a heartbeat. There'd be no bartering for time, she knew. Bridge wasn't going to gloat. He wasn't going to ask her for her last words. She'd been a thorn in his side for months. She'd given him a chance to eliminate her, and he wasn't going to risk squandering it.

Which meant Keira had only one option left.

She moved on instinct, swinging, and clamped a hand onto the rifle's barrel. As Bridge pulled the trigger, the sight aimed square at her face, Keira sent every last shred of energy into the gun.

The energy and the bullet collided midbarrel. The rifle shattered.

Searing heat burned through Keira's hands as shards of hot metal sliced into her. Bridge lurched back, a grunt catching in his throat. He still held the grip, but the rifle's front assembly collapsed into smoking shards.

Keira had nothing left in her. Exhaustion weighed on her like she'd been draped with loops of iron chains. But she forced herself to move. To lunge toward Bridge, no matter how unsteady her feet were, or how raw her lungs felt, or how badly her hand hurt. She slammed into him, making him stagger back again, and reached for the gaps in his armor.

His elbow hit her ribs, driving the air from her. And then he pushed her again, slamming her into a wall so hard that her back spasmed. She fumbled for a gap of skin—anything, any shred of contact—but her vision was swimming. Bridge drew back a fist, and Keira knew there was nothing she could do to stop it.

Suddenly an arm wrapped around Bridge's neck. It yanked him back, and some of the pressure disappeared from Keira's chest. More hands appeared, this time around the helmet's edges. Knuckles bulged white, and the helmet slid off as Bridge's face was uncovered.

He was grizzled. Dark circles ringed his eyes. Gray stubble covered old scars. His lips were pulled back to show very square teeth, bared in a ferocious snarl.

"Now, quick!" Mason yelled, and Keira realized the arm around Bridge's neck belonged to him, as he fought to pull the mercenaries' leader away from her.

She thrust out her hand. No time for subtleties: she slammed her entire palm into the center of his face. He swung his fist toward her just as she pulled.

Hot energy poured back into Keira. The fist landed squarely on the side of her cheek. But she'd stolen all of its momentum before it could reach her. The glove grazed across her skin, closer to a caress than a punch. Then Bridge's eyes rolled back into his head. He collapsed, boneless.

They all staggered back. Mason released his hold on Bridge, his hair sticking to the sweat on his face. Dane and Marlene stood next to him, both holding on to the helmet they'd wrestled off Bridge's face.

And there was light again, Keira saw. At some point, she'd stopped needing to use her spectral sight, and she hadn't even realized. Adage stood a few feet back, clutching Mason's phone in both hands, its flashlight on. He held it above his head, using it to light the scene.

"Keira." Mason crossed to her in a few short steps. Shaking hands reached up to hold her but stopped before properly touching her, as though he was afraid she would shatter. "Oh," he whispered, frantic eyes darting over her face, then to her body, then back up. "Oh, Keira."

"Hey," she said. She smiled and tasted the blood leaking over her lower lip. Then she tipped toward him, too unsteady to do anything else.

He caught her, gently pulling her against his chest, and held her so tenderly and desperately that she felt her heart break.

"You'll be okay," he whispered. His hands turned into fists in her clothes as he supported her. "We're going to be okay. Just… just sit a moment. Here. We'll get a chair…"

She wanted to rest. Desperately. Her body was on the edge of breaking, and she knew she'd be taking it past the point of no return if she didn't give it some time.

But time was something they'd never had. Not since they first entered Artec's central office.

Thoughts snapped through her, discordant and strange, but only one floated to the top.

"Harry." She pulled back from Mason. She'd left a smear of blood on his shirt. She'd have to apologize for that later. Keira blinked, trying to see the room through distortion caused by the dust and the darkness and her own blurred eyes.

Dane and Marlene had already crossed to the space where the doors had once been. And they were digging through the rubble.

Keira gasped as she staggered over to join them, Mason and Adage close behind her. She caught sight of Harry's pale arm first. Then a flash of limp, dark hair.

"No, no, no," she whispered. She didn't think she had any strength left to help move crumbling concrete, so she dropped to her knees beside Harry and gripped his arm. The rune on her palm reacted. There was still energy traveling through him. *Thank mercy.*

She began funneling the excess she'd stolen from Bridge back into Harry. The healing runes she'd painted across him were smudged and blurred, but she thought she saw little sparks darting between them as they began to work.

Dane, Marlene, and Mason worked together to lift the largest slab free, revealing Harry. He groaned, his legs pulling up close to his chest, as Mason dropped at his side. "Don't try to move yet, okay?"

"Am I dead?" Harry asked, and his eyes peeled open, bleary.

"No," Mason said, feeling for his pulse with one hand as he searched for injuries to Harry's head with the other. "Not yet."

"Shame," Harry mumbled, and closed his eyes again.

Keira stayed where she was, slowly feeding her energy into him. Adage hovered over them, stoically holding the light, even though his glasses were so covered with dust that she thought he wouldn't be able to see much of anything.

Then, inexplicably, a cheery pop tune began to play.

They all paused, turning to stare at the fallen guards. None of them were moving. The song echoed strangely in the half-collapsed research room. It took Keira a second to recognize it. She fumbled for her mobile.

Zoe had programmed the song into Keira's phone as a custom tune for her number. Only, Zoe almost never called her, preferring to text whenever possible. Keira blinked at the name on her screen, then, feeling as though she'd somehow tripped and fallen into the wrong dimension, pressed the *answer* button. "Zoe?"

"Oh, hey, hi! How's it going?" Zoe's voice was high and tight with stress. "I hope it's good, because stuff's on fire here."

"What…?" Keira blinked, wishing her brain could be a little better at pivoting. "Fire…?"

"Yeah. Stuff's on fire."

Keira thought she could actually hear flames crackling in the background of the call—though it could have been rapid footsteps as well. Zoe was breathless, like she was running. Keira frowned. "The server room's on fire?"

"Sure. And other stuff. All of it. The whole thing's on fire." Zoe took a gasping breath. "They set the whole place on fire."

Keira's heart plunged. They only knew of one way out, and that was the elevator. She switched the phone to speaker so the others could hear.

"I think they wanted to smoke us out," Zoe said, and paused to take a quick, gasping breath. "Or…burn us in? One or the other. But all back there, the offices and reception and everything, that's gone. Fire. All of it."

"Oh." Keira pressed her thumb to her temple, trying to think. If she made a shock wave of energy, would that be enough to push back the fire? Just enough for them to run through? But then, there were no stairs that they'd seen, and the elevator would be consumed, likely broken—

"I'm following the cat," Zoe added. "Kinda banking on the buck wild hope that she knows where she's going and can reconnect us.

Anyway, just wanted to let you know. Fire. On everything. I hope things are better there because they're *not* super great back here."

"A wall fell on me," Harry said from the floor. "It was pretty cool, I guess."

"Love that for you, buddy," Zoe said, and Harry gave a thumbs-up that he wouldn't be able to see. The call disconnected.

"Okay." Keira ground her thumb into her temple, as though extra pressure might make her think better. "Okay, okay, so…"

"There's got to be another exit," Mason said.

Marlene's sallow face was lit up eerily by Adage's light. "I'm not so sure about that. It's part of my job to think about fire safety regulations for the café, so it stuck out to me. There's no visible suppression system. No escape signs. And no hint of emergency exits. I very seriously think the elevator might be the only way out."

"Zoe managed to get in touch with a contractor who was involved in the construction," Mason said, staring at the walls around them, a grim realization drawing over his face. "He said the building was a disaster waiting to happen. This must have been what he meant."

"Because Schaeffer doesn't care about anyone except himself," Keira said, a numb resignation filling her. "Everyone here is disposable to him. And so he started a fire."

"But…" Mason glanced up at her. "Schaeffer would still be inside this bunker, correct?"

She saw what he was leading to. "He is. Which means there *must* be a way out. One that he, if no one else, can reach." Keira glanced from Harry to the others. "Can Harry move?"

"I'm worried about his ribs." Mason's face was pale, and dust left stark marks at the frown lines surrounding his eyes. "I don't know if there are fractures or breaks. He *shouldn't* move. But we don't have an option."

"I'll help," Dane said.

They each took one of Harry's sides and pulled him up. He grimaced as he stood but didn't make any sound. His expression fell back into the familiar, flat planes, though he seemed unsteady as Dane helped support his weight.

"Right." Keira glanced back at the research lab. The five guards lay there, still and silent.

It was pure foolishness to worry about what would happen to them.

But she still couldn't stop herself.

She scooted to the nearest guard. Her right hand ached with the burns and cuts she'd gotten from the gun, so she used her left to unclip the communication device from his belt.

"Five of your men are in the research lab," she said, holding the button to activate the channel. "More in the offices. All alive. If anyone can hear this, you need to get them out while there's still time."

She dropped the device without waiting for an answer. Then she took the jacket Mason offered her, wrapped it around her injured hand, and let him help her up and guide her toward the chasm where the doors had once stood.

The lights in the hallway had been taken out too, leaving it in pitch darkness. Adage held the phone up high, lighting their way as well as he could. Mason helped Keira climb over the rubble, while Dane and Marlene followed behind her with Harry between them.

Together, they stepped back into the hallway. There was no going back. Their only remaining option was forward.

CHAPTER 38

KEIRA MOVED AS QUICKLY as she dared. Every step jarred the aches and pains running through her. Blood left an acrid taste in her mouth. Her hand throbbed with every small movement, and she held it pressed against her shoulder, above her heart, to slow the bleeding.

Mason held her carefully, supporting some of her weight and helping her keep her balance, but even he was breathless. She'd taken his energy. She'd taken from all of them. They were exhausted, but they couldn't stop.

A crossroads appeared ahead. Keira paused at it, trying to see down three identical unlit pathways.

Wait...

Not entirely unlit. A light bobbed along the passage to the left. Footsteps moved toward them, and dread crashed through Keira.

She couldn't survive another confrontation. She might have just enough left in her to buy the others some time, but...

A tail flicked through the light, casting a snakelike shadow, and the dread evaporated. "Zoe!" she called.

"Hey!" Zoe called back, panting. Her sweat-streaked face came into view. The runes bled together, lines of black ink trailing down her cheeks and dripping from her chin. She grimaced as she caught up to them, staring at Keira incredulously. "What happened to your…?" She gestured to Keira's face, her finger sweeping in a circle to encompass it.

"Huh?"

Zoe shook her head. "Don't worry about it. The blood-soaked-ghoul look suits you." She raised her light. "Is Harry back there? You still alive?"

"Apparently," Harry said. He didn't sound enthused about it.

Zoe's mouth scrunched up as she took in their powdery dust coating and strained expressions. "You all look like garbage," she said bluntly. "So, we have a plan?"

"Try to find Schaeffer," Keira said. "And hope he has a secret way out."

Zoe glanced back in the direction she'd come, her mouth working unhappily, and Keira knew they were thinking along the same lines. It wasn't in any way a good plan. But Keira could smell the smoke on Zoe's clothes, and the hallway seemed slightly warmer than it had when they'd arrived.

"Cool," Zoe said, facing forward again, resolute. "So, which way?"

Daisy twisted around Keira's legs, rubbing them happily, then began trotting down a hallway. Keira turned back to her group—exhausted, hurt, afraid—and gave them the fiercest smile she could muster. "This way."

They couldn't move fast. Even with the urgency of a spreading fire on their heels, Harry's condition meant they couldn't handle much more than a steady walk. Mason supported Keira, and she could feel his glances, filled with concern. She kept her face neutral. He didn't need to know how badly she hurt.

Zoe and Adage both used their lights, holding them up to illuminate the cold steel passageways ahead. Daisy led the way, her tail high and her ears alert. She took them around turns and corners and past countless doors without any hesitation. Keira didn't know how she could sense where to go when Keira herself had no knowledge of the bunker's layout, but she didn't want to jinx it by questioning it.

A faint haze began to bleed across the floor. Adage cleared his throat, then cleared it again. Keira could smell it, too—the acrid tang of char and burned plastics. She suspected the solid metal doors separating the different sections might have collapsed.

She didn't want to think about what would have happened to the shopping mall above. She could only pray that Mikhail had evacuated everyone, as she'd made him promise.

The hall ahead ended in a final door. It looked no different from any other door in the space, but Keira felt thick dread rising in her stomach as Daisy came to a halt and sat, staring up at it.

She knew what would be behind the door. Schaeffer's offices.

They'd lost the element of surprise somewhere along the way. She'd have to face Schaeffer with only the very small reserves she had left.

I knew, before going into this, that there might not be anything I could do. I knew, fully, that this might kill me.

I'd just hoped to leave a path for my friends to escape through.

Keira raised the access card and pressed it to the panel. The light flashed red. Of course: Mikhail was high ranking, but he wouldn't have been given access to Schaeffer's space. Schaeffer alone would have that privilege.

She wore Mason's jacket around her injured hand but unwound it then. Her fingers were stained red, and fresh blood welled as the pressure relaxed.

She raised that hand and used it to smear a rune on the door. *Unlock.* The bolts held strong for the first mark, so she repeated it, creating a circle around the card reader. *Unlock. Unlock. Unlock.*

The panel's lights flickered, then went out. Something inside the metal clicked. Keira nudged the door with her foot, and it drifted inward.

The room was dark. Zoe craned forward, extending her phone over Keira's head. The weak, harsh white beam flashed over a solid wood desk and rows of bookcases.

It was a space very reminiscent of Schaeffer's office at Artec's research center. While the employees were treated to sterile metal and impersonal furniture, Schaeffer's space was luxurious. Carpet indented under Keira's feet. Hardback book collections filled the shelves. A laptop, sleek and expensive, lay on the desk's leather surface. Everything was pristine, except, inexplicably, small patches in the ceiling that looked like they'd recently been replastered but not yet painted over.

Keira stepped into the space, hungry eyes scanning its corners. No sign of Schaeffer.

"Oh," Zoe whispered, gaze locking in on the laptop. She shoved her phone into Mason's hands and unhooked her backpack from her shoulder. "Gimme a minute with this."

Keira didn't have time to watch as Zoe opened the laptop's lid. There was another door in the back of the office, this one already open a crack. Keira crossed to it, Mason following closely and providing the light.

The door led to a private living area. It was built like an apartment, with a kitchenette, a bed, and a bathroom. All were just as luxurious as the office space.

She'd seen these areas before, through Daisy's eyes, when they'd gone into the air ducts. Schaeffer had been living here ever since he fled the research tower.

Keira checked in every space a human could hide—inside the closet, in the narrow gap beneath the bed, inside the bathroom. All empty.

Of course he's gone. If Schaeffer had a private escape route, he would have used it the moment he realized Keira had breached Artec's center. Schaeffer was very likely long gone, probably in his car on a highway, too far out of reach for Keira to even think of chasing him.

The sting of failure was painful. After everything—after putting her friends' lives at risk—she had still managed very little more than to wound Artec.

The employees might use the chaos as a way to escape the

company. The fire would likely destroy the bulk of Artec's central location. But it wasn't the end, like she'd needed it to be. Schaeffer was both the head and the heart. As long as he remained out in the world, the monster would never die.

At the same time, that knowledge came with a glimpse of freedom. There *was* a way out. They only needed to find it.

She returned to Schaeffer's main office, where Zoe was hunched over the laptop. She had multiple devices plugged into the laptop's USB drives and was intently watching something on the screen.

Someone had pulled the leather executive chair out and sat Harry in it. He slumped back, limp hair covering half of his face and sticking to his skin, his eyes closed as he took shallow breaths. Dane and Marlene leaned against the desk, arms around each other, looking drained. Adage still held the phone, though he had let it drop to his side. None of them could take much more.

Keira turned to her little cat, who had not yet led her wrong. "Where's the way out?" she asked, but Daisy had lost focus. She stood beneath one of the bookcases, reaching to bat at a bookmark tassel hanging from one of the titles, her tail twitching with each swipe.

They were on their own for this one.

"We need to find the exit," Keira said, speaking to the rest of the group. "Schaeffer probably didn't want anyone else knowing about it, so it's likely concealed. Our best odds are in this room or the living quarters back there. If we can't find it here, we'll go back to the hallways and start opening other doors. I don't think it'll be far. Not if Schaeffer planned to use it in emergencies."

"Heard," Marlene said. She gave Dane a quick squeeze, then pushed off the desk and began feeling along the shelves.

"I need a minute here," Zoe said. "But Dane might have some ideas for where to look. Old family houses like his have a million hidden passages, I'll bet. He'll know all the good hiding places."

Dane grunted, but he didn't disagree. He began stomping on the floors, moving methodically over them. Apparently, if he was put in charge of a secret escape route, he'd conceal it under the carpet.

Mason moved to the back wall, which held multiple display cases with glass covers. Adage joined Marlene at the bookcases.

Keira, trying to cover ground as effectively as possible, peered up at the ceiling. The repaired patches in the plaster seemed significant. But they were too small for a person to fit through—the size of her fist, not much larger—and looked recent. Schaeffer was lax about his employees' safety, but not his own. Any emergency hatch would have been installed when the basement offices were built.

Keira turned away and began opening desk drawers, working by the light washing off the laptop's screen, as she hunted for a concealed switch or button to activate.

Zoe mumbled something at her side, and Keira couldn't help glancing up at her. "Didn't the worm get to install properly in the data room?"

"Oh, no, that took off beautifully. It's probably infecting some employees' home computers right now, and I honestly pity them for it. But this laptop was kept off the main network. It's a security measure. Something Schaeffer apparently is pretty fond of, incidentally. This thing is a beast to crack into. But…if I can just…"

She trailed off. Keira left her to it and focused on clawing stacks of paperwork out of the lower-right drawer and prodding around the base and the back for anything that felt like it might be a cover.

The room was growing noticeably warmer. Trails of smoke had begun to bleed in beneath the door. The others must have sensed the growing urgency too. Their searches were becoming less meticulous, and more desperate. Mason and Adage both left the shelves and disappeared into the apartment space. Only Daisy seemed oblivious; she'd successfully gotten her claw stuck in the bookmark tassel, and kept tugging at it, apparently confused about why she couldn't get free.

Keira couldn't stand watching her. She'd emptied the desk without finding anything, so she left it and jogged over to pry her little cat's claw free.

There was something strange about the title. As Daisy tumbled away, unhooked, the whole row of books shifted. Almost as though the set had been glued together.

Their titles, gold on fabric binding, seemed innocuous: *Aquatic Sciences,* volumes one to twelve. But it went past innocuous. It was generic. And, more than that, nothing Keira had learned about Schaeffer indicated he was even passingly interested in water or the things it held.

She pressed her hands into the tops of the books, leaving streaks of blood on the pristine page edge. And she pulled.

The whole row shifted as one. It moved just a fraction, then froze, as though it had hit a block. Keira pulled harder, and she felt a latch click.

The shelf rattled as it began moving toward Keira on hidden runners. She stepped back, giving it room.

"Clever cat," she whispered to Daisy, who had lost interest in the books and was now meticulously cleaning her posterior.

"A door concealed in a bookcase," Dane said, sounding both incredulous and disappointed. "I would be ashamed to stoop to such a cliché."

The others all left their tasks, except for Zoe, who was wholly absorbed in the laptop, and Harry, who didn't seem to care about anything as long as he was allowed to rest. Mason and Adage returned from the apartment. The group stood around Keira, watching as the bookcase began shifting sideways, revealing a hidden passage.

It was only a few feet deep. At its end was a massive steel door with a small circle of glass set into it at head height.

Keira moved forward first, as Adage stepped up behind her, raising the light. It glared off the glass for a second, turning it into a mirror, and Keira caught a glimpse of herself. Zoe's assessment of *blood-soaked ghoul* wasn't too far off. She'd tasted the blood on her teeth, but more of it had trickled down from her hairline to coat her face. It left her streaked in crimson, the lines blurring into the rapidly smearing runes. It was no wonder Mason had looked worried.

Then Adage adjusted his light, and Keira strained to see through the glass.

It was incredibly thick—at least six inches, she guessed—and distorted her view of the space beyond. She'd been hoping to see stairs or, failing that, a passageway. Anything that indicated the door was the last barrier they'd have to contend with. Instead, she found herself looking into a single room.

It was square, and not large—ten feet in each direction at the most. The walls, floor, and ceiling were concrete. They seemed to be made of one continuous expanse of the material, with no seams or gaps visible.

Some sort of machine stood in the corner, a little larger than a person. Beside it was a shelf with two books, a hand-crank lamp, and multiple small devices Keira couldn't identify. On the floor beneath the shelf were four stacked trays of water bottles, a bucket with a lid, boxes of nonperishable food, and a roll of what looked like bedding material. A chair sat against the back wall.

Together, those items took up most of the small space. Although Keira subconsciously noticed all of them, they weren't what her attention was most focused on.

A man stood in the center of the room, facing Keira, as though he'd been waiting for her. Adage adjusted the light again, and Keira found herself staring through six inches of impenetrable glass at the person she'd gone through hell to find.

Schaeffer.

CHAPTER 39

SCHAEFFER'S EYES GLINTED DIMLY as the light shone across him. Keira caught him recoil as he saw her before he quickly masked his reaction.

Despite everything, she still felt a twinge of satisfaction that the sight of her had gotten a response. The blood-soaked-ghoul look had its upsides.

Then Schaeffer smiled, and every single one of the room's implications sank in.

"What is it?" Adage asked. The opening in the bookcases was too narrow for more than one person to stand in, and the door's window was small. Adage shuffled as he tried to see over Keira's shoulder.

"It's Schaeffer," she said, and heard her voice crack at the end. "He never had an escape route. Instead, he has an escape bunker. A room he can lock himself into for days—maybe even weeks—until he's rescued."

The devices on the shelf would be used to radio for help, to make sure he wasn't forgotten. He had light. Water. Food. He even had books, to while away the time.

"But—" Adage sounded lost. "The fire—"

"He'll be safe inside." Keira swallowed around the lump forming in her throat. The glass was too thick to just be for show. "I'm pretty sure he built this room to withstand anything. The whole building could collapse in an inferno around it, and he'll be sheltered and safe as he waits to be dug out. There's even a machine in the corner to keep the air breathable."

It felt so much more excessive, and so much more elaborate, than having an escape route. But it also made perfect sense. An escape route meant a second way *in*, one that could be discovered by accident at any time. No matter how well it was hidden or how securely it was locked, it introduced a level of vulnerability that Schaeffer wouldn't tolerate.

There had only ever been one entrance to Artec's headquarters. And Schaeffer had positioned his office as far from it as possible, forcing any unwanted entities to battle their way through both the staff and the mercenaries to get to him. That gave him plenty of warning that they were coming. Plenty of time to seal himself away into a cube that was designed to be as impenetrable as money could make it.

Keira glanced back. The tense, drawn faces of her friends were barely visible behind Adage, watching her. Waiting for her next instruction. Waiting for her to lead them out of the situation she'd brought them into.

The smoke trailing in underneath the office door was growing thicker and darker.

Frustration and growing panic snapped through the exhaustion. She raised her bleeding hand. Her numb fingers danced across the metal as she drew the unlocking rune. Again, then again, then again, growing faster and more frantic until her fingertips ached and half of the door was covered in her blood.

The metal stayed unyielding. There was no subtle click, no sign it was working.

The barrier was just too large, she knew. Too difficult. The rune worked on locked doors and locked drawers, but not on two feet of solid concrete. There wasn't even a handle she could tug at.

"I…I…"

They were out of time. She wasn't just smelling the smoke anymore; she felt it, aching in her lungs with every breath. The room was stiflingly hot.

She turned back to her friends. Their expectancy was fading into dread and resignation as understanding sunk in.

There was no way out.

If they were lucky, the fire would use up all the oxygen and suffocate them before the flames reached their bodies.

And Schaeffer would get to watch every second of it.

She never should have let them come with her. They were good people. They'd wanted to help her. To help their town. This price was too high.

"Got it!" Zoe yelled.

The group jostled as Zoe aggressively shoved through them,

using her elbows to make room. She carried Schaeffer's laptop, facing outward and held above her head like a prize. In the dim passage, the screen felt painfully bright.

"I'm a genius," Zoe announced, sounding immeasurably pleased. "You can shower me with praise later, if you like. Right now, all you need to know is I cracked some of the nastiest encryptions I've ever seen. And I've gained access to Schaeffer's email account."

There was a second of resounding silence. Keira tried for a feeble smile. "Does his email account have a magic button that somehow activates a secret fire suppression system we didn't know this building had?"

"Save the snark for a time when we're not about to burn to death," Zoe said, flashing Keira a grin to show that she was still friendly. "No. But the email account *does* let me send an official message to every Artec employee, ostensibly from their own boss. It's certified and everything. They're going to take it seriously."

"Um." Keira blinked rapidly, trying not to notice the way the smoke was stinging her eyes. "I know you said no snark, but…"

"Your big problem—the problem you couldn't figure out how to solve—was getting all the research destroyed. Remember? Because, even if you eliminated Schaeffer, someone else at some point in the future might pick up where he left off. And you'd have no way of stopping it. We can get rid of the digital files, but the physical papers are still out there."

"Right," Keira said, still not following.

"Well. People in this company know better than to ignore an

order from Schaeffer. He's made sure of that." Zoe adjusted her hold on the laptop, squeezing in next to Keira, even though there really wasn't any room. "You think he can hear me?"

Keira glanced at the window. Schaeffer had drifted closer to the glass. His arms were folded over his chest, his earlier smile vanished into a cold, wary expression.

"Yep," she said. The door would be too thick to hear through, but she suspected Schaeffer had an audio transmitter hidden somewhere. He'd want to stay abreast of what was happening in his office while he was in the bunker.

Zoe held the laptop up so it could be seen from the window. Its screen held an email draft. The cursor hovered ominously over the *send* button.

"*Urgent: For Immediate Action*," Zoe said, reciting the message, since the glass was inches thick and might blur the words. "*We have been exposed. Destroy all files associated with Artec immediately. I repeat: all papers, current and archival. Do not leave anything that could be found in an upcoming investigation. Consequences for failure to comply will be severe. You have one hour.*"

Zoe lowered the laptop so Schaeffer could see her face over the top of it. Her eyes were sharp and bright and frighteningly intense. "You're going to open this door," she said to Schaeffer. "If you do, we'll make you a deal. You won't be harmed in any way. We'll give you your laptop, and you can delete this email without it being sent. Your bunker is big enough for all of us to wait inside for rescue. And once rescue happens, we'll part ways, with no one being hurt."

Keira felt an immense rush of pride for Zoe. It was a desperate plan. She didn't think Schaeffer would go for it. But, at the same time, it was the smartest thing any of them could have thought of.

"I repeat," Zoe said, raising her voice. "It's a trade. Our lives in exchange for your research being left intact. I know you value it above anything else. It's taken the better part of your life to build. It's the difference between you having a legacy that will never be forgotten and you fading into obscurity. If you don't open the door, I'll hit *send*, and all that history will be wiped away within the hour."

Schaeffer's face twisted into something ugly and angry. He reached inside his jacket pocket.

Shock hit Keira. He might actually do it.

Maybe Zoe's instincts had been right. Mikhail had noted that Schaeffer cared about his legacy above anything else. It was why he'd guarded Artec's secrets so closely—not from fear of ridicule or legal repercussions. But because he didn't want any competitors taking his hard-won discoveries.

He'd been prepared to commit atrocities to guard his company. He'd been prepared to kill…and kill again.

Maybe he would also be prepared to do the opposite. Maybe he would show mercy, at the threat of losing it all.

"You have our word you won't be harmed," Zoe said as Schaeffer drew a small device out of his pocket. "And that's not just an empty promise. If there's a dead body in that box when it's pried open, the rest of us would spend our lives in jail. So. You know. We have an incentive to be nice."

Schaeffer pressed something on his device. Keira thought she heard a very quiet but very ominous click coming from somewhere behind them.

Behind, not ahead. It wasn't the click of the door opening. It was...

Her mind flashed back to when they'd first entered the room. She'd noticed small patch jobs in the ceiling. Each one was no larger than a fist. The work had looked recent.

There are rumors he's installed a doomsday device, whatever that means, Mikhail had said.

Explosives.

In anticipation of a worst-case scenario, he'd installed explosives throughout the building to demolish it and everything inside.

And he'd just activated them.

CHAPTER 40

"RUN!" KEIRA YELLED.

She threw her arms out, shoving into the group behind her, forcing them toward the office. They stumbled and yelled as she drove them back. Zoe lost her grip on the laptop, and it tumbled to the floor.

Booming sounds echoed through the walls. Like immense fireworks. Like rolling thunder. Like an apocalypse, bearing down on them. Wave upon wave of it, growing louder as it drew nearer, as Artec's entire offices were brought down.

Harry was still slumped in the office chair, elbows on the armrests. He lifted his head as Keira shoved the group into him.

Daisy frisked out from beneath the desk and vanished into Keira. The nearing explosions were deafening.

"Hands on me," she screamed.

Mason and Zoe responded quickest, pressing their palms into

Keira's exposed skin. The others fumbled to reach her. Hands on her arms. Her neck. Mason's on her cheek, a final tender caress.

Daisy existed inside Keira, a little spark of extra energy. Keira hadn't yet drawn from Zoe, who still had a full charge. The others were close to empty, but there was some there. Some she could take, if she no longer feared pushing it too far. If their situation was so dire that she had no choice except to race to the cliff's edge and try to stop herself just before tipping over.

That was what she did.

She pulled everything she could from them, and everything she could find left in herself. As the waves of detonations reached the offices, as the ceiling above them exploded in a wall of fire, as an avalanche of concrete came down toward them, Keira sent all that energy out as a shock wave, slamming it into the crumbling structure.

————

Everything was pain. Everything was darkness and sparking, sizzling lights in the back of her eyes. Every inhale choked her.

For a while, that was all there was.

Then hands pulled on her. Small tugs, urging her to move.

She couldn't remember where she was. She couldn't remember why she couldn't see, or why she hurt, or why she could barely move.

But…there had been something she needed to do. Something that mattered more than anything else.

The others. She couldn't remember their names. But they were important, and she'd needed to make sure they were safe. Were they?

What had she done to them?

The hands pulled again, and a voice spoke. "Move. You have to move. Come on. Please."

Mason. His name rushed back to her, and with it came the memory of his face.

Yes. He was one of them. One of the ones worth fighting for.

Even breathing drained more from her than she could afford, but she rolled toward the hands. With their coaxing, she began to crawl.

Upward. Every inch had to be fought for. The ground wasn't steady. The air was choking her.

And then other voices joined Mason's. Voices she didn't recognize. Hands caught under her arms, hauling her up. Her feet stumbled over rubble.

She faded out again.

———

Keira couldn't tell how long it took her to wake. But when she finally opened her eyes, it was night.

She was alive. Somehow.

And she was out of Artec's basement.

Her throat and mouth were parched. Her head throbbed. But it no longer hurt to breathe. Her hand twitched, but it couldn't flex far; it had been swaddled in thick bandages.

She was somewhere quiet and warm. Some very distant light—a

streetlamp?—came through a window. It ghosted over the edges of forms she couldn't quite make out.

A hand rested on her shoulder. It only took her a second to remember the name this time. *Mason.* She was lying with her head on his lap. When she tried to move her legs to ease the aches, her toes hit something solid.

The van's door. She was back in the van.

"Hey," Mason said, his voice raspy and rough around the edges. He squeezed her shoulder lightly. "There you are. Can you sit up? We have water."

Two of the nearest forms shifted, and the streetlamp's light revealed them in slivers. Dane and Marlene.

Still alive.

A miracle.

"Where—" Keira pushed herself to sit up. It was awkward, trying to find things to lean against when she couldn't see her surroundings. Her tongue didn't want to form sounds properly.

"Hey-o," Zoe called. The enthusiastic greeting didn't match the utterly bone-tired tone she gave it in.

Zoe's voice was followed by a softer, "Hello, child. We were worried." Adage. He and Zoe sat in the van's front seats. Keira, Mason, Dane, and Marlene were slumped against the walls in the back storage area. Which left…

"Harry," she croaked. "Where's—"

"He's fine. Don't panic." Mason still managed to add a smile to his voice. He pressed a cold bottle into Keira's hand. "Here, drink. I have painkillers, too, though we're close to running out."

348

As she raised the bottle and drank desperately, someone turned on the van's lights. They all groaned and flinched against the sudden brightness.

"Sorry, sorry," Zoe said, and turned it off again. "Just thought it might be nice to see again. Guess the painkillers aren't helping anyone else's headaches either."

"The switch near the indicator," Marlene mumbled, leaning back against the wall. "It's a dimmer light."

There was a second's pause, then a soft golden glow came on above them. That was better. Keira finally got a clear look at her companions.

They were all ashen. Soot and streaks of dirt gave both their clothes and skin a muted gray tinge. They were barely recognizable underneath it. The only source of color came from spots of blood on their clothes. They looked drained, like hollow memories of themselves.

She'd taken every scrap of energy she could without killing them. And she'd very much toed the line on that last part too.

"I'm so sorry." Speaking hurt, but she needed to say it. "I had to take more energy than I should have. I never... It wasn't supposed to..."

It wasn't supposed to get that bad.

But she'd known it might. She'd known better than any of the others could have.

Marlene flicked her hand, a weary batting away of the apology. "You broke us out of a collapsing building. We can deal with this."

"And you did say the energy comes back," Adage added from the front seat.

"Yes. Slowly." Keira grimaced, then swallowed more water. Her throat was still raw. "It might be a few weeks before any of us are fully back to our normal levels."

"Well." Dane sighed. He had his eyes closed as he leaned back against the wall, Marlene against his shoulder. "A few weeks is nothing."

This was probably very similar to how he'd felt during the years his ancestors had been feeding from him, Keira realized.

"What happened?" she asked. She remembered everything up to the detonation, but after that was a blur.

"We've been trying to piece that together. Everything was chaos, so the details are foggy." Zoe shuffled around in the driver's seat and slung her arm over its back so she could face them. Streaked blood ran down one side of her face, though it looked dry. "Best that we can tell, the explosions took down not just Artec's base, but most of the shopping mall over it, as well. We ended up in… well, it wasn't exactly a crater…"

"A pocket?" Mason volunteered. He was close to Keira. Close enough that she could feel his warmth. "We could see daylight, but it was a long way above us. We tried to climb out, but it was unstable, and none of us had much strength to move. The first responders arrived quickly—we could hear the sirens—but it took them nearly half an hour to find us."

"They hauled us out," Zoe continued. "There were a couple times when we thought the rubble was going to collapse again and crush us all, but they got us up."

Mason nodded. "The shopping mall was largely gone. Parts of it had collapsed into the ground, and what was left was on fire."

"More and more firefighters and rescue workers were arriving," Zoe said. "And they were searching everywhere, probably because it was a mall in the middle of the day, and they must have expected the fatalities would be in the hundreds."

"In the confusion, we slipped away," Marlene said. "We mostly had to drag you. Harry, too. But we got to the van, and when we thought no one was looking, drove out. I don't know if that was the *right* choice, but we figured it would be risky to have our names connected to the mall's collapse."

Keira nodded. In the immediate aftermath, they would probably be treated like victims, just casual shoppers who were caught up in the disaster. But if an investigation was ever launched…

"And Harry?" she prompted. His absence was hanging over her.

"Cheltenham Hospital," Zoe said. "He complained, but Mason said he needed scans."

"We told them he got hurt in a home renovation job gone wrong," Marlene added. "I don't think they believed us. But he backed up our story, and it's what we're sticking with."

"He might need to be in for a couple of days," Mason said. "None of us were family, so we weren't allowed to stay. But he'll text us once they know more."

Zoe pulled a face. "His mother's going to kill us."

"You should have probably been seen by someone there too," Mason said to Keira. His eyes glanced from her bandaged hand to her face. "But I couldn't ask you, since you were unconscious, so I used the chaos to sneak you out instead. You've always been clear about your stance on hospitals."

"Thanks. That was the right call."

She was starting to feel more like herself again—in tiny, fractional ways. She was still thirsty, but she knew she'd be sick if she drank any more, so she capped the bottle and turned it over in her hands instead.

Harry was in the hospital. She could see scrapes across Mason's chin and jawline. Marlene had bandages around her forearm, and hints of red bled through.

But they were all alive.

And that was already more than she could have hoped for.

There was only one member of their party who wasn't accounted for. Daisy. Keira had taken the little cat's energy, as well.

She felt for Daisy's presence. It took a second, but she found her, buried deep inside. In Keira's mind's eye, Daisy was curled up somewhere dark and warm, sleeping deeply. She didn't wake, not even when Keira called to her, but Keira couldn't blame her. She'd be back, Keira thought. She just needed time.

"What happened with Schaeffer?" Keira asked.

Zoe shrugged. "He's still down there. We didn't tell any of the rescuers about him. He can dig his own way out, the horrible, miserly lump that he is."

"I'm sorry," Keira said. "That email was a brilliant idea. It might have even worked if he hadn't installed the explosives. He just saw those as a more efficient way to solve the threat. It was a good play, though."

"I'm honestly kind of relieved he didn't take us up on it," Zoe said. "Can you imagine being trapped in a box with that guy for even just one day?"

"Ugh," Marlene muttered.

"We're told to show forgiveness wherever possible," Adage said gently. "But I simply can't. Not today."

Keira chuckled with them, then felt her smile falter.

"What is it?" Mason asked. He was watching her like a hawk.

She made herself smile for him. "Sorry. I'll get over it. Just…that email. The one telling the employees to destroy everything. That might have been enough; it could have wiped out most, if not all, of Artec's physical research. And I knocked the laptop out of Zoe's hands before she could send it. That was our biggest breakthrough, and it's gone."

None of the others seemed as bothered as she felt, though. In fact, as she glanced about the van, they were all smiling at her.

"Check your phone," Mason suggested.

She fumbled in her pockets to pull the mobile free. It held a single message. From Mikhail.

How did you pull that off?

Following that was a photo. It was blurry and taken from a distance, and Keira had to enlarge it to figure out what she was looking at. When she did, her breath caught.

The photo was of Artec's research tower. The one hidden behind an abandoned development, hours away. One of Mikhail's contacts inside the company must have sent it to him.

It showed the tower burning.

"You're working with a professional here," Zoe said. She

flicked her short hair, then grimaced, apparently having sparked her headache again. Her wicked grin only grew wider, though. "There was no way I was going to play games with an email that important. The version I showed to Schaeffer was a copy-paste job. I'd already sent the original two minutes before. *And* confirmed company-wide delivery. Schaeffer thought he had a chance to save Artec, but there was no way I was ever going to let that happen."

"Zoe." Keira gaped at her friend. "You really—"

"You're allowed to call me a genius now, if you like."

"Genius. Genius, genius, genius."

Zoe beamed, pleased. "Thanks. I have my moments. If you want another totally genius idea, how about this? There's a place that serves pancakes, and it says it never closes, and it's only ten minutes away."

Keira hadn't realized how ravenous she was until that moment. That was probably a side effect of the lost energy: her body was scrambling for whatever fuel it could get.

"We're kind of a mess," she hedged, glancing down at her own clothes, which were grimy with cement and splatters of dried blood.

"It's a pancake place that stays open twenty-four hours," Zoe said. "And it's currently two in the morning. Have you seen the kinds of clientele diners get at two in the morning? We're fine. Probably won't even be the weirdest thing they've seen this week."

"I could go for some pancakes," Adage said.

"With stacks of butter," Marlene, half asleep, mumbled.

Dane and Mason both nodded at that thought, and Keira turned back to Zoe.

"Yes, you continue to be a genius. Let's go."

———————

The server blinked at them a few times as they walked through the door but handed them menus and showed them to a corner booth without missing a beat.

For the next hour, they focused on working their way through plate after plate of pancakes. They barely even spoke, except for a few mumbled sounds of appreciation as fresh food arrived. They were all too tired to do much else.

But they were happy. Keira felt it. Despite the grime, despite the dust, despite the exhaustion and the long drive home still ahead of them, everyone radiated a quiet satisfaction.

Artec's base of operations was gone. Its research tower was in cinders. Schaeffer was trapped, and while he would almost certainly be dug out within a day or two, for at least that night, he no longer felt like a threat.

Sometime around three in the morning, Zoe borrowed Mason's phone and began picking through news articles.

Two bodies had been recovered from the mall's ruin. Rescue workers predicted they would find more.

Keira's mouth turned sour, even though the pancake inside was painfully sweet. "Does it say who?"

"No, nothing detailed yet." Zoe put her phone aside. "I've

nudged some contacts; we'll see if they can get anything more. My guess would be they're mercenaries from Artec's level…not customers from the mall, though."

"The fire alarm sounded before the real fire was lit," Mason added. "There should have been plenty of opportunity for shoppers and store staff to escape."

She hoped they were right. The deaths were going to live on her conscience no matter what. Even if they were the mercenaries. But innocent mall-goers? That would be so much worse.

Sometime around four, Adage fell asleep in the corner of the booth, his face pressed to the window's glass and his snores whistling. They'd mostly given up on eating by then, though none of them felt ready to return to the van.

At four-thirty, Mason's phone pinged. He smiled when he read the message and turned it around for Keira to see.

"*Hospital sucks,*" she read out loud. "*Nurses won't let me play my music. Got a stupid cast and now Mum's taking me home. Would rather have been left in rubble. Regretfully, Harry.*"

"A cast?" Marlene asked. "On his ribs?"

"Wrist," Mason clarified. "I noticed he was holding it carefully. He just never said out loud that it was hurting him."

"Not Harry's style." Zoe shrugged. Her hair was a mess of coils and spikes and flattened portions, all tinged gray. In a weird way, it suited her. "He complains, but only about things that aren't important. Any genuine suffering is relished."

Adage began to slip from his place against the wall, jolting awake with a grunt.

Keira reached across the table and patted his shoulder reassuringly. "Sounds like it might be time for us to go home too."

———

Dawn ghosted along the horizon when Marlene and Dane dropped Keira, Mason, Zoe, and Adage off at the parsonage. They waved goodbye to the pastor as he shuffled through his door, then Keira reached for Mason's hand and found his was already outstretched, already waiting for her.

Even without discussing it, they'd known they didn't want to be alone that night. The three of them moved slowly as they made their way toward the cottage. Flickers of movement shimmered through the mist. With her energy so low, Keira found it harder to see the ghosts. Instead of fully formed beings, they were hazy. Like a blur of movement in the back of an old photo. They watched her, though. Some even walked alongside the group as they passed through the cemetery.

Keira's cottage door hung open. The mercenaries had torn through it. Her clothes had been pulled out of the wardrobe and left in piles on the floor. The mattress lay askew, the blankets scattered. Even the kitchen cupboards were open, and the plates had been swiped out, many of them shattered on the floor.

Keira just sighed. "I'll fix this in the morning."

Despite the chaos they'd left, she doubted they would be back. Not with their leader missing and Schaeffer locked away. For the first time, she felt like she could rest without keeping one eye on the windows.

The three of them shook out the blankets, making sure there were no pieces of broken tableware inside, and then they collapsed together on the rug in front of the empty fireplace.

Keira was asleep as soon as she closed her eyes.

CHAPTER 41

THE CAFÉ WAS PACKED.

It was busy on a good day and, somehow, became busier on a bad day. Everyone wanted to talk. Everyone wanted updates on their neighbors and friends. And through unspoken but universal agreement, the café was where that happened.

Keira, Zoe, and Mason were lucky to get a narrow table near the back. It was a squeeze, but it put them in a sheltered corner where they could watch the rest of the town flow in and out. The door rarely stayed closed for more than a minute at a time.

Three days had passed since they'd torn through Artec's base. Three days since the mercenaries had swarmed the town. It dominated the chatter around them, but it was hardly the only pressing news.

Jensen had been discovered deceased in The Home, lying in a pool of his own blood in the foyer. And Gavin Kelsey had been identified—dead, miles away from where he was last seen, burned up at a power station.

For a town as quiet as Blighty, just one of those topics would have been talked about for years on end. But all three of them had collided in the one week, and it seemed to be more than most people could handle.

They'd barely reached their seats when two women shuffled up to them. They ignored both Keira and Mason and zeroed in on Zoe.

"Hi there, Zoe," the first woman said. "I'm glad we caught you. We wanted to see if you knew what was happening."

"You and everyone else in this town," Zoe said, her expression falling.

"Exactly," the other woman added, as though Zoe hadn't spoken. "I know you're all into that government conspiracy stuff. And we thought, well, those people who came through our town seemed like they might be part of some secret operation or something. And then Gavin died, and it feels way too much to be a coincidence. And I know I always used to laugh at you for believing in this stuff before, but it's gotten real now, and I thought, if anyone's going to know what's going on, it's going to be Zoe."

Zoe stared up at them, her lips drawn into a tight, unhappy line, and then she sighed. "Nope. It was just what the police guy said. Burglars were casing the town. We probably scared them off, though, so I bet it's going to be fine now."

The two friends shared a confused glance.

"But—" the first one started. "What about Gavin—"

"Absolutely nothing weird about it." Zoe's expression remained dead. "Just an awful coincidence. Trust me, I dug into it, and I found nothing. You can relax."

"Huh." The friends shared another look, then, without saying goodbye, left.

"This is agony," Zoe whispered, and Keira gave her a sympathetic smile.

For once in her life, people were coming to Zoe about conspiracy-related news. And, even worse, Zoe knew the full extent of what had really happened.

And she couldn't tell anyone.

It was probably the biggest sacrifice she'd ever made for Keira, greater even than risking her life in the mall.

"Here," Marlene said, appearing at their side. She carried their three drinks, as well as a plate of muffins they hadn't ordered, and unloaded them all onto the table.

"I didn't realize you'd be back at work already," Keira said, leaning toward Marlene and keeping her voice down. "Are you doing okay?"

"About as okay as I ever am," Marlene said, a crooked smile appearing at the corner of her lips for just a fraction of a second. Dark circles hung around her heavy eyes and her skin seemed paler than ever, but her movements had lost none of their sharp efficiency. "We're too busy for any of the staff to take time off. It is what it is."

Someone called to her from near the counter, and she vanished back into the crowd before Keira could say anything else.

Three days wasn't much time to recover from their energy losses—or other injuries. Harry was back home, his arm in a cast, and was being doted on by his mother. He texted them occasionally. Apparently, Polly Kennard claimed that she would "never forgive them" for what they'd let happen, which he said meant she'd frown at them sternly for a few days, and then everything would be fine again.

Keira herself had spent most of the first two days just sleeping. Mason would occasionally wake her to make sure she ate and drank, but for the first day, especially, she'd felt like her body was peeling apart at the seams.

Repeatedly drawing energy and then forcing it back out again so many times within one afternoon had done damage. Clumps of hair were falling out. Her gums bled. Headaches had become a constant companion.

But, she thought, those symptoms were slowly starting to recede. The nausea was nearly gone. Her heart was no longer skipping beats. She'd have to be careful—there was no way she could survive a repeat of that day—but as long as she didn't use any energy for a while, she hoped she would be all right.

Two days of solid sleep had been a luxury. But there was still work to be done.

"So, updates." Zoe pulled out a binder that didn't at all fit on their small table. Keira and Mason pulled their drinks to safety as Zoe slammed the folder down and flipped through its pages. "Let's start with the big one. Schaeffer's out."

Keira's throat caught. She'd known he wouldn't be trapped in his bunker forever, but it still wasn't news she was ready to hear.

"Apparently, they got him out yesterday," Zoe said. "But there's a big clampdown on information leaks while the authorities investigate what went on, so it was kept quiet. He's currently being kept detained while the police work out whether there are any charges to lay."

"Detained is good," Mason said. "If he isn't able to contact anyone else from Artec, it will be harder for him to maintain control."

"Funny you should say that," Zoe said. "Because we also have some updates there."

Keira craned forward. She'd been reading Zoe's messages in the brief patches she'd been awake the previous two days, but there had been shockingly little news.

The media had latched on to the shopping mall collapse, and it made headlines across the country. That was quickly tapering off, though. With so few shoppers present on the day, there were almost no eyewitnesses to interview, and the police weren't revealing much. The news channels could only repeat the same line over and over: *The investigation is ongoing.*

Four bodies had been found in the rubble. All mercenaries, as far as they could tell. Keira tried not to think too hard about which of the armored figures they might belong to or whether there were more still buried in the mall's ruins.

There had been no news reports at all about the fire at Artec's research institute. It had been too far from any habitation, and so completely forgotten that no one seemed to have noticed it went up in flames.

Other than that, they'd lived the last three days in a state of suspended animation, waiting. For news about Artec. About Schaeffer. About any of it.

"The fact that Schaeffer is being held is a good sign," Zoe said. "The police aren't being dumb about this. First, the shopping mall catches fire; then it explodes; then a man is found in a perfectly preserved survival box in the rubble. They're drawing a link between him and the disaster."

"That's good," Mason noted. "The more eyes are on him, the harder it will be to do anything that might put Keira in danger."

"Or to stitch the ruins of his company back together," Zoe said. "You both remember Fish Face, right? My friend from the forum who was obsessed with the abandoned amusement park and what was being hidden in it?"

"Oh, yeah." Fish Face would live in Keira's mind for the rest of her life, she suspected.

"He sent me photos." Zoe pulled some printouts from the folder and slid them to her friends.

Images of char and ruin filled the pages. Keira leafed through them slowly, absorbing every detail. She saw a burned-out filing cabinet, so twisted that it was barely recognizable. Piles of bricks, coated in scorch marks. A field covered in gray ash, thick enough that it could have been snow.

"He's pretty hyped about this, to be honest," Zoe said. "There's no one there. Absolutely no one. No guards, no employees. Even the fence around it has collapsed. For the first time ever, he's been able to get up close to the tower. What's left of it, anyway."

She slid a final photo over. It was a shot taken from a distance, showing what remained of Artec's research base.

There was nothing but a pile of rubble, scattered over the barren field.

"We told them to destroy the research," Zoe said. "But they didn't stop there. They burned the whole thing to the ground."

"Part of it would be fear of Schaeffer," Keira guessed, scrutinizing the photos. "Your email threatened *consequences* for any failure to obey, and the staff well knew what sort of consequences Schaeffer meted out. But…I don't think that's all."

The tower's blaze had been so furious, so all-consuming, it had come close to erasing the structure entirely. In a strange way, the destruction felt almost gleeful.

"They saw it as their escape," Mason said, finishing Keira's thought. "They saw a way out, and they ran with it."

The sense of relief was immense. At least as far as the tower was concerned, there would be no evidence left that could be picked up by an unrelated party in the future. Nothing that could spark a resurgence of the Reyes Protocol. Over time, nature would creep into the ashen ruins, devouring them. Erasing them from memory. As though they had never been there in the first place.

It wasn't the end. Not by a long stretch. But the tower had been one of the most dangerous, and one of the most pressing, risks of Artec's data leaking.

Artec's base was permanently collapsed, cordoned off with police tape. Schaeffer, at least for the immediate future, couldn't reach Keira.

That left only a handful of loose threads. Specifically, the staff. The high-ranking ones who had been involved in the research. The ones who may have burned their physical papers but who likely stored the same data and calculations in their minds.

"I think we should schedule a meeting with Mikhail," Keira said.

A young man shuffled over to the table, eyes fixed expectantly on Zoe. "Hey, excuse me. You're that girl who's always trying to talk about government psy-ops. Do you think they might have been behind that raid the other night—"

"It was Bigfoot," she said, slamming the binder closed.

The man frowned. "Huh?"

"Or vampires. Yeah…totally, vampires moved into town. You should eat more garlic. Or whatever. It doesn't matter."

"Ugh." The man flicked a hand, dismissing her, and merged back into the crowd.

Zoe sighed dramatically, giving Keira a pained look. "I am never going to emotionally recover from this."

"Sorry," Keira said, reaching over to give her a one-armed hug. "The town might not ever believe you, but you're still a genius to me."

"Okay. That does actually help," Zoe said, and even though she was trying not to smile, some of it crept in. "Let's get that meeting with Mikhail, then."

CHAPTER 42

MIKHAIL WAS ALREADY WAITING for them when they arrived. It was a chilly day, with flecks of spitting rain, and he wore a coat high around his chin. He must have been sitting there awhile; his curling blond hair looked damp. He leaped up from the bench as they stepped out of their car.

That morning marked a week since the events at the mall. They'd asked Mikhail to meet them at the same park he'd nominated for their first introduction. It was an hour from Blighty, but Keira was grateful to be away from the town.

Gavin Kelsey's body had been released by the coroner. His funeral was set for that morning.

Keira had wanted to be respectful, for the family's sake even more than Gavin's. And she suspected her presence would put Dr. Kelsey on edge. He deserved to be able to say goodbye to his son in peace.

Even if her alternative was spending the morning at a largely empty quasi-park off the side of a highway.

She was glad to see Mikhail. She'd sent him messages over the previous days, testing the waters, but he hadn't replied to any except the meeting invitation. He stood stiffly, his arms wrapped around his chest to ward off the cold, as they approached. His eyes darted between her, Zoe, and Mason, as though he didn't quite know where to look.

"Hey," Keira called as they drew near. "Thanks for coming out today."

"Of course." His smile was quick and tense. "Are we okay here, or were you going to make me follow you to a crumbling church again?"

"The Murder Lair is off the table today," Zoe said, slinging her legs over the bench seat so she could sit. "It's a loss for your immune system, honestly."

Keira took a spot at Zoe's side, with Mason next to her. After a second, Mikhail sat opposite, then folded his hands on the table, fidgeting.

"Is this…?" He glanced from Keira to her companions and back again. "I did everything you asked. Back at the shopping mall. I texted the team and I pulled the fire alarm and I chased people out. I did it all. Are you…? Am I in trouble?"

It took Keira a second to catch what he was asking. All of his behavior—the unanswered texts, the nervous fidgeting—made sense.

He was afraid.

She wanted to laugh. She was wearing her Santa Claus sweater under her jacket. On the drive to the meeting, she and Zoe had had a very loud, very enthusiastic contest to see who could count the most cows off the side of the road. She felt like she had to be one of the least intimidating people on earth.

And yet...

Mikhail had seen photos of the research tower burning. He'd watched the shopping mall collapse.

And now Keira, someone who had been inside that explosion, someone who should by all rights be dead five times over, was sitting opposite him.

His estimation of her had started high, when Schaeffer painted her as a terrifying, merciless monster. It had dropped substantially when he'd actually met her. But it was back up again, back to its original levels, and he was genuinely, thoroughly afraid of what she was capable of.

Keira felt bad for him. But, at the same time, it was going to help.

"You're not in danger," Keira said. She folded her arms on the table and leaned on them. "You did everything right. Thank you for that."

"Okay." A nervous smile fluttered up again, and this time it didn't immediately vanish. His posture relaxed a fraction. He really must have been fearing that Keira had summoned him there to kill him. "Good."

"I wanted to get a read of the Artec situation from someone who was involved in it," Keira explained. "What parts are still functional? What teams are still together?"

"Well…" He frowned. "Very little beyond the power plants. You know Schaeffer's being held in custody, right?"

Keira nodded. She knew the police had gotten a court extension on the length of time they could detain him. It was due to run out soon, and she didn't know what would happen then, but she'd deal with it as it came.

"Right. Without Schaeffer, and without the mercenaries looming over us, most of my colleagues have just…vanished. We have no offices to meet at. No projects due to deliver. The power plants are still operating with a skeleton staff, but I'm hearing rumors that they might be shut down if the admin side of the company can't get back online in the near future. As far as the high-level research teams are considered, though, they're seizing this opportunity. Some are hiding. Others have plane tickets booked to get out of the country entirely."

"So there's no work being done on the Reyes Protocol or any similar projects?" Keira pressed.

Mikhail shook his head. "As you saw, our major departments are gone. Low-level staff—staff without any access to the research or even knowledge of what was happening—are still working at the cemeteries and power plants, but right now, those are the only parts of Artec that are still extant."

Keira wasn't ready to call it a victory yet, but some of the heavy weight she'd been carrying in her chest was growing lighter. "And what about the research? Can you think of any colleagues who might have held on to papers or documents? Anyone who might have been hoarding a stash of it in their homes?"

Mikhail gave an uncertain kind of shrug. "It's…possible? But it would have been difficult. Schaeffer was strict about potential leaks, and we were often searched when leaving at the end of a shift. Employees would have been taking a major gamble in smuggling papers out of the office. On the digital side, my computer is destroyed. As is everyone else's who I've spoken to."

Zoe's smile was so wide it stretched her whole face. The worm she'd introduced into Artec's system had been a monumental success. Or a monumental disaster, depending on who you spoke to. It had not only passed through Artec's servers, but it had broken containment and spread outside the company. The news had given up on talking about the collapsed mall; instead, stories about *the worm that threatens to destroy the internet* were making headlines nightly.

Zoe had promised it probably, definitely, almost certainly wouldn't get that dire. But the worm had already chewed through countless personal computers and had taken at least one major bank offline for a few days.

"Thank you, Mikhail," Keira said. She took a deep breath. "I'm going to ask one final thing from you."

He narrowed his eyes a fraction, uncertain. "Yes?"

This was where the unintentional intimidation would help her. "I have a message for your colleagues. It's for every one of them who ranked highly enough to know about the shades and about the Reyes Protocol. As long as they leave Artec and everything they did there in the past, they'll be allowed to live out the rest of their lives. But if any of them starts picking at this scab again—if any of them begin experimenting on their own time or try to pass pieces of their research to other companies—I will come for them."

Keira leaned forward. Mikhail's eyes widened a fraction as he pulled back, trying to maintain the gap between them. Keira's voice came out low and dangerous and icy cold.

"You've seen what I'm capable of. And you've seen how important this is to me. If they ever, *ever* touch Artec's work again, I will find them. And I will hold them accountable for not just what they did, but for every single one of Artec's sins. I showed them mercy before, but I will not show it again. Do you hear me?"

"Yes." His voice was a faint whistle. He didn't even blink. "Yes, I hear you."

Keira sat back. Her smile returned. "Okay. Pass that on. Make sure they understand it, and make sure they know how serious I am. If you do that, I'll call us even. The rest of your life will belong to you, however you want to spend it. But if I learn that the research is starting to spread—and don't worry, the ghosts can sense it, and they'll be able to warn me if that's happening—then I will hold you accountable for it too."

His throat bobbed as he swallowed. "Understood."

"Thanks, Mikhail." Keira stood from the table. "You did right in the shopping mall, and I know you'll do right here again. You're a good person at your core."

She waved as she and her friends walked back to the car. Mikhail gave a very small, very shaky wave in return. He stayed sitting, his hair catching more flecks of rain, even after Keira and her companions had gotten inside and fastened their seat belts.

"Nicely done," Mason said as he turned on the engine.

"Thanks. I am so unbelievably sweaty right now." Keira flashed him a tense smile. It wasn't in her nature to threaten people or to watch them squirm. She'd hated the confrontation almost as much as Mikhail had. But it was necessary. Even if most of it was bluffing.

She'd need to be on the watch for leaking data. That part was true. But the line about the ghosts being able to warn her when it was happening was complete fiction. The range of what they could sense usually faded a few hundred yards from their resting places, and she'd seen no signs of any kind of ghost network that passed gossip from graveyard to graveyard.

But Mikhail didn't know that. Nor did he know that her threat of repercussions was similarly fictionalized.

He believed she was dangerous. He'd follow her instructions. He'd warn the others. From that point on, Keira would have to just wait and watch and hope.

Mason put on some music. A large portion of the tension all three of them had been carrying seemed to have evaporated. It didn't take long for Keira and Zoe to settle back into their game of count-the-cows on the drive home. Keira was losing magnificently when Zoe's phone chimed, and her friend sucked in a sharp breath.

"What is it?" Keira twisted to see her. She'd spent too much of her life on high alert to not worry. "Is it bad?"

"Wait." Zoe's eyes were huge and intense. She scrolled through her message, then typed something back, then read a reply with such hungry intensity that Keira almost couldn't breathe. "Wait…"

"Zo, you've got to start talking before I implode," Keira said, gesturing.

Zoe collapsed back in her seat, her wild eyes fixed on the car's ceiling. "He's been arrested. Properly."

This time, Mason also twisted around in his seat. "Schaeffer?"

"Yep." Zoe lifted her phone again to reread the messages. "It won't be announced until later today, but I have a friend who knows someone who knows someone else. And Schaeffer is no longer just being held; he's been arrested. He's being charged with multiple counts of criminal negligence resulting in death."

"Oh," Mason whispered, whipping forward to face the road again.

"Most of those are related to the mall and the offices beneath," Zoe continued, scrolling. "But he's also being charged for Gavin Kelsey's death, since it happened at the power plant he owned. If convicted, he faces a minimum of twenty years. Potentially life."

Silence fell over them. Keira didn't know exactly what she was feeling, but it was a lot, of everything.

Mason reached across the gap between their seats to find her hand. She clutched at him, squeezing until her fingers hurt, and realized she was both laughing and crying at once.

"I think that's it," Zoe said, and there was a damp, happy thickness to her voice, as well. She wiped at her eyes, smudging eyeliner. "I think he might actually be done."

"Operation Obliterate Artec," Keira said, still clutching Mason's hand.

"Drag the company down without mentioning the ghosts." Zoe nodded. "Bury them under lawsuits instead. In this case, negligence lawsuits."

"Something their reputation will never recover from," Mason finished.

Artec had murdered its employees. But those victims had been taken out by the mercenaries, an intermediary. Artec had been able to hide those well enough that proving them was near impossible.

But it couldn't control the narrative around the other deaths. Not even a little.

Gavin had been electrocuted on their premises. Four bodies had been pulled out of the headquarters' rubble. There was no way to muddy the waters. No way to hide. Even if Schaeffer tried to argue that he wasn't responsible for the deaths, he'd designed an office without a fire escape, without stairs, and without even a basic fire suppression system.

And then he'd built himself a bunker. Because he had fully known how dangerous the basement office's design was.

That alone would be enough to convince a judge of his liability. It proved he'd known the dangers and, instead of trying to fix them, had ensured he would be the only one who would be truly safe.

"I'm taking us to lunch," Mason said, beaming. "Not the café this time. Somewhere on the way home. Somewhere nice, somewhere special. The kind of place that uses cloth napkins. We need to celebrate."

Zoe bounced, too full of energy to sit still. "Yes! Somewhere that serves lobster! At last, you shall both learn the truth about why my middle name is Lobster Disaster. It's going to be a lunch you'll never forget."

"Make sure of it," Keira said, still laughing as she wiped drying tears from her face. "Because I never want to."

CHAPTER 43

NEWS SITES ANNOUNCED SCHAEFFER'S arrest later that afternoon, though the story was buried halfway down the page, beneath updates on *"the computer worm from hell."*

They had a long lunch. Keira had never eaten lobster before, and Mason was very happy to order one for each of them. By the time Zoe was finished with hers, not only was their table covered in shards of crustacean shell, but so were the tables around them. Keira and Mason both agreed that the middle name was very much deserved.

It was already late in the afternoon when they neared Blighty. Keira invited her friends to stay the night at her cottage. Mason offered to get snacks and drinks and make it a party; Zoe wanted to pick up Harry so he could join them.

They dropped Keira off outside the parsonage on the way past. She waved to the car as it turned back onto the road, then faced her cottage and the cemetery surrounding it.

She was grateful for the extra time. She'd been looking forward to sharing the good news with her resident ghosts. As she began to walk along the twisting path, she felt something familiar and dearly missed shift inside of her.

Daisy was awake. And she was ready to be let out again.

Keira placed a hand over her chest, then gently pulled it outward. The cat tumbled free, landing neatly on the ground. Her tail flicked as she stared up at the long grass and tombstones surrounding her.

"Hey," Keira whispered to her. "I'm glad to have you back."

Daisy made a small noise, somewhere between a purr and a chuff, and then frisked into the grass, intent on finding insects to hunt.

The small black cat would return to the cottage when she was ready. Keira would make sure her food bowls were full and the fire was burning for her.

They both needed to rebuild their energy. Especially if she planned to finish her work at Artec's cemeteries.

She kept on. To her left, set back a bit from the path, was a fresh stone marker. The dirt beneath it was still raw and dark. The service for Gavin Kelsey had concluded hours before, and the guests would have returned to Dr. Kelsey's home for the wake.

Keira promised herself she would leave some flowers at the marker. Despite everything, it felt like the right thing to do.

She found it hard to look away from the raw earth as she passed it and didn't immediately see the figure lingering deeper in the cemetery, not far from her cottage. Her breath caught as she recognized the silhouette and quickened her pace. The ghosts would have to wait until later.

Agatha Edith-Whittle's slim glasses and immaculately permed hair caught the light as she gazed over the graves. She clutched a small handbag ahead of herself, her tweed suit's perfect lines at odds with the cemetery's quiet, comfortable chaos. A very thin smile grew as she saw Keira. "Oh, there you are. Good afternoon."

"Hey." Keira, faintly breathless, caught up. "Have you been waiting here long?"

"No, not too long at all." Agatha tilted her jaw toward the scene. "I was admiring your…uh…groundskeeper's skills."

The cemetery was still an overgrown, neglected tangle, and they both knew it.

"My apologies for the unexpected visit," Agatha continued, delicately adjusting her glasses as she turned toward Keira's cottage. "I won't need much of your time."

Keira turned the lights on as they entered her home. It felt good to no longer have to hide the house's presence; the windows could stay open and the lights could be lit as much as she wanted.

She gestured toward the table, inviting Agatha to sit. "Sorry I haven't been in touch," she started, but Agatha shook her head, dismissing the apology.

"Don't be. It's a strange time for our beloved town." Agatha didn't take the offered seat, but instead stood primly, glancing about the cottage. "I wanted to share some news. You may have already heard it; my neighbor, Mr. Jensen from The Home, has passed away."

"Oh," Keira said, and hoped she was making the kind of face

people normally made when they heard surprising news. "Right. I'm so sorry."

"A fall, apparently." Agatha pursed her lips a fraction. "He was found at the base of the stairs, presumably having been startled by the burglars who were casing the town. The coroner thinks it would have been over quickly. He wouldn't have suffered."

"That's good," Keira managed.

"However, his death has caused quite a disruption. Officers have been tramping in and out of his house all of yesterday and today. They're digging up the yard. There are photographers and machines and a whole area has been cordoned off."

"Oh?" Keira said, not daring to say anything else.

"The dust is blowing into my own garden." Agatha sniffed. "Never mind the noise. It's quite a disruption. I've had to postpone our Blighty Propriety Society meeting until next week, and you know Susan will never let me live it down."

"Sorry about that. It sounds like a lot to deal with."

"That aside…" Agatha took a deep breath. "If you remember, before all this strangeness in our town began, I hired you to do a job for me."

"The haunting. Right." Keira tried not to grimace visibly. She'd left rattraps under Agatha's fridge and had planned to return and discreetly retrieve them, but then the Artec situation had taken over and everything else had been swept aside. She hoped the traps hadn't started to smell. "I can come around tomorrow—"

"No need." Agatha's smile was small. "Whatever you did—it worked. The job is complete."

Keira's gamble on the rattraps had paid off, then. "Oh! That's great."

"It is. I'm very grateful. For everything." Agatha reached into her purse. She brought out a pristine envelope and placed it on the table ahead of Keira. "Here is your payment."

"Oh, uh, don't worry about it." Keira tried to nudge the envelope back. "I don't charge."

"You do now," Agatha said, hands clasped ahead of herself as she turned to look through the window facing the cemetery.

It didn't feel right. Technically, Keira had fulfilled the job description: she'd cleared not just one, but five ghosts. But Agatha didn't know that. For Agatha, Keira had just dropped off a few rattraps and let nature take its course. She honestly didn't feel like she could charge for that and still keep her conscience clean.

Her curiosity got the better of her, and she lifted the envelope's flap to steal a glance inside. At first, she thought she must be misreading both the value and the quantity of the notes. Then she did a double take as her stomach dropped. "Oh. *No.* This is too much. Way, way too much—"

"I would have paid a lot more for a lot less."

The words were so soft they were almost a whisper.

The light coming through the window left Agatha's skin strangely pale and thin. She seemed older than when Keira had first met her.

The hairs rose across Keira's arms. She hadn't noticed before, but, lit by the cold daylight, the particular angle of Agatha's nose reminded Keira of someone.

It was impossible. And yet, Agatha was about the right age. But…it *had* to be impossible.

"You knew someone who stayed in The Home, didn't you?" Keira asked, her own voice a whisper.

A wisp of a smile appeared at the corners of Agatha's mouth, then vanished. "My sister."

Keira saw the pale, ghostly faces of the waiting women. She saw them all in agonizing detail. And she saw the one who'd held the gloves, her face distantly familiar.

"She was in remission," Agatha said. Her posture stayed rigid and perfect, but her voice caught as she stared through the window. "She was getting better. She was…she was *supposed* to get better." And once more, so softly that Keira almost didn't catch it, "She was in remission."

Keira found herself staring at a woman she'd thought she'd understood and yet hadn't, not even a little.

"Did you know?" she asked. Her mouth was dry. "That it was Jensen?"

Agatha's nails picked at the hem of her jacket. She took a long moment to answer. "No. Maybe. I suspected, a little."

Rumors about the home and its caretaker had been swirling for decades, Zoe had said. And the accusations claimed that Jensen had kept trinkets from his victims—things the families would have noticed were missing from their returned possessions. The rumors had been so persistent, and so repeated, that Constable Sanderson seemed exhausted at the mention of them.

"You've been trying to get her justice for years," Keira said, as a map of tiny clues wove together.

"I was young when I lost my sister," Agatha said. "My parents never…they never truly came back from it. And I'm not sure I did either."

When the rumors hadn't worked, Agatha had moved in directly next to The Home.

To watch. To wait for answers. To scratch out any little clue, any little detail, about what had happened to her sister.

And she'd pried and dug and stared until Jensen had loathed her so viciously that he would scream if he saw her near the fence.

And still, Agatha had been unable to let go. The police stonewalled her; the town had relegated her story to a local legend. She was so desperate she was willing to hire an alleged spirit medium to visit her home. To exhaust every option.

Keira could only imagine what Agatha thought when Keira had approached the fence to The Home on her first visit, as though drawn there by a magnet. She'd called Keira away. Because, all of a sudden, it must have felt too real. Too alarming.

"I'm so sorry for your sister," Keira said. She meant it. Her heart ached not just for the spirit she'd seen in The Home, but for Agatha, whose whole life had become quietly consumed by the loss. "I don't know if this well help, but she's at peace. She's free."

Agatha nodded softly, still staring out at the graveyard. "I'm glad."

Jensen was gone. As the excavation in the yard uncovered the lost trinkets, the truth about what happened to the victims would become widely known. Most likely, The Home would be demolished. Agatha's search for truth—for closure—would finally be at an end.

Keira hoped it would be cathartic. But she knew it could also very easily feel like being untethered from a life raft. This had been a constant presence in Agatha's life. To lose it could feel like losing purpose. Or even like losing hope.

"If you want to talk," she began gently. "I mean, you're always welcome here, at any time—"

"I have my friends in the Blighty Propriety Society," Agatha said, and her smile held a hint of wryness. "I am a long way from being alone, don't you worry. You may be hearing from them, as an aside; we do like to recommend services we find valuable."

Keira frowned. "Uh…services…?"

"As a spirit medium." Agatha tapped a fingertip on the envelope. "Please do me the honor of accepting your due with grace. I meant what I said. I would have paid a lot more for a lot less."

Keira swallowed around the lump in her throat as she accepted the envelope.

Agatha turned toward the door, then hesitated. "This is unsolicited, and so please forgive me if I am speaking out of line," she said.

Keira shrugged. "It's okay."

"Never let the world make you feel ashamed of what you do." Agatha turned just far enough for Keira to see her eyes through her slim glasses. "Your work brings goodness into the world. It brings healing. Not everyone can say the same."

Through the window, Keira could barely see her ghosts, languidly pacing between the thickening shadows. "Thank you," she managed.

Agatha gave a satisfied nod, then opened the door. Daisy stood on the top step, waiting to be let in. She spared Agatha a brief, curious glance before weaving past her ankles and making her way toward the couches around the fire.

"Well," Agatha said. "Good afternoon, Miss Daisy. And good afternoon to you as well, Miss Keira. Thank you for your time."

"Wait, one last thing." Keira stood, and Agatha paused, halfway out of her cottage. Keira still had an admittedly small mystery hanging over her. "Who told you about me? How did you know I could see ghosts?"

"Polly Kennard is a core member of the Blighty Propriety Society. Her son visits me on occasion. He says…he wishes he could be like me?" Agatha's lips pursed. She seemed disconcerted. "Because I am old, and therefore close to death? I do not understand that boy, but he is well-meaning enough, I suppose. Your name came up during a recent visit."

"Ah." Keira ran her hands through her hair, smiling. Harry had also mentioned Keira and her abilities to Dane Crispin some time before. She should probably ask him to keep it a bit more secret. "Oh, and, uh, sorry, but there are some rattraps under your fridge. I should probably warn you about that."

"Yes, I know." Agatha blinked at her. "I found them a while ago."

"Really? Guess it wasn't such a good hiding spot."

"I don't know why you ever thought it would be," Agatha said, her eyebrows high. "Not when it's common habit to sweep under the fridge at the end of every day."

Keira had no reply for that. She could only smile as Agatha set off along the path, back to Blighty.

The cemetery was no longer empty. In the far distance, Keira could barely make out three more forms meandering in her direction. Their gaits were familiar: Zoe, Mason, and Harry. It was hard to be sure, but she thought Harry might be carrying an enormous store-bought cake, precariously balanced on his cast.

She left the door open for them and went to fill the kettle for tea. It was good to have friends.

EPILOGUE

DAYS BECAME WEEKS. THE town continued to buzz about the intruders, but they never returned, and the conversation slowly simmered down to offhanded comments. The town began to slide back into its familiar routines.

Keira, Mason, and Zoe kept close watch on what remained of Artec. Keira couldn't shake a quiet anxiety that it might still go wrong. That, if she took her eyes off them for even a moment, the company might start pulling itself back together like an undead monster. It turned out that her fear was unfounded. Slowly, a little bit more each day, Artec collapsed in on itself like a dying star.

Zoe, verified genius that she was, had memorized some of the name tags they'd seen while they were moving through the underground office. She'd built a dossier of nearly a dozen confirmed employees, plus an additional two dozen suspected coworkers based on social media connections, and she monitored their movements.

They had all scattered. Some moved to different parts of the country, to put more distance between themselves and Artec. Some, as Mikhail had said they might, traveled internationally.

Gradually, those staff began to pick up new jobs. A few went into engineering or education. Some returned to the companies they'd worked in before Artec had poached them. Zoe watched for any red flags—any jobs connected to cemeteries, mortuaries, or innovating energy production—but nothing concerning cropped up.

It didn't mean there would never be problems. But it was a good sign. Most of the employees were as ready to be done with Artec as Keira was.

———

Two weeks after the mall's collapse, Keira received a final text message from Mikhail.

> I meant it when I said I wanted to do better. I got in touch with the technicians and applied some pressure. The cemeteries are now all offline.

Keira was having lunch with Zoe and Mason when the text arrived. She turned her phone around so they could both read it.

"Wait, seriously?" Zoe said, a smile growing. "He actually did it?"

"We can still take the trip, just to make sure," Mason said.

They'd been planning a four-day road trip to visit each of Artec's cemeteries and to attempt to disable them. Keira felt like she was nearly ready. Her energy was close to the levels it had been before the mall, and the other symptoms—the headaches, the hair loss, the aching gums—were improving, as well. She thought she might be able to push herself again. But if Mikhail was telling the truth, she might not need to.

"Yeah," she said, tucking her phone away. "Let's still go. I want to be certain."

They set out the following morning.

Artec's cemeteries were modern, clean, and sleek. Keira had loathed every one she'd encountered up until then. But as they stepped through the gates to the first plot, she felt herself actually starting to smile.

Hundreds of grave markers spread out ahead of her.

And there were no shades.

"How is it?" Mason asked. He stood next to her, coat hung over one arm, Zoe on his other side. The three of them had spent so long working on the Artec situation together that Keira sometimes forgot that they couldn't see the ghosts.

"It worked." In the distance, she caught sight of a spirit. A proper one—pale, ethereal, and barely visible as it drifted between markers. "I think some of the shades stayed as ghosts. The kind with unfinished business. But this is one of the emptiest graveyards I've seen; most of them moved over the moment they were released, I think."

"And they're not coming back?" Zoe checked. "Artec can't flip a switch and put its batteries back online?"

"No. Not now. They've moved over. And that can't be reversed." Keira inhaled and let the air out in a heady rush.

In the distance, a security guard moved through the graveyard. He pulled up short as he saw Keira. Then, very slowly and very deliberately, he turned around and began walking in the opposite direction.

Once, Keira would have felt like she needed to run. Not anymore. Artec's complex structure of guards and mercenaries had been all but eliminated. At first, she'd harbored some anxiety that the mercenaries might want revenge for what she'd done in the basement office, but she hadn't heard even a whisper from them.

Artec was no longer paying for their services. Their hunt for her had never been personal, not like it had been for Schaeffer. As soon as the money vanished, they stopped caring.

Now…only a handful of individuals connected to Artec knew what she looked like. And they were all very intent on staying out of her way.

"We should still check the rest," Keira said, turning back to the gate. "But I think this chapter might be finished."

Over the following days, they worked through the remaining cemeteries. The scene was the same in each of them. Quiet, undisturbed graves stretched as far as they could see. Sometimes, Keira spotted a lingering ghost. Someone who still had a purpose for being on earth. She made a mental note to return, to see if she could help them.

Every cemetery held restless spirits, but she felt like the ones in Artec's system deserved closure more than anyone else.

Schaeffer's court date was scheduled. He wouldn't appear before the judge for another year and a half. Due to the unique nature of the charges, he was considered a potential flight risk and was denied bail.

The wait was long, but that was good news. Schaeffer would be powerless while he was awaiting trial. And, without him, the Artec ship fully and completely ran aground.

The power plants were shuttered and signs were added warning against trespassing. The international properties—the places Schaeffer had wanted to use for expansion—were put up for sale. Zoe thought it was likely that all of Artec's few remaining assets, including the existing cemeteries, would eventually be sold.

For the first time since arriving in Blighty, Keira got a taste of what it was like to simply exist. She didn't have to count each day; she didn't need to feel she was in a fight against an hourglass that was nearly empty.

She borrowed books from the library and wasted entire days reading them. She spent hours in the cemetery, weeding, as she held one-sided conversations with her ghosts. She walked to town most days and met new neighbors and signed up for trivia night at the pub.

And amid all that, she spent time with Mason. They had proper dates. She watched movies with him, cuddled up on the couch, draped in blankets, while Daisy purred in his lap. They finished jigsaw puzzles; they took walks to their favorite places around town. Mason made her poached eggs in the mornings.

It was everything she'd so badly wanted. And it was every bit as good as she'd hoped it might be.

———

Six weeks after burying his son, Dr. Kelsey closed his practice and left town.

Keira, Zoe, and Mason were sitting on the edge of the fountain in the town square when his car passed them, followed by a moving truck.

"Well," Zoe said, lowering the sandwich she'd been eating. "He was never a good doctor to begin with. But it's going to suck to have to drive to Cheltenham if you need to see someone."

Mason didn't say anything, but some hidden emotion hovered in his expression. Keira had caught glimpses of it before. He was happy with her, and he wore that joy openly. But, sometimes, she caught him lost in thought. As though he was holding on to an idea that still felt too small and fragile to breathe into the world.

"The town could use a new doctor," Keira said.

He blinked at her, startled, then smiled. "I wasn't sure… I mean, I didn't want to say anything if…"

Zoe glanced between them, suspicious. "Wait, are you thinking about going back to med school?"

Mason put his lunch aside. He looked uncertain. "I was close to graduating when I dropped out, and the school said I would be able to return and finish the final semester if I wanted to. But…it would mean being away from Blighty for at least six months. And I'm not sure if I want that. I've just started to build a future here."

Warmth filled Keira's stomach. Mason had looked at her during the last few words, and he didn't try to hide his meaning. He wanted to build a future with *her*.

"Six months is nothing," Keira said, leaning against Mason's shoulder. "Not since we now have the rest of our lives ahead of us. And your university isn't that far, anyway, so we'll still get to see each other constantly. Adage offered to give me driving lessons."

They'd started on the slow and challenging process of getting Keira's existence formally registered. Her parents had kept her an absolute secret when she was born, and the aunt who had taken her in after their deaths hadn't seen any reason to change that. As far as the world was concerned, Keira didn't exist.

That was generally a good thing when hiding from evil corporations. Not so great if she wanted a bank account or a driver's license. There was red tape galore, but they were very slowly, very stubbornly cutting through it.

"Are you sure?" Mason asked. He watched her intently. "I don't want it to be a mistake."

"Do you want to be a doctor?" She stared up at him, meeting his warm green eyes. "Be honest."

He slowly nodded. "Yes. Yes, I always have."

"I'm glad, because you're going to make an amazing one." And that was the truth. She could picture him setting up a clinic in the town. He had seemingly limitless empathy. He was careful and he was kind and he was smart. He might be exactly what Blighty needed. "I can't wait to watch that happen."

Mason smiled, and there was a new, tentative excitement seeping into his expression. "Thank you."

"Ugh, you're both turning into boring adults," Zoe said, and flicked a piece of crust toward a pigeon meandering through the square. "Getting IDs. Getting degrees. Getting *careers*."

"The rat race isn't for everyone," Mason said obligingly.

"It is for you," Zoe teased. "You love conforming to society's expectations."

"Yes. Yes, I really do."

She laughed. "I guess I'm about to be outed as a hypocrite, anyway."

Keira leaned forward, eyebrows raised. "Oh?"

"The general store's owner is talking about retirement. And I guess she said she wouldn't mind if I bought it from her." Zoe flicked her hair, seeming nonchalant. She managed to look like she didn't care for about two seconds, then immediately burst into breathless details. "I think it's doable. Mum left me an inheritance, and I went over the numbers, and it should cover it. And I've basically been running the place for the last year, anyway. I think I can do it. I really think I can."

"Zoe!" Keira beamed. "Yes, of course you can! That's amazing!"

"You're the perfect person to take over," Mason added, looking thrilled. "You're going to kill it."

"Retail is the worst, but it's *my* kind of worst." Zoe cackled, kicking her feet delightedly. "I'm going to start stocking all sorts of weird stuff. It's going to be amazing. I—"

A phone rang. The tone seemed unfamiliar. They all reached for their mobiles, just in case, then Zoe swore under her breath and scrambled in her bag.

"Okay. Quick heads-up." Zoe pulled out a mobile that Keira

didn't recognize. It rang, loud and insistent. "I set up a website for you."

"A…what?" Keira blinked at the phone, utterly lost.

"Well, you made that joke last week about how you could become a professional ghost hunter, and then that lady from the Beeps started pestering me, saying she needed business cards so she could refer you to her friends, and I guess she thought I was the right person to ask about that, and she was probably right because I got carried away and… I made you a website."

The phone was still ringing. Keira stared from it to Zoe again. "What?"

"A website. For you. A professional ghost hunter. And I got you a phone and some business cards as well." Zoe grimaced at the mobile rattling in her hands. "I was going to break the news to you at a better time. I just didn't expect people to call so quickly. Can I answer it?"

Keira squinted, stunned. She looked at Mason. He gave a small shrug in response. "Um. I guess?"

Zoe grinned, then tapped a button and switched to speaker-phone. Her voice immediately became silky smooth. "Good morning, this is Blighty Ghost Agency, where spooky is our business. How may I assist you?"

"Oh, hi." A voice crackled out of the phone, sounding uncertain. "I live in Cheltenham. I don't know if you can help me, but there's an old family graveyard at the back of my property and I've started getting a bad feeling when I go near it. Is that something you can look at?"

"Of course," Zoe said, giving Keira a thumbs-up before pulling a notebook from her purse. "If you give me your address, we have space in our schedule to stop by for an assessment this afternoon."

As Zoe took the details, Keira stared into the distance, quietly absorbing the new development.

Late at night, when her home was quiet and dark, she sometimes thought of what Agatha had said to her. *Never be ashamed of what you do.*

Keira had spent a lot of time trying to hide her abilities. She'd lied about her job by default. She'd felt like her ability to see ghosts had to be a desperate, uncomfortable secret.

But that secret had bled out in gradual drips. Adage knew. Harry knew. And now, so did Dane, and Agatha, and Marlene.

And none of them had turned cold toward her, like she'd feared.

Maybe she could do more. *Help* more.

And maybe this wasn't a path she needed to fear.

"Congratulations, Keira," Zoe said, tucking the phone away. "You have your first official booking." She gave a grimacing smile. "Sorry, again, for not asking you sooner. I thought you might need a bit of a nudge to get here, is all."

"That was a fair assessment," Keira said, shaking her head. "But we are *not* keeping that slogan."

"But spooky *is* your business!"

"And yet, no."

Mason chuckled. "You said the address is in Cheltenham, right? I can drive."

"And I can bring some funky-looking equipment and talk about cold spots and orbs," Zoe said. "I've seen *all* the ghost-hunting shows. I know exactly how to please the crowds."

"You sure you're both up for this?" she checked. "You've already had firsthand experience on how it might take more than just one afternoon to clear a ghost's unfinished business."

"Which is why you'll need a good team," Zoe said, gesturing to the three of them. "We've done this before. We know how you work, and you know we'll have your back."

"Always," Mason agreed. "We must have broken at least half the country's laws by now. I'm sure we can squeeze in a few more, if we really try." He smiled at her, and she saw how quietly pleased he was. "In all seriousness, it's a joy to watch you work. I'd love to come."

"All right," Keira said. Her heart felt full enough to burst. She reached out and found both of their hands, showing them how grateful she was. "Let's go find some ghosts."

DON'T WALK ALONE, OR THE STITCHER WILL FIND YOU.

Enjoy this glimpse of
Where He Can't Find You, available now!

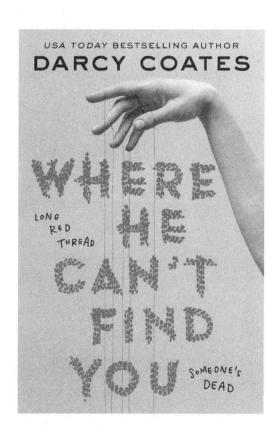

ONE

〜〜〜

"DO YOU WANT TO SEE SOMETHING BAD?"

Abby woke with icy sweat plastering her clothes to her skin. Her breathing came in rough gasps as she stared into the darkness flooding her room.

The nightmares were always the first warning. They came before any of the other signs—before the birds that plunged out of the sky, before the streetlights all died, before the sickness.

Before the disappearances.

She reached for her nightstand and turned the clock to face her. Four-fifteen. She watched the second hand tick forward, making sure it was still keeping time. Technology always broke when things were getting bad.

She'd been having nightmares for nearly two weeks. This one was the worst, though—a memory from that night at Jessica's house. It was supposed to be a girls' sleepover, but Abby had been the only one who arrived. She and Jessica had sat at an empty dinner table for half an hour, no parents in sight, before Jessica had asked the damning question.

Do you want to see something bad?

It was Abby's first time facing a dead body.

Not her last, though.

Now, her mouth was parchment dry. Sweat stuck her hair to the back of her neck as she slid out of bed. The wooden floorboards creaked as she left her room and crossed the hall to reach her sister's.

Hope lay on her stomach, one arm thrown above her head, her blankets tangled.

The window over her bed was open an inch. Hope liked to feel the cold air at night, but they weren't supposed to keep any part of the house—doors, windows, anything—unlocked after dark. Moving silently so she didn't disturb her, Abby slid the pane closed and fastened the latch.

At the opposite wall, near the door, was Hope's desk. It was covered with equipment, including a webcam, a ring light, and a computer that could handle the editing software she needed to piece together her videos. Even with technology becoming so unreliable, Hope was serious about making this a career. And Abby thought she might just have a chance.

When Hope first started posting videos, it had felt like she was yelling into the void. She'd get a handful of views but no likes. No comments. She later admitted that she was on the edge of giving up when her first fans found her. Just five accounts to begin with—but those five accounts watched every video and always commented, asking for more. So she kept filming. Kept posting.

Now, she had nearly two thousand subscribers. She'd started to get small sponsorship deals. But those five original followers were still there, still cheering her on with each new video, and she always replied to thank them.

Abby hadn't told Hope that the accounts were hers. She probably never would.

She left on silent feet. At the end of the hallway was their mother's room, its door opened a crack. Abby wrapped her arms around herself as she approached and leaned forward.

Moonlight came through the thin torn curtains. It trailed over the edge of their mother's silhouette. She sat on the end of her bed, staring at the wall.

There was just enough light to make out her long unwashed hair. The sharp angles of her thin lips. Her long delicate nose.

Abby hadn't made a sound. Hadn't even so much as breathed. But her mother seemed to sense her presence. She turned, suddenly, her eye flashing in the cold light. Abby backed away, her tongue pressed between her teeth.

She didn't let herself breathe again until she was back in her own room. Then she curled up on her bed, her knees drawn to her chest.

There wouldn't be any more sleep that night. She reached for her phone and was grateful when the display came up after only a brief flicker.

She opened the group chat titled *Jackrabbits* and typed: Anyone awake?

A reply came from Rhys. I'm here. And then, almost immediately after, u ok?

He always asked. Every single time. Abby could imagine his shoulders hunching and his eyes darkening, the way they did when he sensed the chance of danger. He was more attuned to threats than any of their group, and *no one* in their group took threats lightly. It left him always on guard, always cautious.

Abby couldn't blame him.

Not after what the Stitcher did to his parents.

All good, she texted, and she knew him well enough to visualize the tightness draining out of him again. She hesitated, then added, I had a nightmare.

Me too, he replied. Bad night.

Yeah. Abby rolled over, bunching the blankets over herself. She might be physically alone in her room, but the group chat stopped her from feeling completely untethered. She needed them, just as much as they needed her.

A new text appeared, this time from Riya. Hey guys. Followed by, Rhys?

He responded with a single question mark.

There was a long pause. Riya had to be taking care with what she wrote next. Abby felt a sense of unease creep into her stomach as she waited. A flicker of static cut over the lower half of her phone's screen, then vanished again.

Then, Riya posted: Can you handle bad news right now?

His response was fast, decisive. Yes. What happened?

Abby's unease redoubled.

I think they found a body. She could picture Riya's face, pinched and tight and frightened. Police just went by my house. Headed toward Breaker Street.

There was a pause as they absorbed the news.

Rhys was the first to reply.

Ok. Let's meet.

Two

ᐯᐱᐯᐱᐯᐱ

ABBY STAYED ONLY LONG ENOUGH TO SLIDE A NOTE UNDER HOPE'S door, saying where she was going.

That was one of their rules: don't leave without telling someone.

Her silver bike waited for her against the house's side. She jogged with it to the street, then climbed on and turned toward the main road.

When people wanted to say something nice about Doubtful, Illinois, they called it a bike-friendly town. What that really meant was that cars were too unreliable. Most of the time they'd work as intended. But sometimes, with no warning, they would stall. Or grind to a halt. Or simply refuse to start.

The town's mechanics would look at a car and say, *It's got the jitters.* That was slang for when they couldn't find anything technically wrong, but it simply refused to work.

And it wasn't just cars. Phones were unreliable. Streetlights went out. Televisions would play static or display a mangled version of two channels spliced together, audio and graphics merging into one.

Things in Doubtful just broke easily.

Not bikes, though. The rubber and spokes and brakes didn't rely on electricity, and so the town's decaying effects left them alone. If you wanted to be certain of getting somewhere in Doubtful, you rode a bike.

Abby's breath came hot and fast, spiraling out behind her like smoke. She moved quickly, air funneling around her body, her legs heating from the exertion, and at that moment she felt as though she could outrun the darkness itself. A streetlight behind her blinked and then vanished, extinguished like a candle being snuffed out. She rode faster.

It was still well before dawn. The houses around her were dark. With the lights out, it was sometimes hard to tell which houses held sleeping forms, and which had been abandoned for years.

A shadow raced toward her, emerging from one of the side streets like a phantom. It skimmed closer until it ran alongside her, matching her pace. In the intermittent streetlight, she could make out dark hair and wild, intent eyes. Rhys.

They shared a look, then turned back to the road ahead.

Don't travel alone. That was another Jackrabbit rule. Rhys could have taken a more direct route to Breaker Street, but he'd taken the longer path to join up with Abby instead.

The road vanished under them. Rhys matched her furious pace perfectly, and they stayed abreast, each turn anticipated, until the rusted sign for Breaker Street rose out of the gloom.

Abby's lungs burned from the exertion, but it was a good kind of ache. The kind that told her she was alive and moving. That her body was strong. She let her bike roll to a halt and put one foot down as she stared along the road.

Red and blue lights flashed, lighting up the asphalt and the washed-out houses. She counted three police cars and an ambulance, all parked askew on a lawn that was long dead and choked with dry, rattling weeds.

Breaker Street was residential but right next to a strip of industrial stores: cube-like buildings with bars over their windows and flat roofs. The area had all been built around the same time—decades before Abby had even been born—and then left to slowly be consumed by neglect.

Rhys gently tapped her arm to draw her notice, then nodded toward the shops across the road. Two figures stood in their shadows. Riya, small and tense and with her dark hair tightly braided, had one arm raised to hail them. Just behind her was Connor, his curly flaxen hair mussed from sleep, his large teeth working at his lower lip as he tried to control his nerves. Abby and Rhys silently crossed the road to meet up with them.

"There's a ladder," Riya whispered as they drew near. Even her warm complexion looked washed out and strange in the frantic, undulating red and blue lights. She nodded to the store behind them, which had once printed commercial signs but had been out of business for more than a decade. It still held advertisements in its fogged windows, promising forty percent off everything. "We might be able to see better up high."

Rhys gazed up the metal ladder bolted to the building's back wall. "Good find," he said.

They left their bikes at the store's back, where they were less likely to be seen. The shops along that stretch of road, right on the outskirts of town, had been left to neglect. Rust flaked off the ladder as Abby climbed, and the wall was full of cracks, zigzagging along the lines of the bricks hidden beneath the concrete, like a map of a hidden city. She reached the ladder's top and swung her legs over the half wall.

The flat concrete roof was barren except for piles of rotting leaf litter gathered in the corners and a stack of old boxes and abandoned furniture clearly intended to be thrown out but then forgotten. The half wall ran around the roof's edges, like a battlement, and Abby held her breath as she crossed the space to get a better view of the streets.

On the other side of the main road, Breaker Street was alive with activity. Abby lowered herself, her arms braced on the half wall, as her three friends took up their places next to her.

Every house along the street looked like it was built from the same mold. They were all Midwesterns with sagging porches and shutters over their windows, and picket fences that sliced the lawns into portions.

They could have looked beautiful once, but Breaker Street had succumbed to time and apathy. The fences leaned and the lawns had lost their color. Children's toys had been abandoned in a nearby yard: tricycles and a small plastic slide now overgrown with weeds.

The police cars had all parked outside one of the worst houses. Pots were spaced about its porch, but none of them held any plants. The shutters were cracked, boards coming loose, and the painted siding was peeled and discolored.

Riya leaned close to the wall, her small hands gripping the cracked concrete, her expression tight. "I pass that house every day," she said. "I've never seen anyone in it."

Abandoned houses weren't uncommon in Doubtful. Properties

were cheap, but there were few jobs to attract new residents. Forgotten *For Sale* signs dotted the town, weathered or tipping over like loose teeth, abandoned where they stood.

Abby remembered how, when she was young and eager to have adventures, she'd wanted to explore some of those empty buildings. She'd quickly learned why that was a bad idea. It wasn't unheard of to *find* things in them.

Figures moved in and out of the house, flashlights in hand. The ambulance's back doors were open, but Abby couldn't tell if anyone was inside. Most of the activity seemed to come from the police. Their uniforms and badges caught the red and blue lights, but their caps were pulled too far down for her to recognize any of their faces.

Rhys had one forearm resting on the wall as his dark eyes took in the scene. "Do you think the new transfer's there?"

One of the deputies had left town nearly six weeks before, bundling his family into his car and tearing out without even putting in his resignation. The town had been forced to hire an outsider. The new transfer and his daughter had apparently moved in just days before, but Abby had yet to see either of them.

"I can't imagine what sort of welcome to town this would be." Connor poked around the pile of abandoned items before pulling something free. He'd found a folded metal chair, red with rust. He shook it out to open it.

"You'll get tetanus," Riya said at the sound of whining metal, without even taking her eyes off the road.

Connor made a faint noise in agreement, but still positioned the chair near the half wall and sat. His pale, densely curly hair absorbed the undulating lights, turning a different shade with each flash.

"There," Riya hissed, rising up another inch. "Look!"

The activity inside the house seemed to have condensed into one room. Flashlight beams cut over one another, bursting out of gaps in the tattered curtains and broken shutters.

Abby craned forward, breath held. She knew what was coming. A part of her didn't want to see it, but a larger, stronger part of her *had to*.

This was how you survived in Doubtful.

ABOUT THE AUTHOR

Darcy Coates is the *USA Today* bestselling author of *Hunted*, *The Haunting of Ashburn House*, *Craven Manor*, and more than a dozen other horror and suspense titles.

She lives on the Central Coast of Australia with her family, cats, and a garden full of herbs and vegetables.

Darcy loves forests, especially old-growth forests where the trees dwarf anyone who steps between them. Wherever she lives, she tries to have a mountain range close by.

HOW BAD THINGS CAN GET

IT WAS SUPPOSED TO BE A PARTY UNLIKE ANY OTHER.

Prosperity Island. Its history is filled with shipwrecks, cannibalism, and a string of unexplained deaths. And now it hosts the party of the century.

A content creator millionaire and more than a hundred of his fans land on the beach. The plan: five days of elaborate games, drinking, and suntanned fun. Among the guests are a woman trying to hide from her bloody and notorious past, and a video journalist hunting for the next big scandal.

The celebrations have barely started when the first guests go missing. Games take a deadly turn. And attendees are forced to question whether they've really been invited to paradise...or whether something much darker is waiting just under the surface.